To/ Maureen.
With ,

CH00736156

ROBERT REID

WHITE LIGHT LIGHT Red fire

A small nation's fight for freedom
from tyranny and a deadly foe

RFR: 15ᵗʰ July 2019

Mereo Books

1A The Wool Market Dyer Street Cirencester Gloucestershire GL7 2PR
An imprint of Memoirs Books Ltd. www.mereobooks.com

White Light Red Fire: 978-1-86151-921-4

First published in Great Britain in 2019
by Mereo Books, an imprint of Memoirs Books Ltd.

Copyright ©2019

Robert Ferguson Reid has asserted his right under the Copyright Designs and
Patents Act 1988 to be identified as the author of this work.

This book is a work of fiction and except in the case of historical fact any
resemblance to actual persons living or dead is purely coincidental.

A CIP catalogue record for this book is available from the British Library.
This book is sold subject to the condition that it shall not by way of trade
or otherwise be lent, resold, hired out or otherwise circulated without the
publisher's prior consent in any form of binding or cover, other than that in
which it is published and without a similar condition, including this condition
being imposed on the subsequent purchaser.

The address for Memoirs Books Ltd. can be
found at www.mereobooks.com

Memoirs Books Ltd. Reg. No. 7834348

Typeset in 11/15pt Century Schoolbook
by Wiltshire Associates Ltd.
Printed and bound in Great Britain by Biddles Books

To Phyllis, Simon, Charis, Kate, Oscar
and Evie – I never really thought I would
manage this. Love you all.

ACKNOWLEDGMENTS

This book has been a journey of over 15 years, and lay unattended to for much of that time. Thanks firstly to Alan Passey, whose gentle kick in the rear got me encouraged to get back to writing it. Keep the cycling stories going, mate!

Thanks to all those who read the first rough version of the story and whose inputs helped make the final version much better. Carole, Manse, Simon, Charis, Phyllis and Alan were all very generous with their time and their gentle critiques. Most important was their encouragement that there was a good story to be told. Particular thanks go to my son, Simon, who provided much detailed input on how the story could be improved and where the narrative had gone astray in either time or place.

Many thanks to my daughter Charis for carrying out a thorough final check of the manuscript.

Grateful thanks to my editor, Chris Newton, who has been extremely patient with the many errors made in the manuscript by a first-time author. Chris's encouragement over many months has been invaluable, and our shared commitment to make the story as good as it could be really helped me push through the times when I was struggling to make progress on the narrative.

Ray Lipscombe designed the book's fantastic cover, which perfectly captures the essence of the story. Great job Ray, much appreciated.

Finally and most importantly, thanks to my wife Phyllis for her forever love and for putting up with a missing husband hiding in his grubby office tapping away at the computer keyboard. Loved you yesterday, love you still, always have and always will.

RFR
March 2019

ABOUT THE AUTHOR

Robert (Bob) Reid grew up in Scotland's beautiful border country. Hawick was home until it was time to go to university in Edinburgh. A degree and a PhD in Chemistry followed. It was in Edinburgh that Bob met and married Phyllis. Work opportunities took them south, and their son Simon was born in Cheshire and their daughter Charis some years later in Swindon. Highworth, near Swindon, became home in 1982. It still is home and has become a special place to Bob and Phyllis.

Bob's career of forty years was initially in technical management, then general management and business consulting. Work generally took priority over creativity. It was during a work break in 2002 that the germ of the idea for this story was first triggered. Bob had always had an interest in Robert the Bruce and Scotland's wars of independence, which partly inspired this novel. Work again took priority and with no time to concentrate on the book, songwriting filled the creative space (see www.bob-reid.co.uk). Semi-retirement in early 2018 created the time, and family and friends the encouragement, to complete this book.

PROLOGUE

The skies were filled with an unreal fire; blue, burnt with amber, red, orange and yellow. This fire was no natural thing. It clawed across the sky, and below it all life shivered and retreated. The land lay scorched, the mountains and glens trembling.

The man stood pale in the false light, a statue, watching. Then he moved, shaking off the stillness, and looked towards the power that shook the world. His clenched fist opened and clean white light leapt to the sky. A huge concussion rocked the mountains. All light was quenched. The sky turned black, then clear and blue. A distant rainbow promised that all was well and God still cared for this lost land.

Alastair Munro fell back, the soft heather a safety net, all power gone, all anger lost. Angus Ferguson was beside him as ever, a reassuring voice, a reminder of why Munro was there, why he must go on, why this was his destiny.

CONTENTS

The Island of Andore

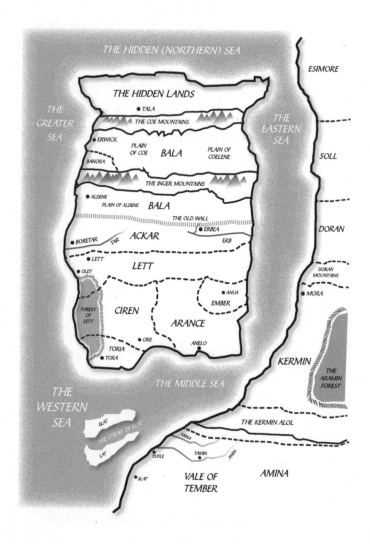

The Country of Bala

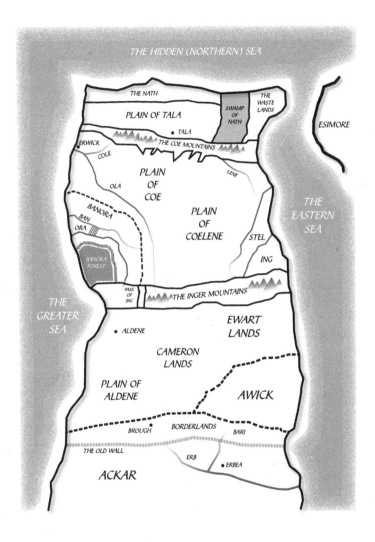

CHAPTER ONE

The Third Age

Few remembered the stories of the days before the end of the Second Age. Those days when all the lands had been under the control of the Council of Five were now wrapped in legends and seemed like fantasy. At that time mankind had been one community, from the frozen north through the tropics to the southern lands, and all destinies had been determined by the Council. Vast machines, powered by substances raped from the depths of the Earth, had travelled the world transporting men and goods to all corners of all the lands. No night had come in those days. A million million lights, powered by endless energy, turned dark to light, and the night shone like the day. In all corners of the world, men strove to replenish the energy that was used. This same energy powered the exploration of the worlds beyond.

In the earliest days of the Second Age, man explored the world and all its corners. In the later days, the planets became the playpen of man. It seemed nothing would halt the march of power as man and his technologies carried him to places where only God had gone before.

God, however, had not agreed to this expansion of man's power, and just as it seemed that nothing could stop the whole solar system being pillaged, He replied. The meteorite storms first fell on the outer planets, where man's foothold was least, but the stony rain fell and fell until all the conquests of man were as nothing. The Council of Five fell as the last of the peoples returned to a badly-bruised Earth, demanding that all the defences of man be exerted yet more strongly against the solar invader. Laser beams leapt from Earth and vast powers of destruction flew to the sky, to no avail. In a few short months mankind was suffering as the dinosaur kings of the First Age had, and like their predecessors only a few populations survived, in hidden caves or remote glens. The meteorites had not caught all life.

Long after the last of the meteorite storms had ceased, the surviving peoples of the world began to explore outwards from their refuges. They found that all trace of the Second Age was gone. No cities remained; no machines to tear at the heart of the land. Day and night had again found their rightful places; all over the world stretched green grasses and woodlands. It seemed that God had decided to re-work His experiment and create a new Eden.

In the early days of the Third Age, all was peace and tranquillity. Man and God seemed to find anew the balance that had been lost. The scattered races started as their ancestors had done in the middle years of the First Age, hunting and farming in small, sheltered, peaceful communities. Again the lands became home to a diversity of creatures as the animal kingdoms re-established themselves in the woods and the grasslands. Where men met other men, they showed respect, trust and hospitality. Over the years the numbers of travellers and explorers grew as man learned again about continents lost in the demise of the Second Age. A new time of peace and exploration began.

As the Third Age grew and man re-established his presence on Earth, the cycles of the previous ages began to be repeated. Explorers rediscovering the old places which had been forgotten also rediscovered greed and envy. Exploration once again became conquest, peace too often destroyed by war.

In the north of the large island of Andore, in the land of Bala, the Third Age grew quietly. There was minor acquisition of lands and some clan disputes, but in general the clans respected the lands of their birth, and never moved far from the villages that had become their homes in the earliest days of the age. Nowhere was this more so than in the western province of Banora. Here the farmlands grew as man again cultivated the inhospitable lands. Herds of cattle and flocks of hardy sheep colonised the rugged moorlands and mountainsides. The people lived in peace and quiet independence.

Sadly the days of peace and harmony were to come to an end for both Bala and Banora at the start of the 14th Century of the Third Age. To the south, the lands of Ackar and Lett had grown in prominence. The 13th Century had seen the many fiefdoms and villages of Ackar and Lett brought together under the Kingship of Dewar the First. Not satisfied with a united kingdom, Dewar the First sought to stretch his power to the lands on his borders. Arance with its rich farmlands to the southeast, Ciren with its coal mines and quarries to the south and Toria with its iron ore and woodlands to the south-west all fell to the armies of Ackar and Lett during the later years of the 13th Century. The wars that raged in the south of Andore lasted for most of the last decade of the century. The kings of the southern lands fought bravely to defend their countries, but their armies were no match for the knights of the Dewar's heavy cavalry, which swept all before it. The many battlefields were scattered widely across the south. It was a decade when the crows seldom went hungry.

In 1297 Dewar the First was killed by an arrow in the final battle at the walls of Tora, the capital of Toria. By 1298, having succeeded his father, Dewar the Second controlled all the territories on Andore except for the rugged northern lands of Bala. Bala had little wealth to attract the attention of the Dewar King. Across the Middle Sea, the rich and prosperous lands of Doran, Kermin and Amina became his next desire. Dewar the Second particularly desired the gold mines in the Doran Mountains, so he led a large army to conquer these southern lands.

The alliance forces of Doran, Kermin and Amina gathered near the city of Tamin, capital of Amina, and the opposing forces met in the Vale of Tember in early July of 1299. The battle of Tember raged back and forth for two months, neither side strong enough to force the other aside. In late August the rains came and the battlefield turned to mire. It was clear no side could win and in early September a truce was made, allowing the armies of Ackar and Lett a safe return across the Middle Sea to their home lands. The southern lands were safe for that winter, but Dewar vowed he would return and conquer.

Early in 1300 an old traveller arrived at the mighty stronghold of Boretar, capital of Ackar, demanding an audience with the King of All the Lands, Dewar the Second. He was greeted by Elan of Ember, King Dewar's Commander in Chief.

Elan laughed. "You demand an audience with the Dewar, old man? Perhaps I will have you flogged to keep my men exercised. The Dewar needs no old man's prattle."

The old man's eyes sparked. "Elan of Ember, you I know, take me to your King." He paused. "Now!" The old man spoke like a crack of thunder and red lightning flashed from his open hand. The portal gate beside Elan flashed with fire and disappeared. Without thought, Elan's sword flew to his hand as he made towards the traveller. But again the red fire flashed. The sword glowed and like the gate, it was consumed by the fire. Elan collapsed, clutching the burnt fragments of his sword in his injured hand. "Take him to the King," he grunted in pain. The guards did so without delay.

Dewar the Second was clearly the son of his father. He was taller than all the other men around him, with a mane of red hair and a temper that mirrored its colour. Dewar was used to the privileges of power. A violent warrior, he thought little of executing any who opposed him. His was a reign of fear, although those who had grown rich under his and his father's time on the Ackar throne were loyal. He did not like being called from his private quarters, so now was not the time to cross the greatest power on the island of Andore.

So it was that the two met, the King dressed as only wealth and power can, and the traveller in his simple black hooded cloak.

"You'd better have good reason to make me break my rest, old man," said King Dewar.

"My Lord King, my name is Oien, and I come to you to seek an alliance. Together we can create a power to rule the entire world."

The King's laugh rolled off the rafters. "I am all powerful in Andore, old man, yet you believe you can offer me more?" The next laugh had a dangerous edge. "Perhaps you will be allowed to polish my sword for me before I take your head off with it."

Again the old eyes glowed, the hand opened, and the red fire flashed to the ceiling in a blinding blaze before being instantly quenched again in the old man's clenched fist.

"Great King, I care little for your power or your sword," hissed Oien contemptuously. "Both are as nothing under the fire. But our ways are linked. If you decide against it then it is of little consequence to me, but your power can help me."

Silence reigned in the Great Hall, and all the men held their breath; their Lord was never challenged. Once more the big man laughed, but this time there was a note of uncertainty in his voice. "So I can help you, but what do you offer in return?" he said.

"The chance to rule all of mankind."

"And who is it that asks me to form this unlikely alliance? With whom shall I rule all of mankind? Who are you, old man?"

"My name is Oien, and I am from times now lost. My power is the old power that once held sway in all the world and all the worlds beyond. That power is the gift I offer to you for our alliance."

The Dewar paused, then crossed the floor and took the old man's shoulder. "Leave us," he commanded his men. In moments they were alone.

"Tell me more, Oien. Who are you, and from whom – or from where – comes this... this power of yours?"

Oien sat down and took off the black cloak. Beneath it his robes were amber like burning embers, and his hair was silver like the moon.

"I am of the olden times, King Dewar, a remnant of a long-forgotten past. In the Second Age all the world was ruled by the Five – all the world and the planets beyond. You remember the stories, perhaps? The Council of Five held all things in their control until the meteorite rains from the skies took them all away. The Five were the masters, but not Gods, and God decided to act to recover His lost world. Of the Five, one was most powerful, and I am he. In the Council of Five I ruled, because I alone understood the nature of the power and how to control it. Everything of that Second Age was fuelled by that power – the red power of othium. King Dewar, it is othium from the province of Banora in Bala that will once again allow us to rule all the lands."

The Dewar was silent. The ghosts of the past were stalking the great halls of Boretar.

At length he spoke. "So, the days of magic return. And all the power can be mine... ours. But why do you need me?"

"Othium is now rare. It is found almost nowhere except in the province of Banora in the land of Bala. The old mines will still lie there under the wild mountains and hillsides of the Inger Mountains. In the old days they were called Am Mondah Ruadh, The Red Mountains. We must own the lands of Bala, and then we can rebuild the glories of the olden days. To take these lands needs an army. You have looked south to build your kingdom, but I need you now to turn your armies north. It is in Bala that real power lies."

Bala was the northernmost country on the island of Andore. In the far south of the island, the kingdoms of Toria, Ciren and Arance were now ruled by the Dewar. Bala lay north of the old wall and until now it had had little to interest the Dewar. Whilst Bala was not a rich kingdom, it was peaceful, and the clan structure was a democracy not copied in the richer lands to the south. The clans selected their chiefs, and they as elders ensured that any disagreement between clans was quickly resolved.

North of the old wall, the Plain of Aldene was Cameron land and James Cameron was Elder. Aldene was the capital of Bala with its castle on a rocky crag looking down on the town, which was surrounded by thick defensive walls. To the east were the lands of Ewart. Bala was bisected by the Inger Mountains; to the west was the Greater Sea and to the east the Eastern Sea. The only route across the Inger was the Pass of Ing. North of the Inger Mountains were the plains of Coe and Coelene. West of the plain of Coe was Banora, which was lightly populated, with scattered smallholdings and farms. The land had known peace and reasonable prosperity for years. The country was wild, but it gave enough for folk to tame some ground and make a living from the sheep and cows they raised and the crops they grew. Winters were raw this far north, and the people were as hardy as the animals they raised.

Alastair Munro had been born on a small farm in the centre of Banora. He was at heart a man of the land and the mountain, and he loved his homeland with a passion. In his early thirties, he wore the features of a farmer, with a weathered face and rough hands. Both his parents had died ten years earlier in a terrible winter that had locked the land in snow and ice for nine months. Since then he had worked the farm on his own.

His father had fostered his love for the lands as together they fished and hunted in the remote lochs and glens of Banora. At night beside the camp fire, his father had told him of the ancient legends of Banora, of the struggles of his ancestors as they strove to tame enough of the land to live from. As long as he could remember, the stunning rugged beauty of the mountains, the quiet peaceful lochs and glens and the spectacular summer sunsets over the Greater Sea had held him in a magical spell.

Alastair had never found the right person to share his life with; there had been girls, some of whom he had grown close to, but none had shared or understood his love of the land, and in time they had all drifted away to softer places.

Angus Ferguson had been Alastair Munro's closest friend since childhood. Some three years younger than Alastair, Angus had also lost his family in the winter of 1290 and since then the two had worked their farms together and become closer than brothers. Indeed the two almost looked like brothers. Both were of medium height, Alastair with light brown hair, Angus with red hair and beard. Matching his colour, Angus was more tempestuous, with less patience than his older friend. Life on the farm had made both men fit and strong, although their innate strength was hidden by their mild and humble demeanour. Like all of the people of Banora, the two men had been taught to show kindness and respect to their neighbours. A stranger meeting the men would have described them as friendly, yet quietly confident.

During the summer months it was usual for the two to head into the Banoran forest with their short bows to hunt the wild deer that inhabited the woods. On other days there would be fishing expeditions to the nearby rivers or lochs. Alastair would smile and tease his friend when Angus's patience would run thin after the fish refused to bite. Angus would rise to the verbal bait as his temper took hold, then as his friend's laughter increased so Angus would throw a playful punch and join the laughter.

Alastair Munro loved the early mornings as the sun rose over the northern hills and on fine evenings he would sometimes climb into the Inger Mountains to watch the sun set over the Greater Sea. Farming here was a hard life, particularly during the winter months, but it was all that Alastair knew and it was how he expected to live out his days, enjoying the different seasons and the ever-changing colours of Banora.

The world beyond Banora held little attraction for Alastair Munro, although he and Angus made occasional trips over the Pass of Ing to take their produce to the markets in Aldene. The large town always felt claustrophobic to the Banoran farmer, who was used to the open vistas of his homeland. The trips to the capital were short and it was always with a sense of relief that he returned across the pass and back to his small farm. On the last visit to Aldene the townspeople were agitated. Rumour had it that Bala's Elders had been summoned to meet in Aldene's castle and that an army was gathering in the south to invade Bala.

Alastair Munro and Angus Ferguson gave little thought to the rumours. Whatever it was that the southern king sought in Bala, it seemed very unlikely that it would be found in their small and beautiful province north of the Inger Mountains.

In the cold late winter days of 1300, soon after Oien's visit, the armies of Ackar and Lett and the conscript armies of Toria, Arance and Ciren were called to gather in the north of Ackar near the city of Erbea, close to the border with Bala. Erbea was Ackar's second city, and with its whitewashed castle and city walls it dominated the surrounding landscape. The river Erb flowed to the south of the city and it was on the plains south of the Erb that the Dewar's forces were camped. The army that gathered was large in number, and although not as magnificent as the force that had crossed the Middle Sea some nine months earlier, it still comprised nearly 50,000 men.

Elan, Duke of Ember, was Commander in Chief of the Ackar and Lett army. It was Elan's belief that the rag-tag clans that populated the northern kingdom of Bala would put up little resistance to a modern army of horse and pike. A tall, proud man with a vivid scar on his right cheek, Elan was a veteran of many campaigns. He had risen to power under the sponsorship of the old King. Once Dewar the First had united the lands of Ackar and Lett he had turned his gaze to the south and east, to the rich farmlands of Arance. In 1290 the Dukes of Arance had raised a large army to protect their border. They met the invaders on the border of Lett and Arance, on the wide, open grasslands to the west of the province of Ember. Notably absent from the defending host was the Duke of Ember.

As the armies engaged, and almost before the first skirmishes were decided, the Duke and his horsemen attacked the rear of the defending army. The result was inevitable and within three days the Dewar's forces controlled all of Arance. The young Duke of Ember's treachery was rewarded, and he became one of the King's senior generals and in time the best friend of the Prince, who was destined to become Dewar the Second.

Elan and his Ember Horse had been at the forefront of the many battles that raged across Ciren and Toria following the occupation of Arance. The light cavalry were a scourge of the foot soldiers defending their lands. Typically, once the heavy cavalry of the knights broke the front lines of the defending foot soldiers, the Ember Horse would follow with irresistible force. Not satisfied with their role in battle, the Ember Horse also terrorised the countryside, raiding far and wide in both Ciren and Toria destroying villages and delivering terror with rape and pillage.

Now, in the year 1300, Elan of Ember was feared across Andore. He was renowned as an outstanding commander of light horse and a brilliant battle tactician. The recent campaign on the Vale of Tember had been his only failure in the series of wars over the ten years that had made the Dewar lord of all the lands west of the Middle Sea. All the lands, that is, except the northern, and until now worthless, land of Bala.

The large town of Aldene lay in a quiet valley two days' ride south of the Inger Mountains. In the latter part of the First Age it had been one of the first of man's settlements, but it was in the Second Age that it became known to all mankind. Here, south of the Pass of Ing, the only route through the mountains, the transports had come to ferry a dull red rock to the far corners of the world. The rock came through the pass from the western province of Banora.

In the 13th century Aldene had become the capital of Bala. The town was surrounded by a stout wall lying behind a perimeter ditch. The grey stone houses and cobbled streets that climbed up to the castle on its rocky crag demonstrated that the town was prosperous, if not exactly rich. Aldene was the centre of commerce for Bala, and the merchants of the town traded with their Ackar neighbours to the south. The castle, with its tall keep, was on the western edge of the town, built on a rock promontory that gave views out over the plain of Aldene to the south and the mountains to the north.

The rumours that Alastair and Angus had heard when they were in Aldene were correct. The Elders of Bala had been called urgently to meet to agree a response to the imminent invasion from the south. Ala Moire was clearly the eldest of the group, hung on a skeletal frame with white hair and a long silver beard and dressed in a white tunic. The old man's features were a startling contrast to the deep blue fire that shone from his remarkably youthful eyes. The rest deferred to the old man, but not out of respect for his age; it was clear that Ala Moire was the leader whom all the others gathered in the room followed and respected.

Into the expectant silence he spoke.

"The time of peace has ended. This new century heralds great danger to our lands, and to the entire world. Many tears and much blood will be shed before we again walk in peace in the sunshine. The greed of times long forgotten returns, and those whose only desire is to rule the lives of men gather on our borders. A storm of great magnitude is brewing, my friends, driven here by the Dewar King. A mighty army gathers near Erbea, and once the cold of winter passes, that army will turn to the north. We are few, but we must defend our lands and our homes. We must fight for every inch of this precious land. Our choices are only three. They are victory, death or slavery, and a slave I shall never be."

The Elder of Ewart spoke out. "Your words are powerful, Ala Moire, yet they will not suffice. The Dewar commands 50,000 troops in Erbea. We are unskilled in war. We have no hope of defeating or even slowing down this invasion. All we can do is hope to treat with them and negotiate some settlement. If this means we bow our heads, so be it. I will not call simple allegiance to a foreign king slavery. Unless the Dewar wants to rape our land, he can have my fealty."

Koren, the Elder of Coelene, voiced his agreement. "The best way to protect my people and my land is to yield to the Dewar," he said.

"I agree." The speaker was Conall Dalzell, The Elder of Awick. Dalzell's lands were in the south east of Bala, running south from the Ewart lands to the Borderlands where Douglas Dougal was the Elder. The county of Awick was mostly dotted with small farms that produced most of Bala's crops of fruit and vegetables. There was no major town in the county, only scattered villages. Dalzell liked his comfort and spent most of his time in his large house near the centre of Aldene. In his early fifties, Dalzell visited his own lands only when he had to deal with some form of land dispute. These occurred intermittently when farm boundaries were contended.

"It is not so simple" said Ala Moire. "The Dewar is driven towards our borders by desires that will destroy our land and all things living in it. We have escaped the aggression of his armies until now because Bala offered the Dewar nothing of value, but now things have changed."

"You talk in riddles, Ala!" replied Ewart. "This land is as it always was, a land of the people who live here. It contains nothing but the land and the people who love it. I see no treasures that should drive the desire of the Dewar."

"No, the treasure, if that is the word, cannot be seen. It lies beneath this land. The Dewar is looking to things that lie beneath us in the province of Banora."

Another voice spoke up. "My homelands are fair in summer and hard in winter and we who live there have a pride in their beauty, but we have nothing to give to a king who rules all the other kingdoms on Andore."

The speaker was the tall and proud Duncan of Coe, the Elder of the Lands of Coe and Banora. It was he who called and led the meetings of the Stewards of Banora. He was the leader of his people, but in Banora, as in all of Bala, no man owned the land; it belonged to the people, and the clan structure with its hierarchy of responsibilities was a democracy that ensured everyone was treated with equity and fairness. Duncan was the Elder of Banora only by the will of the people of those lands, and his first desire was to do his duty for his people in this gathering of the Elders of the Land of Bala.

The gathering was a rare, almost unique event. As long as memory could record, Ala Moire had been the Eldest, the six Elders of the Clans the representatives of their people. Ala Moire travelled the lands ensuring the Elders maintained the order of the Clans. On occasion some of the elders would be called to resolve disputes amongst the Clans. Only once before in living memory had all six met under the same roof.

Ala Moire spoke in a hushed voice, the blue eyes looking into the distance, as if seeing back through the mists of time. "As a few of you know, my birth was in times long past, times that are now only legend. In those days the Council of Five ruled this world and much beyond it. I was one of those Five, and our power was matchless. Yet as we grew in power, it drove us and corrupted us. We lost all sense of humanity and had no care for those swept away on the tide of our excess. The energy that drove our conquests of the world, and the planets beyond, had its roots in these lands.

"Travellers from Boretar tell me that today at the side of the Dewar stands Oien. He too was of the Five, and thirsted only for power over all creation. I had thought him lost in the rains from the sky that washed away the Second Age, yet he, like me, escaped. He has ignored the affairs of man for nearly a millennium, waiting. He still desires untouchable power and has waited for the cycle of life to raise a new conqueror of nations. To rule all mankind requires not just power, but men called to do the bidding of that power. Until the rise of the Dewars, no one man could raise the resources necessary. Today, the Dewar can call on human forces that no one else can gather. With the power of othium, the Dewar and Oien will create again the horrors of the Second Age."

His words echoed in the chamber. The silence in the room only emphasised their impact.

The Elder of Ewart again broke the silence, annoyed. "Again riddles, Ala, and worse, legend. What is othium, and why should desire for it bring an army to our borders?"

"Othium is a red stone found deep within the Earth. Harnessed by those who know, it has awesome power. It is found only in a few parts of this world and in some of the distant planets. Today, probably the only place where this stone may be gathered is in the old mines beneath the Inger Mountains in the county of Banora."

The Elders all clamoured to speak at once. If Bala held such power, why could it not be used to defeat this arrogant King and the army he gathered on their border? Perhaps their salvation lay beneath their feet, in Coe's beloved Banora.

"The power of othium is fickle" responded Ala Moire, "and besides, I do not know how to release its power. In the days of the Second Age, only Oien knew the secrets that could fuel the power. In our hands it would be merely a lump of red rock, even supposing we could find it. Worse, the power of othium is not a power for good – this I know with certainty. I would not be responsible, even if I knew how, for bringing the evil red power back into the world. We must stand together and defeat our enemy; only thus will we protect the whole world from a repeat of the disasters of history."

Again the voices in the room were raised, but quickly they hushed as the door to the room opened. Framed in the doorway was a large man, dressed quietly, yet richly. No clothes could hide the physical power of the new arrival; all those gathered in the room knew him instantly. James Cameron, Elder of the Lands of Cameron, of which Aldene was the capital, was the host to this meeting of the Elders, although only now had he arrived to join them. The Cameron was renowned far beyond the borders of his own lands. He was one of the premier knights in all the northern lands. He had fought the Dewar's armies in Ciren and Toria and had gathered with the hosts of Doran, Kermin and Amina when they had met the armies of the Dewar in the Vale of Tember only a few months earlier. Such was his prowess as a leader and warrior that he had been given command of the southern flank of the great alliance army. Now at last he had returned to his own lands, and his own people.

The group waited silently for the Cameron to speak; no one questioned his lateness, or that he might not know all that had been revealed by Ala Moire. They all knew that in this group only Ala Moire outranked the man who now stood before them. They also knew instinctively that all that had been revealed to them that evening was already known to the Cameron.

Cameron spoke. "Ala Moire speaks important truths. The red stone's power is a path only to despair and destruction. It is not of succour in this time of need. We must instead rely on our hearts and bravery, and on our love for this precious land of ours."

Again the Ewart spoke. "We cannot resist the might of this army, James, they are too many and too skilled in war. We have no chance of success."

"We have our hearts and our land," repeated the

warrior. "If Banora is where the Dewar seeks power, he must cross the Pass of Ing to reach his goal. In those hills and those high passes, a few, if they are brave, can withstand the might of any king and prevail against all."

The debate raged long into the night, but none could outrank the Cameron, nor offer a better alternative to that he proposed. By morning it was decided. The Clans of Bala would gather within the month in Banora, north of the Pass of Ing. The lands of Bala south of the Inger Mountains would, where possible, be emptied of people and most of the nation of Bala would move north behind the mountains, leaving the Cameron lands and the ancient capital of Aldene to the aggressor.

Douglas Dougal, the Elder of the Borderlands, had listened to the endless debate. Dougal was a man of action, and although now in his early sixties he still led his border raiders from his base at Brough across the old wall into Ackar to steal sheep and cattle from his southern neighbours. Brough would be directly in the line of the Ackar forces as they marched north. Dougal was not about to leave his home empty for the invaders to destroy. It was a simple choice as he left Aldene to hurry back south to Brough. He would defend his land.

CHAPTER TWO

Invasion

In the early spring of 1300, Elan, Duke of Ember led the King's armies out from Erbea and headed north to begin the conquest of Bala. The northern territories of Ackar were stunning in the early spring sunshine, with their rolling hills and small, busy villages nestling in the valleys. The snows had now retreated to the far north and the march towards Bala was easy. The mood was light-hearted, despite the imminent threat of conflict. Everyone believed that very soon they would be returning victorious to their homes carrying the booty of war. None believed this more than the proud warlord Elan as he led the troops north.

A day later the vanguard of the army crossed the border at the old wall and entered Bala. Brough was like other border fortifications. On the hilltop a wooden palisade protected the outer ring of the village that huddled inside. The only stone building in the village was that of the Elder. For decades the border conflicts had involved small groups of Reivers raiding each other's lands, north and south. Although Ackar troops from Erbea had gradually pacified the borderlands, there had been no threat from a large army and so Brough did not need defensive stone walls or a castle. Elan was tempted to simply ride past the hilltop village, but then Reivers could attack his baggage train at the rear. He decided it would be good practice for some of his troops to engage in action before they met what he hoped would be a Cameron army further north.

Ember Horse would be of no use in attacking a fortified village, so Elan led a division of Ackar foot soldiers up the hill towards the gate that was the main entrance to the settlement. From the top of the wooden palisade, Dougal's warriors tried to hold back the Ackar forces with a hail of arrows. With shields held tightly in front and over their heads, only a few arrows penetrated the shield wall. The Ackar foot soldiers were elite troops who had fought in many battles and sieges, and this small village would not resist them for long. With well-practised discipline, straw bales were passed up through the Ackar force and torched at the gate of the palisade. The old wood quickly took light, and it was only a few minutes before the gate was breached and the Ackar forces broke through to the village.

The Border Reivers fought bravely, but they were no match for a division of Ackar foot. Douglas Dougal, Elder of the Borderlands, died at the door of his stone house as Elan of Ember drove his sword into the old man's throat. The village was torched with many of the residents consumed by the flames in their small wooden cottages. Brough burned like a beacon on its hilltop, a warning of what was to come.

The army marched for another day, and the scouts riding some ten miles ahead of the first columns reported no sign of a defending army. The villages and small towns they passed seemed to be only sparsely populated. Following the King's instructions, Elan ordered all the settlements to be torched. People who had remained in their villages, often the elderly and infirm, were casually slaughtered where they stood.

For Elan, this easy conquest was bittersweet. He knew these fertile lowlands of Bala were Cameron lands and he had longed to encounter an army, hopefully led by James Cameron. It was in the battle against this army that Elan of Ember would prove himself the greatest warrior, and commander, in Andore. His near failure in the battle of Tember months earlier had given him a bitter hatred of James Cameron and a thirst for revenge. Cameron had been in command of the southern wing of the alliance armies at Tember, his force had first held Elan's brave horsemen at bay and then, with stunning vision, Cameron had used his own small group of cavalry, with his fleet-footed infantry, to inflict a rare defeat on the horsemen of Ember. From this defeat had developed a stalemate on the Vale of Tember that neither army could break, ending with a truce and the retreat of the Dewar's forces back across the Middle Sea.

Elan had been first surprised, then elated, when the Dewar had instructed him to gather the army for the conquest of Bala. Elan had not questioned why, nor had he been much concerned that this new venture seemed to be driven by the strange old man Oien. A burning desire had risen in him to pillage the lands of the Cameron. This would be retribution for the defeat on the plain outside the walls of Tamin. With victory over a Cameron army, and his place in history confirmed, he would return victorious to his King and then deal with Oien. The pain from his badly-burnt hand had largely gone, but the scars remained and the memory of his humiliation burned bright. Yes, victory in Bala first, revenge on the Cameron, and then Oien.

That evening the army drew within sight of Aldene,

the capital of Bala and the seat of the Cameron.
Surely here was a place that would be defended.

The scouts returned well after dark. "My Lord,
there are no defenders at the town and the town gates
lie open to us. Most of the population also seem to
have deserted the town. Only a small number remain
locked inside their houses."

"What?" Elan was astounded. "There is no defence
in the town? No defending army in the surrounding
country? The gates stand open? Like everywhere we
have passed through, it is almost deserted? They
must be deceiving us. These lands are Cameron's, the
greatest of the northern knights, so they say, yet he
places no obstacle in our path? We march unhindered
straight into the capital of his land, and no one raises
as much as a shout against us?"

"They must have withdrawn to the hills, Elan,
I would have." Orridon, the man who spoke, bore
little resemblance to Elan, his older stepbrother.
Both were tall, but while Elan was broad-shouldered
and fair, Orridon was slim and dark, his long black
hair pulled back and tied in tails. He was of the true
bloodline of the Horse Lords of Ember whose cavalry
had terrorised much of Arance, Ackar, Lett and Ciren
more than sixty years before under the leadership of
his grandfather, Ober.

Orridon had been only thirteen in 1290 when his
elder brother had swapped sides in the battle for

Arance and so become a favourite of the old King and his son. Orridon had remained in Ember as Elan was pillaging across southern Andore in the Dewar's wars. The Duke was not popular in his homelands, being held responsible for Arance's loss of independence, although in fact Ember itself had retained a degree of independence and suffered less than the other kingdoms under the rule of the Dewar. Orridon was well known in Ember and better loved than his elder brother. In his eighteenth year, he wanted to explore beyond his home territories. With war still being fought in the south of Andore, he chose to go north. He travelled to Boretar and then on further to Bala. His journey took him to Aldene and then on over the Pass of Ing through the peaceful province of Banora and on to the foot of the Coe Mountains.

Orridon was surprised and impressed by the way Bala was governed. There was no king, and the clan structure was a meritocracy where the people chose elders who ensured that any clan disputes were resolved by compromise, not force. The land belonged to the people rather than the few, as was the rule in the southern lands.

Orridon's year of travel had toughened up the young man and given him a quiet confidence in his own abilities. By 1297 he was a skilled horse warrior. His first experiences of battle had been alongside his stepbrother in the wars in Ciren and Toria.

Orridon had also been with the Ember Horse in the engagements on the Vale of Tember. He had seen first hand the tactical skills of James Cameron and the prowess of Cameron's own light cavalry, The Red Cameron.

"And why, little brother, would you have left these lands unprotected?" said Elan.

Orridon replied, "If the people of Bala have managed to gather a clan army, it can be but ten thousand strong and will have little skill in pitched battle. If Cameron is as good as he is reputed to be, he will know that to stand against us in these open lands would be suicide. In the mountain passes to the north, however, the battle will be very different."

"And what lies to the north? What lies ahead, little brother, to give a place of safe retreat to our enemy?"

Elan was a great instinctive commander, but he gave little thought to preparation. He had marched his army north with the self-belief of one who had rarely known failure. He believed he had no need to understand what lay ahead. He would decide how to deal with the enemy when they met on the field.

"When I journeyed here some years ago, all of these southern lands were filled with people, farmers and merchants, and this Aldene was the centre of all commerce for the land," said Orridon. "To the north, two day's march away, lie the Inger Mountains. They cut Bala in half. To the north west of the Inger lies

Banora and further north the mountains of Coe. At the feet of the mountains the people live, in small villages scattered throughout the lower lands. The only way through the Inger Mountains is by the Pass of Ing. If I were defending this country I would wait beyond the pass, because in those rocky wastes the size of this army will be of little advantage. If we do have to fight, it will be there, in sight of Banora."

"Then so be it," declared Elan. "We might as well enjoy the shelter of the Cameron capital for a few days whilst we prepare to lay waste to the mountains!"

Behind them on the Plain of Aldene, the fires of the burning settlements lit up the evening sky.

Not all of the citizens of Aldene had followed their lord north to the mountains. Some of the richer townsfolk, the merchants who traded with their counterparts in Boretar, thought they would be safer staying in their homes. These merchants anticipated that they would know some of the Ackar nobles in the invading army and could beg for mercy if required.

Gordon Graham was James Cameron's chief advisor in Aldene. In his younger years he had been a renowned warrior and leader of Red Cameron cavalry. He had been mentor and tutor to the young James Cameron as the young man learnt the skills of a warrior. Now in his early seventies, Graham had told his Lord that he was too old and weak to march over mountains and he would stay in Aldene with the merchants.

As Elan interrogated the merchants of Aldene he learnt of the presence of the old man in the town. Gordon Graham was dragged from his rooms. If Elan could not fight the Cameron for Aldene, he would take some revenge here. Essen, a young and ambitious Ackar knight was ordered forward. With a nod from the Duke of Ember the young knight, with a swift swing of his sword, separated the old man's head from his body. It would be a long time before James Cameron found out about the fate of his old friend.

Elan decided he would enjoy some comfort during the few days he would stay in Aldene and commandeered the large house in the centre of the town. One of the Ackar knights found a man cowering in the basement, Conall Dalzell; the Elder of Awick, and he was dragged in front of Elan. Having witnessed the decapitation of Gordon Graham through his window, the Elder was terrified. He pleaded for mercy, promising his lands to the Dewar.

Elan smiled cruelly. "I think you have become too used to living in comfort, Conall of Awick. I have a solution for that." On his orders the Elder was taken to the castle, stripped naked and thrown into the dark pit of the castle dungeon.

Orridon, of course, did not know how correct he was. To the north of the Pass of Ing the clan army had gathered, a ragtag assembly of men numbering about fifteen thousand. These were clansmen, mostly farmers and shepherds, not warriors, although amongst their ranks were the Red Cameron. These were men of war, James Cameron's guard, an elite troop of three thousand men who had followed their chief into many a battle. The Red Cameron were now teachers, and they spent every hour of daylight working with the men of Bala to develop, at least to some degree, the skills with which they could defend their lands. The training was necessary, although in many ways it was only a contingency. James Cameron did not intend to engage all these novices in this battle. He would use the land to his advantage, helped by his small band of professionals.

Despite his confidence in the mountains, Cameron also instinctively felt that the first battle would be only the first. He knew that great forces desired this land, and for that reason he drove the clansmen to learn the rules of combat. He knew that in the days ahead every man gathered here would need to fight for his corner of his beloved Bala.

The men were in small groups of ten to twenty, each working with their Red Cameron teachers. They worked hard and long each day trying to master the sword, the bow and the pike. Angus Ferguson and Alastair Munro spent most of the time developing their skills with the bow. In Bala's bare northern land trees were few, and most of the clansmen favoured sword and pike, but in Banora, near the western seashore, grew large areas of woodland. From there the people of Banora harvested yew for their short bows. Thus the clan army had a troop of nearly one thousand skilled archers.

"I don't suppose it will be quite the same as culling the deer, Alastair," said Angus quietly as they headed back one evening to the tented base camp. "I can't imagine aiming an arrow at another person."

"No, I don't suppose it will, but while we can share this land with the deer, there will be no sharing with those headed this way from Aldene."

"But what does the Dewar King want with Bala, Alastair? He rules most of Andore, and all of it much richer than we are."

"Who knows, Angus, who knows? But Ala Moire must fear the worst. He has ordered all the people, other than the fighting men, to move north towards the Coe Mountains. If we fail to hold the pass here, then all the land of Bala is there for the taking, whatever the reason."

"We will not fail, Alastair. These are our lands and our homes. We cannot let them be lost."

"No, but I fear it will take a miracle to save them, and us."

Without another word Alastair strode off into the gloom, which well matched his mood, leaving Angus contemplating his disappearing back.

Alastair climbed up the slope to join the road leading up to the gap in the distant high mountain known as the Pass of Ing. This was home territory for Alastair Munro, his farm being only twenty miles away. Halfway up the mountain he cut right off the main path and walked down a narrow stream bed before turning up the slope again. After a few minutes he crested a narrow ridge and sat down. The view that opened up was spectacular. The setting sun was sinking over the Greater Sea, and laid out below was Banora and to the north the mountains of Coe. The power of the view, in the dying sunlight, as always, made Alastair catch his breath.

"Aye, we will need more than miracles," he muttered to himself.

"Miracles are usually wrought by those with the desire to make them happen." The voice was soft, and Alastair whirled round. Although he had never met this man, no introduction was necessary. The white hair, the long silver beard and most of all the deep blue eyes told him that this could only be Ala Moire.

Alastair leapt to his feet. "My Lord!"

"Sit, Alastair, let me watch the sunset with you."

They sat in silence for a few moments, and finally, as the last of the light disappeared over the Greater Sea, the old man spoke again. "You have been well taught, Alastair Munro. You can only really appreciate such beauty in silence and with love in your heart. Your father did well."

"I don't understand, my lord? My father loved these mountains, he taught me from his love."

"You speak truly, but what you know is not all there is to know. We are entering a time of great hardship, Alastair. The forces gathered on the other side of the mountain are but the vanguard. Much greater forces will in time be turned on these lands, forces that we cannot counter by skills in arms alone. We need to harness powers that have lain dormant for centuries, powers of good that can stand against the power of evil that is turned towards us. Guard your love of the land, Alastair, your time approaches."

Before Alastair could respond, or question, Ala Moire turned and vanished into the darkness, leaving him alone and puzzled.

It was a bright morning two days later when a Red Cameron scout entered the camp and announced that the enemy forces were only a few hours' march from the foot of the mountains. Angus and Alastair, with others of the army, ran to the head of the pass to look out over the Plain of Aldene. In the distance, plainly visible, was the army of Elan. The size of the advancing horde struck awe and fear into the hearts of the observers. Even at this distance they could pick out details. The flags of the different units of the army flew proudly above the marching troops. The advance force was made up of the proud horsemen of Ember with their wild horse banner prominent at the front. Behind the Ember Horse rode rank upon rank of heavy cavalry, and then followed a seemingly endless stream of infantry and pikemen. For most of the Clan Army the gathering in Banora was the largest single group of men they had ever seen, but compared to the hosts in the plain below they seemed pitifully few.

James Cameron was less impressed by the proud sight. He of course had seen much larger forces. What pleased him most as he surveyed the approaching army was that it had few, if any, bowmen.

As he watched, the army below slowed, then stopped. After an hour of intense activity, the enemy camp was settled and the smoke from cooking fires drifted up into the mountains.

That evening Cameron addressed his army. The message was short and simple. "You have now all seen the forces we must meet. They are many and we are few, but this is our land, and these are our mountains, and the land will be on our side tomorrow, so sleep well, and in the morning be brave and of good heart."

In the misty light of the early morning fifty Red Cameron together with a thousand clansmen, all armed with pike and sword, moved down the southern side of the Pass of Ing. The enemy camp below lay quiet before the waking hour.

John Burnett was one of Cameron's most experienced captains. Burnett had grown up in Aldene and been friends with James Cameron since childhood. Now in his early forties, Burnett had been with his chief through many battles and had earned his place as second in command of the Red Cameron. He knew this fight on the Inger would probably be the most hazardous of his life. Burnett was dressed in the livery of his chief and friend.

Halfway up the south side of the Inger Pass, the path ran between two steep cliffs that rose back towards the mountain peak. Here it narrowed, and in the gap Burnett grouped his forces between bulwarks that had been built in the previous days with rocks from the higher outcrops. The cliff walls lay only fifty yards apart and the two large stone bastions cut the steep path into three channels, each only ten yards wide at its narrowest. The clansmen deployed as they had practised, around a hundred pikemen in each channel forming a tight wedge, half the rest forming a line of pike four deep in front of the channels, the rest held in reserve behind the defensive positions. Confident that his men knew what to do, Burnett stood the troop down and the men relaxed for a short time over a light breakfast.

Gradually the noise from below grew as thousands of horses' hooves beat a rhythm on the hard mountain path. The clansmen had long finished their meal and it was in their defensive positions that Elan first saw them as he led his Ember Horse up the mountain. "At last, there are people in this land," he murmured, smiling. And there in the middle of the ragged group of defenders was the tall man in the white cape with the blue cross edged in red, standing tall under a blue cross banner.

"Cameron!" growled Elan under his breath. "I thought you would keep running. That little army will be of no help to you. The greatest knight in the north, with a beggar army. If only your rich friends in the south could see you now."

Elan halted his horsemen less than two hundred yards from the wall of pikes. Quick words passed through to his commanders. This would be a brief encounter. The horsemen of Ember on their fast plains horses had long been the scourge of pike armies. Each horseman had a short curved sword, many had light axes slung over their shoulders and they all carried the short, light, razor-sharp lance that was their hallmark. The lances were thin and strong, just under seven feet long and perfectly balanced, with a sharpened point and an edge that ran back two feet from the tip. The smiths of Ember had been making these lances for generations and prided themselves that nothing could blunt the edges of their weapons. In the hands of the light cavalry, all of whom were superb horsemen, the lance was the supreme implement of destruction to foot soldiers.

Only minutes passed before the attack formation assembled. No further instructions were needed; they were well practised in this art, although the tightness of the terrain would limit some of their options. Three columns, each with four horses abreast, would charge the defending line and as the charge reached the defending forces each column would swing across the front of the defenders, slashing or throwing the light lances into the packed array of pikemen. The horsemen would swing round back to their own troops, replenish their weapons and repeat the charge. With a hundred horsemen in each column Elan knew that only one, or perhaps two, charges would be needed to break this pitiful wall.

He positioned himself near the rear of the middle column. When his leading troops had wrought destruction on the foot soldiers, he would follow and seek out the Cameron.

The column leaders yelled their war cries and charged. The two hundred yards of ground flashed past under their horses' flying hooves. As they closed on their quarry, the front rows of defenders dropped their pikes and scrambled back over the defensive balustrades, their pikes miraculously disappearing back under the remaining channels of defenders, who pulled on thongs which had been tied to the pikes early that morning. The charging horses, because of their pace and the confused line they now attacked, were forced into the channels between the rocks. Here they met a wall of pikes and were left with no room to turn and slice at the enemy. The force of the charge pressed the leaders further into the spike-filled trap. As the horses fell the horsemen were attacked by the defenders, who moments earlier had climbed up the stony bulwarks.

It was over in minutes. The leaders of the charge were massacred, while those behind were helpless to join the battle. Elan, at the rear of the charge, only got to within twenty yards of the defenders before the returning men and horses of his own attack forced him backwards.

Twenty minutes later Elan looked back at the pike hedgehogs locked between their stone walls. There on the middle bulwark was the taunting figure of Cameron. Elan did not know that it was in fact John Burnett, dressed in his Lord's cloak. Burnett knew it had been a small victory, but a victory it was, and with the loss of only a few tens of clansmen.

Elan screamed at his commanders, berating them for their incompetence. The scar on his burnt hand was throbbing anew. The proud horsemen of Ember moved aside and the whole world seemed to tremble as the Dewar's heavy cavalry moved forward and up the mountain. The great horses, draped in their armour and each carrying a fully-armoured knight, moved ponderously up the steep slope. Where the skills of the Horsemen of Ember had not prevailed, the sheer might of the armoured knights of Ackar most certainly would. Nothing could oppose such an irresistible force. Each horse was almost fully covered in armour plate, as was the rider, in his hand no light lance but a full battle lance, heavy and fully twelve feet long and wickedly tipped with steel. This was a moving pike army, with a sheer weight that no foot defence could resist.

Three wedges formed, each with four horsemen at the head. Slowly each metal wedge advanced towards the defensive channels. But as the cavalry entered the channels, the defenders in front of them again vanished. This time the pikes were left behind as the clansmen retreated up ropes draped from the tops of the cliffs above. Again illusion had helped the defenders. In the time it had taken to call up the heavy cavalry, the Bala forces had pulled back up the mountain, leaving only a few tens of men in each channel. These too quickly vanished over the cliff top, and once there they helped their compatriots to rain stones onto the heads of the horsemen below. Although the falling stones often only succeeded in dismounting the knights, the force of the charge made it hard for those in the rear to avoid trampling their comrades.

Despite all this, the engagement lasted only a few moments before the knights of Ackar were through the balustrades and onto the wider path beyond the narrow cliffs. Here they waited as Elan and his commanders with the Ember Horse joined the front ranks.

Elan felt no pleasure in having broken this first line of defence. Almost one hundred of his elite horsemen had been killed or injured, and more than a dozen of the heavy cavalry would take no further part in this campaign. The loss was but a pinprick to the masses of the attacking army, but Elan knew he had been fooled again by the Cameron, and only a few of the rabble of defenders appeared to have fallen. Elan had broken through, but his pride was seriously wounded and his rage was terrible.

The path up the mountain that now lay in front was quite wide for several hundred yards, wide enough for a reasonable charge of his mounted forces should the opposition decide to defend this high mountain plain. However, half a mile ahead it narrowed again as it neared the crest of the mountain and the Pass of Ing. From this distance the pass appeared narrow, but not very long. It appeared to be wide enough for perhaps six or seven of the heavy horse to meet the opposition in a line, but it was also perhaps only fifteen to twenty yards to the far side, and the path presumably opened out as the road wound down to the lands of Banora below.

Quenching his rage and willing himself to keep calm, Elan turned to his commanders. "Enough, for now we have removed the first barrier no doubt more tricks lie ahead," he said. "We will hold our lines here and move into the mouth of the pass in the morning." Elan knew this was the right strategy, despite his urge to chase his quarry now that he had gained ground. The time would come to finish with Cameron, and it would be in his time, not Cameron's.

CHAPTER THREE

A Fatal Mistake

A raw, damp morning met the waking invaders. The mists clung to the mountain, and the pass, so visible the day before, lay out of sight, shrouded in low cloud. Elan was surprised that it had been a quiet night. He had posted strong pickets all round, certain that the enemy would probe their strength during the night. He had sent a few men ahead and above to the ridges of the surrounding peaks to try to gain intelligence on what lay ahead. Worryingly, none had returned. With no information, the plan of attack became straightforward. This time the heavy horse would lead the force into the pass, followed by the lighter Ember cavalry. Hopefully the brute force of the vanguard would open the way for the following elite troops to complete the slaughter.

Only Orridon questioned this. "Brother, we should lead with the pikemen," he urged. "We must outnumber their men five to one, and we should march through the pass. In this land the fight must be hand to hand, for horses cannot win here."

"We will do as I say!" snapped Elan. "Once we break through the pass we can quickly cover the ground on the other side, and with speed we can eliminate this rabble and deal with their Cameron lord."

"Elan, we do not know what defence is on the other side. We do know that the enemy will have few horses and therefore we can overpower them by sheer weight of men."

"We do as I say!" roared Elan.

Once more the mountains rumbled with the sound of the heavy drumming of hundreds of horses' hooves.

Half a mile away, James Cameron and John Burnett looked up through the same mists to the crest of the pass and heard the noise. "Away then John, and good luck," said the Cameron. He shook his captain's hand and Burnett headed back to the crest.

Contrary to Elan's assumption, the defenders had not had a restful night. Cameron had been relieved that Elan had not carried on with his heavy horse into the pass the day before. The defence had been ready then, but it would have been hard stretched.

Another night's work had enabled them to elaborate their plans and strengthen their resolve. The Red Cameron had spent the night above the enemy. None of Elan's scouts would ever report back. At the pass, the defenders planned for the hoped-for offensive of heavy horse followed by light cavalry. Surprisingly, the pass was to be surrendered cheaply; just a few archers and pikemen would try to slow down the momentum of the attack. The real defence would start some ninety yards from the pass, where concealed holes and trip wires would make the horses stumble. Then the thousand Banoran archers, concealed on both flanks of the downward slopes, would send a deadly rain of arrows into the bunched lighter horsemen as they charged down towards the obvious defensive lines of pike grouped at the entrance to another narrowing of the mountains on the downward path from the pass.

High on the slopes directly above the narrow pass, more preparation had been completed. Tons of loose stones and boulders had been gathered and tied back, concealed on the rocky mountainside. On the high slopes, Burnett was in command.

A small column of horse six abreast, each row ten feet apart, approached the waiting pikemen like the waves of an irresistible sea. The first crash of steel on steel echoed through the hills. This time there was no easy escape route for the first rows of pikemen. The horsemen just rode through them and over them. From the flanks the archers sent a volley of arrows into the advancing foe, with some small success, as a few knights or their mounts stumbled when a fortunate arrow found a crack in the thick plate armour that covered man and horse. The few fallen warriors did nothing to stem the irresistible tide, and within a few moments the leading knights broke through to the far side of the pass. There, as the road opened up beyond the pass, the knights moved aside as the charging Ember cavalry raced through to gain the far side. This time Elan was at the fore, and as the crest was gained he saw the main enemy force gathered, pikes drawn, in the narrowing some five hundred yards away down the mountainside. At the centre of the defending line was a white and blue flag and cape.

"Cameron!" yelled Elan, as he spurred his horse down the slope with his men packed behind him. The battle cries rose over the thundering sound of the horses' hooves, and the cavalry advanced on the waiting pikemen at fearsome speed. Elan sensed a sudden change in momentum, and then saw the stream of barbed arrows that rained on his horsemen from all sides. At the same moment his horse buckled and Elan, despite his prowess, was thrown to the ground. From this prone position Elan watched the charge disintegrate as the horses' hooves tangled in hidden holes and trip wires, whilst from the surrounding slopes a deadly rain continued to fall on the attackers to the tune of a thousand bowstrings. As the vanguard faltered and fell, the attackers still pouring through the pass hesitated, but the press from behind pushed more men and horses into the narrow pass. A signal from John Burnett released the stones and rubble, and to those below it was as if the mountain had collapsed. Many were buried in the rock fall, and the pass was effectively blocked off.

A hundred yards away, Elan watched it all through a mist of rage. All around him were dead and dying Ember troops and their animals. At the crest of the hill the heavy cavalry were trying to manoeuvre down the slope, but their small numbers left them isolated and exposed to the hundreds of clansmen who clambered along the sides of the mountain to the pass. By sheer mass of numbers they pulled the knights down one by one. Through his rage Elan realised that he had to get away from the battlefield. His stupid desire to engage Cameron at all costs had lost him this battle.

A few men quickly gathered round Elan, and with battle axes unslung they moved up the slope away from the field, towards the hidden bowmen. Below on their left the pike hedgehog remained lodged in the lower pass, the blue and white flag taunting them.

Almost at once Elan and his men were on top of the archers, who with no time to restring, and little experience of close combat, either fell to the axe or retreated from the fast running group.

Elan turned to urge his men to greater speed. He started to shout "Quick..." but the command never cleared his lips, as at that moment an arrow pierced his neck and tore open his throat. The great warlord pitched backwards, his burn-scarred hand grasping the arrow. So died Elan, Duke of Ember.

The rest of the group turned towards the bowman who had killed their lord, and hesitated. That was a mistake. All around them arrows thudded into their midst, and in seconds it was over. None of the group would ever leave this high mountainside.

Thirty yards away, Angus Ferguson stared across the field. Little remained moving, and nothing that was worth his arrows. The road below the pass was a wasteland of dead and dying men and horses. Angus felt sick. He now knew that war was not at all like culling deer, and the last one, with the man so close, had been the worst. The shock on the enemy's face as the arrow halted his run would haunt him always. Angus took a deep breath to calm himself; they had had no choice but to defend their homeland. The killing had had to be done.

On the southern side, Orridon looked up at the pass in dismay. Now blocked with tons of rubble, it had become the battlements from which the defenders continued to fire their deadly rains of arrows. The attackers were streaming back out of arrow range, leaving a number of dead and dying men in their wake. The forces of Ackar were moving back off the mountain to their base camp on the plain.

"Bowmen!" Orridon cursed. "Why did I not remember the Banora bow? Would Elan have listened to the warning?"

Orridon immediately took up command. He had been left behind when the first attack was made, to co-ordinate the movements of the rest of the troops through the pass. Now, in his stepbrother's absence, it was natural for him to pick up the reins of command.

Over many hours, stragglers made their way back to camp, many wounded. But none would return from the death road that lay north of the pass.

James Cameron and John Burnett stood on the road amid the scenes of death. The bodies were being gathered into a large heap just beyond the rock fall that now filled the Pass of Ing. Further down the road where the attack had failed, a small group of people, with Ala Moire in their midst, tried to patch up wounded men from both sides. Angus Ferguson and Alastair Munro, with a group of the clan archers, came up the road, bringing more bodies to the pile.

"Stop!" commanded Cameron. "Let me look at that man." He looked down at the body of Elan. The deep scar on the right cheek was confirmation.

"Well, well, my friend, so you didn't get away," he murmured.

Angus spoke next. "Sir, he and these others moved from the road up the slope trying to escape. They killed several of our men, but we had too many archers for them to escape."

"Do you know who this is?"

"No sir."

"This is, or was, Elan of Ember, Commander in Chief of the Dewar's armies. He was one of the great warriors of the northern world. Learn from him. He let his power and his anger cloud his judgement, and all these men" – his hand swept towards the pile of bodies – "paid the price. We were but a small thing he thought he would destroy. How could he fail? With patience and thought, he would not be lying here now. Put him with the others."

He turned to Angus. "What is your name?"

"I am Angus Ferguson and these are my friends, people of Banora."

"And you are Munro," said Cameron, turning to Alastair. "Your time is coming."

Alastair was puzzled; he had never met the Cameron before.

"Angus Ferguson, you and your men have added greatly to this victory. You will stay by my side," said the Cameron.

As night fell, the light from the fire filled the sky. On the plain below, Orridon cursed. Still no one had returned from the far side of the pass. The count now indicated that nearly five hundred elite troops were missing. This was a small number considering the massed force of Ackar, but among them were many of the greatest warriors of the realm, slaughtered by a ragtag army of farmers. Orridon again cursed his stupidity in forgetting the bowmen of Banora. Instinctively he knew what fuel was producing the flames that burned above on the mountain.

High above the Plain of Coe, a strange procession wound its way down from the mountain peaks. Alastair Munro, Angus Ferguson, Ala Moire and a group of men from Banora pulled rough sleds, each of which carried a wounded man. Other wounded enemy staggered behind the sleds blindfolded. Ala Moire had for once countermanded the Cameron, who would have had all the captives killed and added to the fire. Ala Moire had treated them as well as he could, and by ways known only to those of Banora he had brought most of the enemy wounded down to the bottom of the mountains. Only a few of the critically-hurt remained beyond the Pass of Ing.

When the new morning dawned, Orridon was called from his disturbed sleep early and taken to the foot of the pass. There he found about fifty injured men, all that remained from the furious charge through the Pass of Ing. In moments he learned what he had already expected; that Elan would not return from the high mountain. The conquest of Bala, which was supposed to be so easy, had been one campaign too many. Orridon felt little sorrow; he and his stepbrother had been warriors together but never friends. Now it might be his own time for fame and glory.

His musing was interrupted by the thunder of hooves approaching the camp. Orridon had lookouts and defensive positions, so these could only be friends, although he guessed that they might be less friendly when they heard the news.

Orridon left his tent as the visitors arrived. He was not surprised to see the King with the strange old man Oien at his side, followed by the King's own Ackar cavalry, the King's Guard.

The Dewar was far from happy, "Where is that fool brother of yours?" he barked. "He should control every inch of this land by now. Get him."

"He is dead, sire."

"What?"

As Orridon told the story, the King's anger grew. "He was a fool! Cameron is one of the very best, and Elan did not even make it difficult for him. Tomorrow we get the army moving again. This time I will lead, and there will be no mistakes."

"My Lord King, the pass is now blocked and the Cameron has a strong and skilled group of archers under his command. Taking the pass will cost many lives."

"So be it. I will not be halted by a rabble of farmers, no matter how great their commander thinks he is."

Oien spoke for the first time. "There are other ways, sire. Let me talk with Orridon and we will build the plan."

"It had better be good, old man. I am impatient to be rid of these people of Bala. We will meet later and hear what you have in mind."

The fire had burnt itself out during the night, though the smoke and smell lingered in the softness of the early morning. Ala Moire and the Cameron were discussing the previous day's events.

"You should be proud of them James, they held strong against the greatest warriors in Andore, and indeed triumphed," said Ala Moire.

"We won a little battle, with guile and aided by the land, against an impatient foe," Cameron replied. "You know this is no victory, you know the power that gathers on the other side of the mountain. It will not be so easy when they return, be it with might of men – or with might of magic." He paused. "What do we do from here, Ala? We planned a defence in the mountains to protect Banora. The pass was defendable against rashness, but next time... If I were our enemy I would march up on foot and win the day through sheer mass of men. I see no way to delay it, much less stop it."

"We must retreat further, James," replied Ala Moire. "We must be here to fight on another, better day, if there is one. Most important, it is not yet time for the chosen one. He cannot be risked until he himself finds his power. We will move north and follow our people to the Hidden Lands beyond the Mountains of Coe. Only a few know the way to those lands. We can plan and build there, although in so choosing we leave Oien the red power waiting in Banora."

"There is no choosing with but one choice, and we cannot lose all of Bala and more in a vain sacrifice for Banora. So be it, we must start now and follow the others to the Coe and the lands that lie beyond."

The choices fell less easily with the men of the army of Bala. They knew little of the wild northern lands, and of course many had homes in Banora and the regions close by. Those who had come from the southern Cameron lands and the city of Aldene had hoped that they could find some peace here in Banora; they also had no wish to move on yet again. Nonetheless it was clear that many of the families and non-combatants had already started moving north.

Angus Ferguson was among the loudest of the

dissidents. "We have beaten this great army of the Dewar once on these mountains, so let him try again. These are our lands and we will die on them if need be. We have proven this is no great foe, however great his army. Let them come to the slaughter again."

A cheer of support rose, but as the Cameron started to reply another voice cut in, softly, yet with awful certainty. It was Alastair Munro.

"Friends, this land is mine as it is yours. I love it and its beauty beyond all things – the hills and mountains, the lochs and glens, the sky and the forest. This land is my birthright, my love of it born of my father, and his born of his father in turn. I, like you, would die for this place, but not now, when we cannot succeed other than with death. We will prevail over the evil that stretches its claws over our land, but not on this mountain and not in this moment.

"Somehow I know that beyond the pass lie forces and powers beyond our dreams. It is a miracle that we have survived once and wrought such havoc on the aggressor. He will not be so foolish again. If you love this land and your homes, the only way is to preserve yourselves for the fight to come, at a time and in a place where death is not the only choice. For now, I choose the lands to the north."

Alastair stopped, almost as amazed by his own unplanned speech as were those around him. For a few moments, the silence that followed was broken only by the hiss of the fire. Then, with nods and murmurs of agreement, the people began to disperse to ready themselves for the long march north.

As Alastair Munro moved off, Angus Ferguson confronted him. "What right do you have?" Angus snapped. "How can you profess to care for this place when you will walk away from it with your tail between your legs, leaving it to who knows what? I say it is better to die here than to run away and live the life of a coward. I find it hard to believe I heard you say the things you just said."

Alastair sighed. "Angus, I cannot bear to leave, but I know we must. Something deep inside tells me we know little of what is happening here. It is neither the death nor the fight I fear, but that the wrong choice will cause this place to be lost forever. I cannot explain." He shrugged and walked away. Angus stared at the disappearing back of his oldest friend.

It was mid-afternoon, and already the high peaks hid the Ackar camp from the spring sun. Orridon and Oien had talked and planned for much of the day. The old man was impressed by the quiet certainty of the other, so unlike the impetuous fire of his dead brother. Oien learnt of Orridon's time spent exploring the lands of Bala and of his knowledge of the secret routes through the mountains. It was a surprise to

Oien to learn about the ways of the clans that Orridon described. It was clearly a land for the people, with its brave attempt at democracy and fairness, and Ala Moire sounded so like the description of an old friend and advisor, but that could not be; he could not have survived too.

The night was deep black, with no moon, and a myriad stars watched Oien and Orridon pass through the narrow cut of rock to stand above the Pass of Ing. Orridon was searching for ways he had travelled a few years before. It had been a long climb. There had been a number of wrong turnings, some leading to the edges of great precipices where one further step in the dark would have cut the journey very short. At last they had reached the goal and they were now looking down on their objective. Beyond the pass, in the deeper dark of the plain, burned the distant fires of the Bala army.

"Well done Orridon," said Oien. "From here we can clear the land for your army. Go back now and prepare your men."

A tired sun slowly climbed in the eastern sky as Oien studied the land below. He was surprised that so few men hid beyond the boulders sealing the pass, and even stranger was the small group of men he could see moving in the distant camp. Surely so few could not have wreaked the damage of the day before? Still, few or many, it mattered little. Soon the land would be his and the Dewar's.

Slowly from the south, the Ackar foot soldiers emerged. John Burnett, as always in the front line, watched from his shelter above the Pass of Ing. Had he looked high above him at the opposite side of the pass, he would have puzzled at the old man tucked into the edge of the steep rock face. As it was, the focus of his concern was lower and to the front. He knew his task was almost impossible. "Hold the pass as long as you can, then leave and follow us" had been the simple request of James Cameron as he shook his hand. "No heroics John, I want you back here with as many of the men as you can bring. Now is not the time to lose lives."

So his hundred archers were scattered across the sides of the pass and on top of the boulder-blocked central area. Below them in the narrow gap that had baited the trap the day before, the remaining defending pikemen readied straw dummies for the fight, one fake soldier each. Cameron had been right; this time it was not the horses but the infantry. They were certain to win through, but they would come slowly and Burnett thought his bowmen would cause them serious pain before they had to surrender their perches. He did not intend to engage the pikemen; the men with their straw dummies were only there to encourage the enemy to come within arrow range. When the first of the Ackar foot crossed the boulders, the men of Bala would rapidly retreat to the plain and head north to join the rest of the army.

Orridon halted the slow march just out of bowshot. There he told his men to stand at ease and watch.

As Burnett looked down at the stationary, silent army, a shiver passed down his spine. All his senses told him something was not right. He realised that it had gone deathly quiet; not even birdsong broke the stillness. Then in the corner of his eye a movement caught his attention across the pass, and above him he saw an old man in a black cloak. As Burnett watched, red fire flew from the old man's staff and struck the boulder barrier that blocked the pass. The boulders exploded in fragments, and the blast threw Burnett sideways and back onto the sheltered side of the slope.

Through the haze of concussion, Burnett saw the red flame light the pass again and again. Fragments of stone crashed around his little hollow. Then it stopped. Burnett pulled himself forward, keeping very low. From the edge of his sheltered ledge he looked down into the pass. The stone barrier was gone, as was any sign of defenders; no one moved in the surrounding rocks or in the gap further down the mountain. The entire space had been swept clean, and the only trace of the barrier was the scorch marks on the edges of the roadway where the mountain heather still smouldered together with the clansmen's bodies.

To the south a loud cheer rose from the watching ranks of foot soldiers. The day had been won without blood and sweat. The path through the mountain was theirs simply to walk up and secure.

Orridon, in the soldiers' midst, looked thoughtfully towards the high mountain tops. There he could just see the old man retracing the steps of the previous night as he picked his way down to the mountain road. Orridon had anticipated that power and position would be his following the death of his brother, but as he reflected on the event he had just witnessed, he shivered inside at the thought that power had perhaps suddenly become a lot more dangerous. Men Orridon understood and did not fear; the magic Oien wielded was a very different force.

Burnett also now saw the old man more clearly, the silver hair and the black cloak that covered the amber robes. The thought passed through his mind that in another place and dressed in a different colour, the man on the mountain top could have been Ala Moire. The man carried only a staff, and Burnett wondered how he had conjured up the devastating fires. However, the time for observing was running out. Below the foot soldiers of Ackar and Lett were moving through the Pass of Ing and ahead of them, unprotected, lay Banora and the north of Bala. Burnett grunted as he pushed deeper into his mountain hideout, dismayed that he had managed to hold the pass only for a few minutes and that all his men had now been lost to the terrifying fire. Hopefully Cameron had made enough ground during the night to be out of reach of the advancing army. For himself, Burnett would lie up in his hideout for the rest of the day, try to learn something of the enemy, and then under cover of night move north to join his friend and master.

Some twenty-five miles to the north, the army of Bala was making progress as fast as it could towards the Coe Mountains. When the thunderous noise of the destruction in the Pass of Ing reached them, they turned to see the pass erupting like an angry volcano. The flames, even at this distance, were terrifying and shock was etched on every face as each man considered the defiant bravery of the day before, a bravery that could have had them consumed by withering fire.

Ala Moire turned to Cameron. "It seems the rumours about Oien were true," he said. "He, or one with his power and knowledge, travels with the Dewar King. We must move faster, James. We do not know how far Oien's fire can reach. In the days of old we would be far from safe so close to the power of othium."

In the midst of the ranks of clansmen, an ashen-faced Angus Ferguson turned to his oldest friend. He gasped as he saw Alastair Munro shrouded by a field of white, a shower of sparks dancing around him. "Alastair!" he shouted, but as Alastair turned to face him, the power faded and the sparks disappeared. "What was...?" Angus struggled for the words.

Alastair Munro looked sadly back again to the mountains. "An evil has returned from the past, Angus. Our land will be consumed as in days long gone. But this time, fire will beget fire and power will beget power. I will return and cleanse the land – my land."

Angus said nothing. A strange awe filled him as he looked anew at this man he had always known, or thought he had.

A short distance away, Ala Moire also felt the surge of power and saw the radiance surround Alastair Munro. He turned again to Cameron. "His time is coming; the deep love of his land will nurture his power,' he said. 'We must ensure he is safe until he is strong enough to do what must be done."

Cameron nodded and shouted to his commanders, "Faster! We must make the mountains by nightfall."

The foot soldiers in the pass moved aside to let the splendidly-garbed horsemen through. In their lead a tall red-haired figure brushed the slower-moving soldiers aside, nearly trampling a few. Burnett had never seen the Dewar, but he had heard the stories and the description. There was no doubt who this arrogant newcomer was.

The King was closely followed by the old man from the mountain, and the rest seemed to be the commanders of the Royal Guard. The Dewar stopped below Burnett's crevice and shouted to a tall Horse Lord with long black hair pulled back and tied in tails in the manner of the old Horse Lords of Ember. Burnett had already established that this one was Orridon, and he was the general commanding the foot soldier army.

"Greetings, Orridon!" cried the Dewar. "An easy day for you and your men, thanks to Oien. However, your wisdom has been noted and your caution is welcome after your brother's foolhardiness. I think you deserve the chance to prove that you can be a good successor to your brother as my commander in chief of the occupation armies here in Bala."

"Thank you, sire" Orridon quietly responded. "My horsemen are already after whatever remains of the defenders of this place. I hope they can exact some revenge for the lives wasted here."

"Good. Let them give chase, but the remnants of the Cameron army are of no consequence to me. We need now to move swiftly to the heart of Banora so that Oien can seek out that which is hidden."

Orridon did not understand the riddle, but he instinctively knew it was related to the red fire, and once again he shivered. In his hiding place Burnett also shivered; he knew from Cameron a few of the old stories of othium, and although his Lord had cautioned him that the invasion of Bala was to rediscover the old power, still it melted his resolve when considering a foe strengthened by unworldly magic.

Angus Ferguson was in the rearguard of the clan army when one of the Red Cameron came up at speed, his horse foaming with the exertion of the chase. The Cameron recognised Angus, having seen him in conversation with his chief the night before on the high pass.

"You!" he shouted to Angus. "Tell my lord that the enemy horse gives chase – they have not waited by the pass. They will be on you here in the rear within the hour."

Having spoken, the clansman spun the exhausted horse round and headed back south across the open plain. Angus looked to the south, and shading his eyes against the sun he could see far in the distance a dust cloud. Quickly he mounted his stocky Banoran cob and hurried forward to the centre of the strung-out column to pass the message to James Cameron.

Cameron, one of a small number of the clan army who was mounted, drew alongside Ala Moire. "We are two hours from the mountains, Ala, and the enemy are only an hour or so behind," he said. "When we reach the Coe we need to find the secret ways. Sunset is still several hours away. We cannot meet the Ember Horse here in the open plain, it will be slaughter. I will gather the Red Cameron to me here and hold the position for as long as possible, but you must hurry the rest to move faster, I cannot hold a horse army here for long."

Ala Moire looked back down the route they had followed, his blue eyes narrowing as if focusing on the far distance. He turned to Cameron. "No James, now it is my turn to buy us some time. Take the army to the foot of the Coe; you know what you seek there. I have already sent a message to the Guardians, who will have already guided most of the people through the mountain to the Hidden Lands. The army must now follow. I will give us the time to reach the Hidden Lands. Leave me ten archers, the best, and ten fast horses. We will rejoin you before sunset. Now make haste."

Cameron made to object, but one look at the steel in the old man's blue eyes told him this was not the time.

Angus Ferguson and nine Banora clansmen stayed with Ala Moire. Each man had two quivers of arrows and was mounted on a rugged Banoran cob, having rejected the offer of one of the bigger and much faster southern horses captured from the Ember horsemen the day before. Sensibly, each of the clansmen understood that if they needed speed to escape, their mounted skills would be no match for their pursuers, whilst their rugged ponies might be able to cover terrain impassable to the larger, swifter enemy horses.

Angus turned to Ala Moire. "My lord, we are ten strong with a few hundred arrows. Do we plan to slow down our pursuers for long?"

"Faith Angus, we are stronger than you might imagine."

Angus looked north; the clan army had almost disappeared, whilst to the south the column of dust from what had to be at least five hundred mounted men grew ever closer. In a few minutes the pursuing horsemen raced into full view only a couple of miles away on a ridge, and then vanished again behind a higher rise about a mile away.

Ala Moire called Angus and one of the other clansmen to him. "Each of you string one arrow to your bow," he said. The two quickly did as they were bid. "Now hold the arrow towards me." Again they followed instructions. Ala Moire cupped each arrowhead in his hands, and as he did so an intense white glow surrounded each tip. "Now Angus, fire to the south-east as far as you can. Do it!" The other clansman followed the same instruction, but this time to fire to the south west.

The two arrows soared into the distance, their tips still glowing white silver. The arrows flew beyond the clansmen's sharp eyesight, but the bright blue eyes of the old man followed their path until they struck the ground. Ala Moire drew himself up to his full height and drew his outstretched hand from arrow to arrow. Instantly a broad flowing river, fifty yards wide, began to flow through the plain below. The clansmen gasped in awe. Ala Moire's hand then swept along the watercourse and a mist appeared, shrouding the northern bank of the river.

No sooner had the watery barrier and the mist appeared than the Ember horsemen drew into sight on the higher ground. Their leader reined in his frothing mount and glared at the water now rushing between him and his prey. A stranger to these lands, he had no knowledge of this terrain, but as an experienced plainsman he was surprised to find so wide a watercourse here. Slowly he led his troops towards it.

Quietly the watching Ala Moire instructed the Banoran archers to fire at the slowly-oncoming cavalry. The range was close to the limit of the short Banoran bow, but the first two volleys took two of the horsemen from their saddles.

Dismayed, the horde withdrew out of range to consider their options. With their enemy hidden behind the mists on the far side of the river, it was impossible to judge how costly a full attack across the river would be.

Having seen too many of his comrades slaughtered in haste in the past day, the Ember leader was reluctant to charge into the unknown again. Cember was from one of the older Ember families. The long black hair tied back in braids indicated that he was an important Horse Lord. Indeed he was Orridon's senior lieutenant, and whilst much more experienced in warfare than his chief, he shared Orridon's natural caution. Cember instructed three of his men to approach the water's edge on foot to gauge the depth and speed of the water. Although they did not know it, the three men were also going to give him an indication of the shooting prowess of his enemy and their range, or so he hoped.

It did not turn out as Cember hoped. Unfortunately for the troopers, all three were surprised by a completely different enemy. As the first of the three reached the water's edge, a sound like the screaming of wild dervishes erupted on the flanks of the Ember force. Straight out of the mist and the water and into the forward flanks of the Ember troops crashed two columns of horsemen, each fifty strong and all dressed in white with blue crosses edged in red on the breasts of their surcoats. The troops of Red Cameron sliced through the stationary Ember horsemen and then vanished into an eerie silence, leaving two score of the horsemen dead on the plain.

Cember instantly called his men to arms and

formed a defensive circle on the high ground they occupied. He peered at the apparently empty plain around him. How could a hundred riders materialise from nowhere and then vanish as abruptly? He knew the prowess and reputation of the Red Cameron and their skill in skirmish and guerrilla warfare, but what had just happened defied belief. Then Cember's gaze passed over the three troopers who had been mown down as the Red Cameron had appeared to rise from the river. The lead trooper lay in the river, but the water seemed to ignore him, neither breaking nor parting but apparently flowing straight through him. It dawned on Cember that the great river was nothing more than an illusion.

On the north bank, Ala Moire silently cursed the skill of the Red Cameron. His mirage was about to be undone. At his command, Angus and the other Banoran archer let fly two more white silver-tipped arrows into the far banks of the phantom river. The old man's hand again swept from arrow to arrow and instantly a thicker, heavier mist rolled over the river, billowing onto the southern banks and engulfing the Ember horse.

Cember instinctively knew that all was not right, and that this non-existent river and the sudden mist were all too convenient. Equally there seemed no question that the mist was real, as Cember now could not make out the edge of the river. If the Red

Cameron were as they appeared, he and his men were in mortal danger.

Cember called his men to dismount and hurriedly they grouped their horses in the centre of several concentric rings of men. Each ring crouched in the mist with the men's short spears pointing out to an invisible enemy.

Ala Moire turned to the clansmen. "Now go as fast as you can to the Coe, you have done all you can here. Go!"

Angus and his comrades leapt onto their wiry cobs and made haste towards the north, following the route of the clan army. Ala Moire watched the clansmen go; on his larger horse he could soon catch them. He turned back to look at the defensive Ember circles. His mist, impenetrable to the men of Ember, was completely transparent to his blue eyes. He had bought the army at least forty-five minutes, maybe a little more; it might just be enough.

One more little trick might hold the pursuit a little longer. Ala Moire picked up the bow he had taken from Angus as he left and fired a single silver-white arrow into the centre of the river, directly in line with the Ember horse. Then, without another backward glance, he mounted his horse and sped towards the Coe Mountains.

CHAPTER FOUR
Escape to the Hidden Lands

The sun was already low in the sky when the clan army reached the first rocky promontories that stuck out from the base of the Coe Mountains. These strange features at the foot of the Coe had never been explained to James Cameron. Whilst clearly born of the same grey rock as the mountains, the rocky toes sticking out up to a mile from the first proper lower slopes had never looked natural to him, yet their size and complexity appeared far too great to have been fashioned by the hand of man. However it was man's workmanship that the Cameron now sought as he led the army along the face of the promontories. He was looking for a place he had not visited for many years, and which was extremely difficult to find even if you knew where it was.

Night was falling when Cameron spotted what he searched for. Between two of the longest of the promontories were four much shorter toes which stretched out a hundred yards from the mountain base. Cameron steered the army down between the longer promontories towards these smaller toes, which were perhaps a mile away. As Cameron got close to the mountain base he could make out small grey rocks between the small toes. From this distance the grey specks looked like the remaining teeth in an almost empty jaw.

The sun had long ago passed behind the mountain, leaving John Burnett in cold shadow in his small mountain crevice. Below him the vast ranks of the armies of Ackar and Lett and the conscripts still trudged through the Pass of Ing and headed down into the Plain of Coe or moved west towards Banora. Into the evening the procession continued relentlessly.

Burnett, becoming cold and increasingly frustrated with inactivity, decided that from his perch above the pass he could climb higher unnoticed, then cut west before heading down close to the border of Banora and then with luck cut north and east crossing the ford over the river Ola to rejoin Cameron. The move off the pass and over to the lower slopes above Banora was remarkably uneventful and he saw the sun set over the Greater Sea at almost the same time as his chief, miles to the north, was finding the landmark he sought at the foot of the Coe.

As night drew in so the temperature fell, and, more of a problem to Burnett, the closer he moved to the foot of the mountain the closer he came to the invading army still moving down the mountain or setting up their camps on the Plains of Coe and the open land of Banora.

Burnett moved with speed tinged with caution. He held to the slightly higher ground, which although more difficult to navigate was less likely to hold any enemy. Finally, as Burnett moved north and east, he came to the road that wound down from the pass and tumbled out onto the flatter lower ground. This would be the most difficult test, to move across the road undetected. He climbed a little way back towards the crest to find a point where the road swung back on itself to reduce the gradient, and as a train of supply wagons passed, he slipped to the east side of the road. It was now a short drop to the edge of the Plain of Coe. He would move round the foot of the Inger Mountains until he was clear of the invaders and then strike north.

As Burnett reached the foot of the mountains again, he found himself only a short distance away from the outlying tents of the enemy camp. By keeping his distance and working east, he planned to avoid all contact. However, not far from him and a little distance from the other tents was a pitch that drew his attention. The tent was brighter than the others in the gloom, and the light that illuminated the inside appeared to be fuelled not by fire but by a strange amber light. Partly drawn by curiosity and partly by the hope of having additional intelligence to take back to Cameron, Burnett slithered through the plains grass towards the tent. Soon he could hear conversation within it, although it seemed only one person was speaking.

"Well othium my old friend, I am come to harvest you once more, and to renew your acquaintance with the Salt of Elat" said the voice, and gave a muffled laugh. "Then, who knows? Maybe once more we will join together to reach for the heavens. First though, we will give the idiot Dewar the southern lands he covets, and then we will recruit my armies to rebuild all that was taken away from me by the meteorite rains."

Burnett knew he had stumbled across the tent of the old man who had dispensed the fire on the mountain top that morning, the one they called Oien. The fire burning warm inside the tent was of no earthly flame but the magical glow of othium. Burnett had seen enough, and whilst he would not openly admit it, this new world of magic scared him near to death. He hastily retreated to the safety of the lower mountain slopes and headed on east before leaving the mountains and branching north for the Coe.

On the plain of Coe, Cember knew that time was not on his side. Even through the thick mist he could tell that the day was ebbing fast, and although he had no idea what lay ahead across the plain it was clear that he had to try to make contact with the enemy army before nightfall or risk losing it in the dark. The mist still surrounded his men, drawn now into their defensive positions. He was surprised that they had not been attacked again.

He called his men to the saddle; he had to risk a gallop through the mist and across the unnatural river. Hopefully the mist would give his charge protection against the archers on the far side, and once through he could pursue the clan army again. Raising his hand, he kicked his horse into a gallop and raced towards the river, followed by his mounted army.

Two thoughts struck Cember simultaneously as his horse's hooves struck the ghostly water. Firstly, and not entirely to his surprise, the hooves created no splash in the strange river, and secondly he was not the only creature in this misty place. It was the second thought that made him pull back from a full gallop, and as he did so some of his men passed by him.

In that instant a nightmare rose up before them. It was a great black creature more than twenty feet tall, and its huge head held a massive jaw with row upon row of razor-sharp teeth. The monster threw back its head, roared and charged upon the leading riders. The men reacted fast, but the terrified horses responded even faster, rearing up and throwing their riders or simply turning on the spot and heading back the way they had come, crashing into the ranks of their own comrades still moving down to the river.

Cember held his horse's nerve and wheeled the animal to the left, clear of the monster and the increasing confusion in the charging ranks. The monster reached the first of the fallen men, raised its head again and let out another terrifying roar, causing more fear and confusion in the oncoming ranks of horse. Then in an instant the river, the mist and the monster disappeared and Cember found himself looking across the grassland plain at his scattered army.

Few in the world could have created such an illusion. Only one who had seen the ancient charcoal cave paintings from the First Age could have included a Tyrannosaurus Rex in the illusion. Only Oien and Ala Moire had memories that stretched back so far.

Cember cursed. In the clear late afternoon he could see the sun settling in the west and in the far distance the line of the Coe Mountains, where by now the enemy must be moving into defensive positions in the lower slopes. His army of horsemen would have no tactical advantage fighting footsoldiers behind strong defensive lines. His task was doomed to failure; still, at least he could confirm the enemy positions to his master.

Another hour passed before all the horses had been gathered, the injured tended and the force organised for the dash across the plain to the mountains.

The clan army had reached the ground just below the grey slabs in the mountainside when Ala Moire and the small group on their Banoran cobs joined them. Ala Moire advanced through the ranks to join Cameron at the front of the army.

"Well" said Cameron, "you seem to have managed to slow our pursuers sufficiently."

"We should have just enough time, James. The Ember Horse are probably right now fleeing from a monster from their worst nightmares. To business. We need to get the passageways open and get everyone moving to the Hidden Lands before our pursuers get here and can follow our way."

"I have men behind us obliterating the trail and laying a few surprises for those that reach the first of the grey promontories," replied Cameron.

Angus Ferguson and Alastair Munro followed Ala Moire and Cameron up the first few yards of the Coe to reach the strange stone teeth locked into the mountainside. As they approached the grey stones it was clear that these were not natural elements of this terrain. Each was finely polished and fitted like a glove into the slot in which it was located. No gaps could be seen where rock and stone met; not even a sword tip could have slotted between the edges.

Ala Moire reached the first of the grey stones and put his shoulder against it. To the surprise of all of those looking on, the massive stone moved silently backwards, revealing a small entrance with a passage running first to the right and then back into the mountain. All ten of the stones yielded to the same pressure, and soon the clan army was vanishing into the heart of the Coe Mountains, just as their families had a day earlier.

Angus and Alastair, along with Cameron, were among the last to file into the dark passages. The two Banoran farmers were surprised to find behind the stones a force of tall, distinguished warriors garbed for battle. These were the Guardians of the Hidden Lands, and as the last of the army moved away inside the mountain, so the Guardians moved the stones back into position in their slots and effectively prevented them from being moved again by placing wedges into craftily-worked locking points between the edges of the stones and the grey rock of the mountain.

Cameron turned to Ala Moire. "Come, let's go. We have a long walk through the tunnel before we reach the other side," he said. "The Guardians will ensure that any stragglers get passage and the enemy remain barred."

The passageways that Angus and Alastair followed were wide enough for ten men to walk abreast. The walls were alabaster smooth, and every twenty feet or so a flaming torch guided the walkers further into the heart of the mountain. The passageways wound their way forward, often taking sharp defensive turns in their course, but they remained on a flat gradient and as a result the march through the mountain was long but not onerous.

The hours drifted by, and several rest stops punctuated the journey. Silenced with a strange awe at the engineering mastery of the route, no one asked James Cameron how these tunnels had come into existence. He was one of the few in the group who knew something of the history of these secret routes and the Hidden Lands that lay beyond, though he knew only the outline. In the early part of the Second Age, the Plains of Coe and Coelene had been well-populated by a tribe of proud people. The Coelete were a tall, handsome people, sophisticated in their culture and fierce warriors to their enemies. They hunted the plentiful game that roamed the plains and farmed the fertile ground in many smallholdings. They lived their settled existence for many generations, occasionally defending their lands from other acquisitive tribes, but generally unbothered as their society developed and thrived. Then, in the middle of the Second Age, the mineral power that lay in Bala was discovered and the lands of Coe and neighbouring Banora became the desire of much more powerful forces than the neighbouring tribes. The Coelete had no skills to match the might of the powers of the Council of Five and slowly retreated across the plains to scratch an existence on the rocky lower slopes of the Coe. Here, as Banora was plundered for the red stone, the Coelete were left and largely ignored. Their homelands on the plains became the homes and the factory space for those employed from afar to prepare the othium for its journeys south and much further.

Anaton was a young chief of the Coelete who knew the stories of the tribe's proud history, and he despaired at the poverty into which his people had been plunged. It was written in the histories that Anaton was visited in a dream by one of his forefathers and told to search for new homes to the north. Anaton, like all his people, knew that to the north there were only the Mountains of Coe reaching to the sky, and beyond the Coe lay nothing; it was the end of the world. However, he believed strongly in the wisdom of his forefathers and in the power of dreams, so early one spring, with two friends, he ventured north into the mountains. The story of Anaton was long in the telling and his struggles over the mountains a thing of legend. However, after two years Anaton returned alone to tell his tale and to describe to his chief and his people the new land that lay hidden over the mountains, where no people lived and where perhaps the Coelete could again thrive.

Olaton, the chief of all the Coelete, knew that his people could not journey over the mountains and survive to reach these promised lands on the other side. However, convinced of the truth of what Anaton had found, Olaton that self-same day began the task of cutting a passage through the mountain to secure a future on the other side for his people. By the time the long task was completed and the Coelete nation moved through the passageways into the promised serenity of the Hidden Lands, Anaton was an old man and himself chief of the Coelete. Initially the Coelete populated the myriad caves that existed on the lower slopes of the northern Coe, building townships in the shelter of the mountains. Later they moved out and populated the rich northern land, continuing their life of farming and hunting.

The Coelete balanced their needs with the nature of their new territory and managed their numbers so as not to overstretch the natural resources of animal and land available to them. So they survived for a millennium, hiding the routes to their lands behind the grey slabs that had been drawn through the tunnels from the northern Coe. They built broad promontories out from the feet of the southern mountains to obscure their secret. In the rains of meteorites that brought the Second Age to an end, the Coelete already had their shelters made in the caves they had populated when they first arrived in the hidden lands. By the time the people of Bala and the clan army followed the secret routes into the mountain, the Coelete were by far the oldest civilisation on earth.

With no knowledge of this history, there was no possibility that Angus Ferguson or Alastair Munro, nor any other clansman, could have anticipated the wonder that met them on the far side of the mountain as they walked into the morning sunlight. They had found the capital city of the Coelete – Tala.

Darkness was falling fast as Cember and his troop of horse reached the first of the promontories that stretched out from the Coe. To go further into this unknown territory in the dark would be folly, so Cember ordered his men into defensive positions to rest up for the night. His troop formed circles with horses in the centre and resting troopers on the outside, and the sentries would alternate during the night to ensure all received some rest, while also ensuring that any attack could be repelled.

John Burnett, having stolen a horse from one of the outlying posts of the invading army in the plain, had made good progress towards the Coe. It was around midnight when he spotted the defensive rings of men lying between his position and the mountains. Burnett let out a sigh of relief, realising that the clan army must have made it safely to the mountains and from there to the Hidden Lands.

With his horse tethered some way back, he moved carefully closer to the enemy encampment, wondering if there was any possibility of disrupting this group's progress. He was about a hundred yards away when a movement to his right caught his attention. The shadow passed, then reappeared closer. Now Burnett recognised Davy Scott. Scott motioned Burnett away from the resting camp back towards his horse. Out of sight and earshot, Scott told Burnett the plan.

The sun was just rising over the eastern edges of the Plain of Coelene when Cember decided to call his force to the saddle to continue the search for the Bala army. With light improving, the outer defensive rings seemed less necessary and Cember wanted to progress the hunt with pace. Furthermore on this open plain it seemed impossible that a surprise attack could be carried out in daylight.

Yet no sooner had the thought passed than the

impossible happened. The groups of fast-moving horsemen again appeared from nowhere, each group crashing into and through the Ember positions. The attack was not targeted at the men but at the horses of the Ember cavalry. The Red Cameron troopers sliced through the positions and rode the riderless Ember horses away towards the Coe Mountains.

Cember, already mounted, yelled at his men to mount and give chase, but by the time some order was established, the Red Cameron and the captured horses had vanished into the rocky promontories at the foot of the mountains. Cember held his men in place to count the cost of the raid. None of his men had been hurt in the attack and all the attackers also seemed to have escaped harm. However at a quick count a third of his troops had been reduced to foot soldiers, a humbling experience for the proud horsemen of Ember.

Cember still had a mission to fulfil, and on horseback or on foot he was determined to find the fleeing army. So it was that an hour later, with the mounted troopers on both flanks and ahead of the troop of foot soldiers, Cember and his force again moved towards the base of the Coe, following the tracks of their attackers and their lost mounts.

Tala was as big as Aldene, but much more awe-inspiring and unlike any place Alastair and Angus had even dreamed about. The tall towers and the city walls were all formed from the grey stone that was the natural building material on this side of the mountain, but the stone had been cut and polished so that it sparkled in the morning sunlight. The city rose behind them and seemed to have been carved bit by bit from the mountain. The walls merged into the rocks of the mountainside, and even the large houses, many of whose upper floors and roof tops were visible from the exit point of the tunnels, seemed somehow to be a part of the mountain. Indeed, the impression was no illusion. Having conquered the art of tunnelling over the generations as they worked their way through the mountain, it was not entirely surprising that the Coelete employed the same engineering skills to build homes, enabling them to swap the tents of the plains for the security of stone walls.

The clan army had mostly moved out from the tunnel exits and were resting on the plain that lay to the north of the city and on the sides of the roads that led from the tunnels to the city gates. Out from those gates came a small procession led by a tall man dressed richly in long, flowing robes. Most striking was the man's jet-black hair, blacker than a raven. This was Anaton, the current chief of the Coelete; the chief was always called by that name to honour their original saviour. In this way the tribe held a remembrance of how they had come to these lands.

Anaton and his party moved through the clansmen until they reached Ala Moire and Cameron.

"Welcome once more to the lands of the Coelete, Ala Moire." Anaton grasped the old man's hand warmly. "Welcome also to you, James Cameron, it is long years since we last saw you here. Come, we have much to talk about."

A short while later the three men were comfortably seated in the council rooms of the Coelete with several of the other senior chiefs of the nation.

"Ala Moire, we are pleased to have you in our midst," began Anaton. "The Coelete have never forgotten the debt owed to you for warning our people of the stony rains. This debt can never be fully repaid. We are also pleased to be able to help the other clans of Bala in this time of need. However, some problems face us. We are a small nation and we have always lived in balance with the natural resources available to us in these lands. We now have many times our number in refugees and we are already stretched in providing for them. We cannot easily gather supplies from the south; the route through the tunnels deliberately limits that. We can manage for some weeks and maybe even months before we have to restrict food supplies, but when that happens we can expect trouble from our people. Indeed, some of the chiefs gathered here would be vocal today about their concerns, but are silent out of their respect for you. How long do you think your people will need our refuge?"

Ala Moire stood to address all those present. "Anaton, your hospitality is gracious and the respect of your chiefs is an honour. Unfortunately I cannot give you the peace of mind you seek. The problems we face are great. As we speak the lands of Bala are being invaded by an old enemy who is intent on rekindling the power of legends, the power that first drove the Coelete from the plains, the power that forced your namesake to cross the mountains, the power that drove you to pass through the Coe to reach these lands. The women of Bala will be borne into slavery in the hands of an alien army; the men of Bala will be slaves in the mines that will once again scar the beautiful lands of Banora; the children of Bala will be heard, even here in Tala, as they mourn their lost parents and slowly starve to death. In these lands the Coelete will lie safely hidden for a time, but the power that will grow will seek to enslave all peoples, for the Coelete live too near to escape unnoticed. So we must anticipate that for months, and perhaps years, to come, the lands of the Coelete will need to shelter all the clans of Bala."

There was an immediate rise in the temperature of the room and several of the chiefs of the Coelete started to get to their feet to voice their objections. However it was James Cameron who followed Ala

Moire. "Hold your objections, gentlemen, there is no alternative but to secure the people of Bala in these lands. For one thing, returning people to the south will only bring the powers that now reside there north all the faster to explore how to access these new lands. The secret passageways are defendable, but not against an overwhelming force that is careless about the loss of its own men. We must immediately take control of all food stocks and limit each person's consumption so that we can last in relative comfort for as long as possible. We also will need to send parties to the south to scavenge for additional supplies; we may even need to borrow some from the enemy. It will be hard travelling the passageways, but we will need to replenish supplies as best we can.

"We are at war gentlemen, all of us, and none can side-step it. We will be free to live normally, and the Coelete will get their lands back when the enemy is defeated, however long it takes."

Again a few of the chiefs made to rise, but the stare of the Cameron stilled even the most eager. Although he had rarely visited these northern lands, all knew the man's reputation, and his look reinforced all the stories, so none there were going to speak up against him.

Anaton concluded the debate. "Ala Moire, James, we know you both, and we know the honour you carry in your hearts and words. We Coelete are brothers to the clans of Bala, despite the millennium of separation. It is our duty to succour our brother and to fight alongside him to prevent evil overpowering the entire world. We will immediately call a gathering of all the chiefs and give them instructions as to how to preserve our supplies, feed our kin and maintain a balance in the land. It will be hard, but we will do it; we have survived hard times in the past. We will need to supplement as we can from the south, but it should be possible to survive many months with some care of our local resources. I have spoken and the debate is ended – see to it."

And so he dismissed the chiefs. Anaton sat on with Ala Moire and Cameron, learning more about the new world that was encroaching on his doorstep.

As Cember's now somewhat ragged troop, still consisting of several hundred men, marched slowly towards the foothills of the Coe, Cember noticed the strange promontories sticking out from the base of the mountains. The first one they reached stretched almost a mile from the base of the mountain proper whilst beyond this, four shorter promontories, much closer together, jutted perhaps a hundred feet from the mountain base. The tracks of riders and riderless horses led into the gap between the third and fourth promontory. From where he viewed the area, the four short promontories appeared to be separated by only a few tens of yards and opened out again close to the foot of the mountain. The place was an obvious trap, and the clear appearance of the tracks leading into the area was too obvious; they must be bait. Cember halted his troops, sending two riders cautiously ahead towards the jutting walls.

As the two riders reached the first of the four promontories, two tall figures appeared over the ridge of grey rock. Even from a distance Cember was surprised by the height of the men. Both were fully armoured, with long spears, belted swords and bows that reached fully a foot higher than their own remarkable stature.

In two blurred movements the spears impaled Cember's scouts. His troops roared in horror and started to advance towards the promontory and the two strange tall figures. Cember yelled to hold them back, but it was not his call that made the difference; no sooner had the first horse moved forward than its rider left the saddle, skewered by a four-foot-long arrow. The two tall warriors were releasing a terrifying hail of arrows into the middle of the gathered Ember horse.

Cember yelled for the troop to move out of range and take shelter. The nearest was the promontory they had just passed. Cember pulled his horse round and galloped for the shelter of the grey rock. Behind him, at least thirty of his men lay pinned to the ground.

From behind the far away promontory the twenty Coelete warriors continued to fire their deadly hail of arrows an impossible distance. The height of the warriors and the length of the bows gave the archers an unimaginable range. Even as the last of Cember's troop rounded the outlying promontory, the final rider fell. Alain and Gareth, two of the Guardians of the Hidden Lands, smiled knowingly as the harassed Ember troop hurried behind the distant shelter.

It was one of the horsemen, now a foot soldier, who first noticed that the ground he stood on was anything but solid. He ran for shelter from the torrent of arrows, until the rock above him sheltered him from the enemy's arrows. But the sigh of relief was short-lived as his feet sank into the ground. Behind him horses snorted in panic as the apparently firm earth rose around their legs.

Cember, in the middle of the pack, once again pulled his agitated horse away from danger and galloped some distance from the sheltering wall. As he pulled up to assess the difficulty of his men, another movement caught the corner of his eye. From further up the promontory, closer to the foot of the mountains, a mounted troop was rapidly closing on the stranded Ember horse. The white, red and blue of the mounted men's surcoats and the blue cross on the white flag at the head of the troop left Cember in no doubt. This was at least a troop, perhaps several hundred Red Cameron, and Cember had experienced their battle skills in the wars in Amina a year earlier.

As he called his men to him to stand against the charge he realised how few they now seemed. Perhaps there were now only three hundred, but even so that should suffice. Then as confusion built, and the Red Cameron approached, the men nearest Cember fell in another hail of long arrows. The Coelete warriors had, with remarkable speed, crossed the space to the steep grey rock and from the vantage of their high position were now finishing the job started by the quagmire; worse, they were easily picking off the few Ember troops still mobile enough to fight.

Through gritted teeth, Cember called his troop to follow him back onto the Plain of Coe. Behind him, two hundred proud Ember Horse were left to their doom in the Quagmire of Mott, and where the treacherous ground failed, the deadly long arrows of the Guardians of the Hidden Lands finished the job. John Burnett and the Red Cameron did not engage a single enemy, much to their irritation. The Cameron chased the invaders for a few miles before returning to the shelter of the mountains.

Alain son of Lorn shook the hand of the Cameron captain. "Well met, John Burnett. Your lord is on the other side of the mountain and we have instructions to hurry you there. This foe here does not seem too terrible; perhaps this war will not last long after all. Your man Scott's simple plan worked perfectly. My guess is they have left two hundred or more on this field."

"Alain, your archers won this day as well as any plan, but this here is a tiny fraction of the army now to our south. Worse than the army, it marches with the support of magic not seen since the days of legend. Come, hurry me to my Lord."

As the first days of May passed, the armies of the Dewar poured into Banora and the southern edges of the Plain of Coe. Cember with his defeated troop returned to report to a wrathful Orridon. It was no surprise that Cember was moved back into the ranks and his command passed to his half-brother, Elem.

Orridon, not one to miss an anomaly, wondered about the tall warriors with their remarkable bows that had wreaked such havoc on his forces. Orridon thought he knew these lands, but clearly they had secrets still to unfold. When he reported to the Dewar and Oien, the old man asked to interrogate Cember to learn the details around the man dressed in white and the white-tipped arrows. Could it be possible that an old friend and an old enemy had also lived on for so many long years hidden from his view?

John Burnett and the Red Cameron passed through the mountain passageways to join the rest of the people of Bala in the hidden lands of the Coelete. The world waited.

CHAPTER FIVE

𝕰𝔥𝔢 𝒜𝔩𝔠𝔥𝔢𝔪𝔦𝔰𝔱

By late May 1300, Dewar the Second was Lord of Bala and his armies occupied all the land south of the Coe Mountains. The Dewar made his headquarters in the city of Aldene. As in all conquests, the army brought with it camp followers and the associated women and children. These less warlike invaders occupied the towns and villages of Bala and started to build their lives in the occupied land. The Dewar cared little for what had happened to most of the people of Bala; all he cared about was how quickly Oien could convert the mineral resources of Banora into a power he could use to conquer the rich lands in the south, across the Middle Sea.

Orridon was less dismissive of the vanished locals. He knew his scouts had found local people in the far-flung reaches of Banora and in the seaside villages of Ewart and Coelene. In these places the locals were fishermen and plied their trade in the Middle Sea. They cared little for what happened in the outside world and certainly gave no indication of knowing what had happened to their brothers, the farmers and merchants of Bala. Most of the villages and small towns of Bala seemed to have been largely evacuated. In some villages it was clear that the majority of the population had left in a hurry. Orridon guessed that perhaps as many as 200,000 souls had vanished from the country.

Orridon had ridden the foothills of the Coe, past the place where the remains of Cember's troopers still rotted, past the grey promontories, and back through the Plain of Coe to his headquarters at the foot of the Pass of Ing. He did not know what lay beyond the Coe Mountains. Maps simply showed the mountains rolling down to the sea. Orridon guessed that the people of Bala, led by the Cameron, could have scattered themselves along the mid-slopes of the mountains. Caves in the higher slopes may give some shelter and could be defended. It would be a haven for a few months to come, but as the autumn arrived and the first snows fell, the mountains would become uninhabitable.

He did not consider the possibility that they had crossed the mountains. Even now in late May, the top third of the ranges was thick with snow and ice, some of which would never leave the summits. Skilled climbers might be able to reach the summits, but it would be impossible for a large group of people including the old, the infirm and the children.

The lack of a good answer worried Orridon. Cameron, he knew, was a great warrior and a brilliant tactician, and he would not have given up his lands forever. Also there were the tall warriors. Orridon had never heard of these mysterious people who had appeared from nowhere to wreak havoc on his forces. Maybe they knew the location of the people of Bala; maybe there was a way to get to hidden places beyond the mountains. The worry preyed on Orridon's mind.

Oien had moved from the foot of the Pass of Ing into the heart of Banora, and in fact now occupied the farmhouse that had been home to Angus Ferguson all his life. Oien paid little heed to the simple headstones at the rear of the house. He did not know that they marked the resting places of Angus Ferguson's father, mother and sister.

In the early June sunshine, Oien rode alone towards the area where the Inger Mountains began to slope down towards the Greater Sea. This area saw the country change from farmland into forest, as the southern half of the Province of Banora was covered in woodlands and deep, thick forest. It was from these woods that the people of Banora harvested the yew for their short bows. The woods were home to a multitude of wild animals and it was here in the summer months that Alistair Munro and Angus Ferguson would come to hunt the deer.

Oien made for the point where the mountains and the forest met, then climbed easily into the low foothills of the Inger. After an hour's climb up the lower slopes, he ascended through a deep gorge that sliced its way into the higher slopes. Near the top of the gorge he dismounted and began to search the slopes on foot. After a short while he found the cave entrance he had been seeking. As he looked at the weathered entrance, he cast his mind back over far too many years to when he had last stood at this point where the transports had pulled the first load of dark red stone from the mine lying deep inside the mountain.

Oien stood back from the cave face and pointed his staff down into the entrance. A red flame blazed out from the end of the staff, lighting up the deeper darkness in the cave. He stood back and smiled, as around him the raw mountainside gushed with red fire. Flames blazed out of a multitude of cracks in the rock face, then subsided as Oien quenched the staff. The othium was still there, and still able to be activated. All that was needed was the resources to extract it from the rocks that held it captive, and then the real work could begin.

The crack of the percussion was heard by the armies camped around the foot of the Pass of Ing. Soldiers' heads turned to look in the direction of the noise, and they gasped as red flames seemed to leap out of the mountain some five miles to their south.

Oien retraced his steps and remounted for the short trip back to the farmhouse. Tomorrow he would send a messenger to Aldene and get the Dewar to order conscripts up to the old mines in the mountains. It was also now time to bring the other key ingredient up from the baggage trains – the secret formulations containing the purple salt of Elat.

Elat and its neighbouring island Lat sat at the point where the Middle Sea joined the Western Sea. Between the islands the shallows were constricted by promontories jutting west from the islands. In this shallow sea between the two oceans, as the water evaporated during summer, so the sea became much more saline. Over millennia the sea bed had received the remains of lost creatures from the First Age. The dinosaur remains gave the shallows a purple tint, and when concentrated the same colour was reflected in the tiny salt crystals from the Straits of Elat. In the Second Age alchemists had detected the power held in the red stone othium, but none knew how to release or control it.

Oien, as a young man, had looked out from his home in Elat and wondered at the purple sea. At that time he had been an apprentice to Ham, from the neighbouring island of Lat. In the early years of the Second Age Ham was known as one of the great alchemists of his days. Ham had worked tirelessly to understand the power trapped in the red rock and how to capture and control the power. It was to no avail; the othium remained a cold red stone that would explode apparently randomly, emitting bright red, orange and amber flames.

Oien, as apprentice to his master, also struggled with the challenges of experiments to release the power of othium. At times the red rock test pieces could be made to explode when exposed to heat in combination with saltpetre. The material appeared to be more active as a ground powder, although at times the grinding process itself would cause the rock to burn with an intense amber flame. However, often the same experiments simply left the apprentice with a lump of red rock or a pile of red powder.

The activity of othium also appeared to vary depending on the source of the rock. Othium mined from the Doran Mountains, whilst still erratic in behaviour, was more active than the material from the Kermin Alol in Amina. The most active rock seemed to come from the Am Monadh Ruadh, the Red Mountains or Inger Mountains as the locals called them, far to the north on the island of Andore. Wherever the source of the rock, however, none of the experiments yielded consistently positive results, only random events. It was as if the rock itself resisted any attempt to control it.

Late on a cold evening as yet another set of experiments proved useless, Oien in frustration threw his test piece of othium into the purple-tinged Straits of Elat. As the rock flew out over the sea Oien watched in amazement as the dead lump of othium took on a bright amber glow, and then exploded in a blaze of red, orange and amber as it hit the water. By chance he had discovered othium's secret – that its power could be detonated and primed by a small quantity of the salt of Elat.

Over some years Oien developed his skills in harnessing the power of the red rock, and in time the apprentice became the master. In his laboratory on the small island of Elat, Oien experimented with how to control the red rock. It was clear that the salt was the key to triggering the power of othium, but the combination of the two could still be unpredictable. Oien developed more complex formulations. Coating the red rock with oils containing saltpetre and salt resulted in pieces that would only explode on impact. Other secret formulations allowed the othium to slowly release its energy over a period of time. With his research completed Oien had developed formulations that could power machinery, and also create terrifying weapons.

In time, when his control was complete, Oien started to use his power in warfare. Vasel, the King of Elat at the time, had little ambition, and he had a tiny army compared to all his neighbours. Under threat from Oien, Vasel ordered his army to invade Amina across the Middle Sea. With the support of the alchemist's weapons, the small army from Elat quickly conquered all the lands to the south and east of Elat.

In those days othium was still plentiful and could be found in the hills of Kermin, the Kermin Alol and in the mountains of Doran. Being readily available, it was used to build the houses and castles of the locals. Oien learned that arrows tipped with oil, saltpetre and the salt of Elat could cause instantaneous combustion when they struck these buildings. Soon towns and cities across Amina and Kermin were consumed by othium fuelled fires. Othium mines were opened up in the Kermin Alol and in the Doran Mountains. Gold from the Doran Mountains funded Oien's armies. With success in the South and East under his belt, Oien retired the Elat King back to his island and began to lead the conquest of the entire known world.

As his armies, with their othium-powered weapons, destroyed all that stood against them, Oien was surprised to find that the greatest deposits of othium lay below the mountains of the little-known country of Bala, and in particular the mountain ranges of Inger bounding the small northern province of Banora. Not only was he surprised by the quantity of the rock in the Inger Mountains, Oien's experiments had already informed him that this was the most active form of the stone. Having conquered the countries of Andore, Oien then began to tear apart the mountains of Inger to meet his ever-increasing need for the precious othium.

As his power grew Oien was joined by three other alchemists, who had discovered at least some of othium's secrets at around the same time. A fifth alchemist arrived unannounced at Aracene, which now, in the Third Age, was called Aldene, capital of Bala. This young man, whose name was Malama O'Re, was dressed all in white, and had come from the country of Soll which lay east across the Eastern Sea. He said his mission was to help the four men of the council to use power wisely for the good of the nations.

Oien was dismissive; he felt he had all the power he needed in the red stone and the purple salt. Malama O'Re smiled. He opened his hand and a bright white light shone out. Impressed, if slightly discomfited, Oien asked the stranger what he had to offer.

"You have gained great power, master," said the young man, "but great power needs great guidance. I have been sent to provide this guidance."

"By whom?" asked Oien, rather irritated.

"By He who oversees all and guides all."

Malama O'Re became the fifth member of the council, and as the Second Age blossomed so he became the voice of reason in the Council of Five. As othium reserves became rarer on the Earth, the people of the Second Age reached out to the heavens. Oien now led an industrial revolution as othium-powered vessels left the home planet to seek the red stone in the outer worlds.

As the power of the Council grew and the people of the world became subjected to a life of increasing misery in the mines and the factories, only the voice of Malama O'Re stood in opposition. As the planetary expeditions returned to earth and more of the planet was destroyed in the search for new seams of othium, Malama counselled a time of reflection and consolidation. He advised Oien that he was reaching too far and the destruction was now too great to be ignored. In a blinding rage, Oien banished Malama to exile in the far north-eastern lands of Esimore beyond the Eastern Sea. Oien may have contemplated a more drastic solution to the Malama problem, but despite his power he was unsure of the white power which Malama possessed. So as His prophet was banished God had to intervene, and He released the meteorite storms from the sky that ended the Second Age.

With years of exposure to othium, Oien had imbibed the power of the red rock into his very being. Othium flowed through his veins, and he could call the red fire at will. The old alchemist had become immortal. Thanks to the power of his othium, Oien survived the rain of rocks. In the northern lands of Esimore, few meteorites fell.

Tala, the home of the Coelete, was carved out of the mountain, and the caves of the original settlers could still be seen there. Hidden deep in their caves, the Coelete had survived the meteorite storms that had ended the Second Age and in relative isolation their culture had thrived into the dawn of the Third Age. Behind the Coe Mountains, their great protectors, only a few knew of the existence of these people in their Hidden Lands. Bounded by their mountains to the south, the sea to the north and west and the swamp lands to the east, the Coelete remained hidden and secure. Their lands were blessed with warm currents from the Greater Sea and sheltered from the southern winds by the mountains, and they lived in a land of plenty, despite the harshness of the winters. The harvests of sea and land meant that the people had little need to venture into the southern lands of Bala.

Ala Moire, or Malama O'Re as he was known in those days, had first ventured into the far north when tasked by the Council to find new sources of othium. While exploring the lower slopes of the Coe above the promontories, he had spotted a small group of tall warriors stepping out of a grey rock door and followed them into the cave town of Tala. Brought in front of a long-forgotten chief Anaton, Malama explained who he was and what his journey was for. As the rest of the world's people descended into increasing industrial slavery, Malama O'Re decided to protect the Coelete, and never mentioned them to the others in the Council. In his journeys in the far north he created the first maps of the northern territories, which showed the Coe Mountains ending at the waters of the Northern Sea. On maps of the Third Age the Northern Sea had a different name. Lying beyond the impassable Coe Mountains the maps termed this unreachable sea the Hidden Sea.

Years later, from his exile in Esimore, Malama O'Re had ventured back across the Eastern Sea to warn the Coelete of impending destruction from the skies. As doom rained down on the rest of the planet, the Coelete remained safe and well hidden in their mountain caves.

As Angus Ferguson and Alastair Munro helped the refugee people from Bala to set up their camps in the fields below the city of Tala, they could not avoid regularly staring up at the city clinging to the mountains behind them. Coelete warriors patrolled the edge of the refugee camp, not to threaten anyone but out of necessity. The narrow streets of the city could not be filled with crowds, and as rationing had been immediately implemented they wanted no attempt by the newcomers to access the food stores in the city. To the north of the city, over the Plain of Tala and the rolling hills of the Nath, the people were allowed to explore up to the edge of the Hidden Sea. With this freedom they explored their new homeland, but they had to return to the main camp every night before the dusk curfew.

A few days after their arrival, a small group of the refugees was caught trying to enter the camp long after curfew. The group was led by a minor Ewart lord called Craig Baird. Baird's small manor and associated village sat on the Ewart coast and his people survived through their skills in fishing the Middle Sea. The men were also expert sailors. Baird was a vassal of the Elder of Ewart and had been called by his overlord to join the army of Bala. Being out of camp after curfew was a serious offence, so the small group, escorted by Coelete warriors, was marched to the foot of the cliffs and the entry to the city of Tala. Waiting in annoyance were Anaton, Ala Moire, the Ewart, Duncan of Coe and Cameron.

Ewart was short and sharp. "Explain, Craig!"

Apologetically, Baird signalled to two of his men,

who came forward, each holding a basket full of fish. "Lord Ewart, we know the rations for the people are limited, so we went to the north where the sea meets the land beyond the Nath. The sea is plentiful at this time of year but will be frozen come the winter months. My men are experts in catching fish and curing them for winter succour. We did not mean to break the curfew, but the distance to the sea is greater than we thought."

Expecting punishment, Baird was surprised when Anaton spoke first. "We Coelete have never needed to harvest much from the seas other than for special occasions or for entertainment," he said. He turned to Ala Moire and Cameron. "We must use these men's skills to help build our winter supplies and to supplement our current stocks." So Craig Baird and his men became fishermen of Tala.

As May turned to June and the Hidden Lands enjoyed the warmth of summer, Anaton became increasingly concerned about his ability to feed the refugees. He called a meeting of the Chiefs of the Coelete and the Elders of Bala.

"We are proud to host the people of Bala in these troubled times Ala Moire," he said, "but come winter we simply cannot provide for so many. You know that in winter these lands are icebound and nothing moves. The fishermen are boosting our supplies and our reserves, but they will not be fishing during the winter months. Your people are warm in their tents as the sun shines, but they will freeze in the winter. We need to plan now for the months ahead if we are to survive."

Ala Moire let the Chiefs and the Elders debate for a period. Reluctantly the Chiefs agreed that more of the green land of the Plain of Tala could be turned over to growing crops. The Cameron agreed that some of his Red Cameron would raid the plains of Coe and Coelene and rustle some livestock from the south. These could graze through the summer on the Nath.

Then Ala Moire spoke. "Across the short strait of the Eastern Sea lies Esimore," he said. "With summer short, there are few people in this northern land, but there roam vast herds of reindeer. It is not an easy passage through the Swamps of Nath and the waste lands to the east, but the sea trip is short and the sea shallow in the summer. A small band of men could make the journey and return with a herd that will quite happily winter here and provide us with their milk and meat. As for warmth, when the time comes I can supply that."

Duncan of Coe spoke next. "Banoran cobs swim across our lochs and are hardy in the most difficult of terrain," he said. "I propose that I take a small squad of my Banoran men for the journey to Esimore and we will bring back the reindeer."

"Alain son of Lorn, one of the Guardians, and

two Coelete warriors will travel with you; they know the secret ways through the swamps and the waste lands," replied Anaton.

Finally Ala Moire spoke. "Duncan, you will also take Alastair Munro. His time has not come and he needs to learn his power well away from the reaches of Oien."

So the people of Bala helped the Coelete to plant the fields and catch and cure the fish. John Burnett and the Red Cameron raided the southern plains and returned with sheep and cattle. Duncan gathered a small group of Banoran men mounted on their cobs and headed east. Angus Ferguson was furious at being left behind, but he was told that this was at the instruction of the Cameron Lord.

Angus idled away his time helping with the work as required and exploring the Hidden Lands on his cob. One day in late June as he rode along the western edge of the northern Coe Mountains, he saw a team of three planting out a newly-ploughed field. At the far edge of the field a young woman was resting from the back-breaking work. As Angus admired her from a distance, from the corner of his eye he detected movement; it was a mountain lion. These animals were rare this far north, but the invasion of the humans further south had probably driven this one over the mountains to less populated lands. The lion was moving through the lower escarpments to attack the young woman from behind, and she was clearly oblivious to its presence.

Angus was about to shout a warning when he realised that this would not help, as the woman could not possibly outrun the lion. As the beast broke cover he spurred the little cob into a gallop, but as the distances were about equal it seemed unlikely that he could reach it in time.

As the distance closed, Angus drew an arrow from his quiver and let it fly at the lion, knowing it was a one in a million shot. The arrow landed a dozen paces ahead of the animal, and Angus drew a second arrow and slowed the cob to improve his chances. To Angus's surprise the first arrow then flashed and threw a wall of white fire in front of the animal, which stopped and roared before retreating back to the mountain.

Angus did not understand what had happened. He remembered Ala Moire touching some of the arrows in each quiver when they were back on the Plains of Coe, but why he had picked that particular arrow at that particular moment was a mystery that maybe only Ala Moire could explain.

Angus reached the young woman to find that she was shaken more by the sudden fire than by the lion, as she had only seen it as it ran back to the mountain. Sliding from the back of the cob, he took the woman's hand to calm her shaking. Quietly he introduced himself, and hesitantly she told him that her name was Elbeth, and she was the daughter of

James Cameron.

The few minutes it took Elbeth to regain her composure gave Angus time to appreciate the young woman. She was beautiful. Her long light brown hair was pulled back from her face in braids to keep it clear from her eyes whilst she was planting. Angus thought she was in her early twenties, but he had had little experience in assessing a woman's age. Elbeth was tall but slightly shorter than Angus, and as she turned to him for the first time, he looked down into her beautiful green eyes.

"Thank you sir, I am not sure what happened there. The flash of the white light frightened me."

"I am sorry you were frightened," said Angus. "My name is Angus Ferguson." He pointed to the mountain. "The lion was coming for you. I'm not sure where the white light came from, but it saved your life. My own arrows would not have been effective over such a distance."

"So it seems I owe you more than thanks, Angus Ferguson. Please take me back to Tala, where I am sure my father will want to reward you more than I can." But Angus felt her smile was reward enough.

With Elbeth secure in front of him on the cob, Angus rode back to Tala and for the first time was allowed past the city gates and into the mountain city itself. He stared in amazement at the towering houses cut into the mountain which lay on both sides of the narrow streets. Elbeth guided Angus up to the top of the city, where the palace of Anaton was splendidly set back into the mountain behind a fortified outer wall and gate. Although little was said on the short journey back to Tala, for some reason Angus felt a surprising closeness to the young woman.

The pair having been allowed to pass through to the inner sanctums, Elbeth led Angus to an opulent set of rooms on the upper floor, where in the living area James Cameron was in deep discussion with Ala Moire. Elbeth told the story to her father, who in turn thanked Angus, asking him about the strange power of his arrow. Angus shrugged, not knowing how to answer. Ala Moire merely smiled. Cameron told the Banoran farmer that he would be forever in the young man's debt, a debt he could not repay.

With a flash of insight Angus asked Cameron if he could join the training with the Red Cameron, who he had seen most days honing their skills in the plains and on the hills of the Nath. Cameron replied, "This is an easy gift to give, but a very hard honour to earn."

The next day John Burnett called early at Angus's tent and instructed him to ride to the Nath to join the training. So Angus Ferguson took his first small step to becoming a warrior of the Red Cameron.

As June turned to July and the sun shone for long hours over the Inger Mountains, the soldiers of the conscript armies of Toria, Ciren and Arance became the labourers for the Dewar and Oien. In truth, slaves would be a better description. One by one Oien found the openings to the mines of the Second Age and the conscripts were sent underground to clear the debris of millennia and open them up. This was hard and dangerous work, as many of the mine shafts had collapsed or simply been swallowed back into the mountains.

Time and again as Oien searched the old paths through the mountain and probed with his staff, the rocks erupted red fire. This added to the dangers faced by the miners as the interconnected tunnels frequently burned with fire, but Oien cared little for the destruction he caused to those toiling underground.

Below in Banora, the forest was being devastated as wood was brought to the forges that Oien had ordered to be built across the lower ground. One by one large furnaces began to fill the plain as the Dewar's army relocated north to the Plain of Coe and the elite retired south to the comforts of Aldene. As the first of the othium was released from the ground, the smiths began the complex task of forging the iron components demanded by Oien. Supply trains from the south brought the coal and ore that would add fuel to the furnaces long after the initial wood fires had died. In time all the furnaces would be fired by the more intense heat of othium, but it was an unpredictable fuel and it would take time before the smiths could be trained to use it. Oien already knew that the Banoran form of the mineral was the most reactive, but now it seemed even more unpredictable than it had in the past. To create an intense, slow-burning heat required the othium to be activated by particular formulations of the Elat salt. It was clear to Oien that these formulations would have to be refined before the furnaces could safely use the power of the red stone.

From the furnaces wheels of all sizes were crafted and following Oien's designs, the men began to assemble strange machines. The first machine completed was a long and low device with sharp teeth on a wheel on the leading edge. This was hauled up the mountain to the first of the mines, and Oien taught the miners how to load the engine with small amounts of othium and prime this with a few grains of one of the mixtures containing the salt from Elat. Instantly the pistons turned and the toothed wheel started rapidly rotating, decapitating one of the conscripts who stood too close to the wheel.

"This will harvest the red stone far faster than your picks," Oien said to the lead miner. "Now get it down the shaft and bring me up my red stone."

As the smiths honed their craft, other contraptions were assembled and more toothed monsters were manoeuvred into the mines to tear at the heart of the mountain. Othium-powered carts carried the rock to the surface and hauled the wood from the forest.

In early August parts for a larger machine emerged from the workshops in Banora, from where they were transported to the Plain of Coe and assembled. The device was a trebuchet, a vast catapult, built with wooden beams, iron and ropes. It sat on a large base mounted on six massive wheels. Along the length of the machine high beams formed a set of triangles with each of the "A" frames supporting a long wooden spar that ended in a large iron bowl. Coils of rope wound under the base of the machine connected it to a set of cogs and pulleys. The trebuchet was the most feared siege engine of the time and had been used by the Dewar in earlier campaigns in Ciren and Arance. Those had used a single "A" frame and a single spar to launch their projectiles. What was now assembled on the plain however was larger than any seen before, and did not have the large counterweight needed by its brothers to snap the central spars into position to release their projectiles. The complex chain of cogs below the base of the trebuchet was driven by an othium powered reactor. Without the need for the counterweight, this machine could simultaneously deliver three payloads into opposing forces.

Once the machine had been assembled, Oien primed the reactor with othium and a salt mixture.

As the cogs turned, the three long spars bent back towards the ground, and Ciren conscripts quickly filled the iron bowls with large stones. With Orridon and others of the Ackar elite watching, Oien flicked a lever and with incredible speed the spars shot forward, delivering their deadly projectiles far out onto the plain. Delighted with his handiwork, Oien ordered the machine to be dismantled so that it could be transported over the Pass of Ing and reassembled for travel on to Aldene. He knew that the trebuchet was a crude war machine compared to others he could create, but it was the best that could be done for now until the smiths in Banora developed their skills with different metals and his more complicated designs and weapons could be turned into reality.

As Oien and the machine approached Aldene, the King and his retinue rode out to meet the alchemist and his strange contraption. At Oien's request, Dewar had assembled three small groups of Bala soldiers who had been captured in the earlier battles. The three groups stood about 150 yards away across the open ground with 50 yards between them. Oien moved the machine into position with the central spar of the three aimed directly at the central group of captives. He primed a small piece of othium and loaded it into a central reactor chamber. Powered by the othium, the iron ratchets started turning and the beams groaned as the central spars were pulled back towards the ground and held over 90° from their upright position. Into each iron bucket Oien deposited a small amount of othium coated with oil containing saltpetre and the purple Elat salt. Standing back a little, he pressed a lever at the side of the machine. The three spars shot back to their vertical position, hurling their small packages of stone into the air towards the groups of Bala captives. The stones hit the ground within fractions of a second of each other, and on impact the othium and salt combined. Red and amber fire exploded from the stones and the helpless captives were incinerated and reduced to dust.

The King applauded loudly and congratulated Oien. Here was the weapon he needed to bring the kingdom of Amina and its neighbours to their knees and to become lord of all the lands south of the Middle Sea and own all their riches.

Oien welcomed the congratulations, but he knew that the trebuchet had been quickly fashioned and was but a toy constructed to impress. It was trivial compared to the great ships of the Second Age which had been powered by othium to reach out to the planets. While the King planned his conquests across the Middle Sea, Oien planned the conquest of the Universe.

With the last days of August turning to September and autumn, both the Dewar and Oien knew that it was now too late for a campaign in the south. It would be late in the year before the new trebuchet could be transported across the Middle Sea to Amina. Instead it would be moved on to Boretar, for transport ready for the invasion planned for the coming spring.

Oien left Aldene and travelled quickly back to Banora; he had more work to do before the winter set in and stalled his progress. But nature and God have their own powers. In early September, at least a month earlier than most years, winter winds blew in from across the Eastern Sea and all of Bala was covered in a clean white blanket of snow. By the middle of the month, the snow completely blocked the Pass of Ing. As no baggage trains could cross the pass, the coal and ore could not be transported to the north and the mined othium and Oien's other machines could not pass south. The furnaces went out and the soldiers, miners, smiths and conscripts left to the north of the Inger Mountains had no choice but to hunker down for a long, cold winter.

Many of the invading forces had already moved south to camp round Aldene in the slightly less bitter southern part of Bala, or returned to their homes in Ackar and Lett. North of the mountain passes, Oien was livid with frustration – the camps had been well provisioned in the summer months so the winter would not incapacitate them, but it did prevent him from rapidly building his power and implementing his plans. Even with the power of othium the cold and the snow doused every fire, so Oien, with a small cohort including Orridon, crossed back into the southern lands to the comfort of Aldene to wait for spring.

As the small group reached Aldene, it seemed unnaturally quiet. It turned out that the King, his retinue and most of the army had retired to the warmer lands of Ackar and the capital, Boretar. Oien cursed the foolish King, knowing that even come spring it would now take many weeks to bring sufficient resources back to the north to continue his work. However, for once Oien was powerless, so he settled in to pass the winter in Aldene.

CHAPTER SIX

To Esimore and Back

While Oien was reopening the mines, Duncan of Coe
and his small band of Banorans, led by Alain of Lorn,
worked eastwards. Alain knew the ways through
the swamplands of Nath, and having successfully
negotiated them the group entered the waste lands.

This area of the far north-east of Bala was
unknown to most. It had been carved from the rocks
and was little more than a stony desert. Alastair
Munro murmured to himself that in this land it would
be hard to feed a flock of sparrows, never mind a herd
of reindeer. Duncan overheard Alastair and accepted
his point. He sent three of the Banoran troopers with
a Coelete guide back west, ordering them to bring

back forage for the return journey.

The journey to the Eastern Sea was hard but uneventful. The stretch of water between the waste lands and Esimore was surprisingly short and calm, although in winter it would be nigh on impossible to cross as the winds would blow the water into frozen cascades of ice. The short journey across the open water posed no problem to the sturdy Banoran cobs, which were used to enjoying a swim in the lochs of their homeland, and in no time the small group reached the shores of Esimore.

Ahead of them lay mile upon mile of open tundra, looking inviting in the summer sun. As they crossed the tundra, great herds of reindeer moved over the land ahead. It was quick work to cut off a small portion of the herd and drive them back towards the sea.

To the best of their knowledge, few people lived in this barren northern land. It came therefore as a surprise when Alastair Munro, in the lead, crested a small rise to see fifty yards in front of him a group of fur-clad warriors blocking the way back to the sea. The warriors were armed with weapons made from animal bone, and there was no sign of spear or bow. Coe's Banorans were lightly armed with bows and arrows and light swords. The Elder drew the Banorans into a line ready to attack the strange warriors, but Alastair signalled them back to care for the herd and rode on alone towards the opposing group. Alastair was not sure why he had done this, but he knew he meant these people no harm.

When he was about ten yards from the group, one of the strange warriors yelled out and charged towards him, his antler-pronged pike held in front of him. For reasons he could not later recall, Alastair Munro felt anger swell inside him, and he raised the palm of his hand to the onrushing attacker. He felt himself rocked backwards as a strange power rushed through his hand and a white light sprang forward to throw his attacker down to the ground.

Shocked but not seriously harmed, the fur-clad warrior withdrew quickly back to his comrades. As Alastair slowly rode towards the warriors, they stepped back. He was within a few yards of the group when a squat man covered from head to foot in reindeer fur stepped forward and bowed. Only then did Alastair see and feel the white light emanating from him and sparking in the cool evening air.

Alastair dismounted, somewhat bemused, and walked over to the bowing warrior. The man stood up and spoke in a strange tongue, gesturing to Alastair, Duncan and the Banorans to follow him. Gathering the small herd, the Elder of Coe and the Banorans followed the strange group over another low ridge to find a small tented village there in the wilderness.

Alastair felt strangely weak, as though the

release of energy had sapped him to his soul. Duncan and Alastair were led into the central tent of the small compound and made welcome. Alain, who had many years earlier travelled some of these lands, understood a part of their language, which derived to a degree from the language spoken in Soll to the south of Esimore.

Through a mix of broken words and signs, Alain translated for Alastair and Duncan. It seemed that the people of Esimore were few and lived and travelled with the reindeer. They were in the land to protect the animals and only ate the flesh and used the skin of those that died. They could not allow the reindeer in the Banoran herd to be taken from their lands. In return, Duncan and Alastair tried to explain the future of the red fire which consumed all and the needs of the people in the Hidden Lands.

Sulux, the chief of the clan, raised his hands, then again bowed to Alastair Munro. He explained that their legends told them of the ancient times of fire and prophesied that they would return in the future. The legends also told of a man called Malama O'Re, dressed all in white with white fire, who would return to protect them.

Alastair instinctively knew that the chief was referring to the person he now knew as Ala Moire. Alastair Munro, dressed in the way of Banora, wore a kilt, lower leg armour and tartan over his body armour; no white. Through signs and words interpreted by Alain, the chief explained that the white power had come from Alastair when he was attacked. That meant that according to their legends, he was the one come to save them.

The next morning the reindeer warriors helped the small band of Banorans back to the Eastern Sea. On the shore they shook hands and the warriors bowed to Alastair Munro as the reindeer and the cobs again set off to swim the short distance back to the waste lands.

As the group settled for the night before heading back, Alastair sat on the edge of the camp wrapped in thought. He did not understand how the white power had been conjured other than through his rage, and if this was the power that Ala Moire had referred to back on the high Inger, then Alastair was not sure he wanted it. How could power be controlled through rage?

Duncan of Coe walked quietly over to sit at Alastair's side. He knew little, but it was enough. Ala Moire and Cameron had instructed him to be sure to protect Munro above all else on the journey to Esimore. The instruction had been explicit: "Duncan, if you don't bring back the reindeer, make sure you bring back Munro."

The Elder of Coe rested his hand on Alastair's

shoulder. "Alastair, we are living in strange times that I do not understand," he said. "The world seems to be spinning back to the time of legends. I do know that we are living in a time of terror and destruction. I don't know what path destiny has planned for you, but my heart tells me that come the day you may be Banora's only hope."

Next morning as the troopers of Banora rounded up the herd, Alastair was pleased that the Elder of Coe spoke to him with the same rough tongue as he did the rest of the group. The Banoran troopers and the herd of reindeer moved through the wasteland, glad of the forage brought back from Tala by their brothers. Alain skilfully guided the group and the herd back to the edge of the swamplands of Nath, but the swamps, whilst passable in single file by men on horse or pony, were more treacherous for a herd of reindeer. Within minutes, two of them had slipped and drowned in the treacherous mud pools and quagmires.

The group halted short of the swamps to discuss their options. The reindeer could only be guided through the swamp in single file, and this seemed impossible. As the group had travelled, Alastair had noted that the large antlered stag seemed to be the chief of the herd. For a reason he did not yet understand himself, Alastair rode over to the large stag. He felt the white light shimmer across his body as he spoke to the reindeer. The old stag shook his antlers and slowly walked back, touching each of the herd. Alain and Munro took the lead and were followed by the old stag. In single file, the herd, followed by Duncan and the troopers, wove its way through the swamp and on to the broad grasslands of the Tala plains.

It was early in September when the Banorans arrived back below the city of Tala and entered the large refugee camp. As Angus Ferguson greeted his friend back home, the first snowflakes were already starting to fall. The white blanket that would shortly douse the fires in Banora was also going to lock in the Hidden Lands for a long, hard winter. Whilst winter brought hardship, it also brought a time of relative quiet and peace. The people now living in the Hidden Lands would survive through their efforts to stock the winter stores, and the reindeer added to their provisions with milk and occasional meat.

As he had promised, Ala Moire solved the problem of the deep cold. Each person in the camp was given a small white stone which when gently rubbed emitted a deep warmth for both the people and their tents. No one knew the source of these little stones or the magic that powered them. In early August Ala Moire had left Tala heading east with two pack horses, and it was presumed that the magic stones had been gathered somewhere in the waste lands. The people in the city had survived many a winter kept warm by the ingenuity of the builders of Tala, who had dug deep into the core of the mountain and fashioned waterways where the snows from the peaks melted. The waterways ran down deep underground to be fed back up again to provide heat and constant hot water to the people of the city.

On Alastair's return, Angus could not hold back his excitement at the prospect of telling Alastair what had happened whilst his friend had been in the East. When Alastair entered the tent they shared he immediately saw the full set of armour, the surcoat with the white and blue cross and the red edging and the weapons neatly propped up on Angus's side of the tent. "What on earth is this?" Alastair spluttered.

Angus described the rescue of Elbeth, his visit to the palace in Tala and the meeting with James Cameron, and told Alastair about his two months of training with the Red Cameron. The training had been hard and had taken place every day on the fields of the Hidden Lands, but more commonly on the Nath and at times in the swamps and waste lands. He explained that he was becoming increasingly competent with the sword and the short lance used by the Cameron troopers. He had also been gifted one of the horses taken from the Ember riders at the skirmishes on the Plain of Coe. He had been accepted into the troop, and only three days before had been given the honour of wearing the white, blue and red.

As it turned out the training had worked both ways, as the Red Cameron men had learnt to use the short Banoran bow and also now understood the stamina and prowess of the smaller Banoran cobs when tackling difficult ground. Now when training around the swamp, the Red Cameron borrowed some of the cobs. In the past couple of weeks, in part to earn his stripes, Angus joined two Cameron raiding parties that had ventured into the plains of Coelene to rustle some livestock from the south to bolster the supplies for the refugees. In these raids the Red Cameron were also accompanied by a few of the tall Coelete warriors who could travel on foot almost as fast as the horses, although their primary role was to guard the route back to the mountains for the Cameron raiders.

Alastair was impressed and somewhat jealous of his friend's new status. Briefly he outlined his story of the journey to bring back the reindeer from the East, although he left out some parts concerning his role in the adventure so as not to concern his friend. As they were talking Angus was changing from his day clothes into his best attire, which in fact had been worn by his father. The clothes were sturdy rather than fine, but they were presentable in anything but the richest company.

Noting the question on Alastair's lips, Angus explained that he was going into the city to meet with Elbeth. Quietly, although not entirely secretly, the pair had been meeting twice a week ever since Angus had rescued the Cameron's daughter from the mountain lion. The Elder of Cameron knew about these meetings, as he knew most of what went on in the camp of the Bala people, and whilst he did not forbid them, nor did he encourage them. He knew from his own youth and two subsequent marriages that love was a precious thing, yet fragile in times of war. In days of strife love could be a single thread of hope for the future, which none the less could be severed by eternal separation.

James Cameron knew first hand the price paid for love, life and death. It was the memory of Annis, his first love, that had made him hold back from forbidding Elbeth to meet Ferguson. It was a reverse of the current situation; he was to become a great lord and she was the daughter of one of his father's tenant farmers. The spring and summer of 1270 still held warm memories for him. The pair had met secretly on the plains of Aldene. One early autumn morning Annis did not show at their meeting place. Days later James Cameron learnt that the young girl had been taken by a mysterious illness and had died on the very morning they were due to meet. In 1275 Cameron's father followed tradition and the young

Lord was married to Kathryn, the eldest daughter of the previous Elder of Ewart and sister of the current Elder. The couple had happy years together and were blessed with two sons, Rob and Alex, and a daughter, Elbeth.

Cameron was often away from Aldene on campaign fighting with the alliance forces in Ciren and Toria as they continued to resist the occupation armies of Dewar the First. In 1295, Rob, who was twenty, was fighting alongside his father in Ciren when he was hit in the shoulder by an Ackar arrow. The wound became infected and the young man died painfully. When the news reached Aldene, Kathryn locked herself in her rooms and a few months later died of a broken heart. It would be several years before James Cameron returned to Aldene.

As Ciren and Toria fell to the invaders, many of the leaders of the allied armies crossed the Middle Sea to Tamin. It was here that Cameron learnt of his wife's death. In 1297 Cameron met and married Eleanor, who was the widow of a Ciren noble killed in one of the battles against the Dewar. As Dewar the Second's forces gathered on the Plain of Tember in 1299, Cameron was worried about the safety of his new wife. John Burnett was given the task of ensuring Eleanor got safely back to Aldene. So it was in the summer of 1299 that Elbeth first met her stepmother. James Cameron returned to his capital with his other son, Alex, a few months later, once the battle on the Vale of Tember came to stalemate.

The Cameron liked the young Banoran farmer and was impressed by his application in developing his skills as a trooper, but his daughter was very unlikely to be allowed to form a permanent relationship with the young man. As was the way with the daughters of the Clan Chiefs, Elbeth's destiny was most likely to be to marry the son of one of the other Elders, thereby cementing alliances for future conflicts. For now though, remembering his own past and with the people of Bala effectively in exile, the Cameron allowed the young couple their time, but always keeping an eye on them to ensure the relationship did not become too serious. Of course, as had happened since history immemorial, the daughter did not necessarily see things the father's way – and as always, love had its own magic to weave.

As Angus was completing his dressing there was a call, and outside was one of the tall Coelete warriors, asking Alastair Munro to follow him into the city. So the two friends walked into Tala together, Alastair for the first time. As with Angus before him, Alastair looked in amazement at the tall buildings carved into and out from the natural rock of the mountain.

Halfway to the palace at the top of Tala, Angus shook Alastair's hand and moved off down a side passage, no doubt for a liaison with Elbeth. Munro followed the Coelete warrior higher up to the top of the city and into the palace. Guided through the anterooms and on to the upper floors, Alastair was entering the room Angus had been in earlier that summer. Again in residence were Ala Moire and Cameron, but this time Duncan of Coe was also present.

Ala Moire waved Munro to a seat at the table next to the Coe Elder. "Thank you for coming Alastair, and thank you too for your courage on the journey to the East and bringing the reindeer back from Esimore" he began. "Duncan has told me much of the story of your intervention with the reindeer herders of Esimore and how you guided the reindeer through the swamp lands. This must all be very strange to you, and no doubt unnerving. But it is time for me to share with you a history lesson."

Alastair already knew some of the legends of the Second Age from stories his father had told him, but now Ala Moire filled in the detail and more. He started with his own history. "I grew up with my sister in the land of Soll to the south of Esimore. My given name back then was Malama O'Re. From my earliest years I understood that I had been gifted a rare power." He told the story of his journey to Aracene, as Aldene was named then, his unsuccessful attempts to influence the Council of Five and his subsequent banishment to Esimore, hence closing the circle in Alastair's mind regarding the man in white with the white fire in the legends of the reindeer herders.

Ala Moire continued the history lesson. "Several years before I set out for Aracene my sister had gone before me to Bala to marry the Lord of Coe, one of Duncan's ancient ancestors. My sister was also gifted with some of the white power, but it could only be used by her in certain circumstances. As the Coe lands of Banora were pillaged for the othium, my sister and the Lord of Coe raised a small army to try to oust the invaders of the Council. They failed and were captured by the soldiers of the Council and put to death. The Lord of Coe's brother, the new Lord of Coe, sheltered my sister's small family and fled north to the lands of the Coelete. My sister's grandson was with the Coelete nation that moved into these Hidden Lands, and he had inherited some of his grandmother's power, which in part helped the Coelete to anticipate the meteorite storms and enabled them to deepen their mountain hideaway to avoid damage from the stones.

"Early in the Third Age a young man from my sister's line was called to leave the Hidden Lands and venture south. He was the first to visit his ancestral homelands in hundreds of years. He set up a small farm in Banora and built his life there. You, Alastair, are his great-great-great-great grandson, and directly related over the generations to Duncan, who you now sit next to. The power my sister had and that of her grandson have lain dormant over the generations, however it became my task to ensure that the Elders of Coe and Cameron maintained a watch over the small family in Banora, and over the years under the Elders' protection, no harm came to them. I had foreseen long ago that a day would come when one from my sister's line would need to take my role in protecting the world from the reincarnation of the Second Age and the reappearance of the power of othium. I had not foreseen that the power would again be yielded by my old adversary Oien, who I assumed had been consumed by the meteorite storms."

Alastair could not summon a single word to say as Ala Moire continued.

"You remember our conversation above the Pass of Ing? I noted the white sparks and power you shed on the journey over the Plains and I noted the power and passion in your love for your homelands. Your father and grandfather taught you well, although they knew little of the power you were born with. Above all else, I know my time is coming to an end and yours is just beginning. But these are treacherous times, Alastair, and I need time to teach you about His power, which is your gift, your curse and your destiny. We must use this winter wisely to prepare you for the long road ahead."

CHAPTER SEVEN

A Hard Winter

The winter of 1300 to 1301 was the hardest in living memory. The snow and ice stretched from the Coe Mountains south over all of Bala and on into Ackar and Lett. As the land froze, Dewar the Second moved his court south to Anua, the capital of the Province of Ember in Arance. Nothing moved north of the border with Lett. The people, the animals and the plants fought for survival, and many lost the battle.

In snowbound Aldene, Oien paced the castle corridors in a huge anger. If he had had the vehicles of the Second Age he could have used the othium-powered machines to cut a passage south to join the King and at least begin the invasions of Doran,

Kermin and Amina. The winter had come too quickly and too abruptly for the building of any equipment, and only small amounts of othium had been extracted before winter closed all the passes north and south. Oien cursed his luck. He was also worried by the unexpectedly harsh winter, and wondered if once again greater powers were meddling with his plans.

On the Plain of Coe and in the farmlands of Banora, the invading army was suffering more. The forests of the south-west of Banora provided wood to heat the fires, when it was possible to get to the forest. Many of the livestock and many people were literally freezing to death. A few of the invading army suffered somewhat less by sheltering in the requisitioned farmhouses of Banora, including those that had been homes to Angus Ferguson and Alastair Munro since birth.

In the far north, in the Hidden Lands, the Coelete and the people of Bala suffered less. Whilst they had not anticipated the severity of the winter, they were always prepared for long winters and the provisions harvested from the summer fields, the fish, the raided livestock and the gift of the reindeer meant that no one suffered greatly other than enduring the constant bitter cold. The magical white stones treasured by each refugee kept them warm physically and somehow spiritually. In Tala the hot water that pumped through the conduits from deep in the mountain kept the residents as comfortable as they had always been through hundreds of winters.

During the months of October and November Ala Moire and Alastair Munro met regularly, almost always in the same room high in the Palace. The first lesson was related to the nature of power.

"Alastair, you remember the white sparks emanating from you when the othium blast destroyed all those defending the Pass of Ing?" began Ala Moire. "The difference between your power and that of othium is defined in that moment. Oien has learnt to use the hidden power in the red rock through alchemy and science. The power is released through the interaction between the dead cold red rock and the secret formulations incorporating the salt of Elat. The white power that you yield does not come from science or alchemy but from within you. It is a power you have been gifted with by He that has always been and He that will always be. It is a power to make good that which is bad and transform wrong to right. It is a power gifted to you to use, but you do have the choice to use the gift for the good or for the bad. That is a choice you will need to make in the days ahead, and the line between good and bad is not always as clear as you might imagine.

"So I need to teach you how to channel and control the white power. It cannot, or should not, be released in a moment of anger or reflex as you did in Esimore. You need to learn how to call the power to your will when you decide that it is the right time to use it. Used wrongly, the gift will become a curse and will fill your worst nightmares."

Alastair felt a weight of responsibility and anxiety. After all, he was at heart just a simple farmer, with the love of his land burned deep into his soul.

Over the months that followed Ala Moire taught Alastair Munro how to call the power when needed, and Alastair learnt how to quench the fire when it came to his hand unbidden, often when he was annoyed by some trivial incident.

After another heavy snowfall, Alastair and a team of Bala folk were slowly clearing the road from the refugees' tented village through to the gate entry to the city of Tala. The work was hard, tiring and back-breaking, and worst of all very slow. In frustration, Alastair raised his arm and opened his palm to the snowdrift blocking his way. It melted away in an instant, to the amazement of the people who stood nearby. However, as the snow melted, the power also lifted a large stone, which was thrown some way from the cleared road. The stone struck a young boy playing in the snow on the edge of the group. There was a crack and a scream and instantly Alastair realised that the lower bone in the lad's leg had broken. Rushing over, he swept his hand over the broken bone and as the boy's screams turned to sobs, the white light sealed the wound and healed the bone. The people stood in wonder and awe, but for Alastair Munro a lesson had been learnt.

The witnesses to the magic spread the news through the camp and living there became almost impossible for Alastair, as a constant queue of folk with injuries and ailments started to arrive at his tent. When the story reached Tala and Ala Moire, it became clear that Munro could not be left in the tented village. Ala Moire knew that Alastair's love for his people would compel him to use his power to try to heal all their woes, but it was too early and his time had not come. He was moved into the city of Tala to reside in the quarters occupied by the Elder of Coe and his close family. Duncan of Coe, although only a handful of years older than Munro, treated his guest as though he was his son. Of course both men now knew that stretching far back in time, their blood lines were connected.

Duncan of Coe's family were a tight group and initially Alastair Munro found it strange living as part of a family. He had been used to a relatively solitary life on the farm and it had been many years since he had been part of a family. Isobel, Coe's wife, was a gracious lady with a ready smile and she was easy company. It turned out that Isobel had grown up in the north of Banora, and although the two had never met before, they soon learnt that they shared a love of their home land and its mountain vistas.

Often evenings before the fire were spent reminiscing about people they both had known or stories they had been told as children. Ross, who was twelve, the eldest of the children, dreamed that one day he would join the Red Cameron, and regularly insisted that Alastair should go with him to the courtyard outside their rooms to practise with the sword or the bow. The nine-year-old twins, Moira and Leana, loved the make-believe stories that Alastair told them. He settled into family life and reflected that maybe he had missed out in his choice of solitude on the farm.

Living in the city was easy and warm, although Alastair missed the company of his people, and most of all his friend Angus Ferguson. As it turned out, he spent almost as much time with Angus in Tala as he had done in the shared tent. Angus, as a Red Cameron trooper, was allowed ready access to the city and did not need to adhere to the curfew, although the latter had gradually been relaxed as the locals and the refugees came to know, trust and rely on each other.

Alastair often met Elbeth in the rooms in Tala, as she regularly came to the Coe quarters to teach the three children of the Elder. From his room close to the living area Alastair could often hear the children shriek with laughter as Elbeth played some sort of chasing game with them. When Alastair was teaching Ross in the courtyard he would watch as Elbeth braided the twins' hair or worked with them on their writing. Most of all Alastair noticed that when Elbeth was with the children there was always laughter. It seemed to Alastair that it was the young woman's gift to spread warmth and joy.

Elbeth clearly understood her status within the palace, and among the people, yet she was kind and generous with an easy grace and smile. Alastair could understand why Angus would be enchanted in the company of the young woman.

A week or so after Alastair's relocation, Elbeth told him that she was going down into the city that evening to meet Angus, and invited Alastair to join them. As they wound down through the cuts in the rocks that formed the streets of Tala, Alastair was again astounded by the skills of the Coelete builders.

After a short walk down the mountain the pair came to an old inn. The Wild Goose had a narrow wooden doorway which led into a large cave that clearly had existed long before the Coelete had entered the Hidden Lands. Seats and tables had been carved into alcoves around the walls of the cave, whilst the central area was a polished stone floor with stone tables and chairs. Hot water heaters kept the cave warm, and whilst the interior was large it was also somehow cosy.

As Alastair and Elbeth entered the inn, Angus leapt from his corner alcove to embrace his old friend, and a moment later held Elbeth in a longer embrace. Alastair knew instinctively that this was no mere infatuation; the two were deeply in love. Angus and Elbeth did not ignore him as they talked, but their eyes never left each other. Alastair was pleased for his friend, and for Elbeth, but he was also concerned, as he knew this match would never have been allowed back in their normal world. The difference in status of the two was just too great to be contemplated within the clan society of Bala.

Alastair paused, and then dismissed the thought. These were different and strange times, and maybe they would have unexpected endings. After sharing a drink he excused himself and left the lovers to their tryst. As he walked back towards the rooms in the palace he allowed himself a different thought, almost a prayer, and murmured: "If it can be then let it be, if I can influence then let me be wise, and let these two lovers' story find an unexpected happy ending."

As March turned into April, the first spring sun appeared to warm the northern lands. Ala Moire called Anaton, the Chiefs of the Coelete and the Elders to council. Of the people of Bala only the Elders of Cameron, Coe and Ewart were present, as none of the other Elders had managed to escape with the people to the Hidden Lands. John Burnett, as captain of the Red Cameron, was also present.

Ala Moire spoke to the small gathering. "As the April sun warms these lands, so its hand will have been hastening the thaw faster in the southern lands. The hospitality of the Coelete to the people of Bala has been unstinting in its generosity. However, we know that the land of the Coelete cannot sustain the refugee population for the longer term, and indeed it is also possible that as the enemy power grows, our presence here will be detected. It is time for us to assess the situation in Banora, although I fear it will not bring good news."

Burnett spoke first, nodding to his Elder. "Ala Moire, I propose that a small party of the Red Cameron should move south to carry out some raids on the enemy camps and bring back intelligence on the situation in Banora. I request that a small cohort of Coelete warriors should guard the rear of the troop and protect our return route back to the safety here behind the mountains."

Ala Moire nodded his agreement.

Cameron spoke next. "With Anaton's agreement to supply a Coelete rear guard a small troop of Red Cameron can move swiftly, live off the land, raid some of the outposts of the invaders and return to tell us what plans we need to make for the next stage in winning back the lands of Bala. However, I need John here with the majority of the men to continue the training of the Red Cameron and to begin to train the refugee army so that it is ready for a return to face the Dewar invader. I propose that a troop of fifty Red Cameron, led by my son Alex, should venture out to reconnoitre the situation."

Alex Cameron was just twenty and his father was somewhat reluctant to volunteer him for such a dangerous task, painfully aware that Alex's brother Rob had been killed by an Ackar arrow at the very same age. Yet despite his age Alex was already an experienced warrior, having led a troop of Red Cameron alongside his father in the battles on the Vale of Tember. He was of smaller stature than his father but had inherited James Cameron's steely determination. Alex was a good commander and well loved by his Red Cameron troopers. His men respected him more for his personality than his rank.

"We will need Ferguson to be part of the troop," said Burnett. "He is now a fully-trained trooper and knows the land better than any of my other men."

Anaton agreed to supply the rear guard, and so the action was decided and it was agreed that the men should set off in two days' time.

It was a sombre meeting the three had the following evening in the Wild Goose. Angus was excited by the prospect of action as a Red Cameron, while Elbeth was red-eyed from tears of concern for her brother as well as for her loved one. Alastair had mixed feelings; he felt a desire to be going with his friend and a concern for Angus's safe return from what would, by necessity, be a perilous mission.

As the sun began to warm the lands of the Coelete, the spring sunshine was more advanced to the south. In Banora the snow still lay deep but melting, with the meltwater swelling the rivers and streams. The Pass of Ing remained snowbound, but would be passable in a few weeks. Further south, Aldene was surrounded by meadows full of spring flowers, and further to the south in Boretar and Anua the Dewar was calling together his forces for another invasion across the Middle Sea. The Dewar had the great trebuchet that Oien had constructed, and despite the winter a second machine was close to completion in Banora. However, he had only a very small supply of othium and salt. Still it should, he thought, be enough to terrify his foes in Amina, at least until Oien could deliver more firepower; then he would sweep the enemy aside and take the southern kingdoms as his own.

So in late April 1301 a great gathering of armed men moved south to the transports in Anelo, whilst Oien, Orridon, a small troop of Ember Horse and further conscripts, workmen and camp followers moved in the opposite direction, north back to the Inger Mountains and over the Pass of Ing back into Banora.

CHAPTER EIGHT
To Erwick

At around the same time as Oien and Orridon moved north from Aldene, Alex Cameron and the troop of Red Cameron passed through the tunnels under the Coe Mountains and rode out on to the Plain of Coe. The riders were well armed and on fast horses. This time each rider carried a Banoran bow and a quiver of arrows. During the winter the troopers had practised long and hard to master the bow from horseback. Although trees were relatively few in the north, and only the hardiest kinds thrived, there were yew and ash woods along the edge of the Nath and on the borders of the swamplands. The Coelete had long treasured and protected the woods, as they supplied essential materials for use where the naturally abundant stone would not suffice. The trees also provided the wood for the longbows and arrows used by the Coelete warriors. Before the winter set in fully, the Coelete, with some of the Banoran troopers, had crafted enough of the short bows and their arrows to supply a reasonable force of archers. When the Red Cameron practised with their new weapon, the tedious part came after practice, when every used arrow had to be retrieved and returned to the armoury.

So it was that Angus Ferguson and fifty companions rode out into a sunlit morning in the north of his homelands. This was land that Angus knew well, as he had hunted the deer on the plains and fished the rivers and lochs. In those days these lands were relatively sparsely populated, with most of the peoples of the Coe and Coelene plains living in small fishing villages on the coasts of the Greater Sea to the west and the Eastern Sea to the east. Snow still lay on the plains, but green shoots and flowers of spring were pushing through the melting white. Where the snow had melted clusters of snow drops mimicked the white of the snow. In other areas the yellow heads of daffodils were waking up in the morning sun.

The troop moved slowly out to the edge of the grey promontories to survey what lay ahead. Above them the Coelete warriors had climbed onto the lower slopes of the mountains to survey further.

From Angus's perspective the land he could see looked largely unchanged, other than a dark line that marked the horizon. Alain of Lorn came down from the mountain to speak with Alex Cameron, who called Angus forward, as he was the only one of the troop who really knew this land.

Alain spoke to Alex. "My lord, the land ahead for twenty miles or more seems to be open plain. Beyond, however, there appears to be a sizeable camp of tents and crude shacks. Even from the mountain it is difficult to tell who, or how many, live there. Our guess is that this is the overflow camp of the invaders, many more of whom must have seen out the winter closer to the mountains in Banora."

Alex Cameron turned to Angus. "What lies ahead, Angus?"

Angus looked out over the plain. "The central plains of Coe and Coelene are largely just grasslands. To the east and west the rivers run out from the Inger Mountains. To the west, three rivers cut through Banora and the plain, running into the Greater Sea. To the east, two rivers flow down to the Eastern Sea. Both in the east and the west, tributaries from the mountains behind us join the main flows before they reach the seas. If I were with the invader army, then the best land to winter in would be south of the river Ora, where there is access to the forests for fuel. The rivers Ban and Ola further north would be frozen over in the winter, enabling foraging further south for any settlement placed north of the Ola. Most of the homesteads in Banora lie south of the Ora and between the Ora and the Ban. I would anticipate that the better troops would occupy these lands, leaving the conscripts and army followers clustered around the Ola and the foot of the Pass of Ing."

"At a guess, as the distances are not certain, the black tented town is north of the Ola," said Alain.

Cautiously the troop moved out onto the Plain of Coe and set up a staging post a few miles south of the Coe Mountains. Most of the Coelete warriors would remain there to protect any needed hasty retreat. Alain and Gareth of the Guardians would move south when the troopers ventured to raid the enemy encampments. Both warriors had ancient horns hung round their necks. These were fashioned from mammoth tusks that had been found when the Coelete nation had tunnelled their way through the mountains. The horns had long been used to give warning of danger approaching and could be heard over many miles. If a dash back to the Hidden Lands became necessary, the horns would alert the waiting Coelete warriors, who could move south to protect the retreat.

As the sun lowered over the Greater Sea, Alex Cameron led the troopers south for a first raid on the invader encampment. As the troop neared the edge of the camp the evening fires started to burn; although the day was warmer, the winter chill still dominated the evening and night. There was no apparent guard on the camp edges, but then the residents had no expectation or anticipation of conflict. This outer camp was relatively small and clearly only an outpost of the new residents of Banora. The encampment was set between two main thoroughfares with tents and small walkways to the centre and both sides of the main streets. Beyond the campsite, the slow waters of the Ola were just visible in the light of the early moon. Alex Cameron's plan was simple. The troop would split in two, ride at pace into the camp and cause as much havoc as they could.

Alain spoke up. "Gareth and I can go ahead of you to those two nearest fires and as your horsemen arrive we can hand them burning branches to torch the tents," he said. It was agreed.

The two slim, tall warriors slipped out ahead of the troop. In daytime the Coelete warriors would have been spotted some distance away by any passer-by, but at dusk, dressed in their drab, grey clothing, they merged into the deepening dark and became almost invisible. As two burning sticks were briefly waved from the nearest fires, the Red Cameron rode at a fast trot towards the camp. As each trooper reached the fire Gareth and Alain passed up burning brands, and from this point the troopers galloped down the two main streets. The charging horses took the residents completely by surprise and the little resistance was slow to order and largely confused. The blazing torches sent tent after tent ablaze, and the few defenders who managed to gather arms were quickly despatched by arrows from Banoran bows.

At the end of each street the troopers wheeled round at the river's edge and traversed back up the neighbouring street. On this reverse charge the spear and sword removed all opposition.

It took barely minutes for the troopers to race back out to the empty plain to rejoin the two Coelete warriors. Behind them the blaze from the tented town lit the sky and barely a single shelter survived the attack. Many residents also perished in the fire or on the points of the feathered arrows and the sword.

As the troop regathered, Alex Cameron shouted Angus forward. "Ferguson, over to you now. Where do we head for shelter from the night and any reprisal? We can win a short sharp raid, but we can't wait here for them to bring forward reinforcements."

Angus pointed and with the two Coelete easily keeping pace with the horses, the troop dashed north-west. In a couple of hours they reached the banks of the river Cole where it flowed down from the Coe Mountains to join the northerly-flowing river Ola. Where the two met, the Cole cascaded over several waterfalls to plunge down to join the Ola.

The troop set up camp for the night with the rivers north and west of them protecting their flanks. The sentries watched out the night looking back over the plain to where the fires still burned in the far distance. No chase followed that night, and in the bright sun of the new morning still nothing moved over the distant plain. In truth any pursuit, as it turned out, would have had to come from further south. The only seasoned troops, largely the Ember Horse and the foot soldiers of Ackar, were locked between the flooded rivers of the Ora and the Ban.

That morning Alex called a meeting of the two troop leaders, Davy Scott and John Ewart. Joining them were Angus and the two Coelete warriors.

"Where to now, Angus?" asked Alex.

"I suggest a move to the coast," Angus replied. "At the mouth of the Ola lies the ancient fishing port of Erwick. It is unlikely that the invaders will have come this far north and west. From my understanding they would have little interest in fish, and Erwick is difficult to get to without knowing the land. It is well protected by river and sea. In addition the Greater Sea, which the Ola joins at Erwick, has warm currents that should have made even this past winter bearable for the folk of Erwick. It may also be possible to get the fishermen to transport us over the mouth of the Ola, and from there we can raid between the Ola and the Ban and possibly further south into my homelands in Banora."

After a brief discussion it was agreed. From where they had camped it was not obvious to Alex how the troop could cross the waterfalls of the Cole, and the Ola at this point was too wide, and flowing too quickly, for the horses to attempt what would have to be a double swim across the river.

Noticing the captain's worried look, Angus spoke up. "There is a way past the waterfalls, although it is many years since I travelled it with my father."

Alex nodded, and Angus led the troop up into the near foothills of the Coe, the crash of the waterfalls a deafening roar beside them. At the third of the falls a narrow path, only wide enough for a single horse, branched off to the west, appearing to vanish into the third waterfall. Angus remembered it from years ago when he and his father had visited Erwick. The narrow path took a sharp right turn as it closed in towards the water and then a sharp left where it became clear that hundreds of years before, either the water, or man, had crafted a passageway behind the cascading waters. The passage appeared to open out on the western side of the fall. The troop passed through, and as the path initially rose on the western side they looked down on the Greater Sea. Below them, where the Ola flowed into the sea, was the small town of Erwick.

Erwick and its port and harbour sat at the mouth of the Ola facing out to the Greater Sea. It was clear as the troop moved down towards the town that it had been there for hundreds of years. The small stone houses and the cobbled streets were finely crafted from the grey stone of the Coe Mountains.

The two Coelete warriors stopped as the town came more clearly into view. "This is a place of legend" gasped Gareth. "It is said in our ancient stories that as the Coelete worked to build a path through the mountains to Tala and our home in the Hidden Lands, Olaton's brother Calan was concerned that it would take long years to cut through the mountain and the invading hordes from the south would overrun the Coelete before the migration north could be completed. It is said that he took his small family and some friends away from the mountain retreats and headed west to new lands. The builders of this place knew the stonecraft of the Coelete, or were themselves Coelete. I thought as we passed under the waterfall that the passageway looked strangely familiar. It is crafted similarly to the passage under the mountain that leads to Tala. This must be where Calan and his band settled, long years ago."

As the troop paused, a small group of horsemen came out from the town. Whilst well-armed, they were not overtly threatening. Nonetheless the Red Cameron loosened their weapons, just in case. As the men approached, it was clear that they were not of the height of the Coelete warriors, but they were still unusually tall for people from Bala.

As the horsemen drew closer, Alex rode out from his troop to meet them. The lead rider from the group pulled ahead to rein in beside Alex. He extended his hand.

"I am Noren, Steward of Erwick, and I trust you visit my town in peace," he said.

"We do. I am Alex Cameron," Alex replied. "We hope that you and your people may be able to help us in our current mission."

Noren shrugged. "We live quietly here, largely sheltered from the outside world, but fishermen from the south who were working the Greater Sea stopped here on their way home before the winter set in and told us of great unrest in Bala and in Banora to our south. We hope these troubles will not affect us here in this outpost, but we must be cautious. I need to know more."

Noren noted the two tall Coelete warriors. "You travel in strange company, Alex. I have heard of the deeds of the Red Cameron and note your colours, but those two are from the stories our forefathers told of a tribe of tall warriors that live in the mountains in the north and who helped the early settlers of Erwick build our town. You have my attention. Please follow me and we will find you and your men places to rest and shelter for you and your horses. We are not rich here and it will be a squeeze to find beds for fifty men, but what hospitality we can offer is yours. Come."

So the troop rode into Erwick, with the local population staring in amazement at the two Coelete warriors who seemed to have sprung from the pages of their story books.

Once the men had been found rooms and shelter for the horses, Noren led Alex to a large house set in the centre of the town looking out over the harbour and beyond to the sea. In the comfort of the large council room, Alex told Noren about the invasion of Bala, and explained the little he knew about the red stone in the mountains above Banora. He also told Noren about the exodus of the people of Bala to the north and the journey through the mountains to Tala. This part of the story particularly caught Noren's attention.

"So our stories are true, there is a race of people north of the mountains despite what the maps say," he said. "If this is so, then it may also be true that we are distantly related to those people."

Alex responded, "From what Gareth and Alain have said, I think you are right. However we are not here to hide or rest. We need your help to take our fight back to the south and hopefully in time to repel the invaders from our lands."

"We will meet in the morning to discuss what you

require Alex, but be warned over hundreds of years we have set ourselves aside from the politics and troubles in Bala," replied Noren. "We are fishermen, not warriors, and with the harvest of the sea and the fields around the town we are self-sufficient. You will likely find my council men reluctant to engage in anything that might bring attention to our town." With that they parted, agreeing to meet the next day.

The next morning the four councillors of Erwick, together with Noren, Alex, Ewart, Scott and Angus, met in the large council room in what was in effect the town hall of Erwick. It was clear that Noren had, at least in outline, briefed his colleagues. However, from their hostile looks, three of the council members were not very happy about what they had been told.

Whilst Noren was the leader of the council, it was obvious that a slightly younger, more heavily-set man was aspiring for leadership. Erden was of a slightly different stock from the others. Apart from his bulk and his bullish nature he would have passed unnoticed in any town in Bala, whilst Noren and the other three would have stood out, being half a head taller than the average citizen of Bala.

Erden clearly enjoyed the sound of his own voice and liked to use his bulk to bully the rest of the council. He held forth at length. "Why have these strangers been allowed to enter Erwick? They can only bring danger to this peaceful town. They must be forcibly removed! Many times have I advised this council of the need for absolute security in these difficult and challenging times. May I remind the council of a resolution passed only last year in this very chamber..." And so it went on. Noren passed an apologetic glance at Alex, but did nothing to stop the tirade.

There was a quiet knock on the door and Alain of Lorn entered the room, apologising for his late arrival. Erden threw himself from his seat, screaming, "who invited this alien to our lands?" and hurled himself at Alain. With the grace of a ballet dancer, the Coelete warrior simply stepped aside and brought the edge of his hand with practised force onto the temple of the charging Erden, who fell to the floor pole-axed. He was not badly injured, but seemed likely to have a headache for some days.

Noren called some of the people waiting outside the room, and the limp body of the councillor was carried back to his home. Noren openly apologised to the visitors and then added, "Erden is a brute and a bully, but some of what he said was true. What do you want of my people, Alex?"

Cameron paused, unsure of the answer. It was Angus Ferguson who answered instead.

"Noren, we are a small force sent out to test the enemy. We need to find out where their weaknesses are, and we plan to raid their encampments. We have already destroyed one of the outer camps north of the Ola. You may be able to ride out this storm from Banora sheltered in your homes and living from the sea, but the invader has a hunger for conquest and destruction. You may find that your peace here is at best fragile. We would like your help at least to cross over the Ola so that we can test the enemy located in the north of Banora. Better still, we would like your boats to support us in moving down the coast and raiding inland, then returning to move on to another point of attack. Is that possible?"

Noren smiled. "We are fishermen here, not warriors. Our boats fish the near sea and we don't have craft that could transport fifty men and horses down the coast. Even if we did, I doubt many of our villagers would volunteer for such voyages."

A tall man, the youngest in the council, spoke next. He had been introduced as Galbraith and was Noren's eldest son.

"Father, you forget the three craft in the northern harbour. They have not been to sea in years, but once repaired they could easily transport men and horses down the coast, as they once did in our forefathers' time." He explained that in years long gone the people of Erwick had been less peaceful. Their forefathers had been raiders, the scourge of the Greater Sea. Their longboats and warriors had raided the coast as far south as the coastal villages of Ackar and Lett. The warriors had returned with loot and slaves from the softer southern lands, indeed it was likely that Erden was a descendant of one of those slaves and not of the bloodline of the Coelete who had worked with the locals that first inhabited and built Erwick many centuries ago.

He added, "With a few weeks' work the longboats could be ready to sail again. Whilst we may feel remote from the core of the country, we are still people of Bala and we cannot ignore the threat that sits so close to us in the south in Banora. If the Cameron troopers can man the oars, then I believe we can recruit crews from our people to sail the boats down the coast to test the invaders."

Noren nodded. "I was not going to mention the longboats, or birlinns, to give them their correct name, but it seems my son yearns for adventure. So be it, our boat builders will start tomorrow to make the three birlinns seaworthy again and ready them to once more fulfil the purpose for which they were first built."

"What are these... birlinns?" asked Angus, curious.

"The birlinn was the boat of war used by our forefathers and their allies from the western islands to raid down the west coast of Andore," replied Noren. "The raiders controlled the Greater Sea in the latter part of the twelfth century. With their distinctive square sail on a single mast, each boat had eighteen oars and each could easily carry twenty warriors and their horses. During the early part of the thirteenth century larger war boats were developed in Ackar and Lett and the sea raiders retired to their homelands. Today the remaining birlinns are mostly merchant boats travelling the southern sea routes of Andore. It seems the time has come to set them free again on the Greater Sea."

As the Cameron troops were heading west after the night raid on the tented outpost, Oien and Orridon, with a large troop of Ember Horse, were reaching the summit of the Pass of Ing. As they passed the heights, where the remnants of the fight from the previous year still littered the pass, they looked out over the Plain of Coe. In the far distance they could see the smoke still rising from the settlement north of the Ola.

Orridon spoke first. "Maybe we still have work to do to tame these people and these lands."

Oien laughed. "Maybe a little, but once we gather enough of the red rock these feeble people will bow to me, and only to me, as will all the peoples of the world."

Orridon said nothing, but he wondered what the Dewar would have made of such a bold statement.

As the leading group moved down the mountain

pass into Banora, behind them the baggage train stretched back into the plains with more conscripts from Toria and Arance, miners from Ciren and near the rear of the column, wagons filled with the purple salt from Elat, recently harvested from the straits and now being transported to the north.

As the first of the column reached the plain they were met by riders coming back from the north. At the head of this group was Elem, brother of the unfortunate Cember and now Orridon's second in command.

Elem reached out a hand to his commander. "Welcome back to Banora, sir," he said.

"Not much of a welcome when I cross the pass and see what I presume is part of the camp burning in the north," Orridon replied.

Elem looked down under his commander's stern gaze, well aware of his brother now in the rank and file of the Horse. "My lord, we have just returned from there. We gathered the Horse together as soon as the flames appeared on the horizon; however, the rivers delayed our travel. When we arrived the attackers were long gone and few of the camp residents remained to tell the story. From what we can gather a small cavalry troop dashed into the camp and spread fire to most of the tents, killing all who stood in their way. The raid was over in a couple of minutes. Our best guess is that it was a troop of Red Cameron raiding from wherever they are now holed up in the Coe Mountains. Their tracks led west from the camp, but in a quick scout we could find no trace of them."

Skilled in guerrilla warfare, the Red Cameron had left tracks indicating their general direction but then wiped these out a short distance from the burning camp. The two Coelete warriors, who were expert trackers, had followed behind the horsemen to obliterate any sign of their passing.

"So the Cameron is still obstinately skulking in his northern hideouts" replied Orridon. He was still wondering about the disappearance of the Bala army and the people – and who were the tall warriors that had wrought destruction on Cember's troop?

Oien interrupted his thoughts. "Enough discussion, gentlemen. The enemy, if they still have any strength in the north, will bow before us when we unleash the force of othium on them. To achieve that I need to get the miners and the salt into the base camp and start building the machines of power that are needed by your King in the south and by me here, and far beyond."

Again Orridon pondered the naked ambition of this old man who seemed set on ruling the world. Still Orridon held his council; whilst not afraid, he knew he could not exert authority over the old alchemist.

Soon the already busy camps lying below the Inger Mountains and south of the Ola and north of the Ora rivers filled with more conscripts, miners, camp followers, provisions and equipment. Whilst the camps filled and space was limited, the hard winter had also reaped a terrible harvest. Almost one in three of those in the camps that had been locked in by the winter snows had died. Provisions had been almost completely consumed by the time the newcomers arrived. The elite of the Ember Horse and the army had survived better in the houses in the hamlets scattered across the south of Banora between the Ora and the forest. Whilst hampered by the snow, these farming areas had well-stocked barns and warehouses, wood from the forest fuelled the fires in the cottages and livestock was plentiful. The camps at the foot of the pass and those lying between the Ora and the Ban had suffered more severely in the cruel cold of that winter.

The spring of 1301 brought urgent activity to Banora. Conscripts, carpenters and stonemasons started to build large houses for the elite. Most of these were around the base of the Pass of Ing and between the Ora and the forests of Banora. Bridges were built in two places across the Ora, easing the jams at the one ford that gave passage across the river. The small population of Banora had no need of bridges, as the river was crossable most of the year, with only the early spring floods cutting the area off from the neighbouring land. In the foothills of the Inger and between the Ora and the Ban, the great furnaces that had burnt the previous summer were repaired and reconstructed. In the mountain itself, the miners reopened the passageways and the conscripts began transporting the red stone down the mountain. The saw-toothed machines were recovered from the mines and reprimed with othium and salt to resume the task of tearing apart the heart of the mountain. The miners' job was dangerous. Whilst othium was largely inert until primed by the salt of Elat formulations, the red stone was temperamental and could on occasion, without warning, instantaneously combust. As far as Oien could tell, this was a random event with no obvious cause. Again, he wondered if other powers were trying to hold back his progress.

CHAPTER NINE
The Kermin Alol

Far to the south, the Dewar forces had crossed the Middle Sea from the port of Anelo in the south of Arance. The invading army landed unopposed on the beaches south of Tamin, near the small town of Slat. The trebuchets that had accompanied this army were now being transported towards Tamin. A fleet of troop transporters and war boats had attacked the Amina port of Tufle. The Amina fleet had not managed to put to sea, and the invaders had stormed onto the harbour walls. After some vicious hand-to-hand fighting, the Ackar and Lett forces took the port and the town. The Amina foot soldiers who survived the attack on Tufle managed a disciplined retreat back to Tamin.

So the opposing armies again lined up on the Vale of Tember close to Tamin city walls. The coalition forces from Doran, Kermin and Amina replayed the battle of 1299; they were arrayed on both sides of the Amin river, which flowed south from the Kermin Alol and in front of Tamin. Whilst intuitively a river at the back of an army seemed like a trap, the defenders in 1299 had laid underwater passageways that allowed them to retreat across the river to defend the north bank. These passageways were cunningly disguised, and the entrances could be raised or lowered to allow escape or attack as necessary. In 1299 the Dewar armies' attacks had been thwarted by this back-and-forth tactic of the defenders. When the Dewar army drove the opposition forces back they simply used the river for defence, and from the high walls of the city of Tamin they could use arrows and burning pitch to stop encroachment over the river. When the Dewar troops pulled back, the coalition troops used the hidden passages to mount short, sharp raids against their enemy.

In 1299 the result was stalemate, and a truce was agreed. The Dewar, somewhat humbled and wounded but not defeated, headed back to Boretar, cursing the Red Cameron who had been at the front of many of the cavalry charges out from Tamin. As the opposing forces again took their positions, the Dewar announced, "Today is a different day, and it will have a different outcome."

So the armies lined up against each other, and after a few violent clashes the coalition forces retreated behind the river. Looking across their protective barrier of water, the leaders of Amina, Kermin and Doran smiled as they saw the two great trebuchets being moved into position on the south of the river. They wondered what the Dewar hoped to achieve by throwing stones at their impregnable city. But on the other bank the armourers, whilst still fearful of their new weapons, were now practised at the art of priming the red stone without causing it to explode in front of them.

The leaders of the coalition were dumbstruck as the first othium bombs hit the city walls with a force that drove huge wedges into the outer stonework. Some of the city walls still contained residual othium blocks, which exploded, intensifying the blast from each impact.

The second round of charges exploded in the midst of the Amina knights, killing many cavalrymen and their horses. This was an unholy attack, somehow appearing to use wizardry to pull down the city walls. The bombardment lasted an hour, and by the time it was over the defenders had been forced to retreat, leaving many dead and injured lying around the broken walls of Tamin.

The force and speed of the attack had left the river crossings undefended and still visible just below the waterline. The retreat became a rout as Ember Horse and Ackar cavalry crossed the river and charged into the fleeing coalition infantry. Red Cameron and Doran cavalry managed to slow the invaders, but with the numbers stacked against them they too had to break off and head for the protection of the hills to the north.

As the sun slipped behind the shattered city of Tamin, the invaders pulled back. The battle had been won decisively. That evening the Dewar rested in the royal rooms of the palace. Tamin was his, and it had taken barely a day to banish the memory of the weeks of frustration of 1299.

The next morning, at the Dewar's instruction, the thousand defenders captured in the battle were dragged into the plaza in front of the castle gate. Determined to make a statement, and show his intent, the King had his soldiers take every twentieth man and hang him from the city walls. The rest were herded out of the city and across the river and dispersed amongst the units of the conscript forces of Ciren and Toria.

The Kermin Alol marked the boundary between Amina and Kermin. This hill country started thirty miles north of Tamin and stretched for another fifty miles before opening out into the Kermin plains. During the night, and through the next day, small groups of infantry made their way into the hills of the

Alol. Many of the soldiers were injured, often with burns from the othium explosions. The commanders of the retreating army hoped that the natural barrier of the Alol would give them some respite and time to regroup. It was also a strategic defensive position from which to hold the Dewar back from spreading his power further north into Kermin.

As the stragglers made it back to the hills, it was clear that several thousand men had been killed or captured in the battle for Tamin. Most severely depleted were the knights of the Amina heavy cavalry. It was a significant loss, but the knights would not have added much to defence in the Alol as this was ground for infantry to defend.

After a week enjoying the luxury of the King's Palace in Tamin, the Dewar called his captains to a conference to plan the next phase of the conquest. His scouts had brought back the news that the remaining forces of Amina, Kermin and Doran had pulled back into the Kermin Alol and seemed to be scattered in the hill country there. The Kermin Alol did not reach great heights, but the hills were steep with narrow valleys cutting between the slopes, many with small rivers flowing through them. Under interrogation, captured Kermin troopers told the Dewar and his captains that the Kermin Alol was passable and could be used to reach the plains of Kermin with their rich farmlands beyond. The Dewar's scouts added a caution: the valleys were also ideal for ambushes. So with rough plans of the land from the scouts and captives laid out before them, the captains set out their strategy to move through the Alol and gain more riches in Kermin, and from there on to capture Mora and the gold mines in the Doran Mountains.

It was agreed that after another week's relaxation in Tamin, the army would move out in three separate groups. Each wing would move through a separate valley, one to the east, one central and one to the west. The Dewar, with most of the baggage, the elite horse and the precious trebuchets, would pass through the central valley with their flanks protected from any attack by the forces east and west of them. If the defence was stout in the central valley, the trebuchet would be used to clear the ground for the Lett foot soldiers and the Ackar cavalry. Once through the central valley, the invaders could then move east and west to squeeze the coalition defenders from north and south.

So with the warmth of a late spring sun making the countryside glow, the Dewar army headed north towards the Kermin Alol. A substantial force remained in Amina, both to protect the conquered lands and to begin the process of gathering taxes from the people of Amina and further bolster the King's riches and his war chest.

From the heights of the Alol, the leaders of the defending forces could see in the distance the preparations for the march towards them. The kings of Amina, Kermin and Doran had all moved north through Kermin and were guests of the King of Kermin in the great city of Mora, which sat at the foot of the Doran Mountains. This was a place of refuge, with vast open lands to the south of the city and the river Mora in front.

The river Mora flowed from the Doran Mountains and wound its way around the city on its way to the Middle Sea. The Mora, unlike the Amin, was wide at this point in front of the city and was only accessible across three large bridges which could be retracted from the south and drawn up on the land in front of the city. This made the city largely impregnable from a normal frontal attack, although the kings reflected on the wizardry that had caused Tamin to fall so quickly and wondered just how secure they were. The natural defences of the city could also be a trap, as there were few passes through the Doran Mountains at their backs and even these were only passable for a few months in summer. It was these restrictions in movements through the mountains that had brought the kings of Kermin and Doran to a peace treaty twenty years earlier that allowed the standing army of Doran to be permanently stationed in Kermin.

With their kings safe in Mora, the coalition forces were under the control of their commanders, Silson, Duke of Amina, Arin, First Lord of Kermin, and Ishca of Doran. These three reported to Coran, who wore the colours of the Red Cameron. Coran was James Cameron's younger brother and had been his second in command during the 1299 wars. It was in fact Coran who had led many of the Red Cameron charges that had defeated Elan's Ember Horse and stalled the progress of the Dewar armies in 1299. When his brother had left to return to Bala, Coran, with a small troop of Red Cameron, had stayed with the forces in Amina.

Coran, unlike his brother, was not of great physical stature. An illness in childhood had nearly been fatal, and an arrow wound received in the battles in Ciren, where his nephew Rob had died, had damaged his left leg, so he walked with a distinct limp. Nonetheless, despite his handicap, Coran was an outstanding horseman and like his brother, was recognised as one of the finest commanders of the age. His position as leader of the coalition forces was not given from birthright but from his reputation and his knowledge of defensive warfare in hill country. The other three leaders were great men in their own right, but in terms of war they deferred to the man from Bala.

As Coran watched the Dewar army move out from Tamin, he saw them split into their three sections.

Coran's spies from Tamin returned, all leaving the city disguised as poor farmers until they reached their horses stabled at nearby farms. The spies reported as best they could on the apparent plan of the invaders to march through the Alol in three separate cohorts, with the Dewar and the elite troops moving through the central valley. As with most armies of the time, the defenders were largely foot soldiers with leather coats for protection and equipped with sword and pike. By contrast, the standing army of Doran was largely made up of mounted warriors equipped with lance, bow and sword. Many of the elite knights of Amina had been killed in the othium attack two weeks earlier. Since the fall of Tamin, the defenders had been reinforced as Kermin foot soldiers and more Doran cavalry had been ordered south from their bases at Mora.

It was clear from the distance over the plain below the Alol that the attackers would not reach the hills until dusk, so any attack would likely follow the next day at the earliest. Coran knew his soldiers would give a good account of themselves in the Alol, a land they knew well. His concern was with the fire-spitting trebuchets. From the experience of the battle for Tamin, if the trebuchets were brought into engagement they could wipe out defenders in narrow valleys without any engagement of the forces on the ground.

After a quick discussion, the three lords departed to move their forces into defensive positions – Silson to the west, Arin to the east, and Ishca remaining in the centre. With some reluctance Ishca allowed his cavalry to be dispersed into three units, with each unit supporting the larger numbers of foot soldiers. With the trebuchets foremost in his mind, Coran told the others that his Red Cameron would carry out a night raid on the baggage train at the rear of the moving forces and try to destroy the machines before they could be brought to wreak havoc on the defending armies.

So it was that a small group of thirty horsemen moved out of the Alol at dusk, not dressed in the normal Cameron surcoats but in dark grey over their armour, so that in a few tens of yards they blended with the deepening dusk.

As the troopers moved away from the hills Coran knew this could be a suicide mission, but he also knew that allowing the attackers to bring the trebuchets into play would cause far greater death and destruction. Coran also hoped that the invaders would be careless, thinking themselves safe on the flat lands south of the Alol. There would be sentries, no doubt, but hopefully none of them too alert. Each trooper in the band had a number of packages attached to his saddle, each containing a mix of sulphur, charcoal and potassium nitrate. This mixture and the containers, known as

Doran combustibles, had been given to the troop by Arin. In the foothills of the Doran Mountains the miners had invented this mixture some years earlier and used it in their excavations of the gold mines of Doran, from which came much of Mora's wealth. The gold of Mora was well known, and as well as the rich farmlands, the possession of the gold mines was a major goal of the Dewar's invasions.

The troopers slowly approached the large tented army camp. Some distance from the rear of the camp, twenty of the troopers moved forward on foot with their Doran combustibles strapped round their waists. The approach to the rear of the baggage train was largely uneventful, as most of the warriors on guard seemed to be forward and facing the Alol, from which the risk of attack seemed greatest. Near the rear were the trebuchets and three wagons loaded with red stone and bags containing an unknown substance.

The few guards were quickly despatched and the combustibles were placed in the trebuchets. It quickly became obvious that they carried too many of these devices, so Coran decided to load some in the wagons containing the red stone. Three short whistles alerted the remainder of the troop waiting with the horses that all was ready. The troop now rode at speed towards their comrades – no need for silence now. The men on the ground lit the fuses on the combustibles while those on horseback came racing in with the other horses to bring the troop at speed away from the camp.

The thirty men were moving rapidly east of the camp rather than heading directly back to the Alol when the first combustible fired. The mixture was not tightly constrained, so it did not explode but had more of an incendiary effect. One by one the packages burst into flame and the fires rapidly consumed the wooden frames of the arms of the trebuchets.

Coran had anticipated this type of destruction. What he had not anticipated was the huge concussion that occurred moments later. The wagons exploded in vast fireballs, obliterating all within a hundred yards. The devastation included a significant number of the army followers' tents, and some of the soldiers were killed. Indeed the Dewar, in his expansive and rich headquarters tent, avoided the destruction by only a few yards.

Coran and the troop, now some distance away, stopped in surprise to look back at their handiwork. Carelessly the Dewar had loaded the othium stone and the salt of Elat mixtures in the same wagons. The incendiaries had not maximised the priming of the red stone, so the power was less than it might have been, but the fires were enough to trigger significant explosions. Coran smiled, seeing that much of the rear of the baggage train was being consumed by the fires. Then the troop galloped east at speed, putting themselves far out of reach before any of the Dewar army could mount to give chase. Once far enough east, and before encountering the Dewar's eastern army, the troop turned north into the east of the Alol, to the camps in the hills now occupied by Arin and the soldiers of Kermin.

"Well met, Coran," said Arin, welcoming Coran into the camp. "I'm not sure how you did that down there, the combustibles are useful in removing blockages in the mine shafts, but I have never seen them deliver that power."

"I don't understand either," responded the Bala general. "The trebuchets simply burned, but whatever was in the supporting wagons was far more powerful. Maybe some of the wizardry we saw at Tamin was stored in the wagons. Anyway, at least now we can meet the enemy on an even footing, as he will not have his wizard's power to threaten us. Indeed it seems to me that you should send some fast riders north to the mines to equip us with more incendiaries. With a long fuse and a good throw these devices could cause significant disruption to any charge the enemy could make against our positions."

"It will be done immediately," came the reply.

In the Dewar camp, the King was incandescent with rage. Why had his precious war machines been left undefended? Were the guards asleep at their posts? Several of them were executed to make his point. Whatever his rage, the Dewar now faced a ground war in the Alol without the strategic benefits of the othium. He despatched fast riders back to Bala with instructions for Oien to urgently replenish the ammunition and to send more trebuchets to the south.

The war in the Alol raged on through the summer months, but the forces of Amina, Kermin and Doran, with their superior knowledge of the land they defended, continually thwarted the offensive thrusts made by the army of the Dewar. Coran appeared to be everywhere when a breakthrough was likely. The Red Cameron were once again the scourge of the enemy, with their lightning raids on the flanks of the three Dewar armies. East, west and centre, the defences held. The hills and rivers created opportunities for ambush and barriers against attacks. As importantly, the incendiaries sent from the mines of the Doran Mountains, whilst not having the power of othium, were sufficient to halt and disrupt the charges of mounted knights and the slower advances of the foot soldiers. As in 1299, the result was stalemate, and in the late summer of 1301 the Dewar returned to Tamin to await the delivery of the munitions from Bala. The 1301 wars in the Alol are described in detail in the history of the Kermin Alol, 1270 to 1303.

CHAPTER TEN
The Sea Wolves

While the Dewar was easily winning the battle at the gates of Tamin, in the far north, in Erwick, the birlinns were being put to sea to check their seaworthiness. By late spring Galbraith and his shipmates had the boats ready for action. Now a plan was needed for the best deployment of the small fleet. The raiders and Noren, Alex, Angus, Galbraith and Alain met to plan the sea campaign. Erden was notably absent from the discussions, and indeed from the town itself.

The raiding party on the three birlinns was small – fifty Red Cameron and their horse – but they were some of the most feared guerrilla fighters, and legendary in Andore and beyond. Their tactic in general was simple – fast horseback raids in and out before the defence could muster a response. They relied on speed and surprise. The most obvious targets would be the enemy camps between the Ban and the Ora or further south between the Ora and the forest. With no better intelligence, the decision was made to carry out a fast raid into the land between the Ban and the Ora. Alex Cameron was heartened by the decision of many of the young men of Erwick to man the oars of the birlinns so that the raiders would be fresh for the lightning attacks.

It was Noren who suggested a rather extreme option. "In the stories from the past our ancestors used to raid down all the Greater Sea and into the Middle Sea," he reminded his comrades. "They took slaves and ransoms from the lands of Toria and the islands of Elat. Many years ago I travelled to Boretar, the capital of Ackar. The river Tar flows close to the city and our stories tell of our raiders pillaging the city in the distant past. With fifty horses you cannot hope to gain the city, but you could cause concern for the citizens living around it. Our ancestors, so the stories tell, had dozens of birlinns and hundreds of warriors. But a fast raiding troop focused on destruction of farms and outposts could cause havoc with the local population."

It was agreed: the raiders would anchor in the mouth of the Ban and quickly raid south, return to the boats to move on to the mouth of the Ora and raid between the river and the forest. Then, if the troop remained intact, they would travel south down the Greater Sea and then sail up the Tar and raid the Dewar heartlands. It was a daring and perhaps impossible plan, but Alex and Angus agreed they had to try it, and the next morning the three birlinns set sail south.

In Banora, Oien was yet to hear of the Dewar's misfortune before the hills in the Kermin Alol. News had reached him of the success at Tamin and the role played by the trebuchets. He already had instructions from the King to build more of the machines and transport them south. The construction of these was under way in the furnaces between the Ban and the Ora and east of the forest that was supplying the wood for the fires. The smiths were toiling at their forges to create the iron frames and wheels for the new trebuchets.

For Oien it was a frustratingly slow process. He wanted to move onto much more sophisticated machinery, but it was clear that it was going to take time for the smiths to learn the techniques he needed to develop the stronger iron necessary for the larger equipment. It would take much longer for them to learn to form large constructions from the new materials, steel, aluminium and titanium, which had produced the huge machines of the Second Age.

Whilst frustrated by the speed of progress, Oien had waited a long time for the right moment to re-enter the mainstream world and try again for domination. He needed to be patient; after all, the successes of the Second Age had not been created in a few years.

In the Inger Mountains above the forges, the mountain seemed to be breathing fire. The miners were successfully increasing the stores of othium, but the stone itself was behaving with much greater volatility than Oien remembered from the olden days. With the constant risk of explosion, despite the threats from the old man, the miners were extracting the rock slowly and with great care. Military resources in the area were relatively limited; a significant troop of Ember Horse remained under Orridon's command and there was a small number of Ackar foot soldiers still acting primarily as guards on the perimeters of the inhabited area. Most of the conscript soldiers of Toria, Ciren and Arance were now no more than slaves, helping the miners, loading and moving the stone and assisting the smiths in the forges.

With no obvious threat from the north, the Ember Horse spent much of their time on the plains training. Orridon often wondered where the Bala army and most of the people had vanished to. He occasionally led training sessions near the foot of the Coe Mountains, but these yielded no evidence or information on where the forces of Bala had found safety and security. Orridon was slightly unlucky, as a couple of times his training runs had brought his troop close to the Coelete camp on the plain where they were waiting for the return of Alex and his small force. Over hundreds of years, the tall Coelete warriors had moved through the mountain to learn what was happening elsewhere in Bala and occasionally to return with livestock raided from the local farms. They were, however, experts at camouflage, and unless Orridon had ridden straight into their camp he could never have seen them. Indeed had he done so he would have been met with a small but formidable foe, and he would probably have regretted finding them. As it was, the Coelete remained undetected. Erwick also remained safe from any Ember Horse raid, hidden as it was behind its rivers and waterfalls.

The birlinns landed at the mouth of the Ban around the same time as the Dewar was planning the army's departure from Tamin. Alex and the Red Cameron disembarked from the boats. It had been agreed on the journey south that the two Coelete warriors, with Angus and Galbraith, would venture on foot along the river bank to scout out the situation to the south and east.

A day later the four returned, and Alain reported: "The land appears to be heavily populated to the west of the Pass of Ing where most of the settlements appear to be. Further north and west, beyond the point where the Ora and Ban flow towards each other and constrict the land, there appear to be a multitude of forges working to produce some form of machinery. It seems that whatever they are digging out from the mountain is being brought to storage areas between the main camp and those forges. To the west, new bridges have been built and wood from the forest is being transported into the same area. Most of the activity seems to be concerned with the construction of large machines with metal wheels and bases supporting timber frames." None of those present had encountered a trebuchet. Alain continued, "They clearly do not anticipate any attack as the forges, and indeed the camp, are only lightly guarded. It would appear that we can do most disruption by dampening the fires of the forges and then, separately perhaps, slow the transport of the wood through from the forest."

Angus Ferguson was unusually silent as he looked up at the Inger towering over his homeland. The red and amber fires that seemed to spontaneously erupt from the mountain filled him with dread. His country seemed to be filled with red fire.

The next morning the fifty Red Cameron rode out along the southern bank of the Ban. Angus led the group, as he knew the land intimately. The going was relatively easy until the Ban moved south towards where the Ora flowed. This narrow stretch was mostly bog, but Angus, having been brought up nearby, knew the dry routes through the swamps.

As the land opened out again south of the bog, the troop could see in the near distance the smoke rising from the smith's forges. Alain and Gareth travelled with the troop to this point. As the troopers returned, the Coelete warriors would slip behind to cover their tracks and hide the safe routes through the swamp and back to the birlinns.

There was no grand strategic plan here. The idea was simply to race into the area where the forges were built, remove any resistance and use the flames from the forges to torch the smiths' workshops. The troop split in two to cause maximum confusion and then sped over the open ground to the forges. The minimal resistance was quickly eliminated, and most of the smiths, being craftsmen, not warriors, simply downed tools and ran at the sight of the fast-approaching cavalry. Each Cameron trooper carried a long loop of cord strapped to his saddle, and in each forge these were wrapped round the smith's fires to pull them to the ground. The wooden structures quickly caught fire and were destroyed.

A few of the troopers lit brands from the forge fires and tossed these onto the large piles of wood waiting to be moved forward for construction of whatever machines were being imagined. It was a typical Red Cameron guerrilla tactic, in with surprise and quickly out again.

Its work done, the troop turned and raced back to the southern edge of the bog. Angus moved into the lead and they again charged through the dry areas in the bog to reach the open space beyond. Behind them the two Coelete warriors covered up the tracks and followed.

Elem was in charge of the Ember Horse in the settlement, and as soon as the fires were noticed and the frightened smiths entered the tented encampment he had a troop of one hundred Ember Horse quickly to the saddle. They raced to the forges and the wood stores, but all they found was charred ruins. Knowing the enemy had come from the north, the Ember Horse gave chase.

Elem was more in the mould of Elan than Orridon and he furiously raced his horsemen into the area of the bog. His was the first mount in the chase and the first to slip up to its haunches in the sticky mud. Elem scrambled off his mount and managed to hold the riders racing behind him. Clearly there was no quick way to the other side of the swamp and the raiders would now be long gone. One of the Ember Horse would have a long walk back to the camp. Elem knew he would have a difficult conversation with Orridon when he returned, but of more concern was how to explain this to Oien.

When Elem returned to the main camp, Oien was already there and demanding answers. Elem started to explain, but the old man halted him, and with surprising strength threw one of the Ember Horsemen from his saddle, mounted up and rode forward to see for himself. Elem and a few of the Horse rode behind at a safe distance. The old man's rage was clear, with flickers of amber flame sparking from the alchemist's cloak.

When Oien reached the forges, it was obvious that the damage was significant but not irreparable. Some of the conscripts would need to be pulled from the mines to rebuild the forges, which would take a little time. The smiths would need to be bullied back to their work, but that would be easy. Oien reminded himself that he had time; these were just the first steps in his conquests.

However, incompetence needed to be punished. The old man turned to Elem, his eyes blazing. "You are meant to be protecting this area – were you and your men asleep?" Elem started to respond, but he got no further than "my lord" when a narrow bolt of red fire shot out from Oien's opened hand and burnt a line across the Horse Lord's eyebrows. Elem collapsed in pain. "Maybe that will remind you to keep your eyes and ears open!" snapped Oien as he mounted his horse and rode back to his homestead south of the Ora. Tomorrow he would instruct the conscripts to get back to work rebuilding the furnaces and forges.

Oien was near the bridge that crossed the Ora heading to his now substantial living quarters when a fast rider dressed in the livery of the Dewar caught up with him. The rider, one of many sent in relays from Amina, explained what had happened on the plain in front of the Kermin Alol. Oien fumed, "What sort of idiot is he? His weapons and the othium were more precious than any of his troops. They should have been guarded with soldiers' lives, and the salt and red stone should never be kept in close proximity in transports." He explained the events of the day and sent the rider back south to inform the Dewar that he would get his weapons, but it would take some time.

Back at the mouth of the Ban, the Red Cameron rejoined the birlinns for the short journey south to the mouth of the Ora, where it flowed wide and deep into the Greater Sea. The birlinns could easily travel some way inland on the mighty river. This was very much home to Angus Ferguson, so early the morning after the previous raid he quickly guided the troop to the edge of the Banora forest. Skirting the forest edge, the troop moved quickly east to where the logging stations were. Here the forest was being torn down to feed the furnaces on the plain. There were no enemy deployed to protect the logging stations and the foresters had no intent of fighting a well-armed raiding party. They moved in and out fast, the way of the Red Cameron, and the harvested wood was set on fire before the troop retreated back to the birlinns.

However, being so close, Angus wanted to see his family homestead, and with a couple of troopers as support he rode east towards the Inger Mountains. Some distance from his home, Angus was dismayed to see that the relatively humble abode was in the process of transformation. He did not know that Oien himself had established his living quarters there, and all around the simple farmhouse, construction work was under way to extend and expand it.

It then suddenly struck Angus that part of the construction work was extending the dwelling out over the land at the rear of the house where his parents and sister were buried. He felt a sudden surge of anger. The temptation was strong; a short gallop across the fields and Angus could at least halt the work that he felt was destroying his heritage. Fortunately, other factors held him back. The land between the Ora and the forest was open and offered little cover for retreat, unlike the bog further north.

His eyes shining with mingled grief and fury, Angus turned his horse and rode back to the main troop and the birlinns. It was now onwards to Boretar.

Boretar was Ackar and the Dewar's capital, and its

magnificence had made it one of the wonders of the known world. The city was rich, due to its merchants and the access the city had via the river Tar to the Greater Sea. Ships from across the world filled its harbours, bringing in merchandise from distant lands and leaving with holds crammed with the wool, wood and grain that were the harvest of the rich lands of Ackar and Lett. Above the walled city and its gates stood the castle, the home of the King, and its upper parapets were clad in gold so that on a sunlit day they shone like a lighthouse. Boretar was designed to be impressive and impregnable to anything less than a huge army supported by siege engines.

The three birlinns made good time moving south from the Ora to the Tar. Wind and weather were favourable, and it was only three days before the vessels found a sheltered cove just north of the entrance to the Tar. With the volume of shipping moving in and out of the river mouth it would have been foolhardy to sail upriver towards the city.

A plan had been discussed on the journey south, but local intelligence was needed. By night Alex, Angus and Galbraith travelled cautiously towards the city, dressed as simple travellers. They were lightly armed and hoped to pass openly, but unnoticed, towards the city.

By morning they were only a short distance from the city gates and merged with the crowds taking their wares and produce to Boretar's markets. However the city was not their objective. Close to the main gates they left the crowds and moved south to the river and the port of Boretar. Like all ports, it was constantly busy with boats loading and unloading and sailors and dockhands shouting and joking. It was a normal port scene and the trio simply mingled with the crowd whilst unobtrusively studying the shipping in the port.

As the Dewar's conquests had brought peace to Andore's southern lands, most of the ships sailed to and fro with little in the way of armed protection. Only those from more distant lands carried warriors and defensive equipment. These ships, travelling from the far south, were more likely to be the target of the marauding pirates who still worked the southern parts of the Western Sea.

Alex, Angus and Galbraith noted that the wide boats that had travelled the short distance north from Toria carried the liquid produce that this south-western land was famous for. This was the intelligence that the three sought. The Torian boats had another advantage: as they were travelling a relatively short distance and usually with the prevailing south-westerly or westerly wind behind them, they had few oarsmen and mostly relied on sail power. The distinctive twin-sailed boats were wide and their hulls were filled with barrels of wine, brandy and other spirits. For their plan to work, however, Alex and Angus also had to find an escape route.

The trio headed back west, this time staying on the paths that followed the north bank of the river, thereby avoiding the main road that led back to the main city gates. About half a mile from Boretar, their search was rewarded. They came across a run-down and apparently disused boatyard with a small dock. The timbers of the dock were in a poor state, but the inlet was largely hidden from the main flow of the river. The visitors had learnt enough; their plan could work. The three made their way back to the coast where the birlinns waited.

Early the next day, one of the birlinn left the shelter of the cove. It was barely light as the boat crossed the mouth of the Tar and headed down the coast of Ackar and into the waters west of Lett. The boat kept close to shore to avoid the main traffic passing north towards the Tar. Stealth was needed if the vessel was to succeed in its mission without detection. On board Galbraith was in charge, with a small group of the Cameron warriors sitting centrally.

The first phase of the plan needed luck and skill. That luck came late in the day when a twin-sailed vessel approached, heading north slightly out of the main shipping lane to look for a mooring place where it could ride out the night before heading on to its destination in the light of the following morning.

Sitting as close as it could to the shore, the birlinn was hard to see against the dark background.

The Torian vessel anchored a short distance away, its occupants probably thinking that the birlinn was also mooring for the night. A century earlier the merchant vessel would have run as fast as it could from the single-mast birlinn, but the days of the northern sea raiders were long forgotten and a number of the old square-sailed vessels still carried goods between Olet on the Lett coast and Boretar. The Torian ship's captain imagined that the boat moored nearby was on its way back from Boretar with produce for the markets in Olet.

As darkness fell, the birlinn left its position and quietly came alongside the other vessel. Within moments the Torian boat was taken and the birlinn had crept back to the sanctuary of its cove north of the Tar estuary. The Torian boat would sail north the next day as if it had simply stopped overnight to ensure safe passage in daylight. The boat was now crewed by Galbraith and the men from Erwick. The Torian crew had already been taken north, held captive on the birlinn.

It was late the next day when Galbraith gave the order to ship the anchors and move the captured boat out into the main stream. Whilst sitting at anchor for most of a day might have appeared suspicious to any close passer-by, the crew had been told to pretend they had imbibed too much of the ship's cargo during the night and any curious onlooker would simply think that they were inebriated and could not continue their journey until later in the day, when they had recovered.

Galbraith needed to make perfect time, as it would also be suspicious if the boat was seen to cross the entrance of the Tar rather than enter the river and head into Boretar.

As dusk settled in again the Torian boat slipped unheeded across the mouth of the Tar and made landfall in the cove where the birlinns were moored. During the night the wine barrels were removed from the Torian boat and those containing brandy and stronger spirits were laid across the bottom of the hull. These were then covered with dry wood gathered from the nearby woodlands. By dawn the boat was ready, and with Galbraith again at the helm it made its way openly into the mouth of the Tar. With other vessels moving up and down the river, the deception needed to be effective.

Half a mile from the main port, Galbraith made it appear that there was a problem with the steering mechanism and moved the boat towards the northern shore. Both sails were lowered and the boat was guided along the northern river bank, from where it could slip into the inlet that led to the disused boatyard. Any passing boat noticing the move would likely assume the captain had a problem with the rudder and was looking for a landing place to make some quick repairs before continuing the short trip to Boretar's main port.

In the boatyard, Galbraith and the sailors were met by Angus, Alex and Alain. The crew's job was done, and in small groups they headed back west to the birlinns.

It was around midday when the sailors arrived back at the cove. This was the signal for John Ewart and Davy Scott to leave their shelter with a small band of the Red Cameron. Some of the warriors, together with Gareth of the Coelete, stayed to guard the birlinns and ensure that the Torian ship's crew did not try to escape. The instructions to Alex's lieutenants were simple and typical Red Cameron tactics. They would carry out a fast sweeping raid out to the north of the cove, then circle back again, creating as much havoc as possible before returning to the boats. On returning from the raid the birlinns were to leave their shelter and return as fast as possible back north to Erwick.

The Red Cameron did their job well, and when they returned to the cove they had left a swathe of rich farmlands and prosperous villages burning. Seeing the smoke to the north, troops from the garrison at Boretar were sent to investigate. It was early evening when they returned to report that a raid had been carried out, but who was responsible was unknown, and there was no trace of the raiders. For once the Red Cameron had attacked without wearing their distinctive surcoats, in order to keep their anonymity.

As the troopers from the garrison headed back down the road to the city gates, Angus, Alex and Alain, further downriver, were slowly moving the Torian boat out from the inlet. This was the second part of the plan, and again timing needed to be perfect. Luck remained with them, as a wind picked up coming directly from the west and the tide turned, so the main channel was now flowing upriver. At its stern the Torian boat towed a small rowing boat.

Once into the stream, Angus and Alex raised the sails on the boat and lit the kindling sticks that sat between the brandy barrels and the dry wood on top. As the sails filled and the boat picked up speed, the two jumped off the boat to join Alain in the rowing boat. They quickly crossed back to the land and to the horses tethered behind the boathouse. There was no time to wait to see the impact of their plan, as it would be a long and treacherous journey on horseback and on foot back north to the shelter of Tala and the Hidden Lands. Angus and Alex were mounted, but the tall Coelete warrior easily kept pace on foot.

Almost a week later, two messengers arrived

simultaneously at Tamin. They were both quickly led to an audience with the Dewar. The first messenger was from Oien, and his message described the raids in Banora and informed the King that the damage that had been done was not catastrophic but would delay transport of further weapons to the front line at the Kermin Alol. The King roared his irritation at the messenger. With no more othium and weapons, the stalemate in the hills was likely to continue until the spring.

However, if that was bad news, what followed from the second messenger was worse. Unknown raiders had pillaged lands just to the north of Boretar and escaped, probably by sea. Worse was to come, as the messenger reported the second incident. A fireship had been sent into the docks at Boretar, presumably by the same raiding party, causing chaos.

It turned out that the sea wolves had more luck than they could have imagined. Whilst Alex, Angus and Alain reached the safety of the shore, the fires in the Torian boat had smouldered. The strong wind and current had driven the vessel rapidly upstream towards the port. As the boat entered the harbour the flames grew, but those on the jetties were slow to spot the danger. Suddenly the barrels with the spirits joined the conflagration, the sails caught the fire and the entire boat was a flaming torch. In the port a large boat was being repositioned midstream, and the fireboat hit the other amidships. The impact was heard across the city. What followed was a larger explosion and fire ripped from the stricken vessel. This ship was bound for Amina and held iron balls, othium and salt of Elat formulations which were being sent to reinforce the dwindling supplies that the King had left after the battle for Tamin. Whilst the two materials were segregated on the boat, the fire that started to engulf it activated the othium. The resulting red flames spewed out across the port, some of the sparks crossing the city walls and sending fire through the lower city of Boretar. Much of the port and the lower city were now no more than ash.

"Can this be true?" roared the King. He grabbed the messenger by the throat and would have extinguished the man's life with his bare hands, had it not been for the nobles at his side restraining him. Calming himself, the King demanded "Is the port functional? Can it still bring my munitions from the north, or are we now bound to use land transport? That will add weeks to getting my supplies here!"

The trembling messenger reported that the port would be out of operation for at least a few months as the main jetties would need to be rebuilt and the burnt-out wrecks of the moored ships removed. "Months?" roared the King again. "So now I have to wait on the idiots in Banora to build new equipment and mine new resources, and I need to wait on them to be transported here over land!" He knew that the fighting season was nearly over and he would not be able to take the Alol or the Kermin lands until the next spring.

"Who could have done this?" Dewar spluttered.

Melnar, Overlord of Lett and one of the Dewar's senior commanders, dared to speak. "My lord King, no one stands against us anywhere south of the Inger Mountains," he said. "Any uprising from the southern lands would have been noticed by your sheriffs or governors and stopped. It is several years since we had any uprising in Toria, Ciren or Arance."

"The fireship was a T-T-Torian ship," said the trembling messenger. Melnar struck the unfortunate man and sent him sprawling to the ground, then turned back to the King. "My son Orimir is Governor of Toria and a loyal subject of your majesty," he said "His lands would not support any attack on Boretar and his people would have no cause. I think this attack was spawned much further to the north. We know the Cameron led the Bala army into the northern mountains. From the description of these raids, they are in my view the work of the Red Cameron. They have all their hallmarks – fast horsemen riding in and out before any defence can be organised. Lord King, the culprit here lies somewhere in the northern wastes of Bala. He is James Cameron."

The Dewar again grabbed the unfortunate messenger by the throat. "You will go now, faster than you can imagine possible, to Banora, and you will tell that fool Orridon that when I return to Boretar I want to receive the Cameron's head on the end of a spear. Now go!"

With relief that they still had their own heads, the two messengers departed for the north. Now Dewar turned to Melnar. "I need to go back to Boretar to assess what damage has been done," he said. "In any case, without the alchemist's weapons we will just be sitting here through the winter without a chance to bring our army to battle. You will take charge in my absence. And be sure you are not as careless as those in Boretar and Banora. Remember, it is another Cameron who lies skulking in the Kermin Alol."

A few days later, another messenger arrived from Boretar. The Torian sailors had been released some distance north of the Tar and had made their way back to the city on foot. They were interrogated by Sir Roger Eld, the captain of the King's castle and the most senior noble in Boretar. The Torian sailors, fearful for their lives when they learnt of the destruction their ship had caused, told the Lord everything they knew, which in truth was not a lot. All they could confirm was that the raiders were not from the south and by their speech and language must have come from the far north. They also reported on the two tall warriors who were with the party, saying they were of a people unknown to them. Melnar's suspicions were confirmed; if it was not the Red Cameron, then it was a force sent from Bala to disrupt the conquest of their lands.

Having suffered the ignominy of being felled by Alain, Erden had skulked for a few weeks and had hardly left his home. Brooding alone, he was being eaten up by the fires of resentment he felt towards Noren and the other councillors of Erwick. He had watched from his window as the birlinns left their harbour. Finally, after much procrastination, he decided that the best way to get his revenge would be to travel south and share his knowledge with the invaders. The next day Erden left Erwick on foot.

Erden was a man of the town, and not a horseman, nor was he fit, so it was a long climb before he looked back over the town and then passed through the passage under the waterfall to come out looking over the Plain of Coe. Erden had never left Erwick, so he had little idea where to go other than south. For two days he walked, largely sticking to the banks of the Ola, which at least provided him with water. The cheese and bread he had brought with him was soon gone, and he wondered how long he could survive in this empty land.

On the third day, Erden noticed horsemen in the distance. Uncertain as to whether to draw their attention or to hide, he chose the former, feeling that death at the hands of the unknown riders was likely to be less painful than death through hunger. His decision would not have mattered, as the horsemen had seen the lone walker and rapidly rode up to find out who he was and why he was there. It was a group of Ember Horse, checking for any activity from the north. The group was led by Elem, and the bright red scar above his eyes was prominent.

Elem dismounted and with sword drawn, inspected the weary traveller. "Name?" he snapped.

A very scared Erden gave his name, insisting he had vital information to give, but despite the threats he would say no more until he could talk to the leader of the invaders. Elem was tempted to force the information from the man, but he paused, the pain above his eyes reminding him what happened if you crossed Oien. So it was that strapped over the back of a horse, Erden made a less than dignified journey south to Banora.

With Erden safely secured in his tent, Elem sent word to Orridon and Oien, and they were soon interrogating their new guest. Erden told of all that had happened at Erwick, of the Red Cameron and the tall Coelete warriors. It was now clear that the raids in Banora had been carried out by Cameron's men.

While Erden was being questioned, a rider from the south arrived to deliver the news of the raid on Boretar. Oien fumed once again at the stupidity of keeping othium and salt formulations in close proximity. Orridon anticipated the response of the King. He confirmed that Erden could lead him through the paths north of the Ola so that the Ember Lord could wreak vengeance on those who dared to attack the Ackar capital. Elem was sent to ready the Ember Horse for a raid to the north.

Orridon was bored with riding endlessly and aimlessly across the plains, and the prospect of action thrilled him. However he again thought about the tall warriors and wondered where the Bala people had sheltered through the winter. It was difficult to believe that many could have survived the last winter in the Coe Mountains.

As Elem was gathering the horsemen, the three birlinns passed the mouths of the Ora and Ban. With a favourable wind at their backs, the boats were making good speed back to Erwick. In the absence of Alex and Angus, John Ewart and Davy Scott were in charge of the returning raiding party. Galbraith captained the lead boat, as he had the greatest knowledge of these often treacherous northern waters.

On making landfall in Erwick, the raiders were welcomed home by Noren and the people of Erwick, who celebrated the return of their sons and husbands, many of whom had been crew on the birlinns. Galbraith briefed his father and the council on the raids. After a day's rest Scott sent Gareth and three troopers up to the passage through the waterfalls to see if their return to the Hidden Lands could be arranged. The timing, or Scott's premonition, had been perfect. As the Coelete warrior looked out over the plain he could see the horsemen in the distance, probably still some hours from the pass through to Erwick. Gareth despatched one of the troopers back to Erwick to alert the rest of the men and the citizens of the town.

Had Orridon, Elem or Erden been sailors, it might have occurred to them that the safest approach to Erwick was by sea or along the wide river Ola. However they were all men of the land, and Erden was a townsman and not a warrior. Erden had outlined the road through the foothills that led to Erwick, but had not given any details of the narrow climb through the hills or of the single track that led below the waterfalls.

So Orridon and the Ember Horse slowly climbed out from the plain and up into the hills via the narrow track. Elem led the troop, whilst a cautious Orridon rode near the rear at the head of his household troopers. It quickly became clear to Orridon that this was not the place for a battle on horseback, and he slowed the column, which was by now largely in single file. Sending Erden, Elem and a few of the horsemen ahead through the path under the waterfall, Orridon could only hope that their arrival had gone unnoticed.

Clearly this was a forlorn hope, as at that moment a scream came from the far side. Erden, who was leading the way, was the first to fall as an arrow from a Banoran bow took him from the saddle on which he had been so uncomfortably perched. Elem was next, as John Ewart's archers continued to punch holes in the unprotected horsemen. As the front ranks retreated, Davy Scott's archers hidden in the higher hills to the east sent a rain of arrows down on the stationary horsemen strung out along the narrow path. As troops fell all around, Orridon had little choice but to call his men to retreat back down the hillside. He did not want to suffer the fate of his brother Elan.

Orridon pulled back, several of his force already lying dead on the foothills. As the Ember Horse retreated back down the hill, a tall figure stood at the top of the path leading from the waterfall and blew a single note from his horn. Orridon heard it, but took little notice. It was only as his troop rode out into open ground that the reason for the signal became clear. The remaining horsemen were again following the Ola south when the rear riders began to tumble from their mounts. This time the arrows were not from the short Banoran bow but were much longer, and flew from some distance across the Plain of Coe. It was time to leave, and fast. Orridon led the remaining horsemen at a gallop south towards the shelter of Banora.

At the path under the waterfall, it was time for farewells. Scott shook hands with Noren and Galbraith. "You have done well, and my Lord Cameron gives you thanks," he said. "With the Dewar's horse defeated you should be able to live through the coming winter without threat. John and half of our men will remain with you in Erwick to give some added protection. However the enemy now know how to approach here and you may need to seek protection in the Hidden Lands come the spring."

Noren nodded. "With your men and the protection of the passes, hopefully we can continue to live in peace, but if we are attacked from the river or the sea we now have the birlinns to help our defence."

Scott and Ewart embraced. "Take care John, the enemy knows we are here and this could be a dangerous outpost," said Scott. "At my lodgings in the town you will find some well-cared-for homing pigeons that have been looked after by Galbraith's wife. If you find yourselves in peril, then release them and they will find their way back to Tala to alert us, and hopefully we can get forces here quickly enough to support you."

Scott and half the Cameron troop made their way down through the foothills to be met by the Coelete warriors, who greeted Gareth. Led by the Guardian, the Cameron troop made their way back to Tala, leaving the Coelete warriors waiting to meet Alex, Angus and Alain and hopefully bring them safely home too.

While the birlinns embarked on a fast journey north, Alain, Alex and Angus travelled more slowly. As Alain would clearly be conspicuous to the people of Ackar the three travelled mainly by night, keeping relatively close to the coastline but away from the fishing villages that dotted the Ackar coast. Angus and Alex might have travelled faster and more openly without Alain, but the Coelete warrior was essential because his horn could be used to signal, if required, as they moved into the more dangerous lands of Bala and the north.

The trio lived off the land and by occasionally poaching livestock. The land of Ackar was largely open farmlands, but a long strip of woodland followed the coast about a mile or so inland. This part of the ancient forest which had once covered all the land served as a windbreak, giving some shelter for the farmlands from the winter winds and rains that blew in on the south or south-westerly gales. The woods gave the travellers shelter and enabled them to rest during the day, making small fires on which to cook their provisions. The nights were for travelling, and although the woods meant the two horses largely walked, the cover they gave the travellers was more important than speed.

A few days later the three men left the land of Ackar and entered the Cameron lands of southern Bala. They kept to the west of the capital city, Aldene, and then headed for the western edge of the Inger Mountains, hoping to cross by routes known to Angus before cutting into the forest below and then heading east again. This was going to be the most dangerous part of the journey, as the lands ahead of them were now full of the enemy. In addition even the lower slopes of the Inger were dangerous, as othium eruptions continued to happen regularly and randomly across the whole mountain range.

The instability of the red stone was also worrying Oien. In the Second Age othium had been largely stable and inert, until primed with the mixtures of the salt of Elat. It seemed to Oien that the ages had somehow made the stone less stable when either exposed to vibration or perhaps just to the air. At the back of Oien's mind was the constant niggle that some other power was again trying to disrupt his plans.

When the travellers reached the southern base of the Inger Mountains, Angus had a difficult choice. He could keep to the southern foothills and try to make a crossing over the Pass of Ing or hold close to the western shoreline, hoping the surrounding mountain would hide the two horsemen and the Coelete warrior. He chose the latter, recognising that it meant they would have to cross lands that they had raided only a few weeks earlier. Angus hoped that the enemy would have relaxed over the weeks as no more attacks had followed the raids, but he also recognised that the route he had chosen would mean crossing at least the Ora and possibly the Ban and Ola before they could strike north across the Plain of Coe to reach Alain's warriors, who were hopefully still there waiting for his horn call.

Angus knew the time for slow, careful travel had passed, and with a land filled with enemy forces they would need to move quickly to avoid detection. Whilst the forest at the foot of the Inger would provide some cover, from there they would have to ford the rivers, which would hopefully be low during the summer. He decided to remain close to the western shore and move down into the forest that covered the mountain foothills. It was clear that the earlier raid in the forest had caused only minor disruption to the felling operation. The three travellers could see from a distance that the logging base had largely been rebuilt and wood was stacked ready for transport to the smithies, forges and workshops on the other side of the Ora.

They decided to make a quick night-time dash across the open land and try to cross the Ora to the west of the bog between the Ora and the Ban which had protected their retreat from the raid a few weeks earlier. They reached the western edge of the bog just as dawn broke over the Plain of Coelene. It was wet where they camped that day, but with the bog as protection they were not disturbed.

Again they could look over to the east, to the area of Banora that lay between the Ban and the Ora. In the distance they could make out large constructions of iron and wood. The purpose of these was not clear from their position and Angus proposed that by cover of night he should move closer to find out more in order to inform Ala Moire of the invaders' activity in Banora. He would travel with Alain, who would wait at the edge of the bog for his return.

As dusk fell, Alain and Angus moved carefully along the narrow paths that allowed passage through the swamps. Angus then travelled a short way across the open land until he could get a better view of the activity. Dark was closing in and the red fires on the mountain cast an eerie red light. There appeared to be no guards this far from the workshops, although no doubt there would be some closer in, and if they were mounted Angus would have little chance of outrunning them.

He could see that the forges appeared to be turning out huge iron wheels which were being assembled onto iron and wooden frames. One of the machines appeared to be moving without any horsepower or manpower. In the centre of it was a red glow of fire which Angus presumed was somehow linked to the fires in the mountain. In another forge, long iron tubes were being fashioned. Angus had no idea what their purpose could be. Despite the disruption and destruction of a few weeks earlier, the workers had clearly been busy day and night.

In the weeks following the destructive raids, Oien had decided to abandon the building of trebuchets, despite the command from the King. Under close supervision the smiths had begun work on more complex weapons. When the long tubes that Angus spotted had been fully formed they would be mounted on the frames already completed. The cannons, when assembled, would prove far more destructive and powerful than the simple trebuchets that had been initially planned.

When he had seen as much as he could, Angus finally returned to where Alain was waiting and they rejoined Alex.

The route north that Angus planned next carried some risk, as once they crossed the Ban and the Ola rivers they would have to travel north across the Plain of Coe. Angus hoped that like the Ora, the rivers would be low. The Ban, Angus knew, flowed slowly past the swampland. The Ola he was less sure of, but the horses could swim and Alain seemed to have no trouble with the rivers.

Crossing the Ban turned out to be relatively easy, but it was clear that the land between the Ban and the Ola leading south towards the Inger was well populated, with campfires burning across the south where the Ban split off from the Ola. This forced Angus to head further north than he would have liked, as the Ola was the largest river and where it was still fed by tides it could be treacherous and deep.

Crossing the open land by night, the three finally reached the Ola close to the border of Banora. To the south the land was blackened, and the trio realised that they were only a short way from the camp they had destroyed on their first raid south. From a distance it appeared deserted; it was probably viewed as too remote to be worth defending and it lay on the wrong side of the river for the workforce to cross south to the forges.

The three headed south towards the burnt-out camp site. Luck was with them, as several small rowing boats lay tied up against the southern bank; presumably these were transport for workers from the south who had not returned to the camp on the far side before it was destroyed. Careful to ensure there was no movement on the far shore, the three men crossed the river with the horses swimming alongside the boats. Landfall was uneventful, but it was with great care that they approached the camp. Fortunately it was deserted.

Although it was still dark, Alex suggested that they should stop for the rest of the night and most of the following day. Whilst most of the camp had been destroyed by the fires, some small areas had survived. These would give shelter, and as long as no one occupied the camp by day, the travellers would be well hidden. In addition a few small stores had been left undamaged, and the food and drink that remained would make their stay more pleasant after days living off the land.

By late afternoon, Alex felt it should be safe enough to risk the short dash north. As they headed out from the destroyed camp, Alain spotted a small group of horsemen following the river some way to the south, almost certainly a troop of Ember Horse. They looked far enough away for the trio to avoid detection. However it was at this point that their luck ran out. As they broke out from the wood they almost collided with two Ember troopers who were slowly following their companions, clearly wounded. Both men quickly spurred their horses to the gallop and shouted to their comrades some distance away. Alain took one rider from the saddle with an arrow, but the other raced south, raising the alarm.

Clearly there was no point now in caution, so the three raced north towards the towering Coe Mountains. In the distance the horsemen had turned and were giving chase. Whilst their pursuers were still a fair distance away, the horses that Angus and Alex rode had travelled far and were not at their fastest. The pursuing troop of horse was slowly closing the gap. Even from a distance it was clear to Alex that there were far too many riders in the chasing troop to consider stopping to engage with them.

As Orridon and his troopers closed in Alain gave three clear blasts from his horn. Orridon instantly recognised the sound and called his men to a halt. He made his decision just in time. As his troop reined in, long arrows pierced the ground some fifteen yards ahead. Whilst his riders could outrun the fleeing strangers, they could not outrun the longbows of the tall warriors. Gareth had returned from Tala to join the cohort on the plain.

"Well met, brothers!" said Gareth. "Now let's take the passage north. After the destruction we delivered a day or so ago I doubt your pursuers will be too keen to chase forward to meet us. Let's go."

The group, surrounded by the Coelete warriors, headed quickly for the grey promontories that splayed out from the mountain and soon reached the entrance to the passage through the rock. Gareth and Alain's brother guardians were on watch and at a single blast from Gareth's horn the hidden doors opened and the band passed through.

Orridon and his horsemen followed at some distance, but as they drew closer to the mountain again they were met with a hail of long arrows. Orridon knew this was where Cember and his troop had been attacked. As he and his troop moved cautiously forward they could see only a few Coelete warriors. Orridon realised that the rest of them must have somehow escaped inside the mountain. He turned his troopers round and headed back for Banora.

The following day a depleted troop of Ember Horse arrived back at their camp. Orridon was instructed to report immediately to Oien. He was not looking forward to the meeting, knowing that Oien was the more senior in the eyes of the King.

Oien showed little emotion as Orridon reported on the disasters of the past week. His attention sharpened only when Orridon described the disappearance of the retreating group into the solid rock of the Coe Mountain. "I wonder" murmured Oien to himself. "The north was mapped by Malama O'Re in the Second Age before he was banished. The maps showed the Coe Mountains reaching the sea with no land between." He looked at Orridon. "The Dewar is returning to Boretar to review the situation there after the raid. You are instructed to report to him there. I am requested to join you on the journey as we have machines to deliver to your King and I want them well protected. We leave in the morning."

As the sun rose the next morning a strange procession left Banora and headed up through the Pass of Ing over to the Plain of Aldene and onwards towards Boretar. The baggage train appeared well protected by a large force of Ember Horse, but it concerned Orridon that with the losses over the past weeks he was leaving only a small troop of Ember Horse behind to protect the conquered lands, although there were also the troops from Ackar and Lett and the conscripts of the southern lands. Orridon had left his nephew Idula in command. Although young and inexperienced, Idula was of the royal lineage of the Horse Lords of Ember, so he would command respect from the troopers. He was also, despite his age, a proven warrior, if not a proven commander.

A casual observer watching the baggage train move out across the plain would have been puzzled. The great machines were moving without the aid of man or horse. A dull red glow emanated from the centre of each machine, and the massive pistons driving the wheels seemed to turn by magic. As in the Second Age, the first of the great war machines were again treading their path south through Bala.

As Angus, Alain and Alex emerged from the tunnel through the mountain, they were met by James Cameron and his daughter, together with Alastair

Munro. Elbeth raced over to greet Angus, who leapt from his horse to scoop her up in an embrace. James Cameron looked on in mild surprise. Despite his attention, it seemed these two were getting too close.

Alex dropped from the saddle to shake his father's hand. Once released by Angus, Elbeth ran to her brother, while Angus greeted the men. Alain bowed to the others and turned to leave.

"Wait!" the Cameron called, "I have to take you to the palace to report to Ala Moire and others. There will be time later for all of you to freshen up and rest."

Cameron led the way as the group walked up through Tala's narrow streets. Some way short of the palace, Elbeth whispered to Angus, let go of his hand and slipped off on her own. The others continued to the palace and entered the hall where Angus had first asked to be allowed to join the Red Cameron. As last time, seated in the room were Ala Moire, Duncan of Coe and Anaton.

"Welcome back" said Ala Moire, rising to greet them. "Alex, you have done well and your father should be proud of you. Your trooper, Davy Scott and Gareth have given us details of the early raids and the planned attack on Boretar. That was a brave, if somewhat reckless adventure. Now you need to tell us the rest of the story." Gareth had already told the three about the skirmish in the hills above Erwick.

Alex reported on the raid on Boretar, the release

of the fire boat and the journey north. Ala Moire nodded. "The fire boat was a clever plan, although its impact was more than you could have imagined," he said. The three had not waited to see the result of the destruction delivered by the fire boat. "I wonder at Oien transporting salt and othium together. Either he is getting careless or the pressure on him from the Dewar is making him too hasty."

Cameron spoke. "One of the Red Cameron has just returned from a spying mission south and passed through Boretar on his return. His report indicates that the fireboat started an othium fire which caused significant damage to both the port and the lower city. I think you will have made the Dewar an angry man."

Alex turned to Angus. "Banora is for you to report on, Angus," he said. Angus told the others about the journey north, including the red fires belching from the Inger, the monstrous self-propelling machines and the tangle with the Ember Horse.

"Metal tubes mounted on large wheeled vehicles, is that what you saw?" asked Ala Moire.

"Correct."

"Good, and well done again – you may all leave us now."

Anaton held up his hand. "Wait, I have a last question for Alain. Did the Ember Horse see you move through the secret passageway?"

"I don't think so as our archers held them some

distance away, but they'll know we didn't climb the mountain and no doubt in time they'll come seeking an answer to our disappearance."

Finally the three companions left, Alain to go back to his home and family in the city. "Till next time" he said and shook their hands. Alex left too, thanking Angus for his guidance in the raids. Alastair was keen to learn more about his friend's adventures, but before he could ask, Angus had taken him by the arm and led him to the Wild Goose. At a corner alcove Elbeth was waiting, and as they entered she ran over to embrace her man.

Alastair and Elbeth had become good friends whilst Angus had been in the south, so Alastair would have been welcome to stay, but he could see that the lovers needed time alone. "I have other business to attend to, and I'm sure you don't need my company just now," he said, smiling. "Angus, I'll tell you all about the summer in Tala when we meet in the morning."

In the room in the palace, there was a thoughtful silence for some minutes after the others had left. It was Anaton who spoke first. "I am concerned that the enemy are getting closer to guessing where we are and possibly locating the passage," he said. "It would take a significant force, and they would lose many men in fighting through the tunnel, but I am concerned that the red fire may make invasion much easier for them."

"You are correct, Anaton," replied Ala Moire. "If Oien has his machines, then defence of the underground would be difficult. We can only, I think, hope that for now the Dewar will remain set on conquering the rich lands of the south and leave us, as he sees it, locked up behind the mountain. If we have another winter like the last one then in a month or so travelling to here will be challenge enough, never mind supporting an army to make an attack."

"Nevertheless I will deploy a small troop of warriors to the southern slopes of the Coe to deter too much snooping," replied Anaton. "My warriors can hold even a large force some way back from the mountain. I will also have a troop held ever ready on this side to move quickly through for defence if needed."

Cameron spoke. "We will also hold a troop of Red Cameron ready to move the instant word comes to us of any threat. Ala, I have not heard of these machines with long metal tubes on them. What is this new peril we face?"

Ala Moire sighed. "Oien is repeating his own history. First he builds trebuchets that can hurl othium fire at the enemy, then, more devastating still, he is building cannon that are powered by othium and do not need horse or man to move them. They can fire iron and stone balls or othium bombs at the enemy and cause great devastation. Once his smiths learn their art and can fashion machines from other materials, he will build more terrifying instruments of war, and from there the transports that will move men and equipment to the field far faster than any horse can. We must hope that his mind is locked in the glory of the past and his eyes are on the riches of Amina and Kermin and the gold of the Doran Mountains. For now he needs the Dewar and his armies, but with the southern lands conquered he can dispense with the King, as he will have gold enough to buy his own armies. That plan worked in the Second Age with different forces, and it looks as if he hopes to repeat history. We can only hope his greed leads him and the Dewar south and that they leave dealing with us for another day."

Duncan had remained quiet, listening to the conversation. Now it was his turn. "From what you say Ala, we simply wait here for our doom to arrive on our doorstep. I would rather we led the army south now to see if we can retake the land of our forefathers. We have some weeks before the snows come and if they are moving forces south then they may be weak in Banora. James, we cannot sit here in comfort waiting for the red fire to break through to Tala."

James Cameron paused before replying. "Duncan, you are correct in your thoughts but not in your timing.

As you all know, winter is not a time for campaigning, or at least so is the conventional wisdom. If the Dewar is true to form he will winter in Boretar, unless the old man can persuade him otherwise. Coran, my brother, is leading the forces of Amina, Kermin and Doran. By both fast horse and homing pigeon we have been swapping messages.

"Coran and Silson, the Duke of Amina, believe it is possible to mount a winter campaign to retake Tamin. If their plan proceeds, we would then mount a winter campaign south from here. Whilst the snow would make a large raid south challenging, we know the Banoran cobs can get through even deep snow. We would travel with a reasonable force of horse and foot with the cobs leading the way. The Coelete have tools they use to move snow from their walkways, and these could be deployed to clear our way south. We also have the birlinns at Erwick, and history tells us that the sea wolves of the past often raided the coastal settlements in winter. If everything is timed and co-ordinated, we can hurt the Dewar north and south when he least expects it. That is the plan."

James Cameron was not one to be gainsaid, and all nodded. Anaton spoke next. "You will also travel with a large group of Coelete warriors, for now is the time for us to stand alongside our brothers from Bala."

So the plan was agreed. "Tomorrow we start preparations," said Cameron. "We have a month, at the most two, to get ready before the worst of the winter sets in. We probably need to be ready to move within the month."

CHAPTER ELEVEN

Autumn in Tala

In Tala, the first chill of autumn was blowing in on the northerly wind. Alastair and Angus met in the former's rooms, which adjoined the area occupied by Duncan of Coe and his family. Both friends were aware that Elbeth was playing with the three Coe children in a nearby room. Alastair shared his news first, although his adventures had not matched Angus's. Summer had passed quietly; James Cameron had insisted that Alastair should train with the Red Cameron and learn the art of mounted warfare. Alastair had been reluctant, but with little else to occupy him he had in time found he enjoyed the physical exercise and that his skill with the Banoran bow impressed his trooper colleagues to the extent that after horse training, many of them came to ask him to further train them with the bow. Aside from the time training for war, Alastair had spent many hours with Ala Moire, the old man teaching him how to control his inner power.

Training on the horse was a release for Alastair, as Ala Moire's teaching was a great strain. Alastair in some ways resented the gift he had inherited but not asked for. Ala Moire seemed so self-possessed, whilst Alastair could not stop the white sparks flying around his person when he was frustrated at being unable to manage a task set for him by his master. Mostly the exercises involved learning to control the white light by will rather than by instinctive reaction.

Late in the summer Alastair was relieved to be told by Duncan that he was to join him on another trip to Esimore to negotiate with the herdsmen to bring a few more reindeer back to Tala to supplement the winter supplies. This time Alastair brought gifts for the herdsmen in exchange for a few of their herd. Having crossed the Eastern Sea and journeyed a short way inland, the small group from Bala and their Coelete guides camped whilst the Coelete went ahead and sought out the herds. A few days later they returned with a small band of herdsmen and the reindeer. Sulux, their chief, was led into the tent occupied by Munro and Duncan. He told them that, again out of respect for their legends, they brought some of the herd as a gift, but they could not continue to deliver this offering every year.

Alastair thanked the chief and went to his saddlebags, producing a pouch filled with white stones that had been gathered on the journey through the waste lands. As he had been taught, he held each small stone and allowed a small amount of power to seep into each one. Sulux sat in awe as white sparks flickered from Alastair Munro's hand.

Alastair passed the stones to the herdsman and was surprised to find that this time he had somehow absorbed the man's language. He was able to explain to Sulux that the stones were a gift in return for their support. Sulux, under instruction, held one of the stones and with a gentle rub found for himself how it radiated warmth. In the depths of an Esimore winter the stones would protect the tribes, and Sulux recognised that they were no small gift. With a bow of thanks, he and his band departed and the Banorans returned to Tala with the reindeer.

As Alastair finished telling his story, Angus looked at his long-time friend, who seemed somehow older, and more disconcertingly, seemed to have gained some deeper wisdom. Alastair could not share all that he had learnt from Ala Moire with his friend, as much of his new power still felt strange and unreal. Angus then shared all the details of the southern raids and Alastair listened with deep concentration, knowing intuitively that this information would somehow guide part of his future. In particular Alastair concentrated on the descriptions Angus gave of the red fire burning in the mountains of their homeland. As Angus described the scenes on the mountains, he could not help but notice the white sparks that seemed to emanate from all around his friend.

In the clear warmth of a late autumn sun, Elbeth and Angus rode out together, seeking space and time to share each other's company. Since Angus's return the time they had spent together had always been during discreet moments at the Wild Goose or in the palace. As their love had grown the two had become increasingly conscious of the gulf between Elbeth's status and Angus's contrasting lack of position or power.

James Cameron had also been secretly monitoring the developing relationship, and although concerned, he could not bring himself to forbid his only daughter the joy she clearly showed as she fell in love. Elbeth also had her supporter at her father's side, as Eleanor regularly commented on how good it was to see her stepdaughter so happy. Cameron assessed the situation as being a consequence of the war, and felt that once the natural state of affairs in Bala was re-established his daughter would recognise her duty to wed the son of one of the other lords of Bala. Cameron liked the young Banoran and admired his spirit, but at some point he knew he would have to intervene in the relationship and ignore the trouble he would get from his wife.

Despite his attention, Cameron did not know about the pair's planned ride out from the city. Angus and Elbeth had their horses readied in different stables and met only once they were some way from the tented settlement that housed most of the Bala refugees. As they met the two shared a gentle kiss, and with the wind in their faces they galloped off towards the Nath. After crossing through the Nath, they reached the shores of the Hidden Sea, which stretched out endlessly in front of them. The sandy beach was deserted and from her saddlebags Elbeth produced the provisions for their lunch. The venison slabs, the cheese and the wine however went untouched as the lovers lay together with the sand at their backs and the vast blue waters rippling before them. As the waves caressed the shore in a constant tempo, Angus and Elbeth reached deep within their hearts and souls to seek the meaning of the moment and try to understand it.

It was Elbeth who broke the warm silence. "Angus, you must be mine for all time. I love you more than all the world's riches and any other future life I might be destined to have."

Angus was quiet for a moment before speaking. "My love, you know these moments will live in my heart forever, but I cannot see how your father can let us be all that with this love we could be."

Elbeth sat up. "Then we must marry, with my father's blessing or without. I will not live the rest of my life without you by my side, whatever the consequences."

Angus turned to Elbeth and drew her close to him again. The tenderness of the moment stilled their racing hearts, but at the back of his mind Angus wondered how their dreams could be fulfilled, how could they make this magic last.

As the dusk began to fall over the Hidden Sea the pair rode back to Tala, treasuring the time together but both silent with their own thoughts.

The autumn winds were also chilling the residents of Boretar as a strange convoy arrived at the city gates. The huge contraptions that comprised much of the convoy drew crowds to the city walls as news of their arrival spread. Each of four long metal tubes was mounted on a metal base that was supported on each side by three large wheels. There were gasps of wonder when it became clear that the six great wheels appeared to be turning without assistance. The crowds could see the red glow from the reactor at the centre of each machine, but they could not imagine how this could be connected to the movement of the machines.

At the head of the column rode Orridon, who was well known in Boretar. At his side rode Oien, the old man who some recognised from his earlier visits to the city. On each side of the convoy and to the rear rode troops of Ember Horse. Oien and Orridon left the convoy and proceeded on through the city gate. The strange machines were left in the protection of the Ember Horse, although there was little chance of any attack on the open land outside the city walls. The two men expected to find the King in his rooms in the castle, but when they reached the castle gates they were told he was at the port overseeing the reconstruction work there and in the lower city.

The two were led to the rooms of Roger Eld, Captain of Boretar. Eld was a robust man in his mid-fifties who had held the role of Captain of Boretar for both the Dewar and his father. Eld's greeting was cool, particularly to Oien, whom he did not trust; at least Orridon was a warrior, not a magician.

"The King is at the port and has instructed me to show you to your rooms," Eld began. "He will take your reports over dinner this evening, but be warned – he is in a foul mood and he's furious that you have not managed to completely subdue resistance in the north."

Oien sighed. "If the King had heeded my instructions on how to handle the othium shipments, then his campaign in the south would have been successful by now and his port would still be intact."

Eld was about to make a sharp reply, but Orridon quietly shook his head in warning. Clearly the Ember Lord did not recommend an argument with the old man. Instead the Captain briefed the pair on the fireship raid on the port and the ensuing destruction. The two were then taken to their rooms to await the call from the King.

It was early evening when they were summoned into the King's presence, and it took no great insight to tell that the Dewar was in a great rage. It was also clear that although Eld had suggested that they were to report to the King over dinner, all that would be served was the King's ire.

Orridon was the first to taste the royal wrath. "So your esteemed Ember Horse have failed to subdue Banora and the North!" the monarch roared. "Indeed worse, you have been bested several times by the Cameron's rag tag army sneaking out from their mountain retreats."

Orridon started to explain, but the King held up a hand to silence him. "I have my retainers still within the army in Bala and I have had detailed reports of your failings. You do not have the impetuousness of your stepbrother, but nor do you seem to have the competence or the ruthlessness. Maybe I should find a better leader for the northern armies. For now though, you and your troops will protect the war machines on their way south for transport from Anelo across the Middle Sea to Amina, where you will report to Melnar of Lett, who is in command at Tamin. As the port here is out of action we need to move the weapons overland to where transports will be waiting to move them over the sea. With winter coming from the north it is unlikely that Cameron will try to campaign through the snows. We may still have time to deploy the weapons in the south and clear the Kermin Alol of the rebels skulking there under the other Cameron's command. You will send one of your riders north to command Idula to ensure the mines and workers in Banora are well protected through the winter. I want supplies of othium moving south as soon as the snows clear."

With that Orridon was dismissed. The Dewar turned to Oien. "Well old man, your magic seems at best to be unstable and your weapons unpredictable."

Oien tried to be humble. "My Lord King, my instructions were explicit that the salt formulations and the rock needed to be kept well apart to avoid the sort of incidents that have occurred."

The King rose from his seat, fists tightly gripping the chair arms as he tried to control his temper. "You deem to instruct me and have the impudence to tell me what I have done wrong when it is your own magic that has created the destruction of my port and a quarter of my city?" he thundered. As he leaned back against his seat, Oien's own anger rose and amber sparks speckled his closed hand. The Dewar might be King in his land, but he did not have the power to counteract the red magic of the alchemist.

Slowly the King sat down again, "So tell me – what are those monstrous machines that now sit outside the city walls? I hope they are capable of destroying my enemies in the Alol."

Oien explained how the cannon had been used in the second age and how they could spit fire and rock over hundreds of yards to destroy any enemy host armed with sword and bow. "Each cannon has ten times the destructive power of the trebuchets that you have already used successfully, and these are just the start," he said. "Once the smiths in Banora develop their skills, far more powerful weapons will become available, and with these I will once again conquer the world."

The King noted the "I" rather than "we" with some alarm, but he wisely decided that now was not the time to challenge the alchemist. He forced himself to remain calm. "Oien, would you travel some of the way to Anelo with these new weapons and on the journey train my troops? Some of the men who manned the trebuchets are here and will travel with you. They at least have some skill in handling the red rock, so they will hopefully learn quickly, and on reaching Anelo they can train others."

Oien nodded his assent. The Dewar continued, "First, however, you can demonstrate the power of these weapons for me tomorrow on the plain. I cannot travel with you to Anelo, as your progress will be slow and I need to be here to drive on with the repair to the port. Boretar's whole economy is dependent on goods coming in and going out through the port. Currently, with everything having to take the overland routes, our rich merchants are beginning to feel the pinch and are actively talking about moving their trade elsewhere. Men are working day and night on the repairs, but I need to ensure there is no slacking. I will follow you to Anelo in a few weeks' time and hopefully the winter will hold off long enough for us to deploy the weapons in the Alol before the snows fall there."

With a nod, Oien turned and left the King. The Dewar noted that the old man did not deign to bow on the way out of his presence, and again wondered how far to trust the old man, yet he recognised that the alchemist's skills provided him with power and weapons he could not obtain himself or deliver through simple manpower.

Oien returned to his rooms and started working on the complex drawings he had carried from the house in Banora. The parchments he worked on were clearly very old, and each had a strange orange glow to it. In these papers were details of many of the great machines that had powered the Second Age.

Oien detected a presence in the room and spoke openly. "Armon, you took your time in getting to me. You must have received my summons some weeks ago."

The man stepped into the light from the othium lamp burning in the corner. He was tall and as thin as a rake, dressed head to toe in black with a black hood covering his face.

"I am sorry my lord, being discreet in my travel to avoid any contact meant a slower journey than the distance might suggest," he explained. He pulled back his hood to expose a face covered in what looked like black tattoos. The work of the craftsman who created the face was highly skilled, as the darkness of the painting made the face indistinct and it merged into the blackness of the clothing.

Oien spoke again. "I have need of your skills, Armon, to complete a difficult task for me in the far north of Andore."

Most of the common people would find Armon's facial markings strange but would take little heed. The nobility, however, if they had seen Armon, would have hurried away. He was one of the Assassins, a small band of killers whose skills were for hire. They lived in a cave settlement high in the east of the Doran Mountains. The band were one of the few groups left unharmed by the destruction at the end of the Second

Age as they had ridden out the meteorite storms in their cave hideaways. Oien had known the group since the Second Age, when he had occasionally needed to use more subtle approaches than were offered by his use of the red stone. The Assassins were rich, as their customers were generally wealthy nobles who could pay handsomely to rid themselves of some competitor or troublemaker. Their cave dwellings were finely decorated in gold. This was payment extorted from the Doran gold miners. In return the Assassins ensured the miners' families and homes were protected from roaming bandits.

The Assassins' weapon of choice was the skilatu, a long narrow-bladed dagger. When carrying out an assignment or contract, the Assassins would blend in with travellers or pilgrims until they could find the opportunity to carry out their task. By reputation the Assassin never failed to successfully execute a contract.

Oien briefed Armon on his task and the journey he would need to make over the Inger mountains and then over the high Coe. Oien admitted that beyond the Coe he did not know how the land lay and Armon would need to use his wits if he got that far. Crossing the Coe with winter approaching would be a challenge, but Armon had lived in the high Doran Mountains for many years and was well used to difficult mountain journeys. Oien confirmed that

Armon's fee had already been paid to the Assassins, so without another word Armon set out to execute his contract.

It was a bright clear mid-autumn morning as the cannons moved out from Boretar's city walls. This time, alongside Orridon and Oien, the King rode at the head of the procession. About a mile from the walls lay a deserted hamlet whose inhabitants had long since given up a farming life for more prosperous opportunities in the city. The old buildings had never been cleared or reoccupied. A few hundred yards from the buildings, Oien stopped and instructed his men to move one of the machines forward. Then he instructed the gunners, as he now called them, to load the end of the metal tube with a mixture of salt of Elat and a small amount of ground red stone. These were followed into the cannon mouth by handfuls of small round iron balls.

Having overseen the priming of the device, Oien moved to the rear of the machine, where a well-crafted box of shining metal was attached to the long iron tube. Oien opened the door on the side of the box and put in some red stone. An aperture at the top of the box led to a smaller container where the salt formulation was added. Oien slid away the linkage mechanism joining the two containers and from another aperture slid in a small piece of othium, already primed and burning orange. Oien stepped back from the machine as a small rumbling from the box began. It increased in noise, and a moment later the whole beast seemed to roar in discomfort as it blasted the iron balls from the end of the tube. The balls flew towards the empty village, glowing bright red in the air. As they landed each ball exploded, and the nearest houses disappeared in a cloud of dust.

The Dewar, who was sitting some distance away, was impressed, and applauded. However, if this destruction was impressive, what followed was even more so. After leaving the cannon, for so it was called, for a few minutes to cool down, Oien repeated the operation, but this time instead of the iron balls, roughly rounded pieces of othium coated with oil containing saltpetre, were pushed carefully into the mouth of the cannon. The rest of the operation proceeded as previously, but the end effect was quite different. The othium erupted from the cannon as a myriad fire bombs, and as they landed on the far side of the deserted village they exploded. The whole area was engulfed in fire.

A few minutes later, the King rode over to inspect the damage. The fires were still burning, but the explosions had ceased. As the Dewar approached it was clear that not a single brick remained intact in the village. The destruction was complete.

The Dewar smiled and turned to Oien. "Well done,

Oien. I almost pity those in the Alol when we rain this fire on them. Please continue your training on the journey to Anelo, and either travel back once the training is done and report to me in Boretar or I will meet up with you in Anelo."

Oien nodded, and without another word the King turned back to his city and Oien and the war machines began their journey south.

In Tala, as the October moon waned, the cold increased, and although no snow was yet in the air the winds whispered its coming. Preparation for the winter campaign was now well under way. Timing would be critical; move too early and the Bala army might face a much stronger force on open ground, but leave it too late and the winter snows might make the routes south impassable.

James Cameron and the other chiefs fretted over the timing and the weather, but in the meantime the troops were being readied. So too were the various implements which the Coelete used in winter to clear snow from important roads and thoroughfares. The army would be significant, but not too large. Six hundred Red Cameron on their war horses would be supported by two thousand foot soldiers and three hundred Banoran archers mounted on their sturdy cobs. The force would be supplemented by two hundred and fifty Coelete warriors led by Alain of Lorn. Spies from the south kept the Cameron informed, and he knew that Idula was in charge of a larger force but one that consisted of mainly the conscript forces supported by a smaller number of Ackar and Lett regulars and the remaining Ember Horse. Most of the forces of Ackar and Lett were still deployed in Amina, and Cameron hoped that his younger brother could keep their attention on the south whilst he occupied the northern force.

Meanwhile in Erwick, John Ewart and his troop of Cameron, together with a small force of locals, were preparing for a sea voyage, one the birlinns had not made in winter in over a hundred years.

As the preparations for war continued, four riders left Tala heading for the Nath. All four were well clad against the cold and could not be recognised with their hoods drawn up over their heads to give some protection from the cold north wind. The quartet rode through the Nath to the same sandy beach on which Angus and Elbeth had pledged their love for each other. The Hidden Sea was not rippling gently on the shore now but was being whipped up by the winds, and breakers were crashing against the shore line and onto the rocks at both ends of the beach.

Once they had dismounted, they drew back their hoods and Alex Cameron spoke. "I know not what my father will make of this when he finds out, but my love for my sister brings me here. Elbeth has persuaded me that she and Angus must be betrothed before this new campaign begins. I have fought alongside Angus Ferguson and without him I might not have returned from the summer raids in the south. I also know that my father will expect Elbeth to marry into one of the noble families of Bala to secure land and alliances for the future. However I am also sure that my sister's love for Angus is beyond the reach of politics, so I am here to ask us to witness their betrothal."

Alastair Munro, Elbeth and Angus bowed their heads and waited for Alex's next words. The people of Bala had a strong belief in their God, but rather than seeing God as a single entity they believed he was in all things, both in them and around them. Marriage ceremonies would be held in woods, or by streams, and God would be asked to bless the marriages through his existence in the living world around the marriage site. Marriage was completed when the wedding pair exchanged rings, removing them from the third finger of the right hand and placing them on the third finger of the left hand. When a couple became committed to each other, engaged or betrothed, a similar blessing ceremony took place, with rings placed on the third finger of the right hand of each party. Again a blessing would be sought from God within the world around them.

Alex continued, "With the blessing of God through the roaring waters of the sea and the myriad grains of the sand, I commit my support and blessing to this betrothal. I further commit to doing all within my power to help this couple nurture their love and I will sing songs of joy on their wedding day. I ask you both now, in sight of the sea and the sand, to exchange your rings."

Angus and Elbeth each produced a simple copper ring and carefully placed it on the third finger of the other's right hand. Angus had managed to purchase the rings from a copper worker in Tala, but had only been able to afford the simplest of bands. Elbeth and Angus never gave a thought about the simplicity of the rings, having eyes only for each other; they cared only about the symbolism of the moment.

As the two clasped their ring hands, Alastair Munro placed his hands over theirs. A shimmer of white glowed from the clasped hands and white sparks rippled from Munro.

"I too am witness to this moment of promise and I also commit to doing all in my power to support this love and at your wedding day I will dance with joy," said Alastair. He lifted his hands away and the lovers stared in amazement at the rings. The dull copper had been transformed into pure white gold, and the rings carried a motif of joined hands which merged into three engraved words: *Aonaibh Ri Chéile.*

The pair looked quizzically at Alastair. "In the olden tongue it means 'unite' or 'let us unite', he told them. "Elbeth, your father may recognise this when the time comes to tell him of your promises."

Neither knew what to say or what to make of this gift. Simple copper would have been more than sufficient, but now both carried white gold on their right hands.

Alex stepped back, not sure what to make of this unexpected intervention. Alastair smiled and continued, "you are about to spend time apart as we leave for war, and the rings are a special gift. If one of you places their left hand on top of the ring your thoughts will be felt by the other, so that even whilst apart your love can grow and flourish."

Alastair smiled again. For the first time he felt that his power could be a thing for good, and for love, rather than a burden he must carry.

With the ceremony over, Alex and Alastair Munro rode the short distance back to the Nath, leaving the lovers some private time together to share the wonder of the moment and admire with awe the white gold that now glistened on each right hand.

"Elbeth, my love, we must take the rings off before we get back to the Palace in Tala," said Angus. "We cannot let your father know of our betrothal until the time is right."

Elbeth put on a stubborn face. "Angus, we have become betrothed in a ceremony according to the laws and customs of our people." She pointed at her right hand. "This ring will never leave this finger until it moves to this finger." She pointed at her left hand.

"So be it my love, we will face your father together when the time comes," was the quiet reply. With a last kiss the pair mounted and rode back to the Nath to join the others and head back to Tala.

That evening James Cameron, Duncan of Coe, Ewart, Ala Moire and Anaton sat together in the rooms in the palace occupied by the Cameron family. Cameron noted the lightness in his daughter's step as she oversaw the servants bringing the group food and drinks. The discussion was all about the coming campaign and the preparations in Tala, as well as the news from Amina in the south. Over the past month Cameron spies had moved across the lands from the Alol to Boretar and Tala. The Cameron brothers also kept each other informed through carrier pigeons. As a result the commanders in the north and south were well informed about the movement of the cannons and the state of the Dewar's forces in both locations. The timing of the combined forces' movements would be critical if they were to enjoy any success in the planned winter campaigns.

It was only as the meeting was drawing to a close that Ala Moire noted the glint from Elbeth's right hand. He leaned over and whispered to the Cameron. As Elbeth made to leave the room Cameron shouted after her, "Elbeth, you will please come back here as soon as our guests have left." Elbeth knew that her ring had been spotted and she rather breathlessly ran to seek out Alastair and ask him to quickly find Angus.

When Elbeth returned an hour or so later, only James Cameron, Coe and Ala Moire remained sitting in the hall. She carried herself with poise and there was a look of determination on her face. "Show me your hand, girl," said her father. Elbeth held out her left hand, keeping the right behind her back.

"Please don't play games with me daughter, the other hand!" snapped her father. Elbeth held out her right hand, and the Cameron studied the ring.

"I suppose this is a scheme of that Ferguson lad. My dear, a ring on your finger without my blessing means nothing. I should have stepped in earlier. You know this cannot work. When you marry it will be to one of the noble's sons to further cement the alliances in Bala."

As Cameron raised his voice, it seemed that the white gold of the band shone with a light all of its own. Elbeth replied with more determination than she felt, but the glow from the ring fuelled her courage.

"Father, I knew you could not bless this betrothal, but Angus and I are deeply in love and I will only move this ring from my right hand to my left hand when the time comes that we are wed. Without being able to gain your blessing I was blessed in this by my brother, following the customs of our people."

The Cameron was trying to control his temper, and it was Ala Moire who spoke next. "Elbeth, please let me look more closely at the ring."

Elbeth held her hand out to the old man. The white gold seemed to shine even more brightly under Ala Moire's scrutiny.

"I presume Alastair Munro also took part in this blessing ceremony?" Elbeth nodded. Ala Moire turned to Cameron. "James, I think this proposed union has blessing from a much higher power than you and I. Look at the motif on the ring."

Cameron took his daughter's hand and studied the ring more closely. "*Aonaibh Ri Chéile*... what does that mean? I have a faint memory of those words."

"It is many years since I have seen this motto, which used to be engraved on the swords of your ancestors," said Ala Moire. "It is in the old language and means "let us unite". It was the Cameron motto long before the white, blue and red livery of these present days. It also predates your current emblem of five arrows, which you do know about. Angus Ferguson could not have fashioned this ring, and indeed without blessing from a higher power nor could Alastair Munro. Munro has inherited power, but it is usually only enabled when blessed by God for His purpose and His good."

Cameron turned to Duncan. "Can you please ask

my son and the other two to join us?"

Alex, Angus and Alastair had anticipated the request to attend the Cameron, and Coe found them sitting together in the latter's rooms. When they presented themselves it was Alex who spoke first.

"Father, I do not apologise for my role in this blessing. Elbeth and Angus's love means that with or without your blessing, they will be wed. Today they swapped simple copper rings, and when Alastair blessed them they turned miraculously into the white gold you see on both their right hands. Whilst Angus is not of the Bala nobility, he is my friend, and now a proven warrior. Without him I might not have returned from the southern raids. John Burnett has recently promoted Angus to command a troop of the Red Cameron, so in terms of his rank he is as noble as I am. Look how happy my sister is! I will not retract the blessing made in my name, and as your son, also made in our name."

Alastair Munro spoke before James Cameron could reply to his son. "I too added my blessing to this engagement, and I feel the transformation of the rings was given through me, not by me. I believe this union has a higher blessing."

Cameron was not an overtly religious man, but like most of the people of Bala, he did acknowledge that man's actions were to a degree subservient to a higher power. Indeed Cameron had seen first-hand the power of higher forces through his time over the years with Ala Moire. Taking a moment to reflect, Cameron remembered his own loves, those now lost and his love for his new wife Eleanor, who was resting in the room next door. He spoke quietly, turning to Elbeth and Angus, who were now standing together.

"Angus, I can see the joy that you bring to my daughter, and that cannot be denied. We are about to head out again to war, and many things change in times of war. At this stage I cannot bless your betrothal, but I can appreciate the intent. My blessing of a future wedding is for the future and how fate decrees we fare in the coming conflict. For now, be happy in the short time you have together, and we will see what the future holds."

The white rings seemed to glow more brightly with Cameron's words.

As the friends left the palace to celebrate at the Wild Goose, the first snowflakes of the winter started to fall on Tala.

It was some time later when Alastair Munro returned to his rooms in the palace. Ala Moire was waiting for him. "Alastair, it seems your gift has developed further than I could have imagined. Fashioning those rings was no simple task."

Alastair considered his response. "It was strange. It is really the first time that I have felt that my power was for the good, and it required almost no effort from me at all. It was almost as if the rings fashioned themselves."

"And so you are learning an important lesson. Your power is your gift and you can use it for good or for ill, but for the latter it is your will, whilst the former is channelled through you by God. I presume there is a power in the rings other than simple metal." Alastair nodded. "Then I have a similar gift for you."

From around his neck Ala Moire took a silver chain on which hung a white gold medallion imprinted with an emblem of a sheaf of five arrows surrounded by the same words as the rings: *Aonaibh Ri Chéile.* Alastair of course by now knew the meaning of the words, and the five arrows was the emblem used on the official documents of The Cameron. Alastair looked quizzically at the gift.

"Alastair, I am not coming with you to war," said Ala Moire. "I think a winter campaign will test these old bones a bit too much. If I am correct, the rings you fashioned for Angus and Elbeth will allow them to keep in thought contact with each other when they are separated. This device is similar. It will allow James Cameron and his brother Coran to pass their thoughts to you when there is the need. I fashioned the device many, many years ago for the current Lord's forefathers. Both Cameron brothers know of this device, and while the pigeon messengers that we have been sending have some purpose, most of the communications between the brothers comes through me and will now come through you. I have discussed this with Cameron, and he agrees that you should take my place beside him when the army leaves Tala. The first snow is falling and you will be on the move soon, but we will talk further before you depart." Without a further word Ala Moire hung the pendant round Alastair Munro's neck and briefly embraced him. He left the younger man wondering about his role in the days and weeks ahead.

CHAPTER TWELVE
A Winter Campaign

As Tala received its first dusting of snow, autumn rain was still falling in Amina. Melnar had remained warm and dry in the palace in Tamin whilst the troops had spent the last weeks of the summer and the early autumn rebuilding the walls of the city after their destruction earlier that year. Whilst Melnar and his captains remained in the city, the army was camped both in the Vale of Tember and on the plains between the Mina and Amin rivers. It was a damp existence for the soldiers, as the rain seemed never-ending and each day brought dark grey skies. As with any standing army the soldiers trained each day, but with little enthusiasm. They were a large force, but bored by the lack of action and anticipating a cold and wet winter under canvas before the campaigns could start again in the spring.

Melnar, who was more of an administrator than a warrior, did little to dispel the gloomy atmosphere. Like many of his captains and the soldiers themselves, he would have much preferred to winter safely at his home in Lett. However the messengers from Boretar had made it clear that the King intended to bring new weapons to Amina and expected the army to be ready to wipe out the forces hiding in the Alol.

In the Kermin Alol, Coran and his generals had been developing their plans. Coran knew from the messages from Tala and from the Cameron spies that the northern army would leave the protection of the Hidden Lands in the next few weeks. He also knew of the new weapons that were making their way south from Boretar. The forces in the Alol had increased significantly in size over the previous weeks as more Doran cavalry had moved south, together with foot soldiers from Kermin. A significant addition to the defending army was the arrival of a large contingent of elite archers who had travelled from their home territory in the forests in the east of Kermin. These archers were from the Aramin tribes who occupied the large forests that ran from the Doran Mountains south to the Alol. The Aramin seldom involved themselves in the wars of the south, preferring to protect their own homelands when required.

Arin himself had travelled to meet with the Aramin and explain to them the danger represented by this new invasion force. It was clear that if the Dewar army successfully broke through at the Alol, then the home lands of the Aramin would probably be swallowed up by the invaders. In addition Darmon, the leader of the Aramin, recognised that their prowess with the bow would provide little resistance against the magic of the fire that Arin had described.

The forces in the Alol had also been joined by a small contingent of miners from the Doran Mountains. The miners arrived with several wagonloads of the Doran Combustibles as well as other wagons loaded with the raw ingredients necessary to manufacture the incendiaries. The miners brought with them both their skills in producing the incendiaries and their ability to maximise the explosive impact of the devices.

Coran went through the plan again with Silson, Arin and Ishca. In outline it was not unlike the summer attacks led in the other direction by the Dewar's armies. Silson would lead the forces of Amina onto the plain between the rivers and confront the invading force camped on the plain. Arin and Ishca would take the Kermin foot soldiers and the Doran cavalry to the south and west and attack the forces camped on the Vale of Tember. The miners and their incendiaries would accompany both forces, whilst a portion of the Red Cameron would travel with Silson. The Aramin archers would be deployed with both armies, with Darmon accompanying Silson. Coran would take a small force of Red Cameron down from the Alol and lead them along the south bank of the Mina to avoid detection. They would then travel directly south to move along the northern banks of the Amin to the walls of Tamin.

Whilst the walls of the city could withstand a long siege, Silson had explained to Coran that there was a weakness in the defences, as a small portal gate existed in the walls close to the Amin River. This entrance was used by the King of Amina to board his royal barge for travel down the Amin to the port of Tufle on the Middle Sea. The gate was stout and effectively protected by the river flowing close by. To access it, Coran and his men would need to follow a narrow path on the river bank and at times have to wade through the shallows to reach the gate. If their approach was detected, the defenders on the walls would pour hot oil, boiling water and arrows from the ramparts above and make access impossible. Coran's troop, if they could avoid detection, would employ the Doran Combustibles to remove the door.

The plan was agreed, but it was dependent on something that could not be controlled: the weather. Whilst the forces gathered in the Alol were significant, they were still much less than those available to Melnar and the invaders. Coran needed his armies to have surprise on their side. Late autumn campaigns in the rainy season were unusual, and he hoped that the rain, combined with low cloud and mists over the rivers, would hide their intent until first contact was made.

For the next two days, bright autumn sunshine obliged the forces to remain in their camps spread across the Alol. Through Ala Moire, Coran kept his brother in the north informed of their plans and the delay. Fortunately, on the third day the rain, mist and fog returned. If they persisted, the plan was for the coalition forces to move out from the Alol at night and hope that the darkness and the weather would hide their intent.

So on that night the different units moved out from the Alol. In general the forces travelled relatively lightly as they had a lot of ground to cover on the night march. The commanders realised that leading troops into battle following a night march was risky, but it was less dangerous than moving openly across the plains and meeting an alerted enemy in the full light of day. The timing of the engagements was critical, as the different actions had to occur more or less simultaneously to maximise the confusion in the enemy ranks. The weather did not help the coordination of the attacks, as dawn would see only a paling of the dark skies.

It had been agreed that the units led by Arin and Ishca would lead the attack, as their forces had the most ground to cover. They would begin their attack by throwing the incendiaries into the camps on the Vale of Tember, and the light of the fires should be seen by Silson, who would alert his army to move forward.

So it was in the grey mist just after dawn that the Doran miners approached the enemy camp with their incendiaries. Behind them the Aramin archers stood ready, and to the sides of the archers were the troops of Doran cavalry. If luck and the weather stayed on their side, Arin and Ishca hoped for a quick victory over a confused and surprised enemy. The Kermin foot soldiers were at the rear of the attackers and would hopefully be used to drive the enemy back towards the Middle Sea.

The attack began, and in moments the tents across the eastern edge of the encampment were ablaze and the conscript soldiers and those of the Ackar and Lett forces were in panic. Without coherent leadership, the soldiers sought to save themselves and retreated west. As they did so, the Aramin archers played out their role and a rain of arrows fell from the sky. As the panic spread, the Doran cavalry raced through the fires, their swords and lances spreading destruction throughout the camp.

Finally the Kermin foot moved forward in orderly lines. They met little resistance; some half-dressed soldiers attempted to hold them back, while others just turned and ran. It was not long before Arin and Ishca stood across the Amin from Tamin. The underwater stepping stones could not be activated from the south side of the river, so the task was to prevent any escape route from the city. Again the Aramin archers were deployed along the banks. The Doran cavalry continued to harass the retreating soldiers of the Dewar army as they withdrew back towards Tufle and the secure walls of the port.

As soon as the fires lit up the gloom on the south of the Amin, Silson moved his forces forward to the camps lying between the Mina and the Amin. The tactics were the same; incendiaries were followed by Aramin arrows and a rapid attack by the Red Cameron. Whilst a similar panic initially overtook the soldiers camped on the plain outside Tamin, these were mostly the professional army of Ackar and Lett and their captains were quick to restore some order after the initial chaos caused by the surprise attack.

The defenders managed to pull back to the walls of the city and put the Amin River at their backs, hoping that the combined barrier of wall and river would restrict the options of the attacking forces. As the small force of Red Cameron pulled back from the pike wall that the enemy forces had now established they kept themselves out of range of the archers on the city walls. Now the depleted force of the Amina knights rode forward on their warhorses. This was a different prospect from facing the Kermin foot soldiers, and although the knights were mostly clad in armour the arrows from the city walls could still prove deadly.

As the knights halted, just out of range of the missiles from the city walls, the Ackar and Lett soldiers mocked their cowardice – until they were subjected to a hail of arrows from the south side of the river. The Aramin archers, under the command of Arin and Ishca, had reached their target just in time. The forces of Ackar and Lett were now held between the armed might of the Amina knights and the deadly arrows from the south.

Coran and his small troop of Red Cameron had left the Alol ahead of the rest of the forces, as their journey was likely to be slower and more risky. At the same time as the fires lit up the Vale of Tember, Coran and his band reached the portal gate in the city walls. The miner who had travelled with the group primed his combustibles and laid them at the small gate. Melnar and his commanders had raced to the city walls as the first attacks took place, and Melnar hesitated; should he hold his reserve forces in the city to protect it, or release them to try to influence the battle unfolding on the plain? Instinctively he knew that the Dewar would want the city held at any cost, and he also knew that the rebuilt walls of Tamin could resist even the most powerful siege weapons. He decided that it would be better to stay secure within the walls, and if an opportunity presented itself he would open the city gates to allow the forces trapped between the knights and the river to enter the city.

Absorbed in watching the drama unfold on the plain, Melnar did not hear the short blast from far below him at the foot of the city walls. Coran and the Red Cameron were inside the city, and following the back streets mapped out by Silson, the Red Cameron were soon at the main gate. Most of the city's defenders were on the city walls trying in vain to engage the enemy. The gate was only lightly defended, as no one had anticipated an attack from inside the walls.

The Red Cameron swiftly despatched the guards at the gate and swung the big doors open. It now became clear why the other Cameron troopers and the Amina knights had not engaged the forces locked up with the river at their backs. As the gates opened, the mounted troops wheeled round and charged into the city. The defenders on the walls tried to hold back the advance, but Aramin archers from the plain had found their range and the city walls became a place of death for any unwary defender. The Red Cameron threw their combustibles into the lower city, creating further panic as the knights rode through the gates to retake their capital. The Ackar and Lett troops started to move forward to try to stop the attack through the city, but as the horsemen rode into the city their place was taken by rank upon rank of Kermin and Amina foot soldiers, flanked by more of the Aramin archers.

From the city walls it was clear to Melnar that further resistance would simply bring more death. He ordered a white flag to be flown from the city ramparts, and on seeing this signal the troops which were backed up between the walls and the river lowered their weapons.

When it became clear that the enemy had surrendered, Silson, the Duke of Amina, raised his helmet and beckoned Melnar down to meet him. As Melnar approached, the Duke raised his sword to strike down his enemy, but Coran stepped between them. "We have won the city and the plain today, and enough blood has been shed," he said. "Lord Melnar, you are free to go, but only if you lead the troops of the tyrant Dewar back to Tufle and take your invaders back across the Middle Sea to Anelo and their own lands."

Melnar had little choice, although he did not look forward to meeting the Dewar, who he knew would shortly arrive in Anelo to oversee the transport of the cannon across the sea. The hidden paths were raised from within the city and the forces of Ackar and Lett made a sorry procession back towards the sea, flanked by Doran cavalry and Cameron troopers.

A short distance from the port of Tufle, the invading forces had attempted to make crude ramparts in front of the port's defensive walls. Coran rode slowly beside a walking Melnar as they approached the defences. Keeping a safe distance back, Coran allowed Melnar to walk into the port and tell the defenders that they must leave Amina within the week or the coalition forces would seek further revenge on the invaders.

Tufle, sitting at the mouth of the Amin, was the main port for Amina and had been the original disembarkation point for the Dewar's invasion. Still moored in the port were many of the transports that had carried the invaders across the sea in the summer. In addition several of the small, fast war boats that were used to carry messages from Amina to Anelo and on to the Dewar in Boretar rode at anchor in the harbour.

For the next few days, the transports ferried the defeated army back across the Middle Sea. Fearing a meeting with the King, Melnar commissioned one of the war boats to take him to Cire on the southern coast of Ciren, from where he hoped to take the short journey to Tora in Toria where his son Orimir was Governor.

Melnar never completed the journey. Having arrived in Ciren he was taken prisoner by Ciren freedom fighters a short distance from the city. He was a known and important Lord, and his captives hoped he would command a significant value in gold as ransom. From his captives Melnar learned that the resistance in Amina had sparked flames of independence across the southern lands of Toria, Ciren and Arance. The resistance was sporadic and not well coordinated, but the unrest was spreading and the Dewar's control in these southern lands was now often only maintained by force of sword.

The meeting of the commanders in Tala had just finished when Ala Moire felt a warmth from the pendant at his neck. He turned to James Cameron and lifted it. Each brother wore a simple pendant with only the sheaf with five arrows, the Cameron crest etched in the metal. Neither Cameron brother understood how the pendants worked, but their instructions were clear. If they brought the pendant's motif to mind, the charm would warm up and Ala Moire could sense the transmitted thoughts. So it was that Coran let his elder brother know of the success in Amina.

It was now time for the Bala army to make its move, and later that same night Ala Moire passed the pendant to Alastair Munro.

Cameron turned to Ala Moire. "So we have started with success. The first of the snow is starting to fall here and it will shortly cover the rest of Bala. It is time to mobilise. We must have our forces on the move south within the week."

The four great machines embarked from Boretar. They had to be taken around the Tar River and then south through Ackar and Lett. The mounted cannon were very heavy, and although self-powered, the machines could only travel relatively slowly. The smiths of Banora were still learning their craft and could only forge relatively narrow wheels. As a result, if the convoy tried to make too much speed the wheels tended to sink into the ground, which was already wet with the autumn rain.

Oien cut a frustrated figure as he cursed the rain and the slow progress. He knew only too well that success in Amina would depend on the weather. As autumn changed to winter, gales from the east would whip up violent storms and great waves, making passage from Anelo to Tufle impossible or at best extremely dangerous. Fast, slim warships could make the crossing in most conditions, but the cannon would have to be transported across on slow, lumbering transport ships which could not cross in stormy weather.

At the rear of the column rode an angry figure. The

King had ordered that Orridon should ride behind his troopers as a sign of disgrace after his failures in Bala and Banora. Whilst still in command of the Ember Horse protecting the convoy, the proud Horse Lord could barely endure the indignity of riding behind his men and the ugly machines. Each day's travel passed in silence, as the troopers did not even dare look at their Lord, let alone try to converse with him. Oien, at the head of the column, seemed lost in his own thoughts.

The monotony was not broken until the evening rest period, when Oien continued to train the gunners on the use of the cannon. No live practice was held, as Oien had no intention of wasting the othium and salt formulations that travelled towards the rear of the column in horse-drawn wagons. Instead the gunners, as they were now called, went over and over the procedures of loading, priming and working the firing mechanism of the cannon.

It was during one of these practice sessions that Orridon decided he had had enough of riding in the dirt at the rear. Ignoring the King's instructions, he told Oien that he was going to leave the group for a few days to visit his own lands in Ember. Since the death of his brother Elan in the battle at the Pass of Ing, Orridon had been Duke of Ember, but he had never yet visited his own lands in that capacity.

Oien shrugged. He cared little for the Horse

Lord, or whether he stayed or left. He felt the Dewar had been too lenient with the Duke considering his failings in protecting the forges in Banora.

Orridon called Bramdon, a distant cousin and Orridon's current second in command, and instructed him on his responsibilities for the rest of the journey. Orridon said he would rejoin the group before they reached Anelo, but for now he was going to visit his home town of Anua, capital of the Principality of Ember. Without a further word he mounted and rode off to the east, accompanied by two of the Ember troopers.

It was a grey, wet day when Bramdon, riding near the head of the column, noted movement on the plain to the west. A small column of riders was heading in their direction from the borders of Ciren. Bramdon called the Ember Horse to the ready, but Oien stilled him. "These are expected, I think" was all he said.

Slowly two wagons drew into view, accompanied by a group of Ackar cavalry. The two wagons were filled with round polished stones. After the demonstration of the cannon near Boretar, Oien had requested that the Dewar send an order to the quarries in Ciren for additional stone balls for the cannon. These were they.

Oien turned to the Ackar captain. "Only these? I requested at least four wagonloads of stone. Do the rest follow?"

The captain shook his head. "We had five wagonloads, my lord, but on the journey we were attacked twice by Ciren rebels. I lost several men, so I could only properly protect two wagons."

It was then that Oien noted that several of the cavalrymen were injured, although none too seriously. He had expected a trouble-free journey south to Anelo, and this was the first he had heard of the rebel uprisings in the south. He turned to the captain.

"You will now ride back to the quarries and replenish what you have lost. Then return to me in Anelo."

The captain gave a tired salute. "Yes, my lord," he said wearily.

Oien then called Bramdon forward. "We may not have as quiet a trip as I had expected. Stay on full alert, and we need sentries posted around our camp each night."

"Yes sir" was the brief reply. Whilst he would not admit it, Bramdon was terrified by the strange old man.

A couple of days later as the convoy reached the breast of a hill, they suddenly found themselves under attack. A motley bunch of rebels raced out from the trees on either side of the hilltop. The assault was largely uncoordinated and the attackers were relatively easily sent running back to the safety of the trees. Fortunately the rebels seemed to be armed only with swords, axes and spears. Had they had archers in the trees, the situation would have been more dangerous and potentially much more deadly. Bramdon instructed two small groups of Ember Horse to ride along the flanks of the convoy, keeping in sight but being alert for any hint of trouble on the wings.

In the early evening as dusk was setting in and Oien had just called a halt for the day's travel, two of the outriders rode in to warn Bramdon that a larger group of rebels was gathering in the next valley. The scout indicated that the force seemed to be stopping for the night, either to prepare for an attack the next morning or to set an ambush on the next leg of the journey.

Oien smiled and turned to the gunners, who were readying one of the cannon for their usual practice. "Well, I think it is time to see how well your training has come on with some real fire," he said.

The cannon was primed, readied for action and then moved to the hill looking over the next valley. The scout was correct: the group below was gathered round a small number of cooking fires and were settling in for the night. They clearly did not realise how close they were to the convoy. Oien could have instructed the Ember Horse to charge into the valley, but he could not resist trying out his big toy in real combat.

One of the gunners lit the fuse and a fireball of

othium flew out and crashed into the valley some yards from the first of the cooking fires. The explosion incinerated three rebels who were sitting on the perimeter of the camp. The gunners, with many days of practice, were now relatively competent and pulled some levers to raise the angle of the cannon. The second fireball landed near the centre of the camp, with devastating effect. The surviving rebels, shocked by the sudden attack, ran in disarray towards the shelter of the woods, some of them turning into human torches. The third fireball erupted in the woods, tearing down a swathe of trees.

Oien smiled. It had given him great pleasure to wield othium's power once again. He was satisfied. It seemed unlikely that the rebels would come back for more, but none the less he instructed Bramdon to post a stronger guard round the camp for the night. To further enhance their protection, he set othium lamps around the perimeter of the camp. The amber glow from the lights gave the camp an almost otherworldly appearance in the dark of the Arance countryside.

That evening, Oien thought about the situation. The south had been at peace for the last few years, and although the people of Ciren, Toria and Arance had no love for the Dewar, the citizens had prospered as peace had brought more trade to all three countries. The price of that peace, however, was the conscription of half of all young men between nineteen and twenty-four into the Dewar's conscript army. It was a heavy price to pay, and the Dewar's wars in the south and far north seemed remote and of little value to the populations in the three subject countries.

Oien also knew that there had been objections from the nobles that the conscripts were being used as slave labour in Bala and not as soldiers. Maybe this had stirred up more organised resistance. Maybe the Dewar would need to pause in his plans for Amina and Kermin and pacify the uprisings, depending on how widespread they were.

The next morning there appeared no sign of the rebel force, and an inspection of the valley showed only destruction, burnt corpses and devastated woodland. Nonetheless Bramdon kept his scouts out and alert.

The convoy had only just started to move from the overnight camp when a rider came back to report a relatively large group of horsemen heading in their direction. Bramdon readied the Ember Horse, and Oien ordered one of the cannons to be primed. However, as the approaching riders crested a hill, it was clear from the banners that these were cavalry riding in the livery of Ackar and Lett. When the cavalrymen arrived at the convoy, their captain pulled up in front of Oien and Bramdon and explained that he had received orders from the King to ride out from Anelo to find the convoy and ensure it was safely escorted to the port. Clearly the Dewar had been told about the unrest in Ciren and wanted to ensure his precious weapons were not waylaid. The captain also briefed Oien on the fall of Tamin and the retreat across the sea to Anelo. This was a significant blow to the plans for an autumn campaign in Amina and the Alol.

When asked about Melnar, the captain shook his head. The Overlord of Lett had not returned with the troops to Anelo. With no foothold on the Amina coast it would be difficult to safely land the cannon.

Oien sighed. He had waited a long time to regain his power, and still obstacles stood in his way. But he was patient. He could wait till spring again to invade the south and reap the rich rewards of Kermin and the gold of the Doran Mountains.

The captain promised that he and his men would ensure the convoy got safely to Anelo, where the Dewar was expected to arrive in the next few days.

Anua, Orridon's home town, was small but prosperous. The town walls were thick and strong, but although there were many large, luxurious houses, there was no castle. The Principality of Ember had owed allegiance to the Kings of Arance, and Anua did not need major fortifications. When challenged, the Principality relied on the skill and prowess of the proud horsemen of the grasslands, the Ember Horse.

To reach his homeland Orridon had to pass through

Arance, and it was very noticeable that the people of that land did not welcome the Duke of Ember. At overnight stops the three horsemen were ignored by the locals in the inns and taverns by the roadside. Whilst not overtly threatening, the atmosphere was hostile, and the locals talked in whispers whilst the three were present.

When Orridon stopped at a village to get one of the horses reshod, the smith grudgingly accepted Orridon's coin and carried out the work. When Orridon offered more money in return for an explanation of the hostility, the smith drew the Duke furtively into the back of the workshop and spoke to him in a low voice.

"You are not welcome in these parts, my lord," he said. "Our people are increasingly tired of the Dewar and his taxes. That tyrant takes our young men to war but uses them as slaves. Our brothers in Ciren have started to rebel, and word is that Toria is also restless, although Orimir rules with an iron fist there. Here in Arance there is talk, but as yet no action. I think you might find Ember, and Anua itself, may greet your return with coolness."

So it continued for the rest of the journey.

Ember seemed much as it always had, although many of the fields appeared to be untended at a time of year when the farmers should have been ploughing them for winter. At Anua the Duke was welcomed home with civility, if not enthusiasm. In the Duke's absence, Elan's old retainer Letham was administrator for Anua and the Principality as a whole. Letham greeted Orridon more warmly than the people had. He had always had a soft spot for Elan's younger brother, and had known him since childhood. Elan had been a ruthless warrior, but his actions against his own countrymen in the battle of 1290 had left his people with little love for him. It had not helped that Elan had spent most of his life at war with the Dewar armies and passed little time in Ember. Orridon was more of the true bloodline of the Ember Horse Lords and had spent more time in Anua.

Letham largely confirmed the smith's story of rebellion in Ciren, unrest in Toria and rumblings in Arance and Ember. "The people across our lands have been subjected to the Dewar's taxes for ten years, and each year he takes more to fund his wars," he told Orridon. "Across Ember the Dewar also now conscripts fifty per cent of our young men, only allowing a smaller number to train as horsemen. Without our young men the fields get less attention each year. It is worse in Ciren and Toria, I believe. Your older brother is still held guilty in the eyes of many for the subjection of Arance and Ember. Many believe that if we had held the alliance with the King of Arance we would not be now subject to the Dewar's whim. You are being held guilty by association, and also by your position with the King. I know you only have a short time here. Use it to listen to the people before you ride back to the King's army."

Orridon was left to ponder. Elan had been the only southern lord to keep his Dukedom, thanks to his treachery in 1290. Indeed Ember had largely been left in control of its own resources and the Ember Horse were of course important warriors in the Dewar's army. It was news to Orridon that conscripts were now being demanded from the young men of Ember. In Arance, Ciren and Toria the old King had placed overlords from Ackar and Lett to control the subjected countries. Over the years both Dewar kings had gifted land in the territories to the nobility of Ackar and Lett. The local lords were gradually being eroded, with some leaving to move south to Amina and Kermin. As the Dewar's wars raged on more and more taxes were demanded and more conscripts were forced into the Dewar armies, Orridon wondered about his own position; he could still remember his humiliation at having to follow the convoy. Would worse be in store when he returned to the Dewar? He was still, at least nominally, commander of the northern armies and his nephew Idula still commanded in Bala, but his Ember Horse were dispersed, some travelling with Oien, others retained at Boretar to accompany the King to Anelo and the rest in Bala. Part of Orridon's goal in returning to Anua was to add to his own forces, but he had not been informed of the King's increased conscription. This would mean fewer horsemen than he had hoped would have been trained over the past two years.

There was also the old man. Orridon sensed that Oien's alliance with the King was not motivated by a desire to help the Dewar with his conquests but somehow to establish his own power.

Orridon needed time to think; maybe he would need to find a different way in the future.

As Oien and his war machines moved slowly south, more snow was falling in the north. The ground was now white in Tala and snow was building across the plains south of the mountains. With the news of the success in Amina, it was time to move out.

James Cameron, with Alastair Munro riding at his side, led the army through the hidden passageway and out onto the Plain of Coe. Angus Ferguson rode with Alex Cameron in the lead ranks of the Red Cameron. It would be some time before Angus and Elbeth would be able to spend another evening together. All their hopes of maintaining any kind of contact were now pinned on the rings of white gold.

As the army moved onto the plain, the Coelete warriors took the lead. They were well used to travelling in snow, and their teams of Banoran cobs pulled finely-fashioned metal ploughs that moved the snow to the side to enable relatively easy passage for the following horsemen and foot soldiers. The ploughs were a mystery to the people of Tala. They were made from a strange metal, and legend had it that they had been used by their forefathers when they had lived on the plains in the second age. All the people knew was that they had always been in Tala, and each winter they were cleaned and readied to keep the streets of Tala and the roads out from the city passable even in the deepest snow.

If anyone had asked Ala Moire, he could have explained that in the Second Age the snowploughs had been powered with othium and made of a metal which had still not been rediscovered in the Third Age. Somehow the metal had survived the meteorite storms, and had probably been found on the plains by a Coelete raiding party during the Third Age.

As the army moved out onto the plain, a thin, black-cloaked, hooded figure slipped through unnoticed by the Guardians and made his way in the opposite direction along the passageway to Tala. A keen-sighted onlooker might have noticed his oddly-tattooed features. Armon had been fortunate. The assassin would not now have to attempt a hazardous journey over the Coe Mountains.

Cameron's plan was not particularly complicated. He hoped that the winter snow would continue to provide cover as his force moved south towards the Inger Mountains. Whilst the Bala army was of a reasonable size, Cameron knew that it was outnumbered by the combined forces of Ackar and Lett and the conscripts. The movement south would be slow, and he needed their progress to be undetected. He did not want to get to the plain in front of the Ola and find an enemy force in front of him on dry open ground. If the weather held, he hoped to reach the Ola without detection and then deploy his troops. If they were undetected, the plan was for the Red Cameron and the Coelete warriors to make a short, fast insurgence into enemy-held territory. His hope was that the surprise attack would confuse the invaders, allowing the rest of the army free passage across the Ola to retake the northern end of the Pass of Ing, cutting off any retreat. Cameron had two other tricks up his sleeve; John Burnett, and hopefully the birlinns.

In the camps scattered around the foot of the Inger Mountains, the first winter snow was falling. Idula hated these cold winter days in this northern land and wished he could be back in the grasslands of his home in Ember. His uncle had left him in charge of a boring outpost at what felt like the end of the world. With snow now lying on the ground, Idula tried to keep the Ember Horse and the regulars of the Ackar and Lett forces drilled. However it was easiest to keep this training restricted to the lands between the Ola and the Ora, where most of the tents and temporary accommodation were.

Idula understood that winter was a time when armies rested and trained for the next spring's campaign. He largely ignored the conscripts and miners who remained working in the mines extracting the red stone following the instructions of the old man who controlled the red fire. The conscripts were overseen by captains from the Ackar and Lett regulars. The forests to the west were still being harvested for the fires, and the smiths continued to work their forges, creating parts for machines using the drawings that had been left by Oien. Idula was a Horse Lord, and he felt he should be riding free on open grassland; he cared little for the forges or the conscripts, or the smiths and the miners. Ignoring the conscripts would prove to be a mistake.

In Erwick, by letter from a Coelete warrior, John Ewart had been instructed by Cameron on the role his troopers would play in the attacks in Banora. Ewart had a troop of Red Cameron under his command, but this force could only act as a support unit in the Cameron plan. The birlinns would be crewed again by Galbraith and some of the young men from Erwick. A number of the men from Erwick were also prepared to fight and had been taught how to use the Banoran bow proficiently. The birlinns were to travel to the mouth of the Ora. The troops would then hopefully move undetected along the northern bank of the Ora to the bog area that lay in the narrow land between the Ora and the Ban. As well as the men from Erwick, Ewart had two men from Banora, Gareth and another Coelete warrior. These would be the guides through the bog, assuming that the boats made their journey safely. Winter was not a time to travel carelessly on the Greater Sea. Wild storms from the west would bring huge waves crashing into the coast of Bala. The helmsmen would need to hold the boats close enough to the shore to keep position, but far enough away to avoid being swept onto the rocks. Landing at the mouth of the Ora could be equally treacherous. The Ora had been selected rather than the more northerly Ban, as the mouth of the Ora was much wider and hopefully the birlinns could find shelter inland on the river bank.

John Burnett had travelled many miles in the late summer and early autumn. He travelled dressed as a modest merchant and hoped he could explain his journeys, if asked, by saying that he was travelling through the lands trying to develop his wine business in Erbea. Erbea was close enough to the Bala border to explain his accent. However, despite the modest dress Burnett had to travel mostly by night and rest during the day. Had he been captured by any of the

Dewar's men or his spies, he could be a real danger to the Cameron and the army hidden in and around Tala.

Burnett travelled through Toria, Ciren and Arance, meeting with those nobles who had remained in their own lands. He carried a letter from James Cameron stamped with the sheaf of five arrows motif. The Cameron was well known by the nobles, as in many cases he had fought beside them in the wars of conquest. If he was not recognised in person, he was certainly known by reputation. Showing the seal to each lord guaranteed an audience. The letter explained the situation in Bala and Banora and the threat of Oien and the red stone. It also encouraged the locals to start to rebel against the Dewar and regain independence for their countries. The letter had provoked the recent uprising in Ciren and begun the unrest in Toria and Arance. Cameron knew from his spies, who liaised with Burnett, that his man had met with most of the targeted locals. However he had not heard from Burnett for a few weeks, and Cameron could only hope that he had made it safely back to Banora.

The Assassin had taken shelter from the snow on the lower slopes of the Coe Mountains, and was surveying the high mountain above to assess how to cross it as the snow built on the higher ridges. Armon's home was in the high Doran Mountains, so he was well used to difficult mountain travel in winter. The Coe however were a different proposition, and the Doran had never felt this cold in winter. Despite Oien's insistence that the task at hand was urgent, Armon was increasingly feeling that a mountain crossing might not be feasible until spring.

He had been intrigued by the small band of tall warriors he had slipped past on the plain below the foot of the mountain. They seemed to be the only people on the plain, and they somehow seemed oblivious to the snow and the cold. Despite his wide travels, he had never before seen these people and they had never, as far as he knew, been on any Assassin contract.

Armon's ponderings were interrupted by a faint thundering sound, as if many feet were tramping towards him through the rock. His choice of shelter, in a cleft in the rock just above the entry to the hidden passage through to Tala, was fortunate. He slipped deeper into his fold in the rock as below him the grey slabs moved apart and the Bala army, led by James Cameron, emerged onto the plain.

Armon was faced with a dilemma. Was the man he was targeting with this force, or was he still on the other side of the mountain – and what lay there? He had to choose, and silently he slipped inside the entrance to the passageway into the mountain. He was thankful for his black cloak and hood, for against the black rock of the passageway he was as good as invisible. As the last of the foot soldiers moved into the passageway, Armon slipped out unnoticed into the Hidden Lands.

Like all assassins, Armon's first priority was to find shelter unobserved. Instead of turning towards Tala, he climbed a short way up the mountain to find a cave that was relatively hidden and out of the bitter wind and snow. From his hiding place he looked out over to Tala, and was impressed. The walled city, carved from the raw rock of the mountain, made his own cave community in the Doran Mountains seem no more than a cluster of peasant's hovels. The Assassin were rich with wealth gathered over hundreds of years, but their numbers were always few and whilst the interiors of their cave dwellings were richly adorned in gold, they were served by rough paths rather than streets. Tala was a magnificent, full-scale city.

From his vantage point Armon could see the gate into the city and make out the guards, tall warriors like the group he had seen on the plain. Armon was skilled at passing through city gates unnoticed as he had done to meet with Oien in Boretar, but this was completely unknown territory and an unknown people.

He searched the slopes around him and noted a ridge from which it should be possible to drop down onto the city walls. With snow and ice underfoot it would be a tricky traverse, but probably safer than trying to walk through the city gates undetected.

The grey skies quickly darkened this far north, and night has always been the ally of the assassin. Armon used the fading light to pick his way along the ridge, hoping that his black clothing would help him merge with the black rock, although it seemed unlikely that anyone would be observing the mountain. He knew that once he got to the point where he could drop onto the city wall, he would need to take more care. He had not considered an escape route; in general an assassination, if successful and quickly discovered, caused enough commotion to ensure that getting out was easier than getting in.

Concerned that the falling snow that had begun to gather on the ledge would make him more visible, Armon observed the movements in the city for thirty minutes and then moved back to his cave. It was clear that the city was relatively quiet on this winter night. A few folk passed down the streets and the occasional guard moved round the walls, but this was clearly a place that had little fear, day or night. One thing the night venture had confirmed was that it was possible to get to the city wall from the ridge. It was a short jump over a relatively small gap. Another observation was that not far from where he would land on the wall, slightly further up the mountain, was what appeared to be the royal palace. Armon observed the guards round the palace and the many lights that burned in the windows. Completing any contract successfully required time to observe the target and the surroundings. His cave was well chosen, with a deep recess at the rear where he could light a fire to keep warm. Melted snow would ensure that he did not go thirsty, and the occasional animal or bird visitor to the cave or the ridge could provide food. Armon decided to wait and observe for a couple of days before deciding how best to make his move. He still had some concern that his target had moved out with the forces that had left for the plains, but if that was the case he would need to find a way back through the mountain and follow in the army's footsteps.

CHAPTER THIRTEEN

A Killer in the Night

Oien and his convoy reached Anelo a day before the King himself arrived. Thanks to the protection of the Ackar cavalry, there had been no more incidents during the remainder of the journey to the port. But the King, when he arrived, was apoplectic with rage. On his journey south his retinue of King's Guard had twice been attacked by Ciren rebels. The attacks had made little impact on the well-trained and well-armed mounted force, and although a couple of the guard had been wounded they had inflicted much more damage on their attackers.

When Oien was called to the King's presence, he

found the Dewar surrounded by the captains who had led the armies in Amina. The commanders of the King's Guard were also present.

"Where is that incompetent fool Melnar?" was the first demand. No one knew, so the King focused his rage on Melnar's captains. Two of these unfortunates were executed on the spot by the guard commanders. From the rest of the terrified group the King learned all the details of the loss of Tamin and the subsequent retreat. All the captains were demoted back to the ranks, glad to escape with their lives, while members of the guard were given command of the troops. Timon, commander of the King's Guard, was given overall responsibility for the army.

Oien had remained at the back of the room as the story of the loss of Tamin was retold. Finally the King dismissed the assembly with a wave of his hand and beckoned Oien to join him and Timon.

"The cannon are safely delivered, I presume?" was the King's first question. Oien nodded. The Dewar turned to Timon. "Your opinion? We have a peasant uprising in Ciren, unrest across Toria and Arance and we have lost our base in Amina. We have at best a few weeks to regain a foothold in Amina, or we could turn our forces towards the rebels. What do you suggest?"

Timon was well used to dealing with his King and his rages and had largely held his position through his calm in dealing with crises. "My Lord, I have seen at first hand the power of Oien's machines and these would be wasted on the rebels in Ciren," he replied. "It is unlikely that the upstarts can form a well-led, coherent force and so I suggest we have a small cavalry force from Boretar ordered into Ciren to confront that rebellion. The bigger prize is Tamin, and that is where the weapons must be deployed."

Oien coughed. "Your assessment is correct, Timon, but you forget two things. One is that the Middle Sea becomes nigh impossible to cross in large barges in winter, and the other is that there is now no land-based foothold in Amina. My sources tell me Tufle has now been reinforced and any re-invasion there would take more force than we can bring together across the sea. I am as keen as anyone to conquer Amina and gain the riches that lie beyond the Alol, but I fear that winter will overtake us, so I advise that we focus first on pacifying the rebel states on our borders. These are easier targets for winter action. Amina will wait for the spring."

The Dewar crashed his fist onto the table, "Weak and feeble old man, I had those lands in the palm of my hand until that fool Melnar fell asleep in the Tamin Palace!" Amber sparks radiated threateningly down Oien's staff and the Dewar forced himself to calm down. He could order his forces, but he could not afford to pick a fight with the old alchemist.

"Oien, your points are well made, but I believe we

still have enough time before winter weather hinders us," he said in a more conciliatory tone. "In 1299 we did not have a large enough force to take the enemy head on with a landing in Tufle, so we crossed the Middle Sea by hopping to Elat and then Lat and on to land in Amina near Slat, which was not defended. Your trebuchets, with a small force of our army, made the same crossing this spring. I believe we have enough of an army here with transports to make a run down the coast, crossing via the islands and establishing a beachhead on the coast near Slat. If we can land sufficient men and the cannon at Slat, we could at least force the enemy out of Amina and back into the Kermin Alol. We can then pause to let the winter pass whilst more of your precious red stone is delivered, and then we can move again into the Alol with the power of the red fire."

Oien held back his irritation at the King's stubbornness. Whilst anxious about the wisdom of the plan, he had to admit to himself that more than anything he needed to win the south to get the Doran gold that would buy him his own army and enable his own global conquest to begin.

"We will follow your plan, your majesty," was his rather tongue-in-cheek reply.

The harbour at Anelo was packed with troopships and longboats. Some were on the docksides, while others rode at anchor in the bay where the long stone breakwaters held back the worst of the winter storms from the Middle Sea. Small, fast war boats were still shuttling out of the harbour to cross to Amina to drop off and pick up the King's spies. Larger craft lay in the harbour; these had transported the invaders across the sea in the summer and had carried the remains of the retreating army back from Tufle to the safety of Anelo a few weeks before. Dwarfing the other boats were six large transporters that had recently been completed in haste in the shipyards of Olet, the main port of Lett on the Greater Sea. The design for these had been sent to the Dewar whilst Oien was building the cannon in Banora. These vessels needed to be large enough and strong enough to carry the four cannon, the iron and stone balls, the othium and salt supplies. The ship builders in Olet had been working day and night to complete the vessels. The six transporters had left Olet a few days earlier and had clung close to the coasts of Toria and Ciren as they made their slow way to Anelo. They had arrived on the same day as the King rode into the port.

Ramon of Lett, the commander of the fleet, was a seasoned sailor who had commanded the troop ships in the summer invasion of Amina. He was concerned about the vessels. Whilst the design was in principle fit for purpose, the shipwrights had cut corners to build and sea-trial the vessels within the short time available. The hulls were not as deep as the design specified, and there had been no time to fabricate the iron keels that were part of the design. To compensate for this the builders had loaded stones into the hulls. This improved the stability of the vessels to a degree, but meant that even unloaded they sat a little too low in the water. Ramon was also concerned that although the trip to Anelo had been uneventful the vessels were too unsteady in anything but a gentle sea.

When Oien inspected the ships, he discussed the commander's concerns and shared them. Again he tried to persuade the Dewar that the autumn offensive was too risky and the heavy cargos could be lost if a storm blew in as the ships tried to make the crossing to Elat. Again the King insisted that the attack force must be made ready to travel in the next few days.

Anelo became a centre of frantic activity as the troops prepared themselves for war with practice outside the city walls. In the port the troop ships were being readied; many smaller longboats that could carry forty soldiers each, together with a number of larger troop carriers would be the first wave of attack to create a beachhead near Slat. The large transports were being loaded with the cannon and the ammunition. The plan was that these would make their way along the Arance coast and make a short leap across the Middle Sea to Elat and Lat. There were no ports on these islands, but on the eastern sides of both there were large bays with deep water where the transporters could shelter from any storm, and once the army had established a beachhead, the transports could quickly deliver their cargo to join the invasion. The gunners would travel with their weapons.

As the cannon were loaded onto the decks of the transporters, Oien and Ramon again shared their concern about how low the ships sat, even in the calm waters of the harbour. Once the beachhead had been established, Oien and the King would follow the army in a larger fleet of longboats and troopships to reinforce the first wave of the attack.

Oien fretted, torn between his desire to capture the southern lands and his concern that the transporters were increasingly overloaded. He wished he had had more time with the smiths in Banora to train them in the use of other metals. Had he had the othium-powered lasers of the Second Age, the weight on the ships would not have been a problem. Indeed these devices could fire from a ship's deck to clear landing areas. This was not going to be possible with the heavy and unwieldy cannons.

In Tamin, Coran also had spies shuttling across the sea. He knew of the arrival of the cannons and the King and the preparations for another invasion. Tufle's sea

defences had been significantly enhanced following
the port's recapture from Melnar's retreating army.
It seemed unlikely that a direct attack at the port
would succeed and it was agreed that the likely point
of any invasion would repeat the landings of 1299,
and the recent spring, near Slat. Coran's commanders
encouraged him to send a large force west towards
Slat so that any invasion could be pushed back into
the sea.

Coran was undecided. He knew that a large force
would be arriving, and whilst it might be stalled, he
was not certain that a landing could be prevented.
Instinctively he felt that defence was the best form
of attack. Winter was coming, and the progress the
invaders could make was limited. If necessary he
could yield Tamin again and retreat to the Alol, where
the defenders could easily hold out over winter. If
his brother could win in the north, the Dewar and
his armies would be forced to decide whether to win
north or south, or lose one or the other or both.

The other commanders of course knew nothing of
the movement of the Cameron army in Bala. Coran
decided to deploy some of the Red Cameron, a troop of
Doran Cavalry and Darmon with a cohort of Aramin
archers. Coran's orders to Ishca, who would lead
the force, were simple: do not engage in fixed battle,
simply harass the enemy as they land, and if they do
establish a foothold on the beaches, try as best you

can to slow down their progress inland. Coran added, "Ishca, I want you back here with most of these men, no heroics. All you need to do is to slow them down so that if necessary we can move back to the safety of the Alol and regroup over winter." Ishca nodded his confirmation.

Armon had waited and watched. If his target was still in Tala, then he must be in the Palace. Now sure of his footing, despite the snow, he crossed the narrow ridge as he had done each night to make sure of his footholds. A short drop from the ridge and he was on the city walls. With his black cloak and hood, the assassin was almost invisible in the deep darkness of Tala.

He could only guess which direction to take, but towards the Palace seemed the best bet. He reached a point on the walls that was better guarded than the lower reaches and had to constantly slip into the shadows to avoid detection. His choice was rewarded, however, when looking out from the wall he observed an old man in white talking in earnest to a beautiful young lady. Armon watched as the girl left the room and the old man returned to the letters on his desk. He knew he had found his target; this must be Ala Moire.

He dropped down from the city walls onto the balcony of the room. Then, like a ghost, the assassin slipped through the open window, his skilatu in his hand. Ala Moire detected the change in the breeze through the window and turned, but it was too late. Armon drove the skilatu into the old man's back, close to the heart.

Ala Moire let out a scream of agony, but as he fell he released a flame of white from his open hand. Armon was engulfed in a white brilliance and experienced a pain he had never felt before in all his dark life. His black robes fell to the floor, and the tattoos on his face faded to grey. Then Armon dissolved in a sheet of white, gone to join his ancestors.

Elbeth, who had only just left the room, heard the scream and rushed back to the scene. She saw Ala Moire slumped over his desk, and behind him an empty black cloak. In desperation she tried to revive the old man, but it was too late. There was only one thing she could do now. She covered her ring with her left hand and pictured the scene in her mind; she hoped the picture would get through to Angus.

Out on the Plain of Coe, the Bala army was camped. The white tents hid the camp from anyone, unless they rode into the middle of it, and the sentries would have seen to it that no one got that close. It should have been a cold, wet and uncomfortable night for the soldiers, but each had been given a small white stone which when rubbed generated glowing warmth.

Cured meat and fish were the evening meal, and the soldiers found that if they gathered their stones together it was almost like having a camp fire without the give-away smoke and flame.

Suddenly Alastair Munro felt the emblem at his neck glow with an unexpected heat. Ala Moire had not instructed his pupil on how to use the white gold medallion, but instinct overcame hesitation. Alastair put his hand on the pendant and immediately felt Ala Moire's strained thought. "Alastair, my time has come, and with a glad heart I return to my God. It is far too long since I walked the streets of the City of Gold, but now I can return knowing that my work is done and you can finish the task set by our master."

Munro had no way of replying. He could only let out a cry of despair and collapse onto the wet snow.

When Angus Ferguson sensed the images from Elbeth, he immediately rushed across to Alastair Munro's tent. Even as got there, the white sparks emanating from Munro told him that somehow his friend already knew what had happened.

It was a few days later when Sulux and some of his tribe rode into Tala on their reindeer. Anaton of the Coelete seemed to understand what Ala Moire would have wished. He greeted the herdsmen as if they were royal guests, which in many ways they were. Sulux and his people were fulfilling their part of the old legend, that the man dressed in white, who had saved them from destruction in the Second Age, would one day return to Esimore.

So the next day, despite the snow and cold, Sulux and his tribe left Tala with the body of Ala Moire. The procession of the reindeer was accompanied by a cohort of Coelete warriors led by Anaton himself. At the edge of the waste lands, Anaton and the Coelete warriors raised their spears in salute as Ala Moire's body journeyed back to be buried in Esimore. In a different place his soul had already found peace in the golden streets of the land his God had promised him for so many long years.

The following morning Alastair told James Cameron what he knew of what had happened in Tala. Angus, through Elbeth, knew a few more details. Cameron sighed. He knew that the black cloak and the knife could only mean one thing; Ala Moire had been murdered by a paid assassin. Only the old man Oien or the Dewar had the reach and the money to hire one of the black-cloaked men from the Doran Mountains.

Alastair had come to a similar conclusion, and during the night he had let his pain and sorrow ferment into a cold rage. Cameron noted that the other man had somehow taken on a white halo round his body. He had seen that same halo before when Ala Moire acted. The old man had briefed the Cameron, but none the less the great warrior was now slightly in awe of Alastair Munro.

During that day the Bala army made good progress, considering the weather and the snow-covered ground. The Coelete warriors seemed hardly to notice the snow as in small groups they covered the ground ahead of the army to ensure there was no surprise attack or unexpected meeting with enemy forces.

That evening, as the army again rested in camp, Alain of Lorn approached Cameron. "My lord, the scouts tell me we are now only about two hours' march from here to the bridges and fords over the Ola. The scouts confirm your spies' reports that most of the enemy are based around the foot of the Pass of Ing, with their tents and shacks lying largely between the Ola and the Ora. There appear to be little in the way of defensive lines or barriers. My guess is that for most of the year the Ember Horse ride the plains and any threat would be noticed. The Dewar army would assemble for open battle on the Plain of Coe with the river and the Inger Mountains protecting their flanks and rear. It seems there is no anticipation of a winter campaign, as you correctly surmised."

Cameron called together his captains to go over the plan of attack. The men gathered round Cameron's tent, glad of their own white stones. It had been ordered from the outset that despite the cold no fires would be allowed within the camps. As each man arrived, he placed his stone onto a pile placed on a piece of ground cleared of snow. The stones gave a glowing warmth, but still the men gathered their winter cloaks tightly about them.

When Alastair Munro joined the group, he went over to the stones and waved his hand over them. The soldiers were astonished to see the glow increase, while the white radiance reached out to warm them as well as any fire could have.

The battle plan outlined by Cameron was simple, relying, as his brother had at Tamin, on surprise rather than strategy and tactics. Hoping the heavy cloud cover and the light snow would continue to hide their approach, he planned a fast insurgence. The Red Cameron would cross the Ola in three places, across the main bridge in the centre and the fords to north and south. They would be led by Alex Cameron, Angus Ferguson and Davy Scott. Each troop would consist of one hundred and fifty men, while fifty from each troop would remain in the rear with James Cameron and Alastair Munro. If the Red Cameron charge created the havoc intended, then Idula would be desperately trying to rouse his troops to defend their ground. The Coelete archers would line up along the banks of the Ola and despatch their long arrows into the centre of the encampment. Duncan of Coe would take the Banoran horse into the lower

Inger Mountains and use his bowmen to cut off any retreat back over the Pass of Ing. In the hope that Idula would have little option but to pull his forces back towards the narrowing between the rivers and the bogland, the Bala foot soldiers and the Coelete would march over to gain control of the central area.

A key part of the plan was to free the Ember horses from their paddocks on the north of the camp area. Davy Scott and his troop had been given this job. One unknown factor was the conscripts, who were mostly living in humble dwellings around the forest edges and lower Inger to the south of the Ora. Cameron hoped that Idula would see the Red Cameron attack as coming from a relatively small force, seek to get his men to horseback and lead his troops to cut off the attackers' return back over the Ola to regroup with the main force. Cameron could only hope that John Ewart, his troop and the men from Erwick had managed to land and were coming to help their comrades. The army would move out at dawn.

Despite living in one of the best of the cabins that had been constructed at the foot of the Pass of Ing, Idula rose in his normal foul mood. He was used to open grassland and being able to ride free with the wind in his hair. In this godforsaken landscape the grey cloud never seemed to part and the snowfall seemed endless. It would be another grey day, he thought as he left the cabin. For him and his men, it was in fact going to be a very bad day.

Idula heard the horses a moment before he saw the Red Cameron charging towards the buildings. His shouts raised the troops nearest to him and a loud horn blast from a nearby cabin raised the alarm, but it was too late. The Red Cameron raced through the settlement, and now proficient with the Banoran bow, they did not need to engage with sword and lance. Ember troopers grabbed whatever weapons they could and raced for their mounts, but Davy Scott was there first and as the Ember horsemen approached the enclosures their horses were charging towards them in panic. Scott's troopers had lit fires in the horses' straw. Slowed by the onslaught of the horses, the Ember troopers started to drop as long arrows hissed through the falling snow.

A small number of the Ember Horse managed to gather their mounts, and with others on foot they formed a defensive wall round Idula, but with the Coelete arrows raining down the only option was to move back from the river. As they did so, Idula saw the first of the Bala foot with their long pikes start to move forward to cross the river.

Idula despatched riders to cross the Ora and get the conscripts ready to march. The remaining main force of Ackar and Lett regulars had their tents and shacks around the forges to the west, where at least fire was always available. These men had been alerted by the commotion further east of their position, and they were well-trained and well-armed soldiers. The Red Cameron raced past the forges, despatching the smiths and other workers who were only now rising to attend to their furnaces. Despite the surprise of the attack, the Ackar and Lett infantry quickly organised themselves into a defensive formation with sword and pike.

As Angus and Alex Cameron turned their Red Cameron cohorts round, close to where the rivers constrained the land at the entrance to the bog, they saw the now well-armed Ackar and Lett units coalesce and form a steel wall blocking any retreat. The Cameron troopers were now short of arrows, and whilst they could attack the defenders with sword and lance, that was a much more dangerous ploy. As they reined their mounts to a halt they hoped that the Bala foot soldiers would fall on the rear of the enemy. Angus of course knew the routes through the bogland, so there was an alternative plan for retreat.

As he and Alex hesitated, long arrows whistled over their heads to land with deadly accuracy in the defending wall. John Ewart and his troop emerged from the bogland with Gareth and the other Coelete warriors, still firing arrows into the enemy. The men of Erwick, including Galbraith, had travelled from the birlinns with bag upon bag of short Banoran arrows.

So the tide turned. With the arrival of Ewart's force and rearmed, the Red Cameron were again in command. The riders in their distinctive white, red and blue livery now raced in rows across the front of the Ackar and Lett force, and despite the tall shields held in the front row and over the heads of those to the rear, many of the Banoran arrows hit their targets.

Idula reached the two commanders of the Ackar army near the rear of the shield wall and urged them to order their men to march out to attack the Cameron horse. That was easier said than done, as each attempt to move forward was met by more arrows. Almost immediately the rear of the defenders came under assault from the long arrows of the Coelete, and behind the hail of arrows the pike and sword formations of the Bala army were closing in.

Idula looked hopefully to the south, praying that someone had roused the conscripts to join the battle. With them his forces could outnumber the attackers. Idula thought his prayers had been answered as the conscript forces appeared on the banks of the Ora and looked ready to engage, but then he saw that at their head was a tall man dressed in the livery of the Red Cameron.

The conscripts marched across the ford and engaged the relatively undefended flank of the defenders. John Burnett had succeeded in his mission. With forces attacking them on three sides and hemmed in by the rivers, the Ackar and Lett commanders decided that they could not win the day, and forfeiting their men's lives for this desolate land would be a waste. Horns blew the call that all armies hate to hear; the call to lay down arms. The forces of Ackar and Lett were professionals, and on the call their shields were lowered and their weapons placed on the ground. The Bala armies moved back a little, but held their position ready to engage if the call should prove to be some sort of trick.

Idula ranted at the two Ackar commanders, telling them that he was in overall command and the surrender order should only have been given by him. The two soldiers shrugged and walked away. The young man might have been handed command, but he had clearly shown he was not fit for the job. Idula rounded on the small troop of Ember Horse who were with him and sent two of them to find a way south to inform his uncle of the loss of Banora. With the rest of the troop, Idula hoped to make his escape up through the Pass of Ing, fighting his way through if need be.

The troop raced across to the edge of the Ora a short way south of the conscript forces, who showed no appetite for trying to stop the fast-moving horsemen. Cutting east through the foothills of the mountains, he made for the foot of the Pass.

Suddenly a volley of arrows hissed from the sides of the pass and three horsemen fell to the ground. In front of Idula, Duncan of Coe led out a cohort of the Banoran archers mounted on their sturdy cobs. Idula knew his own steed could easily outrun the small horses, but to get through he would need to avoid the arrows. He knew of course what had happened to his uncle Elan when he had faced these tough men of Banora. With no options left, he dismounted and ordered the rest of his remaining horsemen to do the same.

The Coe rode down towards the now dejected Horse Lord, his bowmen still ready to loose another flurry of arrows. Idula was remounted on one of the cobs and his men walked behind, leading their horses back to the Bala base camp, where James Cameron waited.

Cameron, Alastair Munro and the reserve troop of Red Cameron looked down onto the battlefield from a small rise on the Plain of Coe a short distance from the crossing points on the Ola. The low cloud and constant light snow had obscured Cameron's view of the events below, but riders from the reserve had constantly ridden back and forth with updates on the unfolding battle. Cameron knew the day was won, and was relieved that the birlinns had made it safely in time to join the fray.

More crucial was Burnett's mission in persuading the conscripts to change sides. The conscript armies were formed of battalions by country, Toria, Ciren and Arance. Each battalion was subdivided, with each unit under the command of a local junior noble, a sergeant, and overseen by regular captains from the Ackar forces. The sergeants owed their allegiance to their local lords, who in turn had bowed the knee to the Dewar. In Banora the conscripts had been used mostly as slave workers in the mines, forges and forests, and the sergeants had been plotting rebellion for months but had not dared to rise up against their Ackar masters for fear of the consequences to their own lords and their families in their homelands. Burnett had managed to infiltrate the conscript camps with letters from their homelands giving the sergeants instructions to rise up against their masters under Burnett's command. As the fighting had started in the main camp, the sergeants and their men dealt with the captains either by executing them or imprisoning them. Burnett led the forces forward to bring closure to the battle for Banora.

As Idula and the Ackar commanders waited for an audience with Cameron to learn their fate, Alastair Munro turned to James Cameron. "What now? We have won a battle here, but much of Bala still lies in enemy hands."

Cameron nodded. "In the morning we will march the army over the pass and into the Plain of Aldene. I am told the Ing is still passable, but we have little time before the winter snow blocks the passage.

I am hopeful that news of our victory here will not travel quickly south and surprise may still be on our side once we cross over the Inger. We will take the prisoners with us. Whilst this will mean a constant guard over them, without their weapons they will hopefully not cause us a problem. As we march south they will make us appear a much larger force, and that will hopefully dissuade any enemy force from attacking us."

Munro nodded. "I hope the snow and cloud will have broken in the morning so that I can climb into the Inger and look over Banora before we move to the south."

Alastair Munro rose before dawn and was pleased to see stars in the sky as the snow clouds dispersed. From his position at the foot of the mountain, he could see red bursts of fire spouting from fissures in the rock face. As he had done once before in what seemed like an earlier lifetime, he climbed up the slope. Halfway up the mountain he left the main path and walked beside a narrow stream before turning up the slope again. A few minutes later, he crested a narrow ridge and sat down.

It was on this spot that he had first spoken with Ala Moire, and the thought brought tears to his eyes and anger to his heart. The view over the Greater Sea was still spectacular, but below him the red fires seemed to be consuming the mountain. Further below, the Banora forest looked like mighty scythes had cut their way through the trees. In the farmlands and round his own home the forges still burned, fuelled by the wood from the forest and the red othium fires. The small farms that had been the homes of his neighbours were now merely part of the large camp area. His beloved homeland had been destroyed by the invaders.

As the sun rose over the eastern Inger, the sky seemed to reflect the fires springing up from the mountain, burning with amber, red, orange and yellow as if filled with the reflected evil of the mountain. The land lay scorched, and Alastair could feel the mountain trembling as he stood there like a pale statue in the dawn light. Anger at the desolation of his homelands rose in him. The white aura that surrounded him still felt strange, but he could feel the intensity of the power building with his anger.

He raised his clenched fist and opened it, and a blaze of clean white light leapt to the sky. A huge concussion rocked the mountain, and all light was quenched. The sky turned black, then cleared and became blue once more. A distant rainbow appeared, as if promising that all was well and God still cared for this lost land. Alastair Munro fell back into the snow-covered heather, all power gone, all anger lost.

Angus Ferguson had awoken to find himself alone in the tent, and had followed Alastair to the mountain. As he saw the light blaze from Munro's hand, he looked down to see the white gold on his own hand shining with a new intensity. Angus was instantly by his friend's side, and waited for Alastair to recover. The pair looked back down to see that all the red fires were gone, and the mountain seemed to have a new peace. The forges were cold and below in the camps people were praying, many on their knees. The land had not been completely healed, but a cleansing had begun. In time Alastair knew that his people would be able to return to their homes and the cycle of life would continue. It might take a generation or two, but the farmlands would be recultivated, the forests replanted and the remains of the enemy occupation obliterated. Alastair knew this with a strange certainty, and in that moment he also knew he would not return to a peaceful farmer's life. His destiny now lay to the south and a confrontation with the old man, his master's enemy.

Ala Moire had tried to hold back the destruction and greed of the Second Age and failed. God had had to intervene. This time Alastair Munro knew he was the instrument God would use, and he could not fail in His mission.

CHAPTER FOURTEEN

Aldene Liberated –
Amina Defended

In Anelo, the army was nearly ready to leave port, and the troop carriers and war boats were preparing to take the landing force over to Slat. Their task was to forge a beachhead to allow the main force and the cannon to safely disembark. These first-wave troops were mainly foot soldiers and archers, with smaller contingents of light and heavy cavalry. The plan, as before, was to land the force on a beach near Slat and then march towards the town, hopefully pushing any defence from the beaches back to the town. This would leave the shore accessible to the following larger forces of cavalry and heavy horse. Timon would be the overall commander of the invading force and would travel with the cannon. Two senior officers from the King's Guard would lead the initial attack at the beach. Oien and the Dewar would leave in the King's own longboat once the beachhead was established.

The cannons, the othium, the salt mixtures and the cannonballs would be carried on the large transport ships. These were powered with both oar and sail, but they would need to hug the coast before making the short hop to Elat and Lat. When the sea was calm, the transports would then cross to the coast of Amina. Once they were loaded with their cargo, Ramon inspected each ship; two of the transports had slipped dangerously low in the water. On further inspection Ramon found that the stone ballast in the keels of these two had moved on the journey from Olet. The ballast would need to be reset before the ships could set sail.

While the King fretted at the delays, Oien worried about the weather. The King decided the transports could not wait on the repairs and the othium, salt of Elat and ammunition were loaded separately onto the remaining four vessels. The ships settled a little deeper in the water, but Ramon could not refuse an order from his King, so he decided that they would set sail. Thankfully the Middle Sea remained calm as the boats moved slowly along the Arance coast towards the Ciren border, where they would anchor and wait for more clear weather before crossing over to the islands. In case there was trouble on Ciren, the transports were accompanied by a reasonable force of Ackar troops in supporting war boats.

As the transports lay at anchor in a sheltered bay off the Ciren coast, a late autumn storm blew suddenly down from the north, making the Middle Sea a treacherous crossing even over the relatively short distance to Elat. On the third morning the weather seemed to be set fair, although the sea was still rougher than Ramon would have preferred. He hoped that with the fair weather it might get calmer as they journeyed over to Elat, so he gave the order to set sail for the islands.

The convoy moved out into the Middle Sea, the war boats with the Ackar troops in the lead and at the rear of the convoy. Elat and Lat were sparsely populated and Ramon did not expect any military challenge, but to be safe Ackar troops would accompany both parts of the fleet to their shelters. The lead transport carried one cannon and the othium, the second another cannon and the salt formulation. The last two transports followed, each with one cannon and the stone and iron ammunition. The plan was for the lead war boat, with Timon on board, and the first two transports to sail beyond Elat and find shelter in one of the many bays on the northern edge of the sister island of Lat. The remaining war boat and the other two transports would shelter at Elat and all would wait for another clear break in the autumn weather to continue to the beachhead near Slat.

Ramon had sailed these waters many times and his captains knew which sheltered bays were their target destinations. The vessels moving to the more distant island of Lat would need to turn slightly further into the Middle Sea to avoid the shallows of the Straits of Elat.

Despite the choppy water, the first part of the journey progressed without problems, and after only a couple of hours the islands could be seen on the horizon. However, with a seaman's instinct Ramon felt the wind pick up and noticed storm clouds beginning to race towards them from the northeast. The gusting wind and the increasing waves started to force the unstable vessels south towards the Western Sea. The slaves at the oars were now being urged by their overseers to pick up pace and push the boats on to the shelters on the northern edge of the islands.

Ramon considered sending an order out for all the vessels to make a run for the shelter of Elat, but as the storm blew in with clouds and rain the flag messages were unlikely to be seen by the lead boats. Silently Ramon cursed his decision to travel in the rear boat rather than the lead one. His decision had been based on his calculations of the speed that could be made in the sleek war boat and he had imagined that if necessary he could overtake the transports to issue specific orders. Timon had also insisted that he should travel on the lead war boat, as he wanted to be first to join his troops on the beachhead. It seemed pointless to have both commanders in the same boat.

As the seas mounted Ramon's boat came alongside the last transport, which was rolling dangerously from the lateral impact of wave and wind. All that was stopping the vessel tipping over was the stone ballast in the hull. In the distance Ramon could make out the outline of the third transport through the rain, but the first and second were hidden by the storm.

The lead war boat had successfully crossed the deeper water and was now turning south to the sheltered bays in Lat. However, on looking back Timon could see that the transports were making little headway against the wind, and the waves were pounding the ships' sides. Both transports were rolling dangerously, close to being swamped by the growing height of the waves. The captain on the first transport carrying a cannon and the othium was increasingly concerned about his vessel's stability. The constant rolling was causing the stone ballast in the hull to move, adding to the instability of the boat.

Unable to make any headway further into the deeper waters of the Middle Sea, the captain decided to try to use the wind and the waves to race south with the elements and reach the north-eastern tip of Lat. He knew the dangers of the shallow straits and hoped to have enough speed to avoid these and make a safe landfall. It was a brave gamble, but he did not know the danger of the cargo he carried. As the helmsman moved the ship round, the wind and waves picked the vessel up like a toy raft and the boat hurtled straight towards the shallows that lay between the islands. As the transport ploughed forward, the stone ballast moved towards the bow of the ship. With the bow now perilously low in the water, the vessel was uncontrollable, and it raced on into the Straits of Elat.

Had a metal keel been fitted, had the draft been deeper, had the cargo been different, the captain might have survived, but as it was he and his ship had no chance. As the vessel hit the shallows, the bow dug into the sea bed. The timbers could not withstand the impact. The front section disintegrated with a loud crunch, and purple-tinged water flooded the stricken vessel. As the water reached the othium stored in the hold, orange flames started to burst through the decking.

The second transport, carrying another cannon and the salt formulations, followed the lead of the first, with similar results, and it hit the sea bed only ten yards from its stricken sister ship. The damage to this vessel was greater, and it was soon submerged by the incoming waves. The salt of Elat stored on the deck began to dissolve and the purple colour in the water deepened as it spread out. As the concentration of salt increased around the first transport, the ferocity of the othium fires became more intense. In a few moments the heat and the salt caused the othium to reach critical level, and a huge explosion blew both transports into matchwood. The blasts grew in intensity as rock after rock exploded.

The impacts of the eruptions bounced off the sea bed and waves of increasing size exploded north from the straits into the Middle Sea. The storms and wind passed on over Elat and headed out to the Western Sea. The waves racing north from the straits started to coalesce and pick up waters from the now calmer Middle Sea. As the wave radiated out towards the shores of Arance and Kermin, it grew to sixty feet high. It had become a tsunami, and it was unstoppable.

As Alastair Munro and Angus Ferguson moved down from the mountainside, the activity below them had started in earnest. The snow had stopped for the moment and it was a clear, crisp early morning. The conscripts were supervising the Ackar and Lett soldiers who were dismantling their camp, whilst the Bala soldiers were tearing down the forges. A Coelete warrior was sent north to inform Anaton of the victory at Banora and request that the Coelete continue to host the refugee peoples of Bala through the winter. In the Hidden Lands the summer and autumn had been spent storing sufficient provisions for the winter, and Sulux had sent more reindeer as a gift in repayment for the warming white stones. The lands to the south were less well prepared for the Bala winter, and Cameron knew that provisioning the army and the captives would be a challenge. He could only hope that the Dewar had Aldene well stocked ahead of the winter and had also left the Cameron capital poorly defended.

By mid-morning the columns were moving up and over the Pass of Ing and descending onto the Aldene plain. From the top of the pass Cameron could look out over his territories, and was pleased to see that no occupying forces appeared to be stationed on the plain. In the far distance was his capital, Aldene. The column stretched back a mile as the Bala army took the front and the rear of the column with the Ackar captives from the battle in the centre, guarded by the now well-armed soldiers from Toria, Arance and Ciren. Having suffered for years at the hands of their Ackar overlords, the newly-free conscripts were not entirely gentle with their captives, but their sergeants, under Burnett's command, had been told that none of the prisoners should be harmed to the extent that they could not march.

On the sides of the column, Coelete warriors under

the command of Alain of Lorn and Gareth ensured that the flanks remained clear of any threat, and Coelete warriors regularly reported back to James Cameron on the land ahead and to the sides.

Many of the Banoran fighters remained in their homeland to begin the task of repairing the damaged land. Duncan of Coe was commanding these troops, which, if it became necessary, would be a line of defence to the rear of the Bala army. Anaton sent additional Coelete warriors south with provisions for the men remaining in Banora. These would defend the heights of the Pass of Ing if defence was needed and would also keep a watch out over the plains. Raised in the cold Hidden Lands, the Coelete seemed mostly unperturbed by the winter winds.

Galbraith and the men of Erwick returned to the birlinns and headed home to see out the winter storms in the shelter of their small town. Angus Ferguson remained with the Red Cameron, who roamed out at will from the marching column to deal with any enemy forces occupying the plain. None were found. Winter was still in its early days in the south of Bala, and whilst a light covering of white lay on the ground the forces made good speed towards Aldene.

Two days later, in early morning sunlight, the force arrived outside Aldene's town walls and the Bala army deployed to surround the town. James Cameron, with some of the Red Cameron troopers and their captains, rode out towards the town gates to hail the town, keeping out of bowshot. "I am James Cameron, Lord of these lands and this is my capital," he roared. "I require those occupying my town to lay down their arms and leave by sundown. If this request is met, then I guarantee your men safe travel south to your homelands. If you do not surrender by the aforementioned time, then you will not leave here alive. Be aware that this is my town and I know ways into the town that are secret both for defence and attack. I will have no need to storm the town gates or walls; you will suddenly find us in your midst in the middle of the night."

The Ackar knight Essen was commander of the occupying troops in Aldene. "I am Essen and I am now Lord of Aldene," he said. "I know you, James Cameron, and I see you have no siege engines or other means to breach the city walls. Winter is coming and you and your men can freeze on the plain for all I care."

Cameron shrugged and rode back to his men. He well remembered the name Essen. He had been told months earlier of the moment the Ackar knight had decapitated his old friend and mentor Gordon Graham. He also feared for the fate of Conall Dalzell, who had remained in his house in Aldene when most of the rest of the people of Bala had travelled north. Cameron doubted that the Elder of Awick would have enjoyed much luxury in Aldene over the previous eighteen months. Now was Cameron's time for revenge.

Aldene was a relatively small town compared to Boretar. Nonetheless it was prosperous and had stout walls and a protective ditch. On the top of the rock promontory at the west of the town was a strong castle and keep. As night fell, Cameron and fifty of the Red Cameron, including Angus, moved on foot to the west of the town, where the promontory fell away in an apparently sheer rock face. Cameron knew from his spies that despite Essen's bold words, he had only a hundred soldiers in the town. Days earlier the remaining townsfolk had been quietly told that their Lord was returning and on a given signal, likely to be after curfew, they were to arm themselves and remove any defenders from the town walls. Then they were to open the town gates to the host gathered outside.

The small track that wound its way up the rock face was narrow and precipitous. It was also well hidden in the wood at the foot of the cliff and by the scrub that grew on the rock. Cameron knew the route like the back of his hand, and by the time the moon rose he had stationed his force in a small thicket hidden by trees a short distance from where the town wall climbed up to join the outer castle wall. Above them, the castle and keep rose menacingly. Whilst the thicket covered the area with thorns, there was a narrow path leading to its centre. There a small pile of stones and a headstone marked what appeared to be an ancient grave. Cameron pushed on the headstone, and to everyone's surprise it moved back to reveal a wooden trapdoor built into the ground. This led to a tunnel through to the castle forecourt. This route from the town had been created generations earlier as an escape route. The mechanism that drove the headstone had been a gift from Ala Moire to one of the Cameron's ancestors.

Cameron took out a large key from his jacket, pushed it into the well-oiled lock and turned it. There was a click and the trapdoor opened. The troopers crept silently through the tunnel and slipped through another concealed door into the lower part of the castle. The central keep was opposite across a small courtyard. There were few soldiers in the area, as most of the defenders were deployed on the eastern town walls ready to repel any attack from the Bala forces camped a short distance from the main town gate. An attack from the western escarpment was not considered possible. The Red Cameron quickly despatched the soldiers in the lower castle and then made their way to the base of the keep.

Essen, who had commandeered the Cameron's own rooms in the keep, woke suddenly as the door was thrown open. His tenancy had been poor, and the once richly-decorated rooms were now a mess of discarded food and other waste. Cameron's fury boiled over, and as Essen leapt from his bed he felt the knife against his throat. In panic the knight shouted, "I surrender, we yield! We'll lay down our arms!" Cameron did not respond. Instead he pushed the struggling knight out onto the palisade that wound round the upper tower.

A Cameron piper began to play the marching tune of the Red Cameron, and on this signal the townsfolk moved out onto the streets. The few occupying forces not on the town walls were quickly disarmed. The citizens were about to attack the guards at the town gates, but Cameron shouted out from the keep, "I told your commander that he could choose life or death. He chose death for all of you. Put down your weapons now and I may still be merciful."

Soon the Red Cameron had cleared the castle ground of occupying soldiers and opened the castle gates. The troopers now began organising the townsfolk into groups to support an attack on the walls. The soldiers opposite the keep could see that their commander was captured, and all around the walls rang out the sound of steel being dropped onto stone. Slowly the town gates opened, allowing Alex and the rest of the Red Cameron force to enter the town.

Essen again pleaded for mercy. "You made your choice," was the reply, "and you chose death. This is for Gordon Graham, the man you butchered." Cameron drew his knife across the knight's throat and let the lifeless body fall to the ground. At the sight of their commander's death the Ackar soldiers knelt down to show that they posed no threat. They were rounded up by the townsfolk and led out to join the other Ackar captives in the camp outside the town walls. James Cameron was now once again in control of Bala's capital.

Some hours later, one of the Cameron troopers returned to inform Cameron that the emaciated body of the Elder of Awick had been found naked in the castle dungeon. Conall Dalzell was identifiable only by the distinctive tattoos he bore on his right arm.

In the quiet of his room in the castle at Aldene, Angus looked out of the window around the town and sent his thoughts through the ring to assure Elbeth that he was safe and that her home had been secured by her father.

During their time in Tala, Elbeth and her stepmother, Eleanor, had become good friends. Eleanor was only ten years older than her stepdaughter and the two shared a similar sense of humour and would often be heard laughing with each other at some observation or joke. Elbeth also knew that her father had not restricted her time with Angus partly because his new wife had intervened. Eleanor had suffered the pain of loss in war when her first husband had been killed in battle. She often reminded her husband how precious love was, and insisted he did not interfere in Elbeth's love affair.

Elbeth was thrilled to receive Angus' message, and although she knew her father would not approve, she decided to return home to Aldene to try to steal some time with her fiancé. Overhearing Anaton instruct one of his chiefs to move south to the Inger to take supplies and reinforcements to the people in Banora, she decided to make her move.

Despite their friendship Elbeth knew her stepmother was unlikely to give her permission to leave Tala, and it was unlikely that Herlock, the Coelete lord who was in command of the force, would agree to support a runaway. However the Coelete were travelling with a small contingent of Banora men on their tough cobs. These would be responsible for riding with the sleds that carried additional provisions south.

So that day, dressed in plain clothes with her hair tied up under her cloak hood, Elbeth mounted the cob that Angus had left with her and joined the Banora men. The snow now lay deep over the plain of Coe, but this did not impede the Coelete or the sleds pulled by the Banoran cobs. Elbeth brought her left hand to her ring and thought about Angus in Aldene, letting him know that she was on her way.

Two days later, Angus Ferguson asked Cameron if he could have leave to go back to Banora to see how the reconstruction of his homeland was progressing. The Cameron agreed, as he had decided that most of the army would see out the winter in and around Aldene. Angus rode north through a brief snowstorm and crossed the Pass of Ing. At the foot of the Pass, Herlock was overseeing the distribution of the supplies and sending some of the Coelete to patrol the higher slopes. Herlock knew Ferguson and greeted him on his arrival, although with some surprise, as he had expected him to be moving south with the army.

Duncan of Coe arrived at the same moment to meet the Coelete warrior and see to the distribution of the supplies, and he was surprised to see Angus talking to the Coelete noble. Angus began to brief the two on the details of the recapture of Aldene, but he was interrupted by a Banoran cob which raced up from the rear of the column. The rider leapt down and raced into Angus's arms.

Angus held Elbeth close for a few moments until a cough from Coe interrupted their reunion. "Elbeth, this is not a place for you at this time," said Coe. "Although Aldene has been retaken, we have no idea of the capacity of the enemy to regroup. Your father would want you to remain safe in Tala until we are sure that you and the other refugees can move back to the homelands."

Elbeth had inherited her father's steel and presence. "My Lord Coe, your concern does you justice and will be reported to my father, but no harm can come to me whilst I am here with my betrothed."

Coe had known the girl since she was a babe in arms and could see her joy at reuniting with her lover. He knew he might be censured by her father when he found out, but seeing the pair together reminded him of the early days with his own wife, and with a pang of regret he remembered that Isobel and his family were still miles to the north in Tala.

"Your father will not be pleased," was all he could say.

Elbeth smiled at the older man, melting any resolve he had to send her back to Tala with some of the Coelete. "My father will be delighted that I have come home when Angus and I journey back to Aldene," she said.

For two precious days under a clear, cold, blue sky, Angus showed Elbeth round his homeland, the forest and the mountains. Whilst the land was still healing, the views from the Inger over the Greater Sea remained breathtaking. The nights were warm as the pair rested in Angus's now extended cottage, which had remained in good condition despite having been occupied by Oien. It was precious time together as their love grew ever stronger.

The blasts from the Straits of Elat were heard in Anelo, and in the far distance the columns of red fire erupting into the sky could just be seen on the horizon. From the colour of the distant flames, Oien knew that some disaster had occurred to the othium transports. He was about to move down from Anelo's castle, where he, the King and the senior commanders were based. He had decided to commandeer one of the fast war boats to quickly take him south, so that he could assess what had happened.

It was just as he reached the castle gate that the tsunami smashed into the port. Still over sixty feet high and moving at great speed, the terrible wave destroyed everything in its path. In the port, the great protecting walls were breached and the vessels in the harbour were swamped. As the wave continued to rush north, it left the Dewar fleet either sunk or smashed to pieces. The Dewar came to the castle gate and looked down to see that the harbour and most of the lower city were under water. Not only was the fleet lost, but many troops had drowned as the wave overwhelmed the low-lying parts of the city. Any chance of an invasion of Amina had gone.

The remaining transports that had sheltered

in the bays in Elat avoided the wave, as they were anchored south of the impact. Similarly the lead war boat, with Timon on board, had sheltered in one of the bays in Lat. However the concussion of the exploding othium caused landslips all around the surrounding area and the resulting lesser waves made survival of these vessels questionable.

Once the sea had calmed, Timon told the captain of the lead war boat to journey back towards Elat to rejoin the other ships. Ramon and Timon conferred. They still had two cannons and a significant number of troops. They decided that if they could reach Slat and support the troops already on the ground, they could perhaps still establish a beachhead and capture the town itself. The two had not considered that the remaining cannons were useless without the othium.

Further north, the tsunami filled the rivers Amin and Mina to levels never previously seen. The Amin burst its banks and flooded all the low lying areas, but Tamin survived, thanks to the height of the city walls. The Mora also rose high, washing the walls of Kermin's great northern city.

In Tamin, Coran looked down from the castle at the great lake now lying outside the city. Without understanding what had happened, he knew instinctively that the Dewar's war machines had run into some sort of trouble. The explosions and eruptions from Elat could be clearly seen from the walls of Tamin. Coran suddenly regretted his decision to send Ishca and a small force to challenge any beach landing. If the troop transports had been destroyed by the explosions and the wave, then a full force of defenders could easily repel a small landing force.

As he pondered his options, the medallion round his neck grew warm. It was Munro, letting Coran know of his brother's success and the liberation of Aldene.

Coran now knew he must act in some way to reinforce Ishca and repel the invading forces. To his surprise he then saw a small boat working its way upstream on the swollen river. The few docks at Tamin were underwater, so the small vessel had to tie up near the city gates.

Coran raced down to interrogate the crew. It transpired that although the port at Tufle had been swamped by the wave, the force of impact had not been too great as only the edge of the wave had struck it. Most of the ships in Tufle remained intact and seaworthy. Coran sent word to Silson to ready as many troops as possible for departure within a day and then leapt onto the small boat and instructed the crew to make an immediate return to Tufle.

Ishca was following his commander's orders. The war boats carrying the first of the forces from Anelo had made landfall on a beach five miles to the south of the town of Slat. Two troop carriers followed, carrying the cavalry and the heavy horse. The Aramin archers greeted the invaders with volleys of arrows, and many of the first wave of Ackar foot soldiers never made it to the beach.

As the archers' supply of arrows ran low, Ishca ordered the Red Cameron and the Doran Cavalry into the attack. The tactic, as instructed, was hit and run. In Amina the Red Cameron did not have the added weaponry of the Banoran bow, so it was classic cavalry attack with spear, lance and sword. The Ackar forces however were well disciplined and the shield wall was established at the beachhead. Weight of numbers eventually told, and the attackers gained enough of a foothold for the following Ackar cavalry and archers to disembark. Ishca ordered his troops to move back behind the defensive positions offered by the sand dunes on the land side of the beach, and as supplies of arrows came from the camp nearer to Slat, the Aramin continued to slow the attackers' progress.

However, under the protection of their shields the Ackar foot soldiers continued an orderly advance up the beach. The Ackar cavalry also started to attack the defensive lines at the dunes, and Ackar cavalry clashed with Red Cameron and Doran horsemen in a bloody dance of horses and men. The Ackar archers began to find their range, and their Aramin counterparts had to pull further back inland. Gradually the beachhead was secured. Content that the first phase had been successful, the Ackar commanders halted the advance to allow the rest of the army to land.

The following morning at Tamin, a flotilla of small craft came upriver. The disembarkation of the troops was relatively slow, as only the area around the city gate still sat above the floodwaters. Even the flooded river Amin was not deep enough for transporters to load cavalry, but a sizeable force of Amina and Kermin foot soldiers was ferried to Tufle to board the larger longboats. More importantly, the remaining Aramin archers were also moved to the coast.

The longboats of the Amina fleet were of a new design. Having suffered two invasions across the Middle Sea, Silson had commissioned longboats with a reinforced prow and a long, metal-tipped, forward-pointing shaft that could be wound out from the front of the boat to ram invading troop carriers. The foot soldiers and the archers had also been trained in the use of the Doran incendiaries.

Coran quickly issued his orders. He would travel on the longboats with most of the archers and some of the foot soldiers, while Silson would lead most of the foot soldiers on an overland march to Slat. Both forces would carry incendiaries. Silson was ordered to get to Slat without delay to reinforce Ishca's force. The boats would sail down the coast to make landfall behind the enemy. Hopefully, between the two forces, the invaders could be stopped.

Slat was a relatively small town and not of any obvious strategic importance, so whilst a wall surrounded it, the defences were not particularly strong. This left Ishca with a problem as his troops retreated back towards the town. The invading force was only slightly larger than Ishca's contingent, but the invaders now had the benefit of having landed heavy cavalry. Ishca had no foot soldiers to make a defensive stand, and whilst the Red Cameron and Doran cavalry could harass the enemy flanks, they could not make a stand for a pitched battle. Even the deployment of the Red Cameron and Doran cavalry was becoming increasingly risky as the arrows from the invaders were increasingly finding their mark.

The Aramin archers continued to slow the progress of the enemy, but the Ackar cavalry were slowly overpowering the defenders. Gradually Ishca had to fall back towards Slat. His choice seemed restricted by his initial orders. He was planning on making a retreat behind the town and back towards Tamin when a Red Cameron trooper arrived with a change of instructions. Ishca had now been ordered to try to hold Slat until Silson could arrive with his force. Falling back behind the town walls was an option, but the walls would only hold back a forced attack for a short time.

From a hilltop two miles from the beach, Ishca watched the Ackar forces falling into order to march towards Slat. The heavy cavalry were being placed in the lead, with the foot soldiers following. A significant number of Ackar troops remained to defend the beach and protect the landing ground for the forces that the commanders hoped would still cross the Middle Sea. Ishca decided that attack was his best defence, so whilst leaving Darmon and the Aramin troops on the hilltop to engage the heavy cavalry as best they could, he led the Doran cavalry in a loop round the main enemy force to attack the troops left defending the beach. Simultaneously the Red Cameron charged into the rear of the foot soldiers assembling to march out through the dunes towards Slat. The tactic had the desired effect, as the Ackar commanders hesitated between continuing the move inland and protecting the landing beach.

Coran was not to know at the time, but the timing of the departure of the Amina boats from Tufle was to land the killer blow on the invaders. As the boats raced south, the lookouts shouted out that several vessels were visible heading towards the coast near Slat. Ramon and Timon were bringing their fleet over from Elat. A heavy swell on the Middle Sea meant that the transports carrying the cannon and the second wave of the Ackar troops were again struggling to make headway towards the Amina coast. The constant rolling of the ships meant that most of the soldiers on board were suffering from sea-sickness and praying for a landfall they would not make.

The Amina longboats quickly closed in on their prey. As the lead Amina boat approached the first Ackar vessel the incendiaries landed in the midst of the enemy boat, causing small fires to break out. These distracted the captain of the Ackar boat and he missed the change in direction of the Amina boat's attack. The ram at the prow of the attacker had been deployed, and the angle of attack took the ram through the rear of the Ackar boat just on the water line.

A similar tactic was used by the two following Amina attackers, but this time on the transports. With their shallow hulls and heavy ballast, together with the weight of the cannon, the transports were highly susceptible to this form of attack. With holes punched in their sterns, the sea quickly flooded in and within minutes each transport was listing severely. Then, with their bows rearing towards the sky, both transports slid under the Middle Sea. The lead Ackar war boat suffered the same fate.

In the rear, Ramon and Timon watched in horror as their fleet sank. Recognising that they were out manoeuvred and outnumbered, Timon gave the order for the boat to turn and try to outpace the attackers in a race back to Anelo. Coran had no time to give chase as the Amina boats raced for the beachhead near Slat.

The soldiers of Ackar on the beachhead had expected reinforcements from Anelo, and they realised too late that the incoming boats were the enemy's. The Amina and Kermin troops, protected by Aramin arrows, quickly formed into their attack units and advanced. The Doran incendiaries caused panic amongst the Ackar forces on the beach, and most of them simply turned and ran to join their compatriots, who were moving off through the dunes towards Slat. These rear troops were constantly being harassed by Doran cavalry, and one of these riders rode over to Coran to inform him of the situation inland.

Ishca could see the change in the formations on the beach and knew it was time to move his force back to continue to draw the enemy away from the beach. As he was about to issue the order, Ishca heard trumpets calling from behind his position on the hill. Silson and his force were now in the valley below and marching in order up the hill. The Ackar commanders were now facing a battle in front and a defence in the rear. The heavy cavalry could make a charge up the hill where the enemy units had formed up, and the lack of foot soldiers would mean that the light horse on the hill would need to disperse.

As they considered bringing the cavalry forward,

Silson's force lined up on the hilltop. A cavalry charge uphill against a well-armed and well-disciplined force of foot with pike and sword was not really an option. If the Ackar force simply moved round the foot of the hill it would be exposed to the faster light cavalry.

Again the commanders hesitated, and were surprised when a force of Red Cameron raced down from the hill. They were now armed with incendiaries, and when these were thrown into the crowded Ackar foot they again caused panic, though few casualties.

The panic spread as the rear of the force also came under sustained attack from Coran's troops. The Ackar forces fled south and north, but they were easy pickings for the Red Cameron and Doran cavalry. Finally the Ackar horns blew the dreaded notes of surrender.

Most of the surviving Ackar knights were escorted to Slat to be held for ransom. A few of the foot soldiers escaped to the south. By the time Coran rode up to join Silson and Ishca, the battle was over and the first heavy rains were starting to fall. Winter had come to Amina.

Ramon anticipated that the port at Anelo would be out of action following the tsunami, so he made landfall at a small beach on the Arance coast. Timon and the Ackar soldiers disembarked and marched for Anelo. Ramon instructed the crew of the war boat to head north-west back to his home port of Olet. The captain thought there seemed no point in volunteering to face the wrath of the King, but Timon had no option, and found the Dewar in the castle at Anelo. Oien was also present. Timon described the disaster in the Straits of Elat and the destruction of the other transports and cannon by the longboats from Tufle. He also described how the Amina forces had landed on the beaches near Slat and said he presumed that the Ackar land forces may well have been defeated.

The Dewar was incandescent with rage at the incompetence of his commanders. Oien said nothing, but his staff started to shed amber sparks as the alchemist tried to contain his anger. Timon was dismissed and left in a hurry, pleased to still be alive after relating his news, but knowing that his future was now highly uncertain.

Once Timon had left, the Dewar turned to Oien. "Well old man, we now have no weapons, no boats, no beachhead in Amina and no othium, and winter storms are sweeping in from the north. I think Amina and Kermin are safe until the spring when we can begin the campaign again. We need to regroup and rearm ready for warmer days. We need more othium and new equipment, so this time we need the mines and forges in Banora to work through the winter. It may already be too late for you to travel back over the Pass, but with your magic I am sure you can find a way."

Oien resented being ordered about by the King, and amber sparks flickered from his closed fists as he held back an angry retort. Yet he knew the Dewar was correct, and he also knew that he could easily journey back to Banora with his othium power and his anger to keep him warm. The King had forgotten to mention the loss of the salt, but this was of no concern to Oien as his minions on Elat worked through each summer to gather the purple material from the drying straits.

The King continued, "We will travel back to Boretar together and from there fast horses and a troop of cavalry will enable your speedy return to the work in the Inger."

The discussion was interrupted by a knock on the door, and the two travel-weary Ember Horsemen entered the room and told their sorry story. Oien and Dewar were aghast at the news of the battles in Banora and the capture of the Ackar and Ember forces there. It seemed now that winter rearmament was not going to be possible.

The King slammed his fist on the table. "I should have anticipated that Cameron would try something unexpected like a winter campaign, but so should my commanders in the north. It will be best for them if they died in the battle. If they return to Boretar their fate will be much worse!"

Oien picked up the part of the story about the tall warriors who had caused so much destruction to the Ackar armies. Orridon had also mentioned these strange folk. However Oien was still more surprised when the second Ember trooper described seeing the skies darken over the Inger as he rode south and the pure white lightning that followed. Surely the assassin had fulfilled his mission? Oien was sure he had felt the passing of Ala Moire, although that was only an intuition. Maybe his old foe was indeed still alive.

"So much for your promises of power, old man, we are back to where we were when you first arrived at Boretar," said the Dewar. "I wonder if I would have been more successful without your magic."

Oien's control slipped in his anger, and red fire leapt from his staff and his open hand. The King and the two troopers retreated to the sides of the room. "You are nothing without me!" snarled Oien. "You are simply a passing king whose time will leave no lasting mark on the world in the generations to come, whilst I will change the world as I did before in an earlier age."

The King was once more reminded how powerless he was when the alchemist's magic was released. "I apologise," he said. "We have agreed an alliance, so now we need to plan. We will return to Boretar and in the spring we will return north to obliterate the Bala armies and Cameron with them. We will then return here to finish what we have started in the south. We will leave for Boretar in the morning."

James Cameron was sitting in his now better-ordered rooms in Aldene when Elbeth entered hand in hand with Angus Ferguson. As Cameron sprang up from his seat his daughter instantly recognised his anger, but Elbeth also knew her father. She ran across and embraced him. "How good to be home, father!" she said. "Now I can show our home to Angus, who has spent the last few days showing me the beauty of Banora." She ran back to her fiancé's side, and as she took his hand the two white gold rings shone brightly, reflecting their joy at being together.

Cameron was torn. Clearly the two were deeply in love, and their joy and the rings worried him. He could not see how the relationship could reach a happy ending, but nor could he see how to forbid it.

He turned to Elbeth. "You should have stayed in Tala as I instructed," he said. "But as you are here now, you'd better go and get some help to tidy your room and your stepmother's, which if I am not mistaken will not have been treated kindly by the occupiers. Ferguson, you wait here."

As Elbeth kissed her fiancé on the cheek and turned to leave, Alex Cameron, Alastair Munro, Ewart, Alain of Lorn and John Burnett entered the room. Winter was closing in on Bala, and Cameron had more on his mind than his daughter's love affair.

"Sit please, gentlemen," he said. "We need to make some urgent decisions. Obviously winter is gaining a grip over the land and we do not have provisions to sustain our own troops over the winter, never mind the captives and the other forces camped outside Aldene's walls. Anaton is ensuring that supplies reach Coe and his men in Banora, but the Ing is now virtually impassable, so Tala cannot supply us here. Lord Ewart is soon to leave for his lands in the east. They have largely been untouched by the invaders and we may hope that the people there can spare some supplies to help bolster our own reserves here. Alain, can I ask you and some of your brothers to travel with some of the Banoran cobs and go with Ewart to see what reserves you can bring back here? Aldene is relatively well provisioned, as the enemy garrison here has clearly taken all it can from my lands in preparation for winter. Once Alain returns in a few weeks I will distribute the supplies to the Bala soldiers and send them home for the winter to regroup back here in early spring. The Dewar will not wait long to send his armies back north to renew his acquisition of Banora, and although the Inger fires have been quenched I doubt if it will be long before the forges burn again, unless we can make a better defence of our lands. Go now." The Ewart and Alain left immediately for eastern Bala.

Cameron turned to John Burnett. "John, what is the mood in the forces from Ciren, Arance and Toria?"

"They are enjoying having the upper hand over the Ackar captives and they're anxious to fight alongside us to win freedom for their own lands."

"Are you sure we can trust their loyalty?"

Burnett nodded. "They have suffered much under the tyranny of the Dewar and the rebel lords in their homelands have given the sergeants clear instructions that the troops are to follow my orders."

"Excellent. I would like to meet with you and the sergeants first thing tomorrow morning to discuss plans."

As the meeting ended, Alastair Munro leant over to Cameron to tell him the news that Coran had repelled the invasion in Amina and the Dewar's weapons had all been destroyed.

"Good news and bad news, Alastair," replied Cameron. "The Dewar will know by now that we have retaken most of Bala and in the spring he will turn his attention here first so that he can rearm using the old wizard's power with othium. Only then will he look south again. Hopefully we have the winter to prepare, but we will need to be ready for battle as soon as the snows melt in Ackar. It will mean another winter march for our forces, as I plan to meet the Dewar armies in his own lands this time."

It was an odd group that arrived with Burnett at Cameron's rooms the next morning. The conscripts had largely been used as slave labour in Banora, and they were dressed in a strange mix of once expensive but now patched-up clothing. Their armour and weapons had been left in the camp, and as they had been soldiers for the Dewar, their war equipment was in far better condition than their personal belongings.

"Welcome, gentlemen," Cameron began. It was too late to change the 'gentlemen' when a young woman stepped forward from the group. "My Lord, we thank you for freeing us from the servitude of the King of Ackar," she said. "My name is Alluen, and I am daughter of the King of Toria and the wife of Tyros Prince of Ciren. I travelled north with your captain to give proof to the letters he carried from the lords of Ciren, Toria and Arance. By mutual consent I will speak for the lords gathered here."

Alluen had a poise about her that indicated she was used to being in command. At a guess Cameron thought she must be in her mid-twenties. She was of medium height and her brown hair was cropped short. Cameron considered her handsome rather than beautiful. She had a wild beauty and showed a strength of character unusual in one so young. She carried herself with a dignity that came from being the daughter of a king and the wife of a prince.

When she talked about the freedom of her people, her hazel eyes seemed to shine with passion. Toria was one of the smaller kingdoms on Andore, and Cameron knew it was common practice in Toria for the women to be trained as warriors to bolster, when required, the small armies of the kingdom. Alluen must have spent most of her recent years in exile from her homeland. It was clear she hated the Dewar, who had forced so many of her young countrymen into conscription and slavery.

Cameron smiled. "Welcome Alluen. Your brothers here don't look like lords."

Alluen made a slight bow. "My Lord Cameron, you know how the tyrant and his father invaded our lands, you fought alongside us, and you also know that our royal families had to go into exile in Amina and Kermin. Today some of our troops fight alongside your brother in Amina. In our homelands the Dewar demanded hostages and conscripts for his armies. Across Toria, Ciren and Arance the local lords had to submit their sons to the King as well as swear fealty to him. These men here are all of the noble blood lines of their kingdoms. The Dewar would not allow any acknowledgement of the lineage of the conscripts, so they were called sergeants and each held a responsibility to ensure the loyalty of the troops under their command. Each unit was made up of the sons of the families from their individual countries. The Dewar's governors, like Orimir in Toria, demand that the local lords attend an audience every month. Any news of unrest among the citizens or the conscript armies is punished by executing some of the local people.

"A few months ago Tyros and I returned to Ciren from Mora and called on the lords of Ciren to ignore the call to the audience with the regional governor. Tyros has raised a peasant army that is harassing the occupying forces in Ciren, but the cost to our people has been high. Rebels in Arance and Toria have also risen up in rebellion, but the lords of these lands are reluctant to support our cause due to the risk to their people. Orimir is particularly brutal in his punishment of any unrest. However, once John Burnett arrived in our homelands we were able to get the lords in all three countries to sign letters instructing their sons to follow you and your captain. The instructions came from the courts in exile. We are at your command, and we will march at your instructions to defeat the tyrant and regain our freedom."

The Cameron was impressed. This young woman had the steel and grit of a warrior.

As an afterthought Alluen added, "My lords here agree that under Burnett's guidance I will lead our troops to victory over the Dewar." Brave words indeed, thought Cameron.

Cameron nodded. "Alluen, we have a challenge here as winter closes in. We can provision the people of Bala, with some luck, but we will struggle to feed your men and the captives through the winter. I would like you and your lords, with Burnett, to lead your army south to Erbea. The borderlands are in the grip of early winter, but they are rich lands, so you should be able to provision the force as you move south. When you reach Erbea, you must ensure that the garrison there accepts the Ackar and Lett prisoners into the city, and then I need you and your troops to put the town under siege, letting none in or out. Timing is critical – you need to arrive at Erbea just as winter sets in properly. I need the Dewar to be locked in at Boretar by the snow so that he cannot come to the relief of Erbea. To end the tyrant's rule we need to face his forces in a pitched battle, and I am choosing the land between Erbea and the Bala border as the location for that battle. I need you to keep your men fit and ready for us to join you in early spring.

"The Bala army, with the help of the Coelete, will move south before the snows fully melt in the south. With Erbea under siege, the King will have no option but to move his forces north to rescue his second city. So far we have managed to be a thorn in the Dewar's side, but we now need to force his hand."

Alluen bowed again. "We will carry out our mission, my Lord. With the actions we have taken in Banora, it is now victory or death for all the conscripts. I will also send messengers to my husband and get him to try to raise an army from Ciren, Toria and Arance to join our forces."

"As winter will end sooner in the far south, I hope my brother can also raise a force from Amina to threaten Anelo and then march north to join your husband's forces," Cameron replied. "Together we can end the tyrant's reign." He turned to Burnett. "John, I want you to ensure the siege of Erbea is established and then I have another task for you. We will discuss this once our friends here have enjoyed some Aldene hospitality."

Following a lavish repast in the Great Hall in Aldene, Cameron and Burnett returned to the Cameron's rooms.

"The young Princess seems full of fire," commented Cameron.

Burnett smiled. "As we travelled north together with the letters for the sergeants we were attacked by bandits. I don't know who taught her, but she would hold her ground with many of our troopers."

"I'm sure she would. John, I need you to travel with the conscript force to Erbea and ensure my orders are followed. I then want you to go to Anua with Idula as your captive. You will travel with a small force of Red Cameron as a precaution against any attack. The rest of the Ember Horse are captives and will stay here. My spies tell me that Orridon has fallen out with the Dewar and is in Anua. It might be time to try to persuade the Horse Lords of Ember to change sides as they have done in the past. Having Idula with you should facilitate access to Orridon.

"I then require you to make contact with Tyros and encourage him to stoke up more rebellion across the southern kingdoms. Knowing that their sons are in peril should bolster their lords' appetite for war. My hope is that Coran will invade Arance with a force from Amina, and that he will try to cross the Middle Sea as soon as the winter storms abate. If we can unite Amina forces with the rebels, we will have a southern army and we can squeeze the Dewar between the two armies. It will be a dangerous mission John, but I know you will succeed."

"I am at your command, my Lord," said Burnett.

CHAPTER FIFTEEN
The Siege at Erbea

Erbea was Ackar's second city. Its whitewashed castle, surrounded by its equally white walls, could be seen from miles around. The castle hill represented the inner defences, but at the foot of the hill, tall city walls made the city largely impregnable.

Patrick Roth was Lord of Erbea and commanded the Ackar forces in the region. Roth controlled the border lands between Erbea and the border with Bala. In the latter part of the 13th century this had been bandit country. Reivers from the north in Bala had stolen sheep and cattle from the rich farmlands surrounding Erbea. In return the Erbean bandits raided the Bala border lands. Neither the northern nor southern bandits cared much for the authorities of Boretar or Aldene. Nor did they care who they slaughtered in their raids across the border. The prizes for both sides were a wealth of sheep and cattle. These were the lands that Douglas Dougal had raided from his now destroyed hill settlement at Brough.

Roth had been given lordship of the northern counties by Dewar the First, and with an iron hand he had largely subdued the banditry. Ackar troops patrolled the ancient wall that marked the boundary between the countries of Ackar and Bala. Once Dewar the Second had conquered Bala, these patrols became less necessary. To the south and the west Erbea looked out over fertile plains that were irrigated by the waters of the river Erb as it flowed east into the Middle Sea. These lands were the breadbasket of Ackar. To the north and east the borderland's rolling hills provided rich grazing which supported large flocks of sheep and cattle. A small rivulet, the Bari, ran from the hills north of Erbea to join the Erb to the west of the city.

Winter's northern winds had begun to chill the citizens of Erbea, and to the north the hilltops on the borderlands were crowned with snow. It was therefore a surprise when Roth was called from his rooms to the city walls to see a large armed force marching towards the city.

Roth knew from stragglers who had arrived from Bala that the occupying army in Banora had been defeated. He had not expected the Bala forces to continue south as winter set in and so had not sent out any patrols. What he did not know was that a significant portion of the forces descending from the hills were in fact his own captured countrymen.

Looking out from the walls of the city, Roth considered the advancing army. It was marching in an unusual formation. The outer ranks seemed well-armed and formed a square four men deep around the central units, which seemed to be laboured in their movement.

As the force halted out of range of the archers on the city walls, Roth recognised the Cameron surcoats worn by John Burnett. With a trooper carrying a white flag, Burnett approached the city walls.

"My Lord Roth, my name is John Burnett. I come with Ackar captives from the battle in Banora. The armies of Ciren, Toria and Arance now march under my command. If you open the city gates I will allow our prisoners to enter the safety of the city. We will then hold our forces round your walls until my Lord Cameron and his army arrives to support our attack on your city."

Roth laughed. "James Cameron does not have the weapons to breach these walls, and as far as I am concerned you can sit there through the cold of winter and starve. I have enough mouths to feed within my walls. I have no need of more."

"I hope we can change your mind, my lord," Burnett replied. Lowering the flag of truce, Burnett walked back to the front of the conscript army. At his signal Alluen and two of her comrades stepped forward with three Ackar soldiers, their hands bound behind their backs. Roars of outrage came from the city walls as the Erbean soldiers watched Alluen and her comrades draw their knives across the captives' throats and drop them to the ground. Roth's voice rose over the hubbub. "You may kill them all Burnett, but my gates will remain closed!"

Burnett signalled again to Alluen and she made her way to the front again with another captive. Simon Roth was a captain in the Ackar forces in Banora. He also happened to be the only son of the Lord of Erbea. As Alluen raised her knife to his throat, Patrick Roth shouted from the city wall, "Don't kill him! I can pay a huge ransom for him."

"You can take him and the others or you can come and collect his body," replied Burnett. "We have no use for your money."

The Lord of Erbea knew he had no choice. He could not stand on his city walls and watch his only son slaughtered like an animal in an abattoir. Burnett did not hear the order, but as he saw the gates open he held his hand up to still the knife in Alluen's hand.

The front lines of the conscript forces opened to allow the prisoners to march towards the city gates. Alluen held the knife at Simon Roth's throat until the last prisoner had entered the city, then allowed him to follow his compatriots. As Simon Roth walked through the city gates they were instantly closed behind him, not that Burnett had any intention of attacking the city even when the gates were open.

As the gates of Erbea closed, storms from the north were blowing in the snow clouds of winter. The soldiers from Ciren, Toria and Arance built their camps round the walls of Erbea, far enough away to be out of bowshot but close enough to respond quickly to any attempted attack or escape from the city. The conscript forces were under the command of Alluen and her sergeants. They were now very well armed with pike, sword, bow and arrow, having taken all the equipment from the defeated forces of Ackar and Lett. Alluen's force could provision itself from the rich farms that populated the lands close to the city. The army was further reinforced when Red Cameron troopers brought captured horses south from Aldene, enabling Alluen's men to venture further in search of supplies.

Having ensured that Alluen and her men understood their mission at Erbea, John Burnett and his troop headed south, staying close to the eastern coast of Ackar and Lett before crossing the border into

Arance and Ember. A forlorn Idula travelled at the centre of the Cameron troop, dreading the meeting with his uncle. Burnett knew he had many winter miles to travel and hoped that his mission would not end when he arrived at Orridon's home in Anua. Idula, he hoped, was his insurance for a safe passage.

In Anelo work was continuing to repair the port, but there was little to hold the Dewar there for the winter. Timon was stripped of his command of the King's Guard but left in charge of the building works and the defence of the port. The King, with Oien and most of the Ackar and Lett forces, left Anelo to return to Boretar to wait out the winter.

It was on the journey north that the Dewar was informed of the siege at Erbea. His immediate response was to move the forces he was travelling with north and east to try to dislodge the siege; however, as in the previous winter of 1300, the weather seemed to conspire to thwart any plans and as the snows deepened the King realised that the relief of Erbea would need to wait for the spring thaws. At least winter in Boretar would be comfortable, and he would have his revenge in the spring. With Bala now fully under the control of local armies and the forges and mines in Banora cold, Oien also had to hold back his frustration and return for a winter in Boretar.

All the land around Aldene was covered in a thick

white blanket of snow. The Coelete, who seemed to be immune to the weather, continued to use their sleds and snowploughs to keep the supplies from the Ewart lands in the East moving to provision the forces in Aldene. A significant portion of the Bala army had been released to return to their homes for the winter. Similarly in Banora the Coelete continued to travel from Tala to supply the troops still clearing the county of the detritus left behind by the occupying forces.

In Amina the snows covered the mountains of the Doran and the tops of the hills in the Kermin Alol. Around Tamin and the Vale of Tember the winter rain soaked the ground, restricting the movement of armies over the winter. So whilst the snowbound northern lands waited for the spring thaw, in Tufle activity increased. The captured foot soldiers from the Ackar landing forces were forced to work on repairing the damaged troop carriers and war boats as Coran started to assemble his fleet for an invasion over the Middle Sea as soon as the winter storms relented.

As winter took its grip over the lands the world paused, again resting and waiting.

Burnett's troop was met by a strong force of Ember Horse whilst they were still some distance from Anua. Riding at the head of the troop was Orridon. In the centre of the Red Cameron, Idula held a white flag aloft.

Orridon assessed the situation. The Cameron force was large enough to dissuade any banditry attacks, but not large enough to trouble his riders. Then he recognised his nephew in the centre of the group. He ignored the Cameron troopers and nudged his horse through to where Idula sat. The young man opened his mouth to speak, but had not got a word out before Orridon struck him a savage blow. Idula fell heavily from his horse and was followed by Orridon, who gripped him by the throat.

"I left you in charge in Banora and you allowed a ragtag army to beat you in battle!" he roared. "My position with the King is probably ruined beyond repair, and you have the nerve to ride in here in the midst of the enemy. I will have you flogged in the square in Anua. If you survive that, I might let you live."

The Ember Horse had formed a cordon round the Cameron riders, but their lord was left isolated. Burnett slowly moved back and Orridon halted as a Red Cameron lance touched his exposed neck. Orridon thought about shouting to his men to attack, but realised that he would not survive such an order.

Burnett spoke next. "My Lord Duke of Ember, I am John Burnett, second in command to James Cameron and captain of the Red Cameron. Your nephew is here as our captive, but at least he is alive. You and I nearly met before, in the battle on the high Pass of

Ing. I am here at my Lord Cameron's instructions to talk with you, not to fight you. However if your men decide to engage I will ensure that you are the first to die. Please order your men to sheath their weapons and then please lead us to Anua, as I have much to share with you."

Orridon did as requested, and with Ember outriders ready to respond if required, he rode with Burnett back to Anua. Some of the grand houses of the town were built on the remains of the old castle, and below them the dungeons remained. Idula was roughly handled and cast into the damp cellar that lay beneath Orridon's home. Orridon ordered Letham to ensure the Cameron troopers were well looked after and given food and accommodation. He turned to Burnett. "Come, we will talk," he said.

The house sat at the highest point of Anua and the room looked out over the town and further over the wide grasslands of Ember.

"So what have you to say to me, Burnett?" asked Orridon. "Whilst you and your men are here under a flag of peace, you are still the enemy. I might decide my hospitality will be less kind once I hear your news."

"So be it," Burnett replied. "My Lord Cameron has asked me to share with you all that has happened whilst you have been here in Anua and also our plans for the spring. As you rightly state, you are the enemy and I have some reluctance in obeying my orders, in case you use the information to gain renewed respect from the Dewar. However my orders are specific and I will do as I have been commanded."

Orridon listened as Burnett described the battle to retake Tamin, the destruction of the cannon, the impact of the tsunami and lastly the details of the battle Idula had lost in Banora.

Orridon slammed his fist onto the table. "My fool of a nephew! How could he leave the camps in Banora with no guard and no riders covering the plains?"

"My Lord, remember that winter had already settled in the north and our plans for a winter campaign were unconventional. I am not sure that you would have anticipated our attack any more than your nephew did, although you might have been more cautious. To his credit the young man would have fought on, but the Ackar commanders surrendered and with the conscripts changing sides there was little chance of their army winning the battle, so the surrender did save many lives. Your surviving horsemen remain guests of my Lord and are held in Aldene."

Orridon was about to give a sharp reply, but Burnett held up a hand, "I have more to tell," he said. As best he could from his briefing with Cameron, Burnett told Orridon of Oien's role in the Second Age, the murder of Ala Moire and the siege at Erbea.

Orridon had not been told of the treachery of the conscripts. Burnett explained how the uprisings in Ciren and Toria had been sparked by orders from the exiled kings and how these same orders had been passed to the conscripts in Banora.

"Orridon, all of our nations have been subject to the tyranny of the Dewar dynasty and the time has come to end it or to continue to live our lives in slavery, not to the Dewar now, but to the evil of the old alchemist," he concluded.

Orridon hesitated. He had long suspected that Oien was using the Dewar for his own purposes. During his time in his own lands he had learnt how his people despised their Dewar overlord, and by association Orridon and his family were little loved by the people. Over the weeks he had tried to rebuild his position by travelling all across Ember. He had started to win back the respect of the Ember people and had worried how they would react if he simply returned to join the Dewar.

"So you have given me a history lesson," he said. "Now tell me about the future. But first I have two questions. Where did the people of Bala find refuge in the high mountains of the Coe? Secondly, who are the tall warriors who can send their arrows such prodigious distances?"

"The answers to your questions are bound together," Burnett replied. "I am ordered to give them to you, as my lord anticipated you would ask these questions." He described Tala and the Hidden Lands and the history of the Coelete.

Orridon shook his head. "I suspected as much, but we could find no sign of a way through the mountain."

Burnett continued, "The locations of the passages I cannot disclose. However, I have more history for you, ancient history. I assume Ala Moire told my Lord Cameron this story. In the Second Age, as the slaves and armies of the Council of Five occupied the lands in the north of Bala, the Coelete tribes were forced into the mountains. The tribe split into three groups. One group forged the passageway through the mountain, while a second group travelled west past the falls of the Cole river where you were led by Erden and met the arrows of my brothers. The third group headed south and volunteered to work in the Banoran mines. In time this third group either won freedom or escaped the mines. They travelled south and established their homes here in Ember. A small group must have somehow survived the destruction of the Second Age.

"You and the Coelete share a common distant ancestry, probably now only discernable by the black hair that is common to the true line of the Horse Lords and is also a common feature of the Coelete. You have long known that the Ember people are generally taller than the folk of the neighbouring countries. As your ancestors intermarried with the local people, you lost some of the stature of your cousins in the north. However, back in the mists of time you were one people and they were the Coelete."

This was a great revelation to Orridon. "So history has strange tales to tell. Now what about the future?"

It was Burnett's moment to pause. This was the part of his orders he was least comfortable with, as it meant in effect telling the enemy the plans for the spring.

"The army of Bala is not large enough to face an open battle with the forces of Ackar and Lett," he said. "We can win skirmishes and defend our lands where the mountains give protection, but my Lord Cameron now plans to face the Dewar openly on the field near Erbea. The Dewar must look north again come spring to free his second city and to move again to open the mines in Banora. With the freed conscript forces of Toria, Ciren and Arance we may almost be able to match the Dewar's numbers on the field.

"As winter recedes from the south, Coran will lead the forces of Amina across the sea to attack Anelo. The Dewar will face war on two fronts, but more importantly, with your agreement, the rest of my task is to move through to Ciren and help to consolidate and train the freedom fighters in Ciren and Toria so that we can raise a third force that can march north in spring, challenge Boretar and then move on to the battle outside Erbea. My Lord Cameron requests that you hold the Ember Horse here at home and so reduce the Dewar's ability to field troops of light cavalry. Your men are the elite warriors of the Dewar's army and your absence from the field will significantly reduce his capability."

Orridon said nothing. He knew that his stepbrother had changed sides in 1290 and the people of Arance and Ember still blamed Elan for the loss of their nation's independence, the Dewar's taxes, and the sons who were still being conscripted into the King's armies. The Arance nobility in exile must also have been party to the decision to rise up against the King, and must have ordered their countrymen to rebel with the conscript forces in Bala. These were hard choices. Pick wrongly and if the Dewar prevailed, then Orridon would probably have to join his countrymen in exile. However Orridon had witnessed the selfish desire of the old alchemist, and if the Dewar were to prevail, what future awaited his people under Oien's rule?

"Burnett, I need time to consider. I cannot commit to any course of action immediately," he said. "In the past weeks I have learnt more about the reasons for the unrest in Ember and Arance. My fealty has been pledged to the King, but not to the old man. In the meantime, you and your men may enjoy the hospitality of Anua, and you will then be free to continue with your mission to Ciren. Whilst I cannot be on your side, as yet, I will not obstruct you in your mission, nor will I report your plans to the King. As for the spring, we will see."

"I appreciate your hospitality," replied Burnett. "We will rest here for a short time only, as I need to move on whilst the roads east are still passable. I would like you to allow your nephew to travel with us, not as a prisoner but as your representative, as we meet with the rebels in Ciren. I don't want Idula to make commitments in your name, but it would help to be able to say that Ember is considering its position. In addition, when we return to Aldene your men there will need a leader, be it to remain in Aldene as we march or at your command to ride with us."

"That is a strange request, and a hard one. Idula deserves punishment for his failure and more. If you are caught by the Dewar, it will be difficult to explain his presence without giving away my position."

"I understand, but if we were taken by the Dewar's men then Idula would simply revert to being our prisoner and with us under duress. There would be no need to compromise your position."

A few days later the Red Cameron, with Idula, left Anua. Whilst the young man was not entirely happy to be travelling with the enemy, he had been briefed in private by his uncle and knew that at least he was not travelling as a prisoner. He was armed again and told that he could leave the group at any time. However he had clear instructions from Orridon that prohibited any attempt to escape unless Burnett and his men were challenged by Ackar troops. Orridon appeared to be continuing to play a waiting game.

The small troop headed south from Anua and then travelled west through Arance and on across Ciren. With the winter snows now lying deep on the ground, progress was slow. The group also had to avoid the small towns where the local population almost certainly included Ackar forces. However, in the villages and farms where the men rested it was clear that the local populations were severely discontented with their lot under the Dewar's rule. Much of the talk in the inns was around the uprisings in Ciren and of more men joining Tyros's rebel force.

The great forest of Lett which supplied much of the timber for the shipbuilders in Olet stretched much further south, hugging the coast and stretching on through Ciren to the north of Toria. The forest in Ciren was Burnett's destination. Following the summer raids and the destruction of some of his force by Oien's cannon, Tyros had been forced to pull his rebels back to the protection of the forest. The Ciren Prince knew his poorly-equipped rebel force could not resist Ackar and Lett cavalry on open ground. The destruction brought by the red fire on the hills north of Anelo was a harsher lesson in the power that the Dewar now seemed to command.

As the winter closed in, the Prince led his men to the shelter of the vast western forest. It would give them protection from the worst of the winter, and the game that roamed there would more than provide for their needs.

It was late November when the Cameron troop battled on through a fierce snowstorm and entered the forest. They had not travelled far when a lone horseman blocked the path ahead. "Halt!" was the command. "This forest is the territory of the people of Ciren. Strangers are not welcome here!"

It seemed a brave defiance to Burnett and his men, as they could easily have ridden through the lone rider. However a glance at the surrounding trees dispelled any ideas of doing so. A number of men dressed largely in brown and armed with bows and arrows stepped out from their cover.

Burnett raised his hand and shouted out to the lone rider, "I come with messages for Prince Tyros from his wife Alluen. Your Lord knows me and I travel with word from James Cameron in Bala."

"Please dismount, my lord, and lead your horses after me, I will take you to the Prince," was the reply.

It was a long walk, and although the tree cover

had restricted the depth of the snow, it would have been easier to travel on horseback. The lone rider and his men clearly would not allow that option.

After some time, the travellers reached an open space. Deep in the forest a large area had been cleared and tents and other shelters indicated that quite a large population was living there. Tyros and Burnett had met in the summer shortly after the Prince and his wife had returned to their homeland and first raised the rebellion. Tyros greeted the Cameron captain warmly, but his attitude changed in an instant when he saw Idula, for he recognised him as an Ember Horseman. He reached the young man in a few steps and held a knife at his throat.

"Calm, Tyros, he travels with us as a guest," said Burnett. "He and many of his men were captured in the battle at Banora where your countrymen played their part to the letter."

Tyros spat his response. "He and his scum are the reason we lost our freedom. Had they remained loyal to Arance, we would not now be under the tyrant's rule. He has no place in my camp."

Burnett calmly replied, "Idula travels under my protection and with orders from his uncle for his countrymen who are captives in Aldene."

Slowly the knife was lowered and Tyros ordered his men to find food and shelter for their visitors. "He may be under your protection, Burnett, but I don't expect to see him in camp without one of your men at his shoulder," he said. "I have no trust in the Horse Lords of Ember."

Burnett nodded to his men and then walked with Tyros to a large tent which was clearly the Prince's forest home. Burnett again reported on the battles in Amina and Banora and told how the conscript army under Alluen's command was now surrounding Erbea. Tyros listened attentively as Burnett told of Cameron's surprise at meeting Princess Alluen.

"I love my wife dearly and I know from experience she is not one to be argued with," said Tyros. "She will fulfil her mission at the walls of Erbea, but what happens come the spring?"

Burnett explained the Cameron plan to meet the Ackar and Lett forces in open battle around Erbea. Tyros frowned. "You know, John, that it will be close to suicide to meet the Dewar on open ground. The Ackar heavy cavalry will simply ride over and through a pike army. Even if the Dewar lacks the evil red magic, he has overwhelming force at his command."

"We hope to weaken the Dewar by making him fight simultaneously on several fronts," replied Burnett. "You and your men are an important part of the plan."

The winter of 1301 was late in arriving compared to the previous winter, but it was no less harsh for that. From Anelo and Cire in the south to Tala in the north, deep snows locked the people in their towns, cities and homes. Travel through the lands was nigh impossible other than for Burnett, who had his orders to fulfil. Further south in Amina, the snow seemed to play a game with winter rains and the mud-filled roads were no more passable than the snow-covered paths to the north. It was a time for waiting and planning.

It was usual in winter for armies to disperse to their homes and wait for the spring call to arms. Not in the winter of 1301-1302. In Amina the soldiers suffered a cold and muddy existence, but Coran and his commanders still led regular training sessions to keep them occupied and fit. Amina was a rich land, and the farms across the Plain of Tember had more than enough stores to keep the army fed. Supplies also still crossed through the Kermin Alol with further provisions, and Coran had ordered the Doran miners back to the mountains to stock up the supplies of incendiaries. In Tufle the port was busy as carpenters worked on the war boats and transports, ensuring they were seaworthy and ready to embark at short notice in early spring. In the shipyards, additional craft were being built.

Had the workers in Tufle been able to see across the Middle Sea, they would have imagined they were looking at themselves in a mirror, as Timon was overseeing the continued repair of the port, and there too the shipyards echoed to the sound of hammer and saw as new vessels were being constructed ready for a renewed attack on Amina. With small boats still criss-crossing the sea, spies from both sides informed their commanders of the activities in the enemy ports.

Around Erbea, Alluen and her sergeants maintained the discipline in the conscript army and kept Erbea's residents locked behind their walls. Whilst the snow made travel difficult, the horses brought from the north enabled small bands of men to gather provisions from the neighbouring farms and to harvest firewood from the many woods that lay to the west and east of Erbea. It was not a pleasant existence, but the conscript forces, fuelled by their hatred of the Dewar and their success in battle in Banora, had a fierce determination that the siege would hold till spring.

Inside the city, the situation was deteriorating more rapidly. As the conscript army had moved south, most of the residents in the surrounding lands had sought refuge behind the city walls. With hundreds of the defeated Ackar army also now forced into the city, both food and fuel were running short. Patrick Roth had ordered all food to be centralised in the storehouses in the city, and the daily rations were getting ever smaller. The people, already cramped for space, were increasingly huddled together as smaller houses were demolished for their wood. Communal fires were built in the many squares that dotted the city. These were all that were allowed and all that could give the residents some warmth, other than wearing all their clothing and huddling in their blankets. Already some of the older people and some of the wounded Ackar soldiers were dying from cold or from the disease that had started to afflict the population. Each day the conscripts watched as more bodies were dropped out over the city walls.

Roth estimated that the city could maybe just survive until early spring, and hoped that the Dewar would make a quick move to relieve it. He considered surrendering to the enemy, but as they made no move to attack the walls he assumed the siege was in fact the bait to draw the Dewar into battle. That thought gave him some encouragement, as it was clear that the forces camped outside the walls would not give much resistance to a full assault by an Ackar and Lett army. Roth could only hope that this winter would not last as long as the previous one.

In Boretar the Dewar had dispersed his forces, but he had not allowed them to return to their homes. The army was instructed to keep in training but to bivouac in the towns and villages scattered close to Boretar. Many of the elite forces, like the King's Guard, had residences within the city.

With the port again fully functioning, Boretar

returned to some sort of normality. The Dewar saw little of the alchemist, who seemed to keep largely to his own quarters, poring over ancient plans. Whilst some othium and salt had remained in the warehouses of Boretar, there were no remaining machines to exploit the power of the red stone. As a result, the King and his senior commanders made more conventional plans for warfare. There was much debate, as some argued for a renewed attack across the Middle Sea whilst others insisted that the priority must be to break the siege at Erbea. No one seemed to argue for a return to Banora, until Oien arrived unexpectedly at one meeting. The old man listened for a short while and then stilled the discussion with a release of red fire from his opened hand. He let the silence deepen, then announced, "We will march north to Erbea and disperse the rabble forces there and then again north to Banora. Without the red stone and war machines, any attack on Amina will result in another stalemate. We will be ready to march as soon as the weather breaks."

The Dewar's face reddened and he spluttered, "You forget yourself! I am the King and I will decide on our approach to the spring campaign."

Amber sparks flashed from the alchemist's staff. "Following your plan, we have wasted a summer and an autumn. If you had taken care of the war machines and the ammunition, we could now be planning a full-scale attack to the south supported by the cannons. Your insistence that we cross to Slat during the autumn storms has lost us any chance of victory there until we are again fully armed. Any unsupported invasion to the south will simply be held either outside Tamin or again in the Kermin Alol. You will now do as I request."

Appalled by this verbal assault on his King, one of the guards drew his sword. Oien turned at the sound and the red fire consumed the blade down to the hilt. The weapon clattered to the ground. "We will do as I say!" he snarled. "And indeed if Erbea cannot be quickly relieved, then we will leave the population to their fate and move north to Banora. I want slaves from the south and any skilled smiths from Ackar and Lett ready to move as soon as we can. Power is in the red stone and the salt, and this is the only way to conquer the southern lands." He turned without another word and left the room.

It was the first time that the old man had openly defied the King, but despite his displeasure, the Dewar could not see how to overturn these orders, short of killing the alchemist. He also knew that removing Oien would reduce his power to conquer the rich southern lands.

Trying to re-establish some control, the Dewar closed the meeting. "The old man's position has great merit and without his magic we will not be able to prevail," he said. "It is decided, Erbea and then on again to Bala and Banora. Leave me."

After his men had gone, the Dewar sat alone pondering. The old man was becoming a problem to which he could not see a solution.

Further south, John Burnett was again on the move. Most of his troopers, led by Davy Scott, remained with the Ciren rebels, training them in the arts of skirmish and fixed battle. The rebels were brave and keen to learn, but Tyros and Burnett knew that the force was very unlikely to be able to stand against a modern mounted army. However that was not the plan. Burnett, with Tyros, Idula and a small force of rebel archers, headed south to where the great forest stretched into Toria. The Horse Lord had not been party to the discussions between the Red Cameron and Tyros but had been called to confirm that for now his uncle would hold back the Ember Horse. The rebel forces in Toria were less than those in Ciren and they too had moved to the forest for winter shelter. The rebellion in Toria had stuttered to life as Orimir, the Governor of the country, was quick to deploy forces to quash the rebels wherever they could be found. However in late autumn a small force of Torian regulars who had fought alongside the coalition forces in Amina had been shipped to the Torian coast along with a significant consignment of arms. As a result the Torian force was better armed and more professionally trained than their Ciren brothers.

Burnett explained the spring plan to Erin, Count of Toria, brother of Alluen and son of the exiled King of Toria. To Burnett's surprise, Erin introduced a captive. It was none other than Melnar, overlord of Lett, who had been captured by Erin's freedom fighters a few months earlier. He might turn out to be a useful pawn in the game ahead. His mission accomplished, Burnett returned to Ciren and with his troopers and Idula began the risky journey back north. It was time to go back to Aldene, and with the cover of the winter he hoped that the trip home would be uneventful.

It was past midwinter when the weary troop entered Aldene. It had been a long journey, but with the land in winter lockdown Burnett and his men, along with Idula, had returned safely. Idula went immediately to the quarters where his horsemen were held prisoner. Despite restrictions in their movement, the men were well treated and it was a very civil imprisonment. Idula was greeted with little respect by his countrymen, who had assumed he had turned traitor.

Once Idula passed on the orders from Orridon, the atmosphere lightened. Burnett was taken straight to James Cameron to report on the results of his travels. Most importantly, he was able to report that the siege at Erbea was still strongly enforced, and following a short stop on the return journey to meet with Alluen, he was able to confirm the Cameron's memory of the lie of the land around Erbea and the flow of the Bari and Erb, both frozen over again this winter. The Bala army had mostly returned to their homes for winter, but each soldier was required to report weekly to a local lord and be ready for assembly at Aldene within one week of notice being given.

The Coelete warriors were now a common sight in Bala, and now they ranged through the country ensuring that the army could be recalled and ready to march at short notice. The timing would be critical if the Cameron plan was to succeed.

Winter in Aldene had been a blessing for Angus and Elbeth. Whilst Angus had to go on regular patrols and carry out training, they were able to spend much time together and on many evenings Alastair Munro and the two lovers would dine together. Alastair was delighted at seeing the love deepening between the two, but even he was surprised at the light that shone from their rings when they sat close or held hands.

James Cameron remained concerned that his daughter's happiness might need to be cut short if the spring brought normality back to Bala. Cameron also noticed the rings, and the words *Aonaibh Ri Chéile* seemed to shine a message to him whenever he saw his daughter. Ala Moire's words also simultaneously came to mind: "James, I think this proposed union has blessing from a much higher power than you and me. Look at the motif on the ring."

Cameron pondered. Maybe a new time of peace would bring with it new possibilities in Bala, but before that could happen, many battles would need to be won and many plans would need to come together.

CHAPTER SIXTEEN

Spring Campaigns

AMINA & ANELO – EARLY MARCH 1302

In the early spring of 1302 a cold rain was still falling, and the north wind made the Middle Sea too treacherous to cross. Coran knew that small enemy war boats were still risking the crossing to gain intelligence for the spring offensives. He ordered a fleet of Amina boats to monitor the coast and prevent any landings between Slat and estuary of the river Mina.

In Slat, the Ackar transporters from the autumn invasion force were still anchored in the shallow waters just off the beach. Coran and James Cameron kept each other informed by carrier pigeon and through Ala Moire's device, which now hung round the neck of Alastair Munro. The spring campaigns would have to be carefully co-ordinated if there was to be any hope of drawing the Dewar into a battle of their choice. Coran had been told it was now time for his forces to move on Anelo.

In Anelo, Timon was also receiving his orders. The Dewar planned to move north with a large army to first relieve the siege at Erbea and then move on to reconquer Bala and Banora. Timon had been ordered to have the Ackar and Lett troops in Anelo ready to move north within weeks once the roads had cleared. Similar orders had been sent to the Ackar lords ruling Arance, Ciren and Toria. The King knew that the forces that could be mobilised at Boretar would be comparatively small and the rebellion in the conscript armies in the north had to some degree altered the power balance. However the King knew that his knights, the heavy cavalry, had no equivalent in the Bala army. The might of the armoured warriors would obliterate Cameron's puny foot army. His intention was to take sufficient force north to wipe out the conscripts and then destroy the Bala army. Timon was instructed to leave only a small defensive force in Anelo to repel invaders in the unlikely event that the port was attacked from Amina.

It was therefore a surprise when a large force of Ember Horse arrived at Anelo's city gates, led by the Duke of Ember. Orridon was quickly ushered in to meet with Timon. He told Timon that his horse had been ordered south to protect the Ackar forces from rebel attacks when they marched north. Timon knew of the uprisings in Ciren and Toria and was pleased that the elite horse would be protecting his flanks on the road to Boretar and then on to Erbea.

By night Arin and the Kermin foot soldiers, together with Ishca and the Doran cavalry, moved from the Plain of Tember to Slat. Once loaded, one of the transporters headed for Elat. The Kermin soldiers' instructions were to occupy the island and prevent any movement of salt out of Elat. With few defenders, the occupants on the island were mostly Oien's slaves at work gathering the salt. The occupation was quick and without casualties. The other transports and war boats made a difficult crossing of the Middle Sea to land on the borders of Ciren and Arance. There they met with the Ciren rebel forces that Tyros had led south from their winter refuge in the forest of Lett. Together a force of around a thousand now marched east towards Anelo.

Timon was more concerned about the security of Anelo than his master appeared to be. His spies' criss-crossing the Middle Sea had informed him of the winter activities in the shipyards of Tufle. Whilst the sea crossing was dangerous at this time of year, Timon was worried that none of the spies had returned over the past couple of weeks.

It was a clear, calm morning that seemed to be ushering in the new spring when Timon looked south from the castle walls. He was amazed to make out, across the now calm sea, a large fleet of vessels on the horizon. Realisation dawned: Anelo would be the first target for the next phase of the war. Staff officers were rapidly despatched to call the Ackar forces to the harbour. The boats rapidly emerging from the south could not be allowed to reach the port.

On the lead Amina war boat, Coran had anticipated the panic his fleet would cause once they were in sight of Anelo. With the Middle Sea calm, he wanted the Ackar forces to meet his at sea rather than on land. The hastily-assembled defenders would be ill prepared for a sea battle. He ordered the Amina fleet to hold position and wait for the enemy to emerge from the port. Coran was impressed by the speed with which the Ackar vessels were manned and left the harbour. Sea battles were rare and largely replicated the tactics used on land, with fast war boats harrying the enemy and slowing them down so that the larger troop ships could get close enough to throw boarding hooks and engage in hand-to-hand combat on the opposing ships. The Amina fleet was apparently conventionally deployed, with the smaller fast war boats to the front as the first line of attack, followed by the larger longboats and the great troop carriers. However Coran had no intention of playing by the conventional rules; he would use similar tactics to those used off the coast of Slat the previous autumn.

The Ackar commanders were slightly confused, as the Amina war boats held position not far from the troop carriers. Instinctively they felt the Amina force had intended to reach the port and engage on land, and had been surprised by the speed of deployment of the Ackar fleet. This suggested that the attackers were not ready for a sea battle, so with flag signals conveying the instructions, the Ackar vessels hurried into the attack.

Once the Ackar troop ships were in range, Coran released the war boats and the longboats followed. The Amina war boats were not planning hand-to-hand warfare but were manned mostly by Doran miners. Once close enough, the Doran incendiaries were lobbed into the Ackar vessels, creating confusion amongst the sailors and soldiers. This allowed the longboats with their battering rams to charge into the opposing vessels. In minutes, several of the Ackar boats were slowly descending to the depths of the Middle Sea. Simultaneously Aramin archers from the Amina troop ships sent volley after volley of arrows into the Ackar troop carriers, which were now close by. The rain of steel caused mass slaughter amongst the Ackar troopers onboard, and by the time Coran's vessels closed to board the enemy, there were few survivors left alive to engage with. In less than fifty minutes the battle was over and the Ackar ships were either sunk or in the control of Coran's commanders.

From the city walls it was difficult for Timon to see clearly how the battle was unfolding, but the flashes of fire from his war boats reminded him of the attack off Slat, and as the fleet started moving again towards Anelo it was clear that the Ackar navy had not prevailed at sea. Having committed many of his troops to the battle offshore, Timon had a relatively small force now available to protect the inevitable landing at the port. Nonetheless the enemy would find it hard to gain a foothold on land if the defenders held the city walls and made a stand on the port walls.

Timon cursed the fact that most of his remaining defenders were knights from the light horse and heavy cavalry. Whilst effective in mounted combat, these were not ideal troops for a land battle. He needed more foot soldiers, and most of all, archers.

As Timon shouted instructions to his commanders to get them to set up defensive positions on the city walls and in the port, he was distracted by movement to the west. The Doran cavalry was rapidly approaching the western end of the port walls, and behind them in close order marched a significant force of foot soldiers.

It was instantly clear that the Ackar troops would

not be able to reach their defensive positions before the enemy cavalry was upon them. Reversing his orders, Timon called his men back into the city to defend it from the city walls. As he did so a thundering of hooves echoed from within the city and the castle. Ember horsemen led by Orridon rode out through the castle gates, whilst others led by Idula appeared racing towards the city gate. Idula and his horsemen held the city gate open as the Doran cavalry arrived. Idula's men rode under the blue cross banner of the Red Cameron, as did Orridon's.

The battle for the city was short but bloody. The end was inevitable, and as Coran and the fleet disembarked at the port Anelo had surrendered. Coran showed little surprise that the battle had been won with the engagement of the men of Ember. Messages from Aldene had informed Coran that the letters Idula had carried to Aldene gave the Duke of Ember's commitment to fight against the Dewar. James Cameron had released the Ember Horse, and Idula had led them back to Anua. Their presence in Anelo confirmed Orridon's promise and choice of side. Coran had told Ishca that if some of the apparent defenders rode under the Cameron flag then they were to be treated as allies, not enemy.

A week after the capture of Anelo, a large force of cavalry moved north. They made an unusual sight. Doran, Ember and the Red Cameron troops riding together under a Red Cameron flag. Their destination was Anua, where they would wait on instructions to move on to the battle that was in prospect at Erbea. Tyros and the rebels moved west back to Ciren with instructions to harass Ackar contingents that were moving to join the King's forces gathering at Boretar. Further west in Toria, Erin was following the same instructions.

BORETAR – MID MARCH 1302

The snows had largely melted in Ackar and Lett and the Dewar's army was gathering on the plain outside Boretar. The troops that had been bivouacked close to the city were the first to gather. This was a large force of fifteen thousand, comprising heavy cavalry, Ackar light cavalry and foot soldiers. The army was also bolstered by several thousand commoners who had been commissioned from the surrounding towns and villages. These were not warriors, but they were competent archers and all carried bows and arrows. On the fields outside Boretar these men were being taught to fight with pike and sword by Ackar regulars. If the Dewar had learnt one thing from the battle for the Pass of Ing, it was that he needed to have his foot soldiers supported by bowmen.

The Dewar was in a sour mood as he paced his rooms in the castle. His forces were gathering, but too slowly. With twenty thousand men he was fairly sure he would outnumber the Bala army by at least two to one, but the conscripts camped outside Erbea could almost balance the numbers. With the losses suffered in Amina and Banora, the King knew he needed to recall men from Anelo, Ciren and Toria. Small bands of knights and foot soldiers continued to arrive from the south, but each group told of the hazards of the journey with regular attacks from rebel forces. Many of these bands arrived with wounded men in their ranks.

More worryingly, there was no sign of the troops from Anelo. Arin and his men had the city in lockdown and no message reached the Dewar explaining why Timon had not arrived with his men. There was also no sign of the elite cavalry of the Ember Horse. Despite messengers being sent to recall the Duke and his men, no messenger had reported back. The King knew that the situation in Erbea must by now be critical, and he could not wait much longer before moving north to break the siege. In the last week of March, the Dewar and his army headed north.

ERBEA – LATE MARCH 1302

The Bala army had marched from Aldene a week before the Ackar forces left Boretar. Bala was still largely under snow, and the march was slow and tiring. With his spies still active in the south, James Cameron knew the likely timing of the Dewar's march north. He wanted to get his men to the hills above Erbea with time to rest before they had to engage with the enemy. Cameron had gathered a significant force, comprising Red Cameron light horse, many Coelete warriors, Banoran fighters on their tough cobs and the infantry with their long pikes. He knew that even if the rebels in the south had restricted the Dewar's reinforcements and even with the support of the conscript forces, his army would be significantly outnumbered. With no heavy cavalry at his command, Cameron would need terrain that favoured Bala's side, and this was why he had chosen to confront the enemy at Erbea.

Once his troops had settled in their camps on the hills above Erbea, Cameron, with Alastair Munro and his other commanders, rode down to the conscript camp to assess the situation with Alluen. The winter had changed Alastair Munro. He had grown used to his power, although the awe with which his own people now regarded him was still unsettling. Only in Angus Ferguson's company did he feel he still belonged to Banora. He rode towards Erbea dressed entirely in light blue over and under his armour. With the ever-present radiance of his power, the light blue seemed to shine iridescent white as he moved.

Alluen had gathered her sergeants and greeted

the arriving Cameron. "Welcome James," she said. "You can see we have held to our promise. It has been hard over the winter months, but most of my men are fit and ready to reap revenge on the tyrant's army. If you look to the city walls, you can see that winter has not treated the occupants so kindly." The new arrivals looked towards the city just as two more bodies were dropped from the walls onto the pile of rotting remains that lay grotesquely spread across the open ground.

Cameron sighed. "That sight gives me no pleasure. Soldiers understand the risks they take in battle, but many of those will be innocent citizens. Still, we had to bring the Dewar to this ground to fight us here on my terms. Let's go to your tent and agree our tactics for the battle which can now only be a couple of days away."

Cameron laid out the map of the land surrounding Erbea, which had been drafted in Aldene under John Burnett's instructions. The main road that led into Erbea crossed the Erb over a narrow bridge that led to the southern city gates. The road ran through the city, leaving it again at the north gate and leading on to the hills where the Bala army was now camped. The road to the north was bounded by the Long Woods and the North Woods. Running from the south, a second raised track ran to the ford over the Erb to the west of the city, skirting the southern edge of the Long Woods and joining the northern road at the Bari Bridge.

Alluen confirmed that the melting snows had caused both the Bari and the Erb to overflow into the flood plains that lay on both banks of the Erb and to the east of the Bari. Cameron was satisfied that the land would play its part in the battle to come.

As the Dewar was leaving Boretar to lead the army north, a messenger hurried to call him back. A war boat had arrived from Anelo. The Dewar hoped the captain would bring some good news, but he did not. The captain had managed to extract his boat from the sea battle and had witnessed from afar the landings in the port at Anelo. It was now clear why few reinforcements had arrived from Anelo. The King was tempted to turn his army round and march them south, but was sure that Oien would object. It was also clear to the Dewar that he did not have enough men to fight on two fronts, so it had to be north to crush the Cameron and free Erbea. Once Oien could restart the fires in Banora, he would have the weapons to retake the south and squash the rebellions in Toria and Ciren. He had two concerns: firstly, the possibilities of enemy attack from the south, and secondly, the real intentions of the old alchemist.

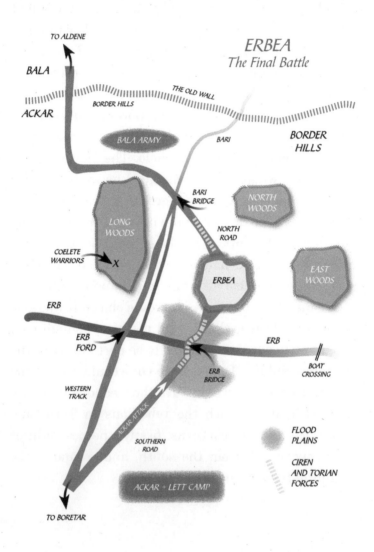

TO ALDENE

BALA

ACKAR

ERBEA
The Final Battle

THE OLD WALL

BORDER HILLS

BALA ARMY

BARI

BORDER
HILLS

BARI
BRIDGE

NORTH
WOODS

LONG
WOODS

NORTH
ROAD

COELETE
WARRIORS

X

ERBEA

EAST
WOODS

ERB

ERB
FORD

ERB

BOAT
CROSSING

ERB
BRIDGE

WESTERN
TRACK

ACKAR ATTACK

FLOOD
PLAINS

SOUTHERN
ROAD

CIREN
AND TORIAN
FORCES

ACKAR + LETT CAMP

TO BORETAR

ERBEA – 2nd APRIL 1302

The massed armies of Ackar and Lett had arrived on the afternoon of the first of April and camped south of the flood plains on either side of the main road leading into the south of the city. Beyond the city to the north and east, on a hilltop, flew the red-edged blue cross flag of the Red Cameron. The Dewar muttered to himself, "That is where we will end this tomorrow. Cut off the head of the snake and the body will vanish."

When that tomorrow came mist hung over the Erb and the Bari, and the city of Erbea was hidden behind a cloud of white. It was clear that the snake would live a while longer, as any charge into the mists was likely to be suicidal. Nonetheless the plan was set and the Dewar's commanders were ready and had their instructions. The absence of the Ember Horse remained a concern, but that could be dealt with at a later date.

Oien nodded to the King and started to walk along the road towards the city. There was something odd about the mist that he could not quite define. It hung over the rivers and across the city, but did not seem to reach far to either the east or the west. It also seemed remarkably static. Maybe Malama O'Re still lived, and this was his creation.

Oien lifted his staff and red fire tore at the white

mist, dispersing it and showing the forces gathering on the far side of the bridge over the Erb. Moments later the mist closed again, like a curtain closing over a window.

Alastair Munro was on the far side of the bridge, and the impact of the red fire nearly made him lose concentration. He saw the mist part for a second, but then with a wave of his hand he closed the brief window.

Munro had been with James Cameron and his commanders on the hill the night before and had been asked if he could create some form of cover as the Bala forces moved to their positions. Oien's misgivings about the mist were correct, although he did not know it had been created by the apprentice rather than the master. Having in many ways mastered his power, Alastair Munro was now as powerful and confident as Ala Moire had promised he would be. His hatred of this enemy was a cold white fire in his soul, whilst his love of his homelands still burnt bright. He was sure that this was the time, and this was the place, to end this conflict once and for all.

It was late morning when the mist suddenly lifted, seemingly of its own accord. Cameron's forces were now in place. The Dewar ordered the attack. The knights of the heavy cavalry would advance on the main road and clear the defenders from the bridge over the Erb. Light cavalry would race along the raised track to the west and then separate, with half the force advancing on the Cameron's hill-top position and the other half turning east to enter Erbea by the north gate. If both attacks could breach the defences, they would meet in the centre of Erbea and then turn north to support the attack on the main Cameron force. This was exactly what Cameron had anticipated. The Dewar was a great king, but not a great tactician.

The Erb Bridge was defended by the pikes of the Ciren and Toria conscripts commanded by Alluen's sergeants. The young Princess herself was with the conscript forces on the north road, ready to resist any attack from the Ackar cavalry on the northern gate. Whilst the conscripts were not elite troops, they had been well trained under their Ackar and Lett overlords. More importantly, they now regarded themselves as freedom fighters for their homelands. Defeat here would at best send them back to slavery under the tyrant. More likely it would mean a painful death.

The pike and shield wall formed the first line of defence some fifty yards south of the narrows of the bridge. Whilst the initial charge of the heavy cavalry crushed the first lines of the defenders, the relatively narrow road created its own problems for the cavalry. Four abreast, the knights charged the front line of the conscript forces, but it soon became apparent that there was no way out from the front. Knights moving off the road to allow the following horse to make contact found themselves sucked into the soggy mud of the flood plains, soaked as they were by the melting snow from the north.

Leaving many of their comrades dead on the road, the Ciren and Torian shield wall slowly pulled back to the Erb Bridge. This created a much narrower front that was almost impossible to penetrate for the large, heavily-armoured horses and their knights, and as more pulled off the road they too were trapped by the mud of the plain. It soon became clear that the heavy cavalry would not breach the hedgehog of pikes locked in the narrows at the bridge. As the horses pulled back, several of their brothers drowned as the weight of their armour pulled them down and they were sucked into the mud.

As the heavy cavalry was advancing on the southern defenders, the light cavalry was racing up the western track to engage directly with the Cameron forces apparently waiting on the hilltop beyond. Capturing the Bari Bridge was the first target before the forces split to attack the defences gathered in front of Erbea's northern gates, with the second force moving to engage the Bala troops on the hilltop. Moving at speed, the riders quickly crossed the ford on the Erb, and with the Long Wood on their left, headed for the bridge. The lead horses had almost reached their target when screams came from the riders in the centre of the force. Volleys of long arrows skewered the riders or their mounts. The distance between the track and the Long Wood had given the impression that any ambush from the wood could be intercepted before any major damage was caused. The Dewar had no knowledge of the Coelete longbows, which could far outreach the range of a conventional bow. The light cavalry paid the price for that ignorance.

As the rear of the light horse turned to retreat, a force of Bala foot charged out from the southern edge of the wood and formed up at the entry to the ford over the Erb. Whilst the cavalry won through again, many were lost to the Coelete arrows or to the mud in the flood plain to the east of the Bari. The Ackar light horse, now isolated north of the woods, had reached the Bari Bridge, but Red Cameron troopers now emerged from the Long Woods and the North Woods. John Burnett led the attack from the west whilst Angus Ferguson and Alex Cameron led from the north-east. It was a short and violent engagement, but the Red Cameron were masters of the hit, run, retreat, hit again tactic of light cavalry, and the Ackar forces retreated. They now faced the prospect of running the gauntlet back south and having to dodge the arrows from the Long Woods.

The sun was a little past its zenith as the bedraggled forces from both attacks found their way back to the Ackar base camp. The Dewar had made the same mistake as the one that had cost Elan his life at the Pass of Ing. Greater force of numbers would seldom win over better tactics and planning.

By mid-afternoon the Ackar and Lett foot soldiers were formed up in ranks to advance along the main road. The Dewar had decided that the Erb Bridge had to be taken, and via the south gate his forces could take the city. This could only be accomplished by might of men and steel. It would be a bloody fight on the narrow bridge, but his foot far outnumbered their opponents, so the loss of men would be worth the gain. Once the city was recaptured Ackar forces could then use the city walls as defence and move to obliterate the Cameron forces still defiant on their hilltop. The western path would need to wait, as foot soldiers would be massacred under a hail of arrows like that which had slaughtered many of the light horse. Again the Dewar cursed the absence of the Ember Horse.

As the Ackar ranks prepared to march, the wind suddenly picked up and black clouds raced in from the west. An early spring storm was about to thwart the plans for the attack. Flashes of lightning were followed by hail and torrents of rain, which battered against the armour of the foot soldiers. It seemed clear that there would be no taking of the Erb Bridge or the city on this day. By contrast, James Cameron saw that the storm had created other possibilities.

Oien looked to the skies and cursed, and amber sparks flashed from his cloak and staff. This storm was beyond even the power of Malama O'Re, and not for the first time Oien wondered if a greater power was intent on stopping his progress.

In Erbea, the winter had not been kind to the inhabitants and the smell of death was everywhere. Starvation and disease had wrought havoc, and the ditches below the outer walls were littered with the remains of the corpses tossed from the city. Patrick Roth had done his best. Strict control of food reserves had limited those dying of starvation, but he had no tools to fight the diseases that became rampant in the stricken city. All he could do was remove the bodies and hope the plagues went with them.

As the mists had cleared that morning and the first engagements had begun, Roth had called the few men he had to the southern city walls to try to harass the rear of the Ciren and Torian troops holding the bridge. The arrows and spears from the walls had made little impact, as the range was too great, and those enemy troops who were within range were well drilled, and held a roof of shields over their heads.

Before the first storm clouds had come in from the west, Roth had seen that his King's intention was for the foot soldiers to take the bridge. Roth thought that perhaps a quick incursion from the southern gate into the rear of the enemy could turn the day. So as the first crashes of thunder erupted in the heavens the noise of the grappling hooks landing on the northern walls was missed. Ciren and Torian soldiers quickly despatched the few defenders left guarding the northern walls and gate. Roth thought the storm had ended the fighting, so his men were not prepared for the attack from inside the city.

Alluen led the Ciren conscripts who had been protecting the northern road south of the Bari Bridge. Whilst the Dewar forces to the south of the city significantly outnumbered the Bala forces, the opposite was now true within Erbea. Following the Ciren troops, the Red Cameron, led by Alex Cameron and Angus Ferguson, swept through the city streets, clearing them of any opposition. For the most part the remaining citizens in the town hid behind their locked doors. As the hail and rain fell, so did the defenders of Erbea. With a fierce desire for revenge on their recent Ackar masters, the Ciren troops had little thought of mercy. The war cries of their home land rang out as they fell like wolves on Roth and his Ackar troops. None of these lived to tell the tale. Erbea was now in the hands of the Bala forces and their allies.

A short distance away on the hilltop the Cameron flag still proudly flew, seemingly defying the storm.

In the cover of the Long Wood, a lone Ackar horseman was sheltering. As dusk fell he stepped out of his cover and crossed towards the Bala camp. He was quickly ordered to halt, and the pickets on the outer edge of the camp led him to Cameron's tent.

Cameron turned as the guards entered with their captive. "Well, well, Koren of Coelene. Where did you spring from?" he said.

Koren was the Elder of Coelene, and one of those in Aldene who had proposed yielding to the invading monarch. He had not joined the Bala army on the Pass of Ing but had crossed back to his home on the east of the Plain of Coelene. Some months later he had been captured by the Ember Horse and forced to swear loyalty to the Dewar. As a result his lands had been gently treated by the invaders and he had joined the Ackar horse with some of his own retainers.

"My Lord, shortly after the invasion in Banora I was taken by the Ember Horse and forced to join the Ackar light cavalry," he said. "I have ridden with them since in Banora and Amina. At the conference in Aldene I could not see how Bala could resist the invader. I was wrong, and the fact you are here and Bala is again free is the evidence. I am not a traitor, I only wanted to do what I thought was best for my people. I am returning to ask your forgiveness and to warn you of a danger you need to face in the morning."

Cameron shrugged. "I could call you a traitor for

deserting your nation, but I may change my mind if you fight at our side in the morning. I know we are far outnumbered by the enemy forces, and we were probably saved today by the storm. They will now try to take the Erb Bridge by weight of men, and we cannot hold that position for long. I have my plans, but what danger do you need to tell me about?"

"I am not privy to the full Ackar plans, but as we moved out to the attack today it was clear that if the heavy cavalry failed then the foot would follow, but as you know the Erb Bridge is easily defended and a lot of lives will be lost winning through that narrow crossing. We passed the baggage train following the army as we moved north from Boretar a few days ago. It seemed strange to me at the time that the wagons moving north, as well as carrying the normal weapons and supplies, also carried at least a dozen boats. That's unusual support for a land army.-

"The Dewar King knows that the fight for the bridge will be hard. He has learnt that the western track is vulnerable to ambush. I think the boats are to be used to ferry troops over the Erb to the east of Erbea. If he can get enough men over the river, then he can avoid the flood plain and move round the city to secure the northern gate. If he can achieve this, then your Ciren force at the Erb Bridge will be attacked from behind, leaving the way across the bridge more easily won."

Koren did not know that Erbea was now in the hands of Cameron's forces, and nor did the Dewar.

The storm had blown over, but the night skies were dark and a light rain kept falling, hiding everything in gloom. In the Ackar camp The King's forces had returned to their sodden tents. Whilst the Dewar knew about Cameron's night attack in Banora, he thought it unlikely that the Red Cameron would venture an approach in the current weather. Scouts and cavalry patrols circuited the boundaries of the Ackar camp, but all seemed quiet.

By contrast, in the northern hills the Bala camp was furiously busy. Instructions were being sent to the dispersed forces in Erbea and the surrounding area. Through Munro, Cameron kept his younger brother informed of the plans for the next day. Bala soldiers, with help from Coelete warriors, were building a stake wall defence on the north side of the ford over the Erb. Alex Cameron and his troop of Red Cameron had been relocated to the north of the Long Woods, whilst Angus Ferguson and his troop were bivouacked in the East Wood with a troop of Banoran soldiers and their cobs. On the southern side of Erbea, Ciren and Torian troopers were busy laying wooden walkways on the marshy flood plains to the south east and south west of the Erb Bridge. Once secured, these passageways were lightly covered with mud and grass. Whilst the Dewar and the Ackar forces rested, Cameron's men had a busy night. He could only hope that preparation and planning would again wrong foot the over-confident King.

ERBEA – 3rd APRIL 1302

Dawn was still more than an hour away as the first activity stirred in the Lett section of the Dewar camp. Horses pulled the twelve boats forward from the rear and a thousand elite Lett foot soldiers lined up alongside the boats for the short march to the east of Erbea and the chosen crossing point where the Erb, swollen by snowmelt, was around a hundred feet wide. On this eastern side of Erbea the Erb cut a deeper channel which left the approaches to the river dry. The flood plains to the west had already gathered much of the overflow from the river. The instructions to the commanders were simple: ferry the troops across the river and approach the city from the east, then if the land was passable circle to the south and attack the rear of the defending force at the Erb Bridge. If that land was impassable, then head to the north and secure the north gate of the city. With troops north and south of the Erb, the Dewar hoped to squeeze his enemy between the two. The attacking force was not large, but it contained many of the best

Lett foot soldiers, men who had won through many battles alongside their King.

As a clear dawn chased away the night rain, the first of the three divisions crossed the Erb and formed up in a defensive position with their backs to the river. The division commanders were cautious, but with the secrecy surrounding the plan they did not really anticipate having to fight until they approached Erbea's walls.

The second division was nearing the far bank when the unexpected happened. A significant troop of Red Cameron was rapidly closing on the Lett force from their shelter in the East Woods, while a short distance behind, Banoran fighters reached the river bank. The Red Cameron were now highly proficient with the Banoran bow, and as the horses raced across the front of the Lett defensive position, arrows, lances and swords punched holes in the enemy line. The line had to hold to allow the second division to land. This meant that the Banoran troop were free to approach close to the Lett line without having to engage.

Banoran arrows hissed through the air as the men in the boats tried to protect themselves under their shields. Fires suddenly lit up the north bank as burning torches were thrown into the nearest of the incoming boats. The third division, still on the southern bank, could do nothing to help their comrades.

Then the unthinkable happened. A second troop of Red Cameron, riding under the blue cross flag, tore into the Lett force on the southern bank. Coran instantly saw that the third Lett division was not in any way prepared for an attack, and the Red Cameron initially wrought havoc. However these were elite foot soldiers, and their commanders quickly established defensive order. The remaining three hundred soldiers formed a defensive wall with shields and started an orderly retreat back towards the main camp.

Coran and his men were not equipped with the Banoran bow, and Coran's orders were normal Cameron tactics – hit, kill and run. By the time a large force of Ackar light horse had arrived, the Red Cameron were gone, leaving the bodies and wounded on the ground the only evidence of their existence.

The Lett troops in transit on the boats and on the north bank were less fortunate. Most of those in the boats died under Banoran arrows or drowned as the torched boats became engulfed in flame and sank. The first division on the northern bank had little chance as the Red Cameron cut them down from their defensive formation and were then joined by a cohort of Torian infantry.

Angus Ferguson called his men back from the fray, leaving the final phase of the slaughter to the Torian troopers. Of the thousand Lett soldiers who had marched from the camp before dawn, only three hundred returned from the killing grounds by the river. The Dewar had to think again. Somehow the Cameron seemed to anticipate his every move, and to his great frustration the blue cross flag still flew defiantly on the distant hilltop.

Oien was furious, and the amber sparks emanating from his cloak and staff emphasised the need for caution. But despite his inner fury, he kept his control. "My Lord King, we need to leave Erbea to its fate, we are wasting time here. With all the Bala forces gathered around Erbea we need simply move east and north and Aldene and Banora can be retaken. With a renewed supply of othium we can quickly rout these usurpers. I have sent orders for salt to be transported north urgently once the cargo carriers dock at Boretar. The fight here is not worth the cost of the delay in rearming with the red rock."

Oien was not to know that very little salt was on its way from the now occupied island of Elat.

The King was forceful in his reply. "I will free Erbea today. My foot soldiers will cross the Erb Bridge and slaughter the rebel conscripts. My heavy horse will simultaneously destroy the Cameron on his hilltop. That is my command. Tomorrow we will move on to Bala."

It would be the type of battle that the Ackar and Lett foot soldiers had won many times, from the conquests of Toria and Ciren to the plains of the Vale of Tember; man against man with sword and shield, where discipline and sheer weight of numbers were usually victorious, although the narrow front line at the bridge would slow the attackers' impetus. The Ackar and Lett forces were lining up. The road to the city was only wide enough for a front of twenty men, and the Erb Bridge reduced the front to only six men wide. Behind the first hundred infantry, the Ackar archers would fill the sky with deadly barbs to reduce the number of defenders and lower their morale. Once the bridge was won, the rest of the foot would pour across to win the southern gate and enter the city. The Dewar would fight on foot with his King's Guard and they would march with the cohort directly behind the archers. The Dewar knew he would be the first to enter and free his city.

On the south side of the bridge, the Ciren conscripts were the first line of defence. They would take the initial impact of the battle. Recognising the constraints of the road and the flood plains on the flanks, Alluen had devised a new approach to the shield wall defence. Pikes used in the Bala defensive formations, the walls of shields and pikes, were effective in an engagement against enemy cavalry but of less use in close combat.

Looking over at the defensive line, the Dewar was surprised to see pikes protruding from the Ciren front lines. He also wondered why enemy forces were positioned on the northern banks of the Erb. The marshy ground had been a trap for his forces the day before and it was unclear how any defence could be mounted through the mud. What the Dewar could see was a Ciren line of shields that equally matched his own front line, other than the pikes. This made no sense, as the pikes would limit the mobility of the front line and leave it exposed to the rush of his men into the battle.

What the Dewar could not see was that the pikes were in the hands of the second row of the Ciren wall, and he did not know that Alluen had a plan.

With the river crossing of the Erb a disaster, the Dewar had to again consider the western path to the Bari Bridge as a way to move his men north of the city. The experience of the day before and the Coelete arrows suggested a cautious approach. A force of Ackar light horse and infantry had been despatched to take and hold the ford over the river, but not to advance beyond it. The Dewar expected his knights on their war horses to clear the hill of the Cameron army and then remove the Bala defences at the ford, allowing the lighter cavalry and foot soldiers to sweep the strange warriors from the Long Wood.

As the Ackar shield wall moved forward on the main road, the western forces reached the ford. The sight that met them was not encouraging. To the northern end of the ford, the Bala troopers had erected a wall of wooden stakes that protected the front line of the defensive formations on the far bank. The light cavalry would need to cross the river and try to outflank the defenders to allow the foot soldiers to engage. The Ackar commanders held off, considering the situation and the risks.

From his hilltop position, Cameron watched as the battle lines formed. It had been shortly after dawn when he had been woken by Alain of Lorn. Coelete warriors had been patrolling to the west of the Long Wood, the only area where the Bala force was now susceptible to attack. Cameron also anticipated the possibility that the Dewar would simply leave Erbea to its fate and move his army north into Bala. In the Dewar's position this is what he would have done, and the Bala forces would have struggled to prevent the invasion. His hope was that the King would be too proud to leave his second city in enemy hands.

As the battle lines formed, Cameron knew that if his army could win here, then Bala would be safe. Alain of Lorn had brought confirmation earlier in the morning. The knights of the Ackar and Lett heavy cavalry had travelled west to cross the Erb near its source and they would be approaching the hill by mid-morning. Most of the Bala army had remained in their camps behind the hill, leaving the fighting around Erbea mainly to the Ciren and Torian troops.

The Ackar and Lett knights were led by Garan, the nineteen-year-old son of the Dewar, and his heir. Garan had inherited more from his mother than from his father, much to the father's irritation. Amelia, Garan's mother, had died when the young Prince was eleven years old. She had been the daughter of one of the senior nobles of Lett and had married the Dewar Prince when she was only sixteen. It had been a good match and the Dewar had greatly loved his gentle wife, who was a good foil to his own tempestuous nature. After Amelia died in 1294, the Dewar had not remarried and in his wife's absence he had no counter to his aggressive nature. Amelia had been the guiding light in Garan's childhood and he still desperately missed his mother. Tall but slightly built and with a mop of fair hair, Garan preferred books and music to battle. He led the heavy cavalry due to his rank and not his prowess in war. The nobles and their knights followed him because they were ordered to, but they had little respect for the young prince.

As Garan's knights looked up from the lower slopes, they could see the Bala forces drawn up in their defensive schiltrons. The schiltron was a defensive formation that John Burnett had devised in the winter in Aldene. The front row of pike men knelt with their weapons' butts wedged in the ground, while behind them the second row held their pikes forward over the front row. The third row of pikes rested on the shoulders of the second row, and so the three pike walls bristled on the hilltop. The defensive schiltron was designed to be almost impenetrable to an attacking force of heavy cavalry.

John Burnett, Alex Cameron and the Elder of Ewart were each in command of a thousand men. James Cameron had not had time to set traps in the lower ground, so he would have to rely on the hill itself to protect his defensive positions. Tall warriors stood between the schiltrons and on their flanks.

Cameron rode along the front line calming his men. "We have travelled far together to have the chance this day to secure our freedom and have peace in the land we love," he said. "Many of our new brothers from Ciren and Toria will die today fighting for the freedom of their own lands. We will draw the knights of Ackar and Lett onto our pikes and send them home bloodied. This is the time for us to win freedom for our land, for our people and for ourselves." Cameron knew that the die had been cast, and now timing was everything.

From his position Cameron could see the Ackar and Lett infantry march in orderly formation towards Alluen's defenders in front of the bridge. The clash of metal on metal could be heard from the hilltop. On the ground, the front ranks of the Ackar infantry fell to Ciren swords. The pikes from the second row of defenders narrowed the killing zone, and two Ciren swords cut into a single Ackar soldier forced to avoid the sharp ends of the pike.

Alluen had been instructed to hold the bridge. The tactic was simple. As the front line of the Ciren defence faltered and fell under the weight of the enemy charge, the survivors slipped from the line and the pikes were moved back to the third line. As men from both sides fell, the bodies on the narrow road slowed the impetus of the attack. The Dewar ordered his archers to engage and the sky filled with deadly barbs, thinning the lines of the Ciren forces in front of the bridge. As Alluen's defenders gradually drew back towards the bridge, the Dewar sensed victory was near.

In that moment of distraction the King did not notice the first of his archers fall to a long arrow from the city walls. Gareth and his band of Coelete warriors were far beyond the range of the Ackar bowmen, and the Dewar's men fell in front of him. For the first time, the Dewar felt fear. As the Ackar archers hesitated, the Ciren and Torian troops stationed on the northern banks of the sodden flood plain seemed to miraculously cross the marshy ground to attack the flanks of the Ackar troops. With little protection the Ackar bowmen were easy pickings, and the first of the King's Guard were soon being sucked into the battle. Alluen's pike hedgehog was now locked in the narrows of the bridge, and engagement with the front lines became a suicide attack for the Ackar troopers. As more Ciren forces crossed the submerged walkways, it became clear that the forward Ackar forces could quickly be cut off. The King and his guard moved forward to resist the attacks on the flanks and to hold the road.

On the western path, the Ackar light horse had hesitated as they faced the pike and stake defences on the north side of the river. As the noise of battle grew from the east, the commanders knew they needed to engage. It was a decision delayed too long. As the first of the light horse charged towards the defenders, they were hit from behind. Orridon and Idula, with a large force of Ember Horse riding under the Cameron flag and the wild horse emblem of Ember, smashed into the rear of the Ackar force.

The Ackar light horse were battle-hardened troops, but they were no match for the wild riders from the Ember plains. Despite the shouted orders from their commanders, they panicked, each man looking to save himself, while small groups retreated back south towards their homeland. The supporting foot soldiers never got their feet wet and had no place to run as they were cut down by the Ember warriors.

At the pike wall, Davy Scott stepped out. Idula dismounted and shook his hand. They had been colleagues in Burnett's winter travels and after a while had become friends. Orridon nodded to Scott and shouted to his nephew, "No time for idle chat! We have work to do and an enemy to chase!"

No sooner had they arrived than the Ember Horse turned to continue the fight to the south. With the ford safe, Davy Scott turned one of his schiltrons north towards the Bari Bridge.

Garan led the first charge of the knights up the hill to attack the Bala schiltrons. Despite his youth and inexperience, Garan recognised that Cameron had chosen his position wisely. On flat ground the weight of a heavy cavalry charge could break the most resolute of defensive lines, but uphill the charge slowed. However it was the tall warriors on either side of the defensive positions that caused the first casualties. The well-armoured horses and their knights were usually protected from incoming missiles, but the long arrows fired from such an unexpected distance had great penetrating power. Many of the first attackers were struck from their horses, or their horses were impaled under them. Garan had been schooled in the theory of warfare, but he had little experience. Theory said that with a first success the foot soldiers would leave their defensive positions to charge on the enemy. The Bala commanders knew better, and as the knights drew back the schiltrons held their hilltop position.

Garan and the Ackar and Lett nobles were regrouping for a second charge when Davy Scott's pikemen appeared, moving north from the Bari Bridge. Garan was left in a quandary. The approaching foot soldiers would not in themselves create a problem, but if they moved into the lower ground they could follow the charge uphill and lock the heavy cavalry between two pike walls. Regardless of the obvious risk, Garan ordered a second charge. As the knights crashed again into the front rows of the schiltrons, they did not see Angus Ferguson's Red Cameron entering the fray from the east. The Cameron troopers were less well armed than the knights they engaged, but they were also much more mobile and content to pick off their opponents exposed on the flank of the heavy cavalry.

The schiltrons again repelled the attack and the bodies of many of the cream of Ackar and Lett nobility were left scattered on the hilltop. As Garan pulled the knights back, Davy Scott's schiltron, now in circular formation, was moving in tight order up the hillside. The young Prince knew he did not want to die on this hill today and rode off to the west with his close retainers. Some of the nobles attempted to break Scott's schiltron, but with Ferguson's Red Cameron hounding their rear and flanks it soon became clear that the depleted force would simply be slaughtered if it remained in the field. The Bala army shouted insults as the knights dispersed.

The battle at the Erb Bridge was locked in a mass of killing. The King's Guard had now identified the sunken paths and were engaging the Ciren troops moving over the marshy ground. Alluen's pike were locked in the narrows of the bridge, and despite the loss of men were just holding back a breakthrough.

Then, as Alastair Munro stood watching in horror from the city wall, a familiar voice spoke. "Alastair, it is time to end this madness. Use the white arrows." Ala Moire was still guiding his apprentice from beyond the grave.

Alastair felt a strange glow, and looked to his shoulder. Two of his arrows were shining white in their quiver. The distance seemed impossible, but he could not ignore the whispered instruction. He knew there was no need to aim, and simply shot both arrows in rapid succession.

Oien, from his position near the rear of the Ackar troops, had noticed the figure on the city walls and the light that seemed to shine around it. Again he wondered if his old enemy had somehow escaped the assassin's knife. Too late he saw the white lights shoot through the sky. He raised his staff, and red fire shot out over the troops. It deflected the second arrow, but the fire came too late to tear the first from the sky, and it hit the ground in front of the Dewar.

As the baffled King looked on, a slow rumbling began around the place where the arrow had struck, and it quickly grew until the ground was shaking violently. In the road before them a great crack appeared. The horrified Dewar and his men turned to flee, but they were too slow. Before they had covered two paces the crack had become a yawning chasm, and with cries of despair, the Dewar King and a dozen of his guard fell helpless into the depths of the underworld.

With their King lost and cut off from any retreat, the Ackar and Lett soldiers at the forward line slowly laid down their weapons. The battle for the Erb Bridge was over.

With the chasm making their advance impossible and their King gone, the Ackar and Lett army started to pull back towards their base camp. It turned into a hazardous journey as Coran and the Red Cameron attacked the retreating soldiers. The camp held no refuge either, as Ishca and the Doran cavalry had already destroyed much of the baggage train and the reserve units. The retreat became a rout. With their own cavalry dispersed, groups of foot soldiers laid down their weapons, whilst others tried to escape to the south, in the desperate hope of seeking sanctuary back at Boretar.

Red fire flashed in bursts as Oien tried to protect himself from the cavalry's onslaught. Realising that his own position was becoming increasingly perilous and that the fire identified him, he slipped into one of the remaining wagons in the south of the Ackar camp. The Cameron and Doran cavalry now ignored the camp and continued to round up prisoners and to chase down units trying to escape south.

As the fighting ended, no one paid any attention to the old beggar in black leaning heavily on his staff as he shuffled down the southern road.

James Cameron entered Erbea by the northern gate and was greeted by Alluen. He dismounted and bowed to the young princess. "You should be very proud of your warriors, Alluen," he said. "They have succeeded against all the odds, thanks to your tactics and deployments."

"My Lord, I am glad to see you safe, we could not have held the bridge much longer. Indeed until Munro's arrows came I thought we would be overwhelmed by the Dewar force. There were simply too many of them. I was very close to ordering our retreat back behind Erbea's walls."

Cameron nodded. "You will please join me and the others later to plan what we do next. You should also know that your husband and brother have gathered an army and wait at the gates of Boretar."

Dusk was falling as the Cameron commanders gathered again after their disparate actions. Last to join was Orridon, as his Ember Horse had raided far to the south to harry the retreating Ackar cavalry. Idula continued with the chase, forcing the Ackar troops to fight a rearguard action whilst moving south.

James Cameron rose from his seat to greet the Duke. "Welcome Orridon, and my thanks. You and your men enabled Coran to win Anelo, and it might not have ended happily at the ford without your intervention." The two former enemies shook hands. Cameron continued, "I have news for you from the King of Arance."

Orridon stiffened. Ember was a province of Arance and it was his brother's treachery that had enabled Dewar the First to conquer Arance and send the King to exile in Tamin.

"The King has agreed that once we sign peace treaties, Ember will be ceded from Arance and become an independent country again," Cameron went on. "The past will be forgotten and your people will be the first to gain independence."

Orridon was taken aback. He murmured his thanks.

"Now, on to business," Cameron continued. "We have won a great victory here, thanks mostly to the Ciren and Torian warriors. Their brothers now wait at the gates of Boretar, and in the morning we march south to secure peace. The new King is not like his father or grandfather, and I believe if we show our mettle in front of the gates of his capital, we can force his hand to set treaties for peace. I have no wish to rule the lands in Ackar and Lett, but we now need agreement to seal the independence of our countries, both north and south."

With a strong force left behind in Erbea under the command of Angus Ferguson, the allied armies marched on south to Boretar.

CHAPTER SEVENTEEN
The Peacemaker

It was a warm spring day, and under the shelter of a large canopy four long tables formed a square. The canopy was emblazoned with the emblems of the Dewar Kings, but around the outside flew the flags of Amina, Toria, Ciren, Arance and Bala. At the front flew the blue cross of the Red Cameron and the wild horse of Ember.

Around the table sat the kings of the southern lands, returned from exile. Tyros, Alluen and Erin sat with their respective kings. In the centre of the square of tables a smaller table was positioned with quill and paper on the table top. At this smaller table James Cameron, Alastair Munro and Orridon took their places.

The first paper of the day was signed by Orridon and passed to the King of Arance, who added his signature. The signatures sealed the right of Ember to exist as an independent country whilst promising, in the event of conflict, its alliance with Arance. Orridon, who admired the democratic system in Bala, had refused the title King of Ember but would retain his title as Duke.

The assembled lords fell quiet as Idula led Garan into the enclosure. The Ember Horse had captured the young Prince as he tried to make his way south to Boretar. With most of the nobles of Ackar and Lett now also prisoner, Garan had surrendered the city on his arrival. With the Prince's capture and the scattering of his father's forces, there was little option. The surrounding army, commanded by Erin and Tyros, had no siege equipment, but as they were bolstered by the arrival of the Ember Horse and Ishca's Doran cavalry, it was clear that there was little chance of a break-out from the city. Tyros had accepted its surrender a day earlier and had ordered that there should be no entry by the surrounding forces. The city gates remained closed.

Garan looked frightened as he came in and visibly shook as he was led to his seat. James Cameron offered his hand to the young man. Relief swept over Garan's face; maybe he was not here to be tried for the sins of his father and grandfather. Cameron offered the youth a seat, which he took. Cameron remained standing and addressed the gathering.

"My Lords and Lady, we are here to settle a peace, not to persecute men for the sins of the past. None here want dominion over the lands of Ackar and Lett. There has been enough destruction and death in the name of the Prince's father and grandfather. Now is the time to agree a safe and secure future for all of our lands." He turned to Garan. "My Lord Prince, we would all be pleased to attend your coronation as Dewar the Third. The coronation has already been arranged for fourteen days hence. None of our troops will enter the city, by command of Tyros and myself, and your people can remain safe within their walls provided you agree to sign the documents in front of you."

Garan's shoulders sagged, but there was relief on his face. He would be signing away his birthright, but he knew he had little option.

There was a long list of documents to sign. Garan was to sign under his future title of King Dewar the Third and the documents were all dated 24th April 1302, after his coronation.

On reading the first document, Garan looked over to Cameron in puzzlement. "You need to sign these as King, not Prince in waiting," explained the older man. "The thirteen days are to allow you time to order the withdrawal of your troops occupying the towns of

Anelo, Cire and Tora in the south. None of your forces remain in Amina. The peace treaties we are signing will come into force on the twenty-fourth, and if your occupying forces are not back in Ackar and Lett before that date then they will be considered outlaws to peace and be denied safe passage back to their own lands. Once you have signed the treaties, the armies of Ciren and Toria will move south to Lett's southern border to uphold your order, with force if required."

Garan read the first document, which guaranteed in perpetuity that Ackar and Lett would hold Amina as a free and independent kingdom. An added catch clause promised that Ackar and Lett would come to the aid of Amina in the event of any attack on their sovereign kingdom. Garan signed, and the paper was passed to the King of Amina, who countersigned. Cameron and Munro signed as witnesses to each document. The same followed for each of the southern kingdoms.

The last document had a sting in the tail. The wording was the same as the rest apart from the last clause, which stated that to protect its border Ackar and Lett would agree to the border being moved south of the old wall. Bala was to be gifted the lands up to the northern bank of the Erb River. This of course included the city of Erbea.

Cameron noted Garan's hesitation. "Your people and those north of the Erb will be treated as citizens of Bala with full rights," he said. "I will appoint a Bala lord as governor in Erbea. Bala has suffered greatly under your father's greed and we need to create a wider border between our countries. You will also notice that the clause allows for the return of the northern territories to Ackar and Lett after the passage of one hundred years' peace."

Garan signed.

The treaties made on the plain outside Boretar were designed to herald a new time of peace for the lands. The agreements intrinsically linked the security of each country to the others, and an invasion of any of the lands would require all to come to its aid. Since Kermin and Doran had not suffered much under Dewar the Second, they were not included in the signatories, although their existing pacts with Amina largely locked them into the same agreements.

Those in the crowd which had gathered some distance from the great treaty signing paid little attention to the old beggar in their midst. Oien was careful, as he was known in Boretar. Over his normal clothing he had covered himself in black rags. From a distance he could only guess at what was happening round the tables, but he knew that the Prince would not resist the demands of those gathered before him.

Oien paid more attention to the Banoran man who sat alongside James Cameron. From his dress this was the archer from Erbea's walls who had halted the Dewar attack. Clearly it was not Malama O'Re himself, but someone who had somehow taken on his mantle.

Few in the crowd would talk to the filthy old beggar, so his questions about the person dressed in light blue remained unanswered. There was little more to learn here. The armies that could have helped Oien to conquer the world were defeated. For the first time the old alchemist felt his many years. It was time to return to Banora. With a supply of othium nearby, he hoped he could recharge his energy and rekindle his hopes.

Once the signings were completed, King's messengers were dispatched with royal orders for all occupying troops in Ciren, Toria and Arance to move back inside Lett's borders within ten days and await further orders. The troops were promised safe passage. Having followed the dead King's call to arms for the northern war, the Ackar and Lett forces left in the southern countries were actually relatively few in number. Cameron expected little resistance to the orders, but nonetheless a troop of Doran cavalry travelled with each messenger.

Erin, Count of Toria, asked Cameron to hold the messenger who was destined for his home city of Tora. "I think we need to send a bigger force to my homeland," he said. "Orimir has been ruthless in squashing the local rebellions in Toria. As we travelled through the forest in March to join Tyros's army we saw little movement of Ackar troops responding to last month's call to assemble with the King's army at Boretar. Orimir has the grip on power in Tora and behaves as if he were a king himself rather than a subject of the Dewar. My fear is that he will ignore the young Prince's orders and try to gain control of Toria for himself. With your permission I would like to take my men and go with the Doran cavalry to ensure Tora is released from occupation. I only have a few hundred men, but I know some of Tyros's Ciren warriors will join us, and as we travel south the local freedom fighters will add to our numbers. With our men on foot, we may not be able to get to Tora and report back before the twentieth of April, but I do not wish to send the Doran cavalry on a suicide mission."

Cameron nodded; he had heard of Orimir's reputation and his ambition. "Go Erin, and go quickly," he said. "Good luck."

As an afterthought, Cameron called over Alain of Lorn and explained the situation. Erin was surprised to see a troop of the tall Coelete warriors line up beside his men as they prepared to march south.

A week later, a group of Doran horsemen rode back into Boretar to confirm the withdrawal from Arance and Ciren. As the Ackar and Lett occupiers crossed the border the Ciren forces moved south, taking up defensive positions on their side of the border. Alluen and Tyros hoped that the exchange of land would remain peaceful, but they also recognised that there were still seven days before the treaties became official.

To the east, Idula and a large force of Ember Horse ensured that the few Lett forces left in Arance passed peacefully back to their own lands. With a day to go before the coronation, no word had come back from Erin and Alain on the situation in Toria.

The 24th of April dawned with clear blue spring skies, and in Boretar the pageantry for the coronation was already being readied. The day before, Garan had travelled to the Lett capital of Olet, to be greeted with festivities. It was Ackar tradition that the King in waiting was feted by his subjects in Olet before returning on the King's barge to Boretar for the formal crowning in the city castle.

It was early morning when a weary Doran cavalryman rode into the Bala camp seeking James Cameron. Cameron and Alastair Munro quickly arrived at the large headquarters tent in the centre of the camp, and the trooper told his story. Erin's troops had arrived at the southern edge of the Forest of Lett on the 18th of April. The King's messenger, with Alain of Lorn and some of the Coelete warriors, had approached Tora. As instructed, the messenger had stopped a short distance from the closed city gates, while the Coelete waited on the hilltop some distance back with their longbows at the ready. The messenger had shouted to the city wall that he had a message from the Prince for the Governor. Orimir could see that he was out of range of the strange tall archers on the hill, and with a cohort of well-dressed companions, he rode out from the city. Taking the messenger's papers, he slowly read the instructions, then with a cry of rage he drew out his sword and decapitated the messenger.

It was a mistake. Immediately the long arrows soared into the sky and four of the nobles fell from their horses. Orimir limped back to Tora with a Coelete arrow in his shoulder.

The following day, Erin and the Torian army drew up on the same hilltop. Erin rode forward a short way and announced to the city that Orimir's action was treason and all in the city were now outlawed. He told the citizens they had until noon the next day to surrender before he would lead his troops to attack. By way of warning, a volley of Coelete arrows flew up over the city walls, impaling two unwary defenders.

On the morning of the 20th the city gates were opened and a delegation of nobles walked out under a white flag. Erin held his ground and let the small group come to him. As they approached, he recognised a number of the group; they were junior lords of Toria who had helped Orimir in order to gain position and wealth.

Erin nodded to the leader of the group, who was the son of one of Toria's exiled nobles. Whilst they were all traitors to their country, Erin resisted his instinct to take revenge. After all, they were under a flag of peace.

The leader explained to Erin that the city was surrendering. Orimir and the other Ackar nobles in the city had been executed during the night, and the Torian lords gathered here now represented authority in the city. The gates were open for the Count of Toria to be welcomed back to his home. What would have been the last battle in the wars for independence never happened.

Cameron let out a sigh of relief. With Toria secure and the peace treaties coming into force that day, maybe a longer peace could be won.

The citizens of Boretar were lining the streets, dressed in all their finery. In the castle the kings and lords from all the lands crammed into the Great Hall. Most were not there to celebrate the coronation, but to ensure it took place. On completion of the ceremony, the peace treaties would become law across the lands.

As the King's barge drew up at Boretar's port, great cheers rose from the crowds. Garan stepped from the barge, looking swamped by his regal robes.

None, it seemed, greatly mourned the passing of his father. Across Ackar and Lett, the ordinary folk were tired of the wars of aggression of the Dewar dynasty. They had lost too many fathers, brothers and sons on foreign soil. It was clear that the new King was no warrior, and most of the population thought that a good thing. Maybe for the first time in generations they could have a good king rather than a warrior king.

As he walked up the central isle of the Great Hall, the future King looked much younger than his years. Garan knew his sudden rise to the throne was only grudgingly being accepted by the Ackar and Lett nobles. They were used to ruling, and it was hard for them to accept this frightened youth as their King. However, the succession was part of their sworn fealty to the old King and the promises would be honoured. The fact that the Bala army remained camped outside their city encouraged them to keep their vows.

As Garan stood on the top step in front of the King's throne, Roger Eld stepped forward to place the crown on the Prince's head. The ornate and ancient crown of Ackar glittered with gold and precious stones. As the Captain of Boretar moved to place the crown on the young man's head, Alastair Munro stepped forward, to a gasp from the crowd. He laid his hand on the Prince's head before the crown was placed, and his cloak and clothing shimmered in sparkling white.

Garan seemed transfixed and then transformed as white light sparkled around his body. The fear vanished from his face and calmness seemed to settle over him. As the new King Dewar the Third settled on the throne, a strange peace flooded through his veins. A hush descended through the hall as all present wondered what had just happened.

After a quiet moment, Garan rose to address the gathering. The callow youth seemed somehow to have suddenly grown into the royal robes, and his voice reflected his new-found confidence.

"My lords and ladies, I accept this crown and the responsibilities that come with it," he said. "I am not like my father or my grandfather. In taking this responsibility I will expect my people to respect the peace treaties that have now come into force. All of our lands have suffered over the past decades of war and conquest, and to those affected I apologise on behalf of my family. With peace, I want our lands to be partners, making all our countries prosperous through trust and trade. I now commit as my coronation promise that whilst I am King, no armies from Ackar and Lett will seek domination over our neighbours. The treaties are written in ink. I will now seal them with my blood."

Dewar the Third drew a small knife across his thumb and sealed each treaty with a thumbprint. The onlookers were dumbstruck. Treaties on paper came and went, but a promise sealed in blood was for life.

James Cameron was the first to react. He added his thumbprint under his name on the treaty with Bala and as witness to the other treaties. Uncertainly at first, the other signatories on the treaties did the same.

The new King was not done. Rising again from his seat, he addressed his own nobles. "I will not be a warrior king, this you all know," he said. "I am a student and an observer. I have seen the power and the evil that came to Boretar with the old alchemist. Oien's power was a blessing to my father and his ambitions, but for me it is a curse. From now on any use of othium or the salt from Elat will be outlawed, and any use of this evil will be considered treason in my land. The purveyor, however powerful, will face immediate execution. That is the first order of my reign."

The King's words were not lost on those who had experienced the terror of the red fire.

Garan continued, "I am less sure how my rule should treat the magic that seems to be under the control of the man from Banora. Munro, come and kneel for me." Cameron got to his feet to object, but Alastair Munro pressed him back to his seat and walked up to the throne. As he was about to kneel as requested, the King stepped forward and embraced the Banoran.

All of those who witnessed the event told slightly different stories. Most reported a white cloud descending over the pair and said that as it covered them the cloud sparkled as if in joy.

The King stepped back, breaking the moment. He smiled gently at Alastair Munro.

"Thank you, I feel you have somehow anointed me and blessed my coronation," he said. "You, or your power, have given me great faith that my reign will be with a mission for good, for peace and for love."

At the start of the day a timid youth had presented himself for the start of a great journey. In a few short hours the youth had been transformed into a King.

Ala Moire's voice whispered in Alastair Munro's head. "Well done, Alastair. The young King's heart is for good and God is pleased. In future times he will be known as the Peacemaker and will become the greatest of all the Dewar kings."

History would remember Dewar the Third's reign as the greatest of the age, sixty years of peace and prosperity, of law and order, and most of all, of humility and love. His journey had begun.

Days of feasting followed the coronation of the new King. Treaties for trade and cooperation were signed, and there was agreement to stand down most of the armed men across all the countries. In the many ports across the lands the war boats and troop carriers were to be decommissioned and redeployed as trading vessels. In towns and villages, people celebrated. A new century was just at its dawning, and it held new promise for the years ahead.

With summer beckoning, the men of the Bala army needed to return to their fields to plough and plant. The Coelete were impatient to get back to their northern homelands, armed with a new conviction – they were now one of the clans of Bala.

James Cameron rode into Boretar to take his farewells, Alastair Munro at his side. Dewar the Third was busy at his desk writing orders for the demobilisation of the troops at the Lett border. For Cameron his transformation from a prince to a king was still astonishing. He had not discussed this with Munro, knowing that, like Ala Moire, the Banoran would just smile and wave away any explanation.

Cameron shook the King's hand. "It is time for me to return your land to your care and time for my troops to return to their fields," he said.

Garan nodded, "I am sure you will be safe. You and yours are always welcome at my court. I hope we will meet again soon. I would appreciate you educating me in battle tactics. Whilst we have agreed peace, I know some of my own nobles are less than happy, and I need to be better trained in how to deal with any revolt."

"It will be my pleasure, my Lord King. I will

return once I have attended to urgent business in my own capital."

As the pair turned to leave, the King asked Alastair Munro to stay a moment and took his hand. "I cannot thank you enough for whatever magic you performed a few days ago, although I still don't understand your power," he said.

Alastair briefly described his understanding of the events of the Second Age and the role Oien had played in ancient days.

Garan sighed. "I always felt that my father was simply a pawn in the old man's game," he said. "Oien played on my father's ambition and desire for more power and more wealth. What of me?"

It was Alastair Munro's time to smile. Much still depended on the other man's resolve. "You have been anointed by God and He is pleased," he said. "Seek His guidance when you are troubled or unsure. I do not have a crystal ball to tell the future, but with luck and your wisdom you can enjoy a golden age. Farewell, my Lord King. We may not meet again." As the two embraced for what could be the last time, the King again felt the surge of hope transmitted from Munro.

When Alastair returned to the Bala camp, the troops were already preparing to leave. James Cameron approached. "We are ready to go Alastair, and whilst the army will return directly to their home lands and their farms, you and I with some of the others will return via Erbea. With the treaties now in force, I have business to attend to in our new city."

Alastair looked puzzled. "James, it is time for me to return to Banora," he said.

"It is not an order Alastair, but I would be honoured to have you ride with me and help me with my task in Erbea." Cameron smiled; it pleased him that he had a secret he could keep from the other man.

The Bala army marched north towards their home, travelling in ordered units under the command of the Elder of Ewart. Red Cameron troopers and Coelete warriors roamed widely ahead and on the flanks. Treaties may have been signed in blood, but renegade Ackar and Lett troops could still be a threat in the north after they had dispersed from Erbea. In fact the army passed the old wall without incident.

CHAPTER EIGHTEEN

An Uninvited Guest

It was a smaller group that travelled on the north road back to Erbea. James and Alex Cameron were accompanied by Alastair Munro, Alain of Lorn, and Davy Scott, who commanded a small troop of Red Cameron. They were sufficient to dissuade any potential threat, and the blue cross banner carried by the lead trooper emphasised their prowess.

Their flag was seen when the group were still some distance from Erbea. Angus Ferguson was at the city's south gate to greet his friends. Angus, Alex and Alain had become like brothers during the dangerous journey north from Boretar the previous summer, and of course Angus had known Alastair Munro from childhood.

Angus embraced his oldest friend, who seemed to have become more self-contained as his power had grown. Alastair smiled as he took in Angus's look of concern and stepping back from the other's embrace, he grasped his hand in greeting.

Angus was first to speak. "You are all welcome, if unexpected," he said. "I had heard that with the treaties signed, the Bala troops were heading back home."

"They are, Angus," said Cameron, "but I have a task to complete here before we all return to Aldene. Lead us to the council room in the castle and I will explain."

Once the group was seated and food and wine brought to the table, Cameron explained the nature of his task in Erbea. "With the treaties signed, it is agreed that the border with Ackar will now be south of the old wall, here at the banks of the Erb," he said. "It is my promise to the new King that I will appoint a suitable Bala lord as Elder for the region. I have also promised that the people of the land will be treated as Bala citizens with full rights. I have spoken with the other Elders and we have agreed that you, Angus, should be appointed Elder of Erbea and all the land between the old wall and the Erb."

There was a short pause, and then the group burst into applause. Cameron held up his hand and the room quietened. "Angus, you have shown prowess as a warrior in recent conflicts, but I also know you have a love of people and of the land. We can think of no one better to take responsibility for this new region of Bala. You will of course also be our first line of defence should the treaties be broken. Davy Scott will remain here as your second in command. If the Elder of Erbea will allow me, I have other news." Angus was lost for words and could only nod. "I would like to request that the Elder join us for celebrations in Aldene. I have a daughter who needs a husband, and I think I know the man she will choose."

Alastair Munro smiled. He could see the words *Aonaibh Ri Chéile* shining brightly from the new Elder's ring.

Angus and his companions were sworn to secrecy. Aldene was resplendent in the early summer sun and the crowds cheered as James Cameron and his companions passed through the southern gate. This was a celebration of victory, and more – it was a celebration of the expected peace.

There was a scream of joy from the crowd, and a young woman ran out from the crowd to greet the arriving troop. Elbeth knew that Angus had been told to hold Erbea, but she had no knowledge of recent events or that he would be coming now to Aldene. Her father was first to dismount, and Elbeth ran to greet him. After a brief but warm embrace, she turned towards her waiting fiancé, and paused. Her lover seemed older than before, more certain, more confident. She liked the change.

Alastair Munro had dismounted next to her father, and Elbeth could not pass him by. It struck her that her friend had changed even more than her fiancé. The light blue clothing shone in the warm sun, but more than that, the man seemed to shine with power, love and peace. As she embraced him, light flickered between them and she felt lifted by his love.

Elbeth ran on to Angus and as the lovers stood together once more, no one could miss the radiance from the rings shining on their fingers.

Cameron and the group walked their horses towards the castle gate, Angus and Elbeth hand in hand. Cameron stopped at the gate and turned to the crowd gathered in the forecourt. "My friends and countrymen, it has been a hard road these last two years since the invaders arrived in our country. They wanted to take from our homeland and turn it into a wasteland. With the love and hospitality of our Coelete brothers, we found a refuge. With your bravery, we threw the tyrant back to his own land, and there we won a great battle. The new Dewar King is not like his forefathers, and he has promised lasting peace sealed with his blood.

"Peace has been agreed, and all the kingdoms are united in holding it. Today we celebrate that peace.

Inside the castle there is food and wine, enough for all to enjoy." The crowd cheered. Cameron held his hand and added, "Today we celebrate peace, tomorrow we celebrate love. My daughter Elbeth became betrothed to a Banoran farmer when we were exiled in Tala. It seemed to me an unlikely match and not one that could survive a return to our normal life in Bala. However, in the past weeks I have learnt that there is a love even greater than that of a father for a daughter, and it has blessed this union. I have also learned that our humble Banoran farmer has great and noble qualities. I cannot stand in God's way, nor do I wish to. Tomorrow my daughter will wed the newly-appointed Elder of Erbea, if she will have him."

Elbeth threw herself into Angus's arms and murmured, "of course I will!" Then she ran to her father and threw her arms round his neck. "Thank you!" she said, tears of joy running down her face.

"To the banquet then, but make sure you save some of your exuberance for tomorrow."

The crowd cheered. The people loved Elbeth, and many knew and respected Angus Ferguson. No one saw Oien in his beggar's garb watching at the back of the crowd, a jealous scowl on his face.

In Bala a wedding ceremony had to take place outside man's dominion, so the crowds gathered in the meadows outside Aldene's town walls. The meadow was a blaze of colour as the early summer flowers bloomed as if for the ceremony. Angus was dressed in his father's best clothes, those he had worn back in Tala. With his new position he had been offered cloak and garments emblazoned with the motifs of Erbea, but he had refused. At heart he was still a simple Banoran farmer.

Alastair Munro and Alex Cameron stood at Angus's side waiting for the arrival of the bride. Elbeth's appearance drew loud cheers from the crowds. Her father and stepmother walked beside her. Elbeth held Eleanor's hand partly in recognition of the role her stepmother had played in helping her dream come true. On either side of the bride's party rode proud troopers of the Red Cameron with their horses garlanded for the occasion.

Angus felt a tremor of nerves as he watched his bride walk across the meadow towards him. Her beauty seemed to shine like the sun and glitter like the stars. Elbeth's smile calmed his nerves. Their union had seemed so impossible a few months earlier, but now it would become a reality.

Like all Bala weddings, this was to be a simple ceremony. Alastair Munro was to conduct the proceedings and the couple's rings would be swapped from the right to the left hand. Elbeth and Angus embraced and stepped back to exchange the rings. As the two lovers grasped each other's right hands the rings shone with white intensity, dimmed and then reappeared on each of their left hands. Between their right hands a silver quaich appeared with the Cameron motto shining brightly: *Aonaibh Ri Chéile* – let us unite – and united they were.

But then, as the couple lifted the ancient wedding cup to their lips, Munro once again heard Ala Moire's voice from beyond the grave, and this time it carried a warning. "To your right Alastair, evil stalks here in the shadows!"

Alastair spun to his right to see an old beggar pointing his raised staff at the wedding party. Oien! It could be none other. As a flash of red fire left the staff, Alastair Munro pushed his hands forward palms first, then drew them apart. A white wall appeared in front of him, consuming the red flame.

Oien raised his hand and another red bolt shot out, again quenched by the white light. Alastair Munro advanced on the old alchemist, and Oien hurled more and more deadly bolts of red fire. As Alastair closed on him, Oien knew that his red power was as nothing to this white magic. He started to beg for mercy, but Ala Moire's voice echoed in Alastair's head: "It is too late; take him in your embrace. Forgiveness, if it is to be granted, is for a greater power."

Alastair took the alchemist in his arms and felt all the anger and all the lust for power which had corrupted the old man's soul. He placed his arms around the other's neck, clasped his hands and stepped back. The white wall now completely enclosed Oien, and as it brightened in intensity it hid him from view. Flashes of red seemed to bounce around inside the wall and then began to fade away. The wall became a shimmering wave, like a mirage in the desert. Gradually that too vanished, and all that remained where Oien had been was a large piece of dull red rock.

CHAPTER NINETEEN

Homecomings

The festivities in Aldene continued for several days more, although much of the talk was about the strange events that had taken place in the meadow. Wherever they went in the city the married couple were greeted with flowers and cheers. Angus and Elbeth both knew that the time had come to move to their new home in Erbea, but first there had to be a honeymoon.

The two sought out Elbeth's father in the castle to explain their plans. Cameron had been greatly shocked by the attack at the wedding and knew that if Munro had not acted so quickly it would have been a day of tragedy rather than joy. Then he had seen the shining white rings and realised that he should worry less.

Angus spoke first. "James, we need to return to Erbea as we have much to do, but with your permission Elbeth and I would like to spend some time in Banora before I return to my duties."

Cameron moved from his seat and hugged his daughter, then warmly shook the hand of his new son in law. "Of course, and go with my blessings. Stop again on your way back south, for I have tasks for you, Angus, as soon as you return to your city. Alain and the Coelete are also travelling home tomorrow and I am sure they will gladly travel north with you."

The Inger Mountains were spectacular in the summer sun as Angus, Elbeth, Alastair Munro, Alain and a troop of Coelete warriors crossed over the Pass of Ing and descended into Banora. Angus sighed. "This is the land I love, yet I must leave it," he said.

Elbeth put an arm around her husband. "We will return here often. Davy Scott is a strong second in command at Erbea and we will need to be in Aldene to see my father and for you to attend conferences. We will escape here whenever we need quiet time together."

At the foot of the pass it was time for more goodbyes. Alain of Lorn stepped forward and bowed to the couple. "If I may," he said, and took each of the couple's left hands in his hand and brought them up to touch his forehead. The two rings immediately shone. Alain released the couple's hands and Elbeth looked quizzically at Alastair Munro.

"It is a Coelete wedding blessing that has been their custom for hundreds, if not thousands, of years," he explained. "It is asking their God to bless the couple with long lives and love forever, and to keep them safe."

Angus smiled. "I think you have already delivered the last part."

Alain nodded. "Alastair is correct, but I have another gift for you both." The tall warrior then reached to his shoulder and produced one of the ancient horns of the Coelete, which he presented to Angus. No one knew the origin of the horns, except that they were from an animal that had disappeared millennia before. Alain continued, "The Coelete don't have magic, but we have three of these horns and they possess a power of their own. A blast on the horn can carry an immense distance, and it will alert the Coelete to danger. Should you require it, sound a blast on the horn and Coelete warriors will immediately be despatched to your aid."

Alain shook the hands of the others, gave Elbeth a gentle embrace and then stopped to look at Angus. Forgetting protocol, the tall warrior also embraced the new Elder and whispered in his ear, "be safe

Angus, and visit us in Tala with your wife as soon as you can." Then he and the Coelete left, heading north over the plains to their home lands.

A short while later, Duncan of Coe rode out with a cohort of Banoran troopers to greet the trio. "Welcome home my lord, my lady, Alastair. Your homes are ready for your return."

"Thank you Duncan, but lord and lady is a little too formal. Can't we simply remain Angus and Elbeth?"

Duncan smiled and performed a mock bow. "Of course, at your command my lord."

Angus gave the older man a playful slap in response.

The lovers returned to Angus's house and Alastair to his farm. Over the next few days there were many callers and well-wishers. Alastair always felt uncomfortable with the awe and respect with which he was now treated, and he reflected that perhaps life could never again settle back to the way it had been.

After a couple of days enjoying time together in their own lands, Angus and Elbeth decided to journey to Tala and revisit the place where they had first met. Gareth of the Guardians observed their arrival whilst they were some distance from the passage through the mountain. Elbeth and Angus were greeted by Anaton and the nobles of Tala. There would be yet more celebrations over the next few days.

Before the couple left for their journey to the

Hidden Lands, Alastair Munro had sat with them over an evening meal. The three friends were so comfortable in each other's company that there was no need for redundant conversation. Alastair, however, had something to explain.

"As you both know, I have completed a strange journey over the past year. Banora will always be my home, but I know that I will soon be bound for other places. It will take time for me and for the people to see me with my new gifts, and I need to allow them that time. I may not be here when you return from Tala, but I will always be close by. Like the Coelete horn, when you call for me I will come."

The couple were about to argue, but Alastair took their hands and the light blue of his clothes shone brighter than the rings. A silent blessing was given that held great hope for the future.

The day after Angus and Elbeth had headed north, Munro heard Ala Moire's voice again. "Alastair, you have another task to fulfil, and then you will be guided to the next step of your journey. Climb back to the place on the Inger where we first met and take with you some of the salt that is still stored in your outhouse."

The sun was just rising over the northern peaks when Alastair climbed once again up towards the Pass of Ing. Following the well-remembered path, he reached the spot where he had first spoken with Ala Moire. Memories flooded back. To the north the Coe Mountains were bathed in sunshine and to the west the Greater Sea shone, welcoming the new day. Below in Banora the day was starting and the farmhouses' chimneys were billowing smoke. It all seemed to be as it had always been, but of course it had all changed.

He heard Ala Moire's voice once more: "Call your power and sweep your hands over the mountain." Alastair did as instructed and at his beckoning a white mist rose to cover the Inger. As it dissipated, there were further instructions. "Turn to your right and you will find some of the red stone. Draw a shield round yourself and prime the stone with the salt."

Alastair again did as he was told, and found himself with a lump of red stone and a small pile of salt. The othium had been rendered inert. The red fire would not threaten peace again in the near future. By now Alastair Munro had been gifted Ala Moire's memories, so he knew that the distant planets still contained active red stone. He also knew it would be hundreds, if not thousands, of years before mankind could again reach for the planets to threaten its own destruction. He hoped that if others in the cosmos could tame othium's power, God would again ensure His people's safety.

Returning to his small house in Banora, Alastair wrote a number of letters; to Angus and Elbeth, to James Cameron and to the Elders of Bala. He wrote about his journey and the challenges of his inheritance. He described the mission that Ala Moire had laid upon his shoulders. He would come back often, but now it was time to leave for a while to seek his own peace.

In Esimore, Sulux was returning from tending to the herd as it grazed the summer pastures. The lone traveller was dressed in light blue clothing that shimmered white in the evening sun. The old prophesies had finally been fulfilled.

List of Characters

- Alastair Munro – Farmer with a smallholding in Banora
- Angus Ferguson – Farmer with a smallholding in Banora
- Dewar 1st – Late King of Ackar and Lett
- Dewar 2nd – Son of Dewar 1st and King of Ackar and Lett
- Elan of Ember – Horse Lord, Duke of Ember
- Oien – One of the Council of Five in the Second Age
- Ala Moire – One of the Council of Five in the Second Age, when he was known as Malama O'Re
- Ewart – Lord of Ewart in Bala and Elder of Ewart
- Koren – Elder of Coelene
- Conall Dalzell – Elder of Awick
- Douglas Dougal – Elder of the Borderlands
- Duncan of Coe – Elder of Coe and Banora
- James Cameron – Elder of the Lands of Cameron and leader of the Red Cameron
- Orridon – Ember Horse Lord and stepbrother of Elan

+ Gordon Graham – advisor and mentor to James Cameron
+ John Burnett – James Cameron's second in command, Red Cameron
+ Cember – Ember Horse Lord and Orridon's lieutenant
+ Anaton – the first chief of the Coelete nation, and the name given to all succeeding leaders
+ Olaton – an early chief of the Coelete
+ Davy Scott – A Red Cameron trooper
+ John Ewart – A Red Cameron trooper
+ Alain son of Lorn – Coelete warrior and Guardian of the Hidden Lands
+ Gareth – Coelete warrior and Guardian of the Hidden Lands
+ Ham – an alchemist in the Second Age
+ Vasel – King of Elat in the Second Age
+ Craig Baird – minor Ewart lord and fisherman
+ Elbeth – Daughter of James Cameron
+ Eleanor – James Cameron's second wife and stepmother to Alex and Elbeth
+ Duncan of Coe's family – Isobel, his wife, children Ross, Moira and Leana
+ Alex Cameron – son of James Cameron
+ Calan – Olatan's brother
+ Noren – Steward of Erwick
+ Erden – an Erwick councillor
+ Galbraith – Noren's son
+ Elem – brother of Cember
+ Silson – Duke of Amina
+ Arin – First Lord of Kermin
+ Ishca – Lord of Doran
+ Coran – James Cameron's younger brother

- Melnar – Overlord of Lett
- Orimir – Melnar's son and Governor of Toria
- Roger Eld – Captain of Boretar
- Idula – nephew of Orridon & Elan
- Sulux – the head of the herdsmen of Esimore
- Armon – An assassin
- Darmon – leader of the Aramin
- Bramdon – Ember Horse Lord and distant cousin to Orridon
- Letham – Elan's retainer and administrator for Ember
- Timon – Commander of the King's Guard
- Ramon of Lett – sailor and commander of the transporters fleet
- Essen – Ackar knight and commander of the occupying forces in Aldene
- Herlock – a Coelete lord
- Alluen – Daughter of the King of Toria and wife of Tyros
- Tyros – Prince of Ciren and husband to Alluen
- Patrick Roth – Lord of Erbea
- Simon Roth – Son of Patrick and Captain in the Ackar army
- Erin – Count of Toria, son of the King of Toria, Alluen's brother
- Garan – son of Dewar 2nd, due to succeed him as Dewar 3rd
- Amelia – Garan's mother

Main Characters by Allegiance

Banora

- Alastair Munro – Farmer with a smallholding in Banora
- Angus Ferguson – Farmer with a smallholding in Banora

Bala

- Ala Moire – One of the Council of Five from the Second Age when he was known as Malama O'Re
- Ewart – Lord of Ewart in Bala and Elder of Ewart
- Duncan of Coe – Elder of Coe and Banora
- James Cameron – Elder of the Lands of Cameron and leader of the Red Cameron
- John Burnett – Red Cameron, James Cameron's second in command

- Davy Scott – A Red Cameron Trooper
- John Ewart – A Red Cameron Trooper
- Craig Baird – minor Ewart Lord and fisherman
- Elbeth – Daughter of James Cameron
- Alex Cameron – Son of James Cameron
- Noren – Steward of Erwick
- Erden – an Erwick councillor
- Galbraith – Noren's son
- Coran – James Cameron's younger brother
- Koren – Elder of Coelene
- Conall Dalzell – Elder of Awick
- Douglas Dougal – Elder of the Borderlands
- Gordon Graham – advisor and mentor to James Cameron
- Eleanor – James Cameron's second wife and stepmother to Alex and Elbeth
- Duncan of Coe's family – Isobel, his wife, children Ross, Moira and Leana

Ackar and Lett

- Dewar 1st – King of Ackar and Lett
- Dewar 2nd – Son of Dewar 1st and King of Ackar and Lett
- Oien – One of the Council of Five from the second age
- Melnar – Overlord of Lett
- Orimir – Melnar's son and Governor of Toria
- Roger Eld – Captain of Boretar
- Timon – Commander of the King's Guard
- Ramon of Lett – sailor and commander of the transporters fleet
- Patrick Roth – Lord of Erbea

- Simon Roth – son of Patrick and Captain in the Ackar army
- Garan – son of the Dewar (Dewar 2nd), due to succeed him as Dewar 3rd
- Essen – Ackar knight and commander of the occupying forces in Aldene
- Amelia – Garan's mother

Ember Horse

- Elan of Ember – Horse Lord, Duke of Ember
- Orridon – Ember Horse Lord and stepbrother of Elan
- Cember – Ember Horse Lord and Orridon's lieutenant
- Elem – brother of Cember
- Idula – nephew of Orridon & Elan
- Bramdon – Ember Horse Lord and distant cousin to Orridon
- Letham – Elan's retainer and administrator for Ember

The Coelete

- Anaton – the first chief of the Coelete nation, and the name given to all succeeding leaders
- Olaton – an early chief of the Coelete
- Alain son of Lorn – Coelete warrior and Guardian of the Hidden Lands
- Gareth – Coelete warrior and Guardian of the Hidden Lands
- Calan – Olatan's brother
- Herlock, a Coelete lord

The Southern Lands

- Silson – Duke of Amina

- ◆ Arin – First Lord of Kermin
- ◆ Ishca – Lord of Doran
- ◆ Darmon – leader of the Aramin
- ◆ Tyros – Prince of Ciren and husband of Alluen
- ◆ Alluen – daughter of the King of Toria and wife of Tyros, sister of Erin
- ◆ Erin – Count of Toria, son of the King of Toria

Others

- ◆ Ham – an alchemist in the second age
- ◆ Vasel – King of Elat in the second age
- ◆ Sulux – the head of the herdsmen of Esimore
- ◆ Armon – An assassin

Geography of the Lands

In the late 13th century the large island of Andore is home to several independent countries. In the north, Bala has its border with Ackar south at the old wall. South of Ackar is Lett, whilst further south are Toria, Ciren and Arance. To the north east the island is bounded by the Eastern Sea, which separates the island from the eastern lands of Esimore and Soll. To the east and south east is the Middle Sea across which lie the countries of Doran, Kermin and Amina. Lying between Middle Sea and the Western Sea are the islands of Elat and Lat. The Greater Sea runs the length of the island in the west.

Bala

Bala's border starts at the old wall. The Borderlands stretch the length of the wall from east to west. Moving north, the Plain of Aldene runs to the west, reaching the capital Aldene (called Aracene in the olden days). Aldene is the capital of Bala and the home of the Cameron Elder. To the east are the Ewart lands and the province of Awick with their farmlands and small villages. Bala is segmented by two great mountain ranges. North of Aldene are the Inger Mountains and in the far north the Coe Mountains. The only route through the Inger Mountains is the Pass of Ing. In winter the snow means the pass is blocked for several months each year. On the North West side of The Inger is the province of Banora with the Banora Forest in the South West of the province. The rivers Ora and Ola flow out from the Inger through Banora to join the Greater Sea. The Ola flows across the Plain of Coe to its estuary at the small northern town of Erwick. The river Ban branches off from the Ola through Banora. The Cole River flows south from the Coe Mountains to join the Ola in a cascade of waterfalls to the east of Erwick. In the East the rivers Stel and Ing flow through the Plain of Coelene to the Eastern Sea. In the north the Coe Mountains are impassable and the maps show the mountains ending at the Hidden (Northern) Sea far to the north.

The maps do not show the Hidden Lands, the home of the Coelete and their rock city of Tala. The Coelete and the passage through the mountain were at this time unknown to the people of Bala. The lands north of the Inger are hard in winter and populated with tough people working their small holdings. South of the Inger the Plain of Aldene, the Ewart lands and the province of Awick are richer with prosperous farms and small townships and villages. The Borderlands north of the old wall have been the territory of raiders and Reivers for centuries. Bandits from the north, and the south, raid over the border to steal sheep and cattle from their neighbours.

Ackar

Ackar is the richest country on the island with large farms and a busy river port at the capital, Boretar. The Tar river flows through Boretar's port to the Greater Sea. To the north east, closer to the border with Bala, is the second city of Erbea. The Erb flows past Erbea after it has been joined from the north by the Bari. Boretar is the capital of the Dewar kings. Ackar is the most populous of the countries and is rich with the trade that flows in and out of Boretar. Ackar also has the largest army on the island.

Lett

Lett is slightly smaller than its northern neighbour and less wealthy. The capital city is named after the country, Lett lies inland. Olet is the country's port on the Greater Sea and the shipyards in Olet build most of the vessels that ply their trade up and down the sea. The shipyards get their raw materials from the Forest of Lett, which extends down beyond the Lett border into Ciren and on south into Toria. In the mid 13th century Ackar nobles gradually extended their power into their southern neighbour. By 1280 the countries agreed to a union and so Ackar and Lett became the most powerful country on the island, ruled by Dewar the First.

Toria, Ciren and Arance

South of Lett, Ciren and Arance share a border with their northern neighbour. Toria borders Ciren to the west and Arance borders it to the east. Other than Arance these are not rich countries, but the Forest of Lett running through two of the countries and the mines in Ciren are sources of wood and stone for building and extending the castle fortresses in the north. The Torian capital is Tora and the Ciren capital Cire. Arance has rich farmlands and to the east the province of Ember, capital Anua, is home to the fierce Ember Horse Lords. The Horse Lords owed allegiance to the kings of Arance. The Dewar kings sought dominance over the southern lands not simply for their wealth but because they were the stepping stone to cross the Middle Sea to the much richer lands in the south. A key to any invasion across the Middle Sea was to hold the large Arance port of Anelo. In 1290 the forces of Ackar and Lett defeated the Arance armies and by 1296 Toria, Ciren and Arance were dominions of Ackar and Lett, and Ackar overlords ruled in Tora, Cire and Anelo. Anua and Ember remained self-governed but with fealty now sworn to the Dewar King. By 1299, with his coffers swollen by taxes from the conquered lands, and conscription to the Ackar and Lett army now fully implemented, Dewar the Second was ready to embark on more conquest over the Middle Sea.

Elat and Lat

Lying between the southern shores of Ciren and the northern shores of Amina are the twin islands of Elat and Lat. The islands are of little value other than as possible staging posts for crossing the Middle Sea. The water lying between the islands forms a shallow channel connecting the Middle Sea to the Western Sea, the Straits of Elat. However this water is too shallow for any large boat to navigate and holds no value. The islands do however hold a curiosity, as the shallows evaporate in the summer months so the waters turn purple as the salt becomes concentrated in the narrows. In 1299 the purple Salt of Elat was of no value.

Amina, Kermin and Doran

Across the Middle Sea are the rich lands of Amina, Kermin and Doran. These three lands have long lived in harmony with treaties committing each to the protection of the rest. Doran is the most northerly of these lands and is separated from Kermin by the Doran Mountains. Doran's wealth is primarily generated from the gold that the Doran miners extract from the mountains. Kermin to the south possesses rich farmlands. The capital Mora is an impressive city sitting on the banks of the river Mora which flows west from the Doran Mountains into the Middle Sea. To the east of Kermin is the large Aramin forest, home to the Aramin tribes. The border between Kermin and Amina is the Kermin Alol, which is rugged hill country. The hills rise steeply from the valleys, cutting the Alol into several distinct sectors with the trade roads hugging the valley floors. Amina is the southern country, and a rich one. Tamin is the capital, and the Amin river flows past the city walls. Further north the Mina flows south and west from the Alol into the Middle Sea. Amina's port is Tufle, and further south on the coast is the small town of

Slat. The Vale of Tember stretches out from Tamin to the south, and it was here in 1299 that Dewar the Second's armies first fought to try to conquer these rich lands southern lands.

Esimore

Esimore is far to the north, separated from the Hidden Lands by a small stretch of the Eastern Sea. It is largely tundra, with great herds of reindeer roaming free and tended by the few nomadic herdsmen who call the land home.

BV - #0034 - 030619 - C0 - 203/127/31 - PB - 9781861519214